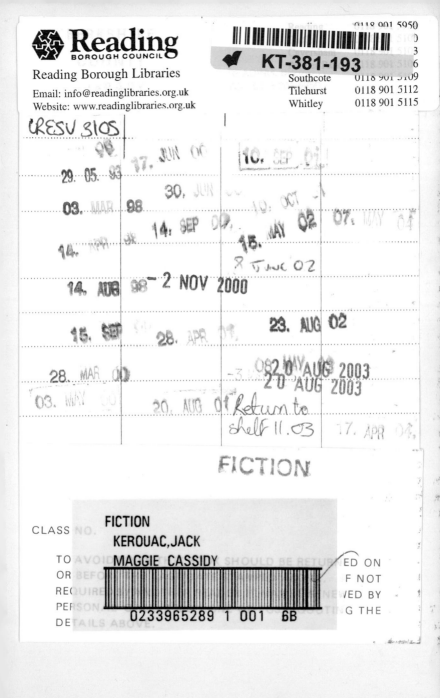

MAGGIE CASSIDY

MAGGIE CASSIDY

Jack Kerouac

ANDRE DEUTSCH

First published 1974 by
André Deutsch Limited
105 Great Russell Street London WC1

Printed in Great Britain by
Lowe & Brydone (Printers) Ltd.
Thetford, Norfolk

ISBN 0 233 96528 9

MAGGIE CASSIDY

I

It was a New Year's Eve, it was snowing in the North. The fellows were staggering down the snowy road arm in arm supporting a central figure who all alone was singing in a cracked sad broken voice what he had heard the cowboy sing in the Gates Theater Friday afternoon, "*Jack o diamonds, Jack o diamonds, you'll be my downfall,*" but not knowing the downfall part of it, just *Jack o* where it broke and yodeled in a western-type twang. This was G.J. Rigopoulos singing. His head hung low like a drunk's as they dragged his shoes through the snow, arms limp and lips hanging out like an idiot's in a tremendous display of complete didnt care attitude that had all the others struggling and slipping in the snow to hold him up. But from his brokendoll neck came the plaintive notes, *Jack o diamonds, Jack o diamonds,* as great thick snow-flakes dropped straight on their heads. It was the New Year 1939, before the war, before everyone knew the intention of the world toward America.

The boys were all French Canadian except the Greek lad G.J. It had never occurred to any of them, the others, Scotty Boldieu, Albert Lauzon, Vinny Bergerac and Jacky Duluoz, to wonder that G.J. had spent his entire boyhood with them instead of with other Greek boys for close companions and soulmates of puberty, when all he had to do was walk across the river and see a thousand Greek boys or go up the Pawtucketville hill to a fair-sized Greek neighborhood and find many friends. It might have occurred to Lauzon that G.J. never ended among the Greeks, to Lousy who was the most sympathetic and thoughtful of the gang; but since everything occurred to him, he never mentioned any part of it—yet. But the love that went out from all four French boys to this Greek boy was fantastic, true-volumed, bleakfaced and innocent of other things in the world and completely serious. They hung

5

on him for dear life, twitching to see each new joke he might choose next in his role as King's Comedian. They were walking under immense beautiful dark-limbed trees of black winter, dark arms twisted and sinuous from sidewalk up; they over-topped the road, Riverside Street, in a solid roof for several blocks past phantasmal old homes with huge porches and Christmas lights buried deep in; real-estate relics of when to be on the river meant and called for expensive building. But now Riverside Street was a hodge-podge running from a tiny brownly lit Greek variety store at the edge of a sand field, with riverward bungalow streets going down; from it to a sandlot baseball field more or less the scene of overgrown weeds, foulballs breaking windows, and October night fires of hoodlums and urchins of the town, to which category G.J. and his gang had, and still belonged.

"Give me a snowball, men," said G.J. snapping out of his drunken act, staggering; Lauzon leaping to the issue handing him the snowball with an expectant giggle.

"What you gonna do, Mouse?"

"Gonna belt that poor poss bowling around!" he snarled. "Make revolutions swim around! Burpers'll raise big legs to poop on southern shores, Palm Miami Beach—" and he threw his snowball with a vicious long whip of his arm at a passing car and popped right in the front a soft plopping exploding snowball that left a star shining in the glass and in their eyes as they all heaved to laugh and throw themselves slapping on their knees, the pop had been just loud enough to attract the attention of the motorist, who was driving an old loud-motored Essex with a load of wood in the back and a Christmas tree and a few logs and a few more in front with a little kid holding up against them, his son, farmers from Dracut; he just turned and glowered briefly and drove on grimly toward Mill Pond and the pines of old tar roads.

"Ha ha ha did you see the expression on his face?" yelled Vinny Bergerac with shuddering eagerness jumping up around the road and grabbing G.J. to haul and push him in a wild laughing hysterical stagger of joy. They were almost falling in a snowbank.

A little to the side, and quiet, walked Scotty Boldieu, head bent in thought as if he were studying a cigarette's tip alone in a room; bulky-shouldered, short, hawk-faced and sleek, a little dark, brown-eyed. He turned to throw a little inward-thinking and courteous laugh with the others in their general uproar. At the same time in his eyes there was a twinkle of disbelief in their antics at his somber side, grave and surprised recognition of them, a kind of leadership of the silent sailing soul in all of them, so, Lousy seeing him thus interior-bemused away from the hilarity leaned his head on his shoulder a second in an old sister's laugh and shook him to see: "Hey Scotty didnt you see El Mouso hurl that apple right on the guy's window, just like when he threw his ice cream at the screen in the movie about the foreclose mortgage at the Crown? Cheez! What a maniac! Zeet?"

Scotty just waved his hand and nodded, biting his lip, and took a deep brooding drag on a Chesterfield cigarette, probably his thirtieth or fortieth of a new lifetime, seventeen years old and bound to sink down to his work in slow, heavy, relaxed degrees, tragic and beautiful to see the snow bedeck his eyebrows and hatless well-combed head.

Vinny Bergerac was as skinny as a stick, screaming all the time, happy; his father's name must have been Joy; inside his crazy-flapping coat of activities and yells with the gang his little thin, wasted body swiveled on inexistent hips and long, white, tragic legs. His face was thin as a razor, sharply handsome, cut with a fingernail file; blue eyes, white teeth, shining, mad eyes; his hair was wet, combed forward to a roll, slicked back with a brush, smooth and dark under his white silk scarf; his eyebrows stood out somewhat like Tyrone Power eyebrows of conscious perfect good looks. But he was a scatterbrained madman from the word go. His laugh crashed and shrieked all over the silent snowy road of huddled holiday workers bending to their work with bottles and packages, noses sniffling in the night. Snow dropped on his head and through the wild steams of his cries. G.J. had risen from his grave of snow, where "That ga-dam rat" he'd fallen, it being soft he sank shudderingly in the cold; now, coming up white, he had Vinny under the belt on his shoulder giving him the whirlaround airplane throw they'd all seen in wrestling matches at the Rex and the CMAC and in their own backyards promoted by themselves—wild, yelling, they danced around the inevitable climax in proud flapping topcoats of adolescence.

They hadnt even begun to drink.

G.J. and Vinny collapsed together in the snowbank, sank, everybody danced and howled; the snow flew, some fell from shivered branches in the high night; it was New Year's Eve.

II

Albert Lauzon turned his sad eyes on Jacky Duluoz, who was unexpectedly pensive beside him.

"Hey Zaaaagg didja see him? Mouse giving him the old flying wedge tackle—what do you call that hold Zagg? Zeet?" This was a convulsive little fizzle giggle in his teeth. "That crazy Vinny had him down did you see that sneaky rat sink him in five miles deep in the zeet? Hey Zagg?" and grasping Zagg by the arm to shake him and make him see what had just happened. But some distant hung-up recollection or reflection had taken hold of the other boy's mind and he had to turn around and look carefully at Lousy to understand what reaction was expected of him at that moment when he had been dreaming. Lauzon's sad eyes he saw, set somewhat close on each side of a long strange nose, something shrouded and hidden beneath a large brown felt hat, the only one in the gang wearing a hat; and revealing nothing but an expectant laugh blazing wildly with youth in the closeup eyes, the long jaw, long mouth drawn to wait and see him. A twinge, a flicker of something, barely touched the corner of Lauzon's mouth as he saw Zagg's long hesitation returning from his own thoughts; some disappointment had come and gone forever in his study of the other boy; and in his own mind Zagg Duluoz had only been thinking of the time when he was four years old and in the red May late afternoon he had thrown a rock at a car in front of the firehouse and the car stopped and the man got out with a great worried expression and the glass was broken, so seeing the flick of disappointment in Lauzon he wondered if he should tell him about the rock of four years old but Lauzon was ahead of him. "Zagg you missed seeing the great Mouse being downed by skinny boy Vinny Bergerac it's sensational!" And Lauzon was giving him hell. "No kidding you was off a million miles then, you didnt see, it'll never be forgotten: imagine the one and only G.J. —look what he's doing now! Zagg you crazy! Zeet!" slapping him and pulling him and shaking him. It was all forgotten in a second. The perturbation bird had flown in, and sat on pearly souls, and gone again. At the edge of the gang trudged Scotty, still alone, still inside.

G.J. nicknamed Mouse and born Rigopoulos, or probably Rigolopoulakos and shortened by his hard-working parents, was now up and unjokingly or trying seriously if possible gravely to brush the snow off his new coat thinking just then of his mother who'd so proudly given it to him last week Christmas. "Easy boys, lay off, my old lady just gave me this cashmere coat here, the price tag was so abnormable I had to put my own immemoriam sign—" but suddenly his vigor and vitality leaped out of him again with the force of an explosion, his interest in everybody was so absolutely boundless it was like a compulsive drunk's leap to rush, to begin anew, exhaust the world, kiss the foundations of the world—"Zagg hey Zagg hey! what's that immemorious word you told me on the Square not on the Square right in front the City Hall the other night, you said you read it in the encyclopediac, Zagg, the word with the monument—"

"—immemor—"

"Immemorialamums— Hayee!" screamed Mouse leaping at Zagg across the arms of the gang and grabbing him with a feverish anxiety. "The immemorials of the world war monuments—six million memorials of the—Wadworth Long-fellow—long far—Zagg what is that word? Tell us *what* . . . *that* . . . *word* . . . *is!*" he yelled with great urgency pulling and pulling at him to show him to the others, with a frantic act of being so excited and so "blafferfasted" as he said that at any moment he would fly into the air from inpent unkeepable explosions of suspense. It was, in his charade, a matter of such great importance that to say the least—"This man must be beheaded at once, call the Tower, twelve sixty-nine, calling the lines in the desk, calling the moon, we got him on our blockheads ready to go, this man refuses to tell us, Boris Karloff and company and Bela Looboosi and us vampires and everybody connected with Frankenstein and . . ." with a sly whisper—"the . . . house . . . of . . . Muxy Smith . . ." At which everybody reared back exploding with laughter and amazement; only a few weeks ago they had carried an old drunk of Pawtucketville home to his house far down River-side Street, and it happened to be a 175-year-old unpainted Colonial house crumbling from hearth to doorstone in its sad sunken field just off a fork of roads to Dracut and Lakeview; it was spooky, night; they stumbled the little old man into his kitchen, he flopped, mumbled; said he heard ghosts all the time in the other rooms; as they were leaving the old man stumbled on a rocking chair and fell and hit his head and lay on the floor moaning. They helped him dragfooted to a couch; he seemed to be all right. But they heard the wind in the eaves, the unused attic upstairs . . . they all hurried home. And the nearer they got home the more G.J., talking excitedly even then, became convinced Muxy Smith was dead, had killed himself. "He's on that couch pale as a sheet and dead as a ghost," whispered, "I'm telling you . . . from now on it's going to be the ghost of Muxy Smith"; and so that in the morning, a Sunday, they had all looked with apprehension at the newspaper to read and see if Muxy Smith had been found dead in his haunted old house. "I knew that moon was out when we met him on that Textile sidewalk—bad sign, we should never taken him home the old guy is half dead," G.J. kept saying at midnight. But in the morning no news to the effect that a bunch of boys had slipped away from a house, leaving a dead man bruised with a heavy object; so they visited each other after church, the French Canadians going to Sainte Jeanne d'Arc on the Pawtucketville hill, and G.J. across the river with his dark-veiled mother and sisters to the Byzantine Greek Orthodox church near the canal, and were reassured. "Muxy Smith," G.J. whispered in the New Year's

Eve snow, "and his immemoriam jazz band is coming on the sheets up there. . . . But what a word! Hey Lousy didja hear that word? Scot? IMMEMORIAM. Forever and ever in stone. That's what it means. Only Zagg could have discovered such a word. Years he studied in his room, learning . . . IMMEMORIAM. Zagg, Memory Babe, write some more words like that. You'll be great. They'll make you honorary chairman of the burpers' convention of general farts in the motors division of the superintendents of Wall Street. I'll be there, Zagg, with a beautiful blonde, a flask, an apartment waiting for your convenience . . . ah gentlemen I'm tired. It was a wrestling match that—how can I dance tonight? How can I go and jitterbug now?" And once again, everything else exhausted for the while, he sang *Jack o diamonds* in that way he'd just learned, sad, incredibly sad like a dog act, or like men singing, floating broken and prophetic in the snow of the night, *Jack o diamonds*, as arm in arm they all scuffled to the New Year's Eve dance at the Rex Ballroom, their first dance each one, their first and last future before them.

III

Meanwhile all this time across the street walking parallel with them was Zaza Vauriselle who but for a prognathic big almost hydrocephalic's jaw and six inches less height could have been Vinny Bergerac's chiseled French Canadian happy smiling brother; he was with the group but for awhile had absented himself to the other sidewalk in the way of one accustomed to walking long distances with gangs, to think, to drive his legs on in a thing of his own, every now and then, too, saying to them, barely heard, comments like "Damn bunch of fools" (in French, *gange de baza*) or, "Aw look the nice girls coming out that house hey."

Zaza Vauriselle was the oldest in the gang, had only recently injected himself via Vinny's invitation, and had made a hit with the rest skeptical or not only because he was such a fantastic fool, capable of any joke, the main joke being, "He'll do anything Vinny says, anything"; and his added value that he knew all about girls and sex from direct experience. He had the same happy thin features, and handsome like Vinny, but was very short, bowlegged, funny to look at, shifty-eyed, heavy-jawed and snorting through a defective nose; always masturbating in front of the others, about eighteen; yet something curiously innocent and foolish almost angelic though admittedly silly and probably mentally retarded as he was. He too wore a white silk scarf, a dark topcoat, rubbers, no hat, and walked purposefully through the two-inch snow to the dance which had been his idea; somewhere down Lakeview Avenue, in some Centreville house where a party of adults was starting, the boys had gone, from G.J.'s house and Zagg's house the final meeting place, to fetch Zaza. It made for walking and rosy-faced excitement holiday-proper; nobody had a car till that summer. *"On va y'allez let's go!"* Zaza had yelled. Now Zaza Vauriselle made a snowball and threw it at Vinny his champion. "Ey, Vinny, go sit on the gadam bowl and shut up before I tear your legs off . . ." Softly, from across the street, with a stupid smile that the others all fondly saw gleaming. G.J. staggered to hear it, whispering, pointing, shushing, "Listen what's he thinking? . . . Ga-dam Zazay!" and ran across the street and dove on Zaza's shoulders and drove him into a snowbank as Zaza, unused to rough treatment, yelled in genuine anxiety "Ey! Ey!" and all sartorial in his coat and scarf was swashed in snow; the others rushing up to wrestle him in every direction, and finally they lifted him to their shoulders horizontal and went on down Riverside yelling and bearing their Zaza.

By now they had reached a deep slope of grass behind a wooden fence, near a near-castle made of stone, with towers, that sat high over Riverside Street. Up the grassy slope, white in the night, began a stone wall built up and in against a cliff, with dry pendant remnant vines now hanging in the snow, gleaming ice; up on top of the cliff, three houses. The middle one was G.J.'s. They were just regular old French Canadian two-story wooden tenements, with washlines, porches, long boards, like Frisco tenements enduring in the fog of the North, with brown lights in the kitchens, dim shadows, a vague sight of a religious calendar or an overcoat on a closet door, something sad and homely and useful and to the boys who knew nothing else the abode of very life. G.J.'s house sat, soared, looked over gigantic treetops of Riverside to the city a mile across the river; in his kitchen in blowing wild storms that would obscure vistas and clank the trees to hit the windows, Jack Frost cracking, raging to come in the door beneath the crack as old overshoes gleamed cold and wet in scuffly slush-halls, as people tried to stop a draft with a folded strip of newspaper . . . in great stormy days when there was no school, and no occasion like New Year's Eve, G J with his long legs strode his mother's linoleum swearing and cursing the day he was born as she an old Greek widow the death of whose husband fifteen years ago left her still in blackest mourning, sat in a rocking chair by the shivering window, with an old Greek bible on her lap, and grieved, and grieved, and grieved. . . . The sight of this house as G.J. rushed with the boys to joys tearing in his brain . . . "Is my mother up?" he wondered— Sometimes she just made long pitiful-to-hear lamentations about the darkness of her life, singing it, as the children heard every word and hung their heads in shame and misery. . . . "Is Reno still home? . . . is *she* gonna take her to that ga-dam woman for that visit. . . . Oh Lord in Heaven above sometimes I think I was born to worry for that unhappy old mother of mine till the day my boots sink in the ground and there wont be no damn saver to pull *me* out—the last of the Rigopoulakos, *elas spiti* Rigopoulakos . . . *ka, re*," he cursed and wrung inside his brain in Greek, squeezing his thighs inside his coat till they burned, taking his hands out of his pockets to spread fingers at the others, bringing his tongue out eloquently to clack his teeth, saying "Thou, thou, thou . . . you cant know!" He felt like howling across the snow and over the twenty-foot stone wall high to his house with its dark and tragic windows except for one brown light in the kitchen that said nothing, showed nothing but death, and but indicated that as ever his mother had begun her vigil with an oil lamp, now in the chair later on the little couch by the stove in the kitchen with a pitiful flimsy bedcover when all the time she had a whole bed in her own room. . . . "So dark that room," grieved G.J., Gus, *Yanni* to his mother, *Yanni* sometimes when she chose to call him by his middle name and everybody in the neighborhood could hear her at sad red dusk calling him to pork-chop supper "Yanni . . . Yanni . . ." A Jack o Diamonds of other broken hearts. And Gus turned to his greatest and deepest friend whom he had named Zagg.

"Jack," taking his arm, holding the gang up, "do you see that light burning in my mother's kitchen window?"

"—I know, Gus—"

"—showing where an old woman this night as all nights when this poor blooder and fubbler tries to go out Zagg and get himself just a little bit of fun in the world"—his eyes tearing—"and not asking so much as that God, in his mercy, munifisessence, whatyoucallit Zagg, should only say 'Gus, Gus, poor Gus, pray to the angels and to me and I shall see Gus that your poor old mother—' "

"—Ah Brigash cass mi gass!" cried Zaza Vauriselle, suddenly weirdly apt so much so that Lauzon laughed his high wild giggle and everybody heard but paid no attention because listening to Gus make a real serious speech about his troubles.

"—that only for a moment my soul and heart could rest to see that my mother—Jack she's just an old woman—your father isnt dead, you dont know what it is to have an old widowed mother who has no old man like your old man Aooway Burp Emil Duluoz come in the house and lift his leg and lay a browsh, it's comforting, it makes the woman—it makes the child, me, realize, 'I got an old man, he comes in from work, he's an ugly old maniac nobody's gonna give ten cents for Zagg but here I am—just two sisters, my brother dead, my oldest sister's married—you know, *Marie*—she used to be my mother's best . . . comforter—when Marie was around I didnt worry like I do now—Oh hell I dont—parade my trouble in front of you guys? Make you realize that my heart is broken . . . that as long as I live I'll have chains dragging me down to the oceans of sad tears that my feet are wet in already at the thought of my poor old mother in her ga-dam old black dress Zagg that—she waits for me! always waiting for me!" A commotion in the gang. "Ask Zagg! Three o'clock in the morning, we come home, we been shootin the bull maybe at Blezan's or saw Lucky on the street and exchanged a few greetings" (in his explanations waving a hand he was eager, thick-tongued, eloquent, his almost-olive skin and greenish-yellow eyes and earnest intensity like something in an ancient bazaar or court)—"and here we come, nothing's happened, but, and it's not too late, but, and there's my Ma— There's my Ma in the window with that light, waiting—asleep. I come in the kitchen I try to sneak, not wake her. She wakes up. 'Yanni?' she cries in a little voice like crying. . . . 'Ya Ma, Yanni—I been out with Jacky Duluoz.'—'Yanni why do you come home so late and worry me to death?' 'But Ma it's late I know but I told you I'd be all right wouldnt go no further than Destouches' ga-dam candy store,' and I start to get mad and yell at her at three o'clock in the morning and she says nothing just satisfied I'm safe and without a sound there she goes in her dark bedroom and goes to sleep and's up at the cracka ga-dam dawn to make my oatmeal for school. You guys wonder I'm known as the crazy Mouse," he concluded seriously.

Jack Duluoz put his arm around him and then withdrew it quickly. He tried to smile. Gus was looking at him for confirmation of all his sorrows. "You're still the greatest right fielder in history," said Jack.

"And the greatest relief pitcher, Mouso, You ever seen his windup you'd die, zeet?" Lauzon coming to him and taking his arm as they all took up the walk again.

"Oh," said Gus, "it's all a big . . . topcoat sale. You cant read it all. Fuggit! I say, I say to you gentlemen, fuggit— I aint never gonna say another word but reach for my oteens of champagne silver biddles, what do you call—big huge decanters of whisky and brew—slup—slip—the whole world is gonna go down my hole before G.J. Rigopoulos says quits!"

They all cheered wildly; and reached the big intersection of Pawtucketville, the corner of Riverside and Moody, swirling with excited snow across the arc lamp and on the yellow bus and all the people shouting hellos from sidewalk to sidewalk.

IV

Down Riverside and to the right Scotty Boldieu lived with his own mother, in a wooden tenement, third floor, you went up there via some outside wooden steps that had the quality of steps in dreams as they rose from ten-foot bushes a jungle of them in the field below and took you swaying up the ladder of flimsy porches with strange-faced French Canadian ladies looking down yelling to other ladies "Aayoo Madame Belanger *a tu ton* wash finished?" Scotty had a room to himself where he spent many hours studiously writing down the summer baseball team averages in red ink in infinitesimal figures and small letters; or just sat in the brown kitchen with the *Sun* and read the sports page. There was a little brother. There was a dead father there too. It had been some big-fisted man with a grim countenance, whose trudgings to work in the morning were like the departure of the Golem across the fogs and seas of his duty. Scotty, G.J., Zagg, Lauzon, Vinny all played an important part in a summer baseball team, a winter basketball team, and an invincible autumn football team.

Lauzon lived back down Riverside Street in the direction they were coming from, down the hill from the Greek candy store at the edge of the sandbank's desert of sand, on a rosy street, among bungalows. Tall strange Lauzon's father was a tall strange milkman. His tall strange kid brother prayed and made novenas at the church with all the other kids his age doing their Confirmation. At Christmas the Lauzons had a Christmas tree, and gifts; G.J. Rigopoulos had a tree too but something sick, scraggly, forever defeated shone from it in his dark window; Scotty Boldieu's mother put up a tree in a linoleumed parlor with the gravity of an undertaker, by vases. In the big Zaza house trees, gifts, window wreaths, confetti . . . his being a typical large French Canadian home.

Vinny Bergerac lived across the river, on Moody Street, in the slums. Jacky Zagg Duluoz lived just a stone's throw from the intersection where they had now stopped. The intersection had a traffic light, it illuminated the snow rosy red, wreathy green. Wooden tenements on both corners had most of their windows shining with red and blue lights; an air of festivity puffed out of their chimneys; people were below in the tar courts talking echoey chatters under clotheslines in the snowfall.

Jacky Duluoz's home was in a tenement several doorways up, on another corner, where the Pawtucketville center-store area seemed always to buzz the most, right at the lunchcart, across the street from the bowling alley, poolhall, at the bus stop, near the big meat market, with an empty lot on both sides of the street where kids played their gray games in brown weeds of winter dusk when the moon is just starting to show with a refined, distant, unseen paleness as if it had been frozen and also smeared with slate. He lived with his mother, father and sister; had a room of his own, with the fourth-floor windows staring on seas of rooftops and the glitter of winter nights when home lights brownly wave beneath the neater whiter blaze of stars—those stars that in the North, in the clear nights, all hang frozen tears by the billions, with January Milky Ways like silver taffy, veils of frost in the stillness, huge blinked, throbbing to the slow beat of time and universal blood. In the Duluoz home the kitchen window looked down on bright wild street scenes; inside, the bright light showed much food, cheer, apples and oranges in bowls on white table-cloths, clean ironing boards leaned behind varnished doors, cupboards, little plates of popcorn left over from last night. In the gray afternoons Jacky Duluoz rushed home, sweating in November and December, to sit in the gloom at the kitchen table, devouring, over a chess book, whole boxes of Ritz crackers with peanut butter smeared. In the evening his big father Emil came home and sat in the dark by the radio, coughing. Through the kitchen door in the hall he rushed down pellmell to find his friends, using the front stairs down the front rooms of the tenement only with parents and company and for sadder more formal runs— The back stairs were so dim, dusty, strange, as if loose-plastered, some day he would remember them in rueful dreams of rust and loss . . . dreams when G.J.'s shadow would fall across a piece of

MC–2

broken leg like pottery in the street, like modern paintings in their keen screaming lostness. . . . No idea in 1939 that the world would turn mad.

On the intersection itself a surprising number of people were passing throwing remarks across the snow. Billy Artaud was striding by at his tremendous pace, short, long-legged, arms swinging, bright teeth shining; he was the second baseman on the team; in the past few months had matured suddenly and was already rushing off to see his steady girl for the New Year's parties in downtown movies.

"There's Billy Artaud! Hooray for the Dracut Tigers!" yelled Vinny but Billy flowed right along, he was late, he saw them.

"Ah you guys whattaya doin?—here it is almost ten o'clock and you're still fiddlin and faddlin down the road when you gonna grow up, me I've got a girl so long you suckers"—Billy Artaud was known also as "Whattaguy"—"Whattaguy with snow all over his coat that Gus Rigopoulos!" he cried, waving his hand contemptuously. "Throw him to the hot night bird!" he cried, disappearing down the long street alongside Textile Institute and fields of snow to Moody Street Bridge and the downtown lights of town, toward which a lot of other people walked and many cars rolled with their chains crunching softly, their red taillights making beautiful Christmas glows in the snow.

"And here comes Iddyboy!" they all yelled with glee as out of the gloom appeared the great figure of Joe Bissonnette who the moment he saw them turned his shoulders into huge bulking phantoms around his sunken and outthrust chin and came forward on padding cat feet. "Here comes the big Marine!"

"OO!" greeted Joe, still holding himself rigidly inside his "Marine" pose, copied of the hulks and bulks of big sea dogs in Charles Bickford films of the Thirties, the cartoons of big Fagans with bull shoulders, the enormous beast who used to chase Charlie Chaplin with a morphine needle, but modern, with a pea cap down over the eye and the fists clenched, the lips curled puffy to show great crooked-bit teeth fleering to fight and maul.

Out of the gang stepped Jacky Duluoz in the identical pose, hunched to bull and his face twisted and eyes popping, fists clenched; they came up against each other's noses breathing hard to hold the act, almost teeth to teeth; they'd spent countless freezing winter nights walking back from the fights and wrestling matches and movies of boyhood like this, side by side, below zero weather their mouths blowing balloons, so that people saw them with a sense of disbelief that in the dark they couldnt check, Iddyboy Joe and Zagg the two big Marines coming up the street to throw saloons to the wind. Some Melvillean dream of whaling-town streets in the New England night . . . Once Gus Rigopoulos had held complete sway and power over the soul of Iddyboy, who was a big-hearted simple stud with the power of two grown men; would dance like a witch doctor in front of him, eyes popping, in summer parks, Iddyboy in his good nature pretending to slaver at the mouth unless he actually did and do his bidding completely like a zombie, and turn on Zagg, at Gus's orders, and chase him howling like a rhinoceros bull through the jungles of the adolescent screamers in afterdark lots; a long-standing joke in the gang that Mighty Iddyboy'd murder at G.J.'s bidding. But now they had subsided a little; Iddyboy had a girl, was on his way to see her, "Rita's her name," he told them, "you dont know her she is a nice girl, up there," pointing, telling them in his simple way, a big red-cheeked robust French Canadian paisan son of a large raucous family two blocks away. On his head too the snow had piled in a little hosanna'd crown . . . his well-combed, sleek hair, his big self-satisfied healthy face full and rich above the dark scarf and great warm coat of New England winter. "Eeedyboy!" he repeated, looking at everybody significantly, and starting off. "I see you—"

"Lookat him go, fuggen Iddyboy, d'javer see him walk home from school weekdays—"

"Hey Mouse, no kiddin hear what Jack's sayin? The first guy out of high school every day, the cellar doors open, the bell's just rung, everybody went back to home room, here comes Iddyboy, man number one, just like a dream he flies out walking long and with big lumberjack steps he cuts over the grass, the sidewalk, the canal bridge, right by the lunch-cart, the tracks, the city hall, now here comes the first high school regular kid out the cellar door, Jimmy McFee, Joe Rigas, me, the fast ones, out we come a hundred yards behind Iddyboy—"

"Iddyboy's already halfway up Moody Street, he not only wants to get to his homework as soon as possible because it takes him six hours to get it—"

"—flying on fast feet he strides past the Silver Star saloon, the big tree in front the girls' school, the statue, the—"

"—here he is"—(Lauzon and Zagg now vying to scream these informations to G.J. and all the others)—"six hours to get it done his homework but he has to eat his three hamburgers before supper and play six games of pish nut with Terry his sister—"

"—no time for any old Iddyboy to hang around and have a smoke and talk in front of high school and let Joe Maple see him and report him to the headmaster, Iddyboy the most honest hardworking never-played-hooky-in-his-life student in United States of America is leading the parade home up Moody . . . Long after him come the girls with their ga-dam bandanas and bananas. . . ."

"—Whattaguy that Iddyboy! There he goes in the snow." G.J. had taken up and was pointing him out. "See the snow hides his ass now. . . . Eeedy-bye oo You Babe OObloo is the salt of the earth, the top of the soup, the—no shit the finest kid that ever walked this God's green if we're gonna be ever saved . . . A little peace before we die, dear Lord," said G.J., concluding, making the sign of the cross, as everybody looked at him out of the corners of their eyes for the next laugh.

And the bright and merry corner was all theirs for a fifteen-minute interlude standing and talking in the youth of their hometown days. "Whattaya say there Zagg," said G.J., suddenly and roughly he grabbed Zagg and pulled him down into a headlock and rubbed his hair and laughed. "Good old Zagg, all the time he's standin there with a big smile on his face . . . what a good kid you are Zaggo—Scotty never had more gold in his teeth with his Kid Faro dealings than you

in your cracky cock-eyed always down in the mouth eyes shine
to show Zagg, that's no kidding Zagg . . . In the interests of
which, burp, brup," lifting his leg several times in a lewd
meaning, "I shall have to apply the headlock to you several
vises tighter till you cry for mercy from Turko G.J. the
Masked Ga-dam Marvel of Lowell decides to ease up and
hand his mercy—back, gentlemen, while I bring Zaggo
Dejesus Duluoz to his ga-dam knees once and mighty for
all—"

"Look, six thousand little kids in Destouches' store buying
up all the licorice and caramels—chewing stones in 'em—
Comics . . . What a life when you think of it— All the little
kids lined up at Boisvert's waitin for beans on Saturday night,
in the cold wind, hey Mouse take it easy," Zagg said from
the headlock below. They stood, all six, Zaza the funny
furious rage of a cat; Vinny suddenly laughing and slapping
Lousy and yelling in his rich throatbroken voice "Good old
Belgium Kid Louso you sen-e-ve-bitch"; Scotty thinking
"You think they'll lend me the money and sign on the dotted
line so I can get that car next summer, never"; Jack Duluoz
beaming, aureating the universe in his head, eyes blazing;
Mouse Rigopoulos nodding final confirmation with himself
that all things would end and end very sadly; and Albert
Lauzon, wise, silent, amazing, spitting soundlessly a little dry
snowflake of spit through his teeth to mark the general peace,
with them and without them, there and not there, child, old
man, the sweetest; all six standing there, silent at last, straight-
backed, looking at their Square of life. Never dreaming.

V

Never dreaming, was I, poor Jack Duluoz, that the soul is
dead. That from Heaven grace descends, the ministers thereof
. . . No Doctor Pisspot Poorpail to tell me; no example inside
my first and only skin. That love is the heritage, and cousin
to death. That the only love can only be the first love, the only

death the last, the only life within, and the only word . . . choked forever.

It was at the dance. The Rex Ballroom; with coat attendants in a drafty hall, a window, coatroom racks, fresh snow spilled on the boards; the rosy girls and handsome boys running in, the boys clacking heels, the girls in high heels, short dresses of the Thirties showing sexy legs. With awe we teenagers gave up our coats, got our brass disks, walked into the great sigh of the ballroom all six with fear, unknown sorrows. The band was on the stand, a young band, some seventeen-year-old musicians, tenors, trombones; an old pianist; a young leader; they struck up the sad lament of a ballad. "*The smoke from my cigarette climbs through the air. . . .*" The dancers met, engaged, shuffled; powder on the floor; lights playing in polka-dots around the hall with its upstairs balcony where cool young sitters watched. The six boys stood at the entrance un-decided, raw, foolish; turning sheepish smiles to one another for support; starting off in a halting gang, down the wall, past the wallflowers, the cold windows of winter, the seats, the other gangs of boys stiff collared and slick; the sudden group of jitterbugs with long hair and pegged pants. A bird of sad-ness whirled slowly around the room with the polkadots, singing love and death. . . . "*The walls of my room fade away in the blue and I'm deep in a dream of you. . . .*"

A jitterbug kid we knew was there. Whitey St. Claire from Cheever Street, long hair, pegged pants, bushy eyebrows, a strange serious interesting look, five feet tall, flashy dissipated rings under his eyes. "Oh Gene Krupa is the maddest drummer in the world! I saw him in Boston! He was the end! Look, you guys gotta learn to jitterbug! Watch!" With his little male partner Chummy Courval, who was even shorter and inconceivably sadder and more glamorous and with a button-down lounge lapel longer than almost his whole body, he joined hands and dug in heels in the floor and they flammed and whammed to show us.

Us, the gang: "What funny guys!"

"Amazing maniacs!"

"Did you hear what he said? Sixteen blondes fainted!"

"What a way to dance—I wish I could do it!"

"Now we'll get to meet some girls and throw em on the couch you babe!"

"We'll smoke them reefers and become big sex fiends you babe! Zeet?"

Whitey introduced me to Maggie. "I tried and tried to work that chick!" I saw her, standing in the crowd, forlorn, dissatisfied, dark, unpleasantly strange. Half reluctantly we were brought together and paraded to the floor arm in arm.

Maggie Cassidy—that in its time must have been Casa d'Oro—sweet, dark, rich as peaches—dim to the senses like a great sad dream—

"I suppose you're wondering what an Irish girl can be doing at a New Year's Eve dance unescorted," she said to me on the dancefloor; I, dope, had before danced only once, with Pauline Cole, high school sweetheart. (*"She'll be jealous!"* I enjoyed the thought.)

I didnt know what to say to Maggie, slavish I tied my tongue to the gate.

"Oh come on—say, you're a football player Whitey said."

"Whitey?"

"Whitey that introduced us, dummy."

It pleased me to be called a name, as though she was a younger sister—

"Do you get hurt often? my brother Roy gets hurt all the time that's why I hate football. I suppose you like it. You've got a bunch of friends. They look like a nice bunch of fellas— Do you know Jimmy Noonan in Lowell High?" She was nervous, curious, gossipy, womany: at the same time suddenly she'd caress me, say, at this early beginning, the necktie, adjust it; or push back my uncombed hair; something maternal, fleet, sorry. My hands clawed into fists to think of her when I got home that night. For, just ripened, the flesh bulged and was firm from under her shiny dress belt; her mouth pouted soft, rich, red, her black curls adorned sometimes the snow-smooth brow; up from her lips came rosy auras hinting all her health and merriness, seventeen years old. She leaned on one leg with the laze of a Spanish cat, a Spanish Carmen; she turned throwing fecund hair in quick knowing sorrying glances; she herself jeweled in the mirror;

I looked blankly over her head to think of other things.
"Got a girl?"

"In high school—Pauline Cole is my girl, I meet her under the clock every afternoon after third bell—" Iddyboy's rapid homeward walk now far away news in this new head of mine.

"And you tell me right away you got a girl!" Her teeth at first didnt seem attractive; her chin had a little doublechin of beauty, if the men will understand . . . that unnamed dimple chin, to perfection, and Spanish—her lip curled, slightly parted teeth charmed and enhanced sensuous, drowning lips, devourous lips; so at first you saw the little pearly teeth—

"You're probably an honest boy— You're French Canadian aintcha? I bet all the girls go for you, I bet you're gonna be a big success." I was going to grow up to walk in sleet in fields; didnt know it then.

"Oh—" blushing—"not exactly—"

"But you're only sixteen years old, you're younger than me, I'm seventeen—" She brooded and bit her rich lips: my soul began its first sink into her, deep, heady, lost; like drowning in a witches' brew, Keltic, sorcerous, starlike. "That makes me old enough ha ha," and she laughed her own incomprehensible girly jokes as I put my hard arm around her soft waist and took her dancing awkward dumb steps under the balloons and crinkly pop funhats of New Year's Eve America and the world orange and black like the Snow Hallowe'en, dumb and swallowing in my ignorance and position in time— People watching us saw the girl, timid, pretty, rather small-faced in a small hair crown but on closer inspection cameolike in choiceness but no paleness eyes therein, the gimlet fires in the beauty showed; and the boy, me, Jacky Duluoz, kid of write-ups, track teams, home and believing goodheartedness with just a touch of the Canuck half-Indian doubt and suspicion of all things non-Canuck, non-half-Indian—a lout—the order of the lout on my arm— They saw this boy well-brushed though not combed consciously, still a kid, suddenly big as a man, awkward, etc.—with serious blue-eyed pensive country-boy countenance sitting in gray high school halls in button-down sweater no water on his hair as photographer snaps line of home roomers— Boy and girl, arms around each other,

Maggie and Jack, in the sad ball floor of life, already crest-fallen, corners of the mouth giving up, shoulders loosening to hang, frowns, minds forewarned—love is bitter, death is sweet.

VI

The Concord River flows by her house, in July evening the ladies of Massachusetts Street are sitting on wooden doorsteps with newspapers for fans, on the river the starlight shines. The fireflies, the moths, the bugs of New England summer rattle-bang on screens, the moon looms huge and brown over Mrs. McInerney's tree. Little Buster O'Day is coming up the road with his wagon, torn knees, punching it through holes in the unpaved ground, the streetlamp dropping a brown vast halo bugswept on his little homeward figure. Still, and soft, the stars on the river run.

The Concord River, scene of sand embankments, railroad bridges, reeds, bullfrogs, dye mills—copses of birch, vales, in winter the dreaming white—but now in July midsummer the stars roll vast and shiny over its downward flow to the Merrimack. The railroad train crashes over the bridges; the children beneath, among the tar poles, are swimming naked. The engine's fire glow is red as it goes over, flares of deep hell are thrown on the little figures. Maggie is there, the dogs are there, little fires . . .

The Cassidys live on Massachusetts Street at No. 31—it's a wood house, seven rooms, apple trees in back; chimney; porch, with screen, and swing; no sidewalk; rickety fence against which in June tall sunflowers lean at noon for wild and tender hallucinations of little infants playing there with wagons. The father James Cassidy is an Irishman, brakeman on the Boston and Maine; soon conductor; the mother, a former O'Shaughnessy with dove's eyes still in her long-lost face of love now face of life.

The river comes between lovely shores narrowing. Bungalows scatter the landscape. The tannery's over to the west. Little grocery stores with wood fences and dusty paths, grass, some drying-out wood at noon, the ring ding of the little bell, kids buying Bostons or penny Bolsters at lunch noon; or milk early Saturday morning when all is so blue and sweet for the day of the play. Cherry trees drop blossoms in May. The funny gladness of the cat rubbing against the porch steps in the drowsy two o'clock when Mrs. Cassidy with her littlest daughter returns from shopping at Kresge's downtown, gets off the bus at the junction, walks seven houses down Massachusetts Street with her bundles, the ladies see her, call out "What'd you buy Mrs. Cassidy? Is that fire sale still on at Giant Store?"

"Radio says it is . . ." another greeter.

"Wasnt you on the Strand program on the sidewalk interviews?—Tom Wilson asked the silliest questions— Hee hee hee!"

Then among themselves "That little girl must have rickets the way she walks—"

"Those cakes she gave me yesterday I just had to throw them away—"

And the sun beams gladly on the woman at the gate of her house. "Now where can Maggie be? I told her a dozen times I wanted that wash hung out before I got back even if it was eleven o'clock—"

And at night the river flows, it bears pale stars on the holy water, some sink like veils, some show like fish, the great moon that once was rose now high like a blazing milk flails its white reflection vertical and deep in the dark surgey mass wall river's grinding bed push. As in a sad dream, under the streetlamp, by pocky unpaved holes in dirt, the father James Cassidy comes home with lunchpail and lantern, limping, red-faced, and turns in for supper and sleep.

Now a door slams. The kids have rushed out for the last play, the mothers are planning and slamming in kitchens, you can hear it out in swish leaf orchards, on popcorn swings, in the million-foliaged sweet wafted night of sighs, songs, shushes. A thousand things up and down the street, deep, lovely, dangerous, aureating, breathing, throbbing like stars; a whistle, a faint yell; the flow of Lowell over rooftops beyond; the bark on the river, the wild goose of the night yakking, ducking in the sand and sparkle; the ululating lap and purl and lovely mystery on the shore, dark, always dark the river's cunning unseen lips murmuring kisses, eating night, stealing sand, sneaky.

"Mag-gie!" the kids are calling under the railroad bridge where they've been swimming. The freight train still rumbles over a hundred cars long, the engine threw the flare on little white bathers, little Picasso horses of the night as dense and tragic in the gloom comes my soul looking for what was there that disappeared and left, lost, down a path the gloom of love. Maggie, the girl I loved.

VII

In winter night Massachusetts Street is dismal, the ground's frozen cold, the ruts and pock holes have ice, thin snow slides over the jagged black cracks. The river is frozen to stolidity, waits; hung on a shore with remnant show-off boughs of June— Ice skaters, Swedes, Irish girls, yellers and singers— they throng on the white ice beneath the crinkly stars that have no altar moon, no voice, but down heavy tragic space make halyards of Heaven on in deep, to where the figures fantastic amassed by scientists cream in a cold mass; the veil of Heaven on tiaras and diadems of a great Eternity Brunette called night.

Among these skaters Maggie performed; in her sweet white skates, white muff, you see the flash of her eye in their pools of darkness all the more strikingly: the pinkness of her cheek, her hair, the crown of her eyes corona'd by God's own bent wing— For all I knew as I toasted my skated feet at Concord River fires in the February Lowell, Maggie could have been the mother or the daughter of God—

Dirty snow piled in the gutters of Massachusetts Street, something forlorn hid in little pits of dirt, dark—the mute companions of my midnight walks from the overpowering lavish of her kisses.

She gave me a kiss upsidedown in the chair, it was a winter night not long after I'd met her, I was in the dark room with the big radio with its throbbish big brown dial that Vinny also had in his house and I'm rocking in the chair, Mrs. Cassidy her mother is in her own kitchen the way my mother three miles across town was—same old big old good old Lowell lady in her eternity wiping the dishes putting them away in the clean cupboards with that little feminate neatness and orderly ideas of how to go about things—Maggie's on the porch goofing in the icy night a minute with Bessy Jones her chum from the bungalow across the street, a big fat red-haired goodnatured girl with freckles and whose inconceivably feeble little brother sometimes delivered me notes from Maggie written the night before school in some brown light of her bedroom or in the morning at pipe keen frost, to hand to him, over the crackly fence, and he in his usual round of days trudged to school two miles away or took the bus and as he rheumy-eyedly weepingly came into his Spanish class which was every morning the second and impossibly dull he handed me the note sometimes with a feeble little joke—just a little kid, for some reason they'd shoved him on to high school through red morning cold parochials where he skipped grades and missed the sixth, or fifth, or both, and here he was a little kid with a hunting rag cap with a Scottish haggle tassel and we believed him to be like our age. Maggie would plant the note in his thin freckly hand, Bessy'd be giggling from behind the open kitchen window, she's taking advantage of the window being open and also putting the empty milkbottles out. Little Massachusetts Street in the cold mornings of rosy snow sun in January is alive with the fragrant whip of blacksmoke from all the cottage chimneys; on the white frozen cap of the Concord River we see last night's bonfire a charred ruinous black spot near the thin bare reddish reeds of the other shore; the whistle of the Boston and Maine engine sounds across the trees, you shudder and pull your coat

tighter to hear it. Bessy Jones . . . sometimes she'd write notes
to me too, giving instructions on how to win Maggie, that
Maggie'd also read. I accepted everything.

"Maggie loves you," etc., "she's madder about you than I
can ever remember her being mad about anybody else" and
in effect she'd say "Maggie loves you, but dont try her
patience—tell her you want to marry her or sumptin." Young
girls—giggly—on the porch—as I sit in the livingroom dark
waiting for Maggie to come back on the chair with me. My
tired track team legs are beneath me, folded. I hear other
voices on the Cassidy porch, some boys, that Art Swenson
I heard about—I feel jealous but it's only the bare beginning
of all the jealousy that came later. I'm waiting for Maggie
to come and kiss me, make it official. While waiting I have
ample time to review our love affair; how the first night she'd
meant nothing to me when we danced, I held her, she seemed
small, thin, dark, unsubstantial, not important enough— Just
her strange rare sadness coming from the other side of something made me barely notice she was there: her pretty looks
. . . all girls had pretty looks, even G.J. hadnt mentioned
her. . . . The profundity wave of her womanhood had not yet
settled over me. That was New Year's Eve—after the dance
we'd walked home in the cold night, the snow was over, just
tight and soft on the implacable frozen ground, we passed
long construction oil flares like avenues and parades on our
way down to South Lowell and the banks of the Concord—
the silent frost on the rooftops in the starlight, ten degrees
above zero. "Sit on the porch awhile anyway—" There were
little children-whimpering understandings between us that we
would join our lips and kiss even if we had to do it outdoors—
The thought of it had begun to excite me even then. But now,
waiting in the chair, and why worry about time, the meaning
of her *kissed* had become all things to me. In the variety of
the tone of her words, moods, hugs, kisses, brushes of the lips,
and this night the upsidedown kiss over the back of the chair
with her dark eyes heavy hanging and her blushing cheeks full
of sweet blood and sudden tenderness brooding like a hawk
over the boy over the back, holding the chair on both sides,
just an instant, the startling sudden sweet fall of all her hair

over my face and the soft downward brush of her lips, a moment's penetration of sweet lip flesh, a moment's drowned in thinking and kissing in it and praying and hoping and in the mouth of life when life is young to burn cool skin eye-blinking joy—I held her captured upside down, also for just a second and savored the kiss which first had surprised me like blind man's bluff so I didnt know really who was kissing me for the very first instant but now I knew and knew everything more than ever, as, grace-wise, she descended to me from the upper dark where I'd thought only cold could be and with all her heavy lips and breast in my neck and on my head and sudden fragrance of the night brought with her from the porch, of some 5 & 10 cheap perfumes of herself the little hungry scent of perspiration warm in her flesh like preciousness.

I held her a long time, even when she struggled to fall back. I realized she'd done it for a mood. She loved me. Also I think we were both frightened later when we'd hold a kiss for 35 minutes until the muscles of our lips would get cramps and it was painful to go on—but somehow we were supposed to do this, and what everybody said, the other kids, Maggie and all the others "necking" at skate and post office parties and on porches after dances had learned this was the thing—and did it in spite of how they felt about it personally—the fear of the world, the children clinging in what they think is a mature, secure kiss (challenging and grown-up)—not understanding joy and personal reverence— It's only later you learn to lean your head in the lap of God, and rest in love. Some gigantic sexual drive was behind these futile long smooches, sometimes our teeth'd grind, our mouths burn from interchanged spittle, our lips blister, bleed, chap— We were scared.

I lay there on my side with my arm around her neck, my hand gripped on her rib, and I ate her lips and she mine. There were interesting crises. . . . No way to go further without fighting. After that we'd just sit and gab in the black of the parlor while the family slept and the radio played low. One night I heard her father come in the kitchen door—I had no idea then of the great fogs rolling over fields by the sea in Nova Scotia and the poor little cottages in lost storms, sad work, wintry work in the bottom of life, the sad men with pails who walk in fields—the new form of the sun every morning— Ah I loved my Maggie, I wanted to eat her, bring her home, hide her in the heart of my life the rest of my days. I prayed in Sainte Jeanne d'Arc church for the grace of her love; I'd almost forgotten . . .

Let me sing the beauty of my Maggie. Legs: —the knees attached to the thighs, knees shiny, thighs like milk. Arms: — the levers of my content, the serpents of my joy. Back: —the sight of that in a strange street of dreams in the middle of Heaven would make me fall sitting from glad recognition. Ribs: —she had some melted and round like a well formed apple, from her thigh bones to waist I saw the earth roll. In her neck I hid myself like a lost snow goose of Australia, seeking the perfume of her breast. . . . She didnt let me, she was a good girl. The poor big alley cat with her, though almost a year younger, had black ideas about her legs that he hid from himself, also in his prayers didnt mention . . . the dog. Across the big world darkness I've come, in boat, in bus, in airplane, in train standing my shadow immense traversing the fields and the redness of engine boilers behind me making me omnipotent upon the earth of the night, like God—but I have never made love with a little finger that has won me since. I gnawed her face with my eyes; she loved that; and what was bastardly I didnt know she loved me—I didnt understand.

"Jack—," after we'd had all our conversations about the kids she fiddled with all day, while I was at school and since I'd last seen her, the gossip, things of high school kids talking about others their age, the stories, rumors, news of the dance, of marriage . . . "Jack, marry me some day."

"Yes, yes, always—nobody else."

"You sure there's nobody else?"

"Well *who* could be?" I didnt love the girl Maggie was jealous of, Pauline, who'd found me standing in the gang of football players one night in autumn at a dance where I'd gone because there was a banquet for the players and a basketball game we wanted to see, boy stuff—I was waiting in the corner for the dance to end, the idea of dancing with a girl

was impossible but I had it concealed— She picked me out
of a corner like young men dream. She said, "Hey I like
you!—you're bashful, I like bashful people!" and drew me
tremblingly excitingly to the floor, great eyes in mine, and
pulled my body and hers and squeezed me interestingly and
made me "dance" to talk, to get acquainted—the smell of
her hair was killing me! In her door at home she was looking
at me with the moon in her eyes, saying, "If you wont kiss me
I'll kiss you" and opened the screendoor I'd just closed and
gave me a cool kiss— We had talked about kisses looking at
each other's mouths all night; we had said we werent interested in such things—"I'm a good girl, I believe in h-hmm—
kissing"—flutter—"but I mean I wouldnt allow anything
beyond that to happen"—like in New England the girls—"but
you've got bedroom eyes, hey. Did I tell ya about the guy I
didnt know who put his arm around me at the Girl Officers'
Ball?" She was a Girl Officer.

"What?"

"Dont you want to know if I asked him to take his hands
off me—?"

"Yeah?"

"Dont be silly, I dont talk to strangers."

Pauline, brown hair, blue eyes, the great glistening stars in
her lips— She too lived near a river, the Merrimack, but near
the highway, the big bridge, the big carnival and football
field—you could see the factories across the river. I spent
many afternoon there conversing with her in the snow, about
kisses, before meeting Maggie. All of a sudden one night she
opens the damned door and kisses me—big stuff! The first
night I met her all I could do was smell her hair in my bed,
in my hair—told this to Lousy, I smelt her in his hair too. It
interested Lousy. When I told him we'd finally kissed the
night before (sitting with him on my bed with the gang G.J.
Scotty Iddyboy sitting in chairs of my bedroom after supper
talking about the team my mother doing the dishes my father
at the radio) Lousy wanted me to kiss him like I had kissed
Pauline. We did it, too; the others didnt even stop talking
about the team. But now Maggie was another matter—her
kisses, an expensive wine, we dont have much, nor often—

hidden in the earth—limited, like Napoleon brandy—pretty soon no more. Marry, love somebody else? Impossible. "I love only you, Maggie," I tried to say, no more success than with G.J. the little boy loves of puberty. I tried to assure her that she would never have cause for jealousy, truly. Enough of singing—I'll sing later—the story of Maggie—the beginning of my jealousy, the things that happened.

The mortality in my heart is heavy, they're going to throw me in a hole already eaten by the dogs of dolor like a sick Pope who's played with too many young girls the black tears flowing from his skeleton-hole eyes.

Ah life, God—we wont find them any more the Nova Scotias of flowers! No more saved afternoons! The shadows, the ancestors, they've all walked in the dust of 1900 seeking the new toys of the twentieth century just as Céline says—but it's still love has found us out, and in the stalls was nothing, eyes of drunken wolves was all. Ask the guys at the war.

VIII

I see her head bowed in thinking of me, by the river, her beautiful eyes searching inside for the proper famous thought of me she loved. Ah my angel—my new angel, black, follows me now—I exchanged the angel of life for the other. Before the crucifix of Jesus in the house I stood attentively, sure of many things, I was going to see the tears of God and already I saw them in that countenance elongated white in plaster that gave life—gave life bitten, finished, droop-eyed, the hands nailed, the poor feet also nailed, folded, like winter cold feet of the poor Mexican worker you see in the street waiting for the guys to come with the barrels to empty the rags the crap and keeps one foot on the other to keep warm— Ah— The head bent, like the moon, like my picture of Maggie, mine and God's; the dolors of a Dante, at sixteen, when we dont know conscience or what we're doing.

When I was younger, ten, I'd pray at the crucifix for the love of my Ernie Malo, a little boy in parochial school, son of a judge, who because he was like my dead brother Gerard I loved with as sublime a love—with the strangeness of childhood in it, for instance I'd pray at the picture of my brother Gerard, dead at nine when I was four, to insure the friendship, respect and grace of Ernie Malo—I wanted little Ernie to give me his hand, simply, and say to me, "Ti Jean, you you're nice!" And—"Ti Jean, we'll be friends always, we'll go hunting together in Africa when we finish school ha?" I found him as beautiful as seven times the pick because his rosy cheeks and white teeth and the eyes of a woman dreaming, of an angel maybe, bit my heart; children love each other like lovers, we dont look at their little dramas in the course of our adult days. The picture—, also at the crucifix I prayed. Every day at school it was one ruse after another to make me loved by my boy; I watched him when we all stood in line in the schoolyard, the Brother up front was delivering his speech, his prayer in the cold zero, redness of Heaven behind him, the big steam and balloon and ballturd of horses in the little alley that crossed the school property (Saint Joseph's Parochial), the ragmen were coming at the same time we were marching to class. Dont think we werent afraid! They had greasy hats, they grinned in dirty holes on top of tenements. . . . I was crazy then, my head ran fantastic ideas from seven morning till ten night like a little Rimbaud in his racks cracked. Ah the poetry I'd written at ten—letters to Maggie —afternoons walking to school I'd imagine movie cameras turned on me, the Complete Life of a Parochial School Boy, his thoughts, way he jumps against fences. —Voila, at sixteen, Maggie—the crucifix—there, God knew I had love troubles that were big and real now with his plastic statued head just neckbroke leaned over as sad as ever, more sad than ever. "You found yourself your little darknesses?" said God to me, silently, with his statue head, before it my hands clasped waiting. "Grew up with your little *gidigne*?" (dingdong). At the age of seven a priest had asked me in the confessional "And you played with your little *gidigne*?"

"Yes *mon père*."

"Well therefore, if you played with your little *gidigne* say a whole rosary and after that do ten *Notre Pères* and tcn *Salut Marie's* in front of the altar and after that you can go." The Church carried me from one Saviour to another; who's done that for me since?—why the tears?—God spoke to me from the crucifix:—"Now it is morning and the good people are talking next door and the light comes in through the shade —my child, you find yourself in the world of mystery and pain not understandable—I know, angel—it is for your good, we shall save you, because we find your soul as important as the soul of the others in the world—but you must suffer for that, in effect my child, you must die in pain, with cries, frights, despairs—the ambiguities! the terrors!—the lights, heavy, breakable, the fatigues, ah—"

I listened in the silence of my mother's house to divine how God was going to arrange the success of my love with Maggie. Now I could see her tears too. Something there was, that was not, nothing, just the consciousness that God awaits us.

"Mixing up in the affairs of the world isnt for God," I told myself hurrying to school, ready for another day.

IX

Here was a typical day, I'd get up in the morning, seven, my mother'd call, I'd smell the breakfast of toast and gruel, the windows were frozen an inch of snowy ice the whole glass illuminated rose by the transformations of the ocean of winter outside. I'd jump out of the sheets so warm soft, I wanted to stay buried all day with Maggie and maybe also just the darkness and the death of *no time*; I'd jump into my incontestable clothes; inescapable cold shoes, cold socks that I threw on the oil stove to warm. Why did people stop wearing long underwear?—it's a bitch to put on little undershirts in the morning —I'd throw my warm pajamas on the bed— My room was lit by the morning the color of a rose coal a half-hour dropped from the grate, my things all there like the Victrola, the toy pool table, the toy green desk, the linoleum all raised one side and sitting on books to make banks for the pool balls that raced track meets when I had time but I didnt any more— My tragic closet, my jacket hung in a dampness like powder from fresh plaster lost locked like adobe closets Casbah roof civilizations; the papers covered with my printed handwritings, on the floor, among shoes, bats, gloves, sorrows of pasts. . . . My cat who'd slept with me all night and was now thrown awake in the empty semi-warm bed was trying to hide himself in near the pillow and sleep a little more but smelled the bacon and hurried to begin his day, to the floor, plap, disappearing like a sound with little swift feet; sometimes he was gone when seven o'clock woke me, already out making crazy little tracks in the new snow and little yellow balls of pipi and shivering his teeth to see the birds in trees as cold as iron. "Peeteepeet!" the birds said; I look outside briefly before leaving my room, in a window hole, the roofs are pure, white, the trees frozen mad, the cold houses smoking thinly, docile-eyed in winter.

You have to put up with life.

X

In the tenement it was high, you could see downstairs the roofs of Gardner Street and the big field and the trail people used gray rose dawns five o'clock January to go flatulate in church. There were old women of the block who went to church every dawn, and late afternoon; and sometimes again evening; old, prayery, understanding of something that little children dont understand and in their tragedy so close you'd think to the tomb that you saw already their profiles sitting in rose satin the color of their rose-morns of life and expectoration but the scent of other things rising from the hearts

of flowers that die at the end of autumn and we've thrown
them on the fence. It was the women of interminable novenas,
lovers of funerals, when somebody died they knew it right
away and hurried to church, to the house of death and to the
priest possibly; when they themselves died the other old
women did the same thing, it was the cups of sugar in eternity— There's the trail; and winter important morning
opening stores and people *hallo!* and I got ready to go to
school. It's a *méli-mélon* of morning everywhere.

XI

I'd have breakfast.

My father was usually away on his out-of-town job running
a linotype for some printer—Andover, near the little crewcuts
there who had no idea of the darkness inherent in the earth
if they didnt see that sad big man crossing the night to go
make his 40-hour week—so he was not at our kitchen table,
usually just my mother, cooking, and my sister, getting ready
for her job at So and So's or *The Citizen*, she was a book-
binder— Grave facts of worklife were explained to me but I
was too proud in purple love to listen— Ahead of me, nothing
but the New York *Times*, Maggie, and the great world night
and morning of the shrouds on twig and leaf, by lakes—"Ti
Jean!" they called me—I was a big lout, ate enormous breakfasts, suppers, afternoon snacks (milk, one quart: peanut
butter and crackers, ½ pound). "Ti Jean!"—when my father
was home, *"Ti Pousse!"* he called me, chuckling (Little
Thumb). Now oatmeal breakfasts in the rosiness—

"Well how's your love affair with Maggie Cassidy coming
along?" my sister'd ask, grinning from behind a sandwich,
"or did she give you the air because of Moe Cole!"

"You mean Pauline? Why Pauline?"

"You dont know how jealous women get—that's all they
think about— You'll see—"

"I dont see anything."

"*Tiens,*" my mother's saying, "here's some bacon with toast I made a big batch this morning because yesterday you finished em all up and you was fightin at the end for the last time like you used to do over Kremel, never mind the jealous girls and the tennis courts, it's gonna be awright if you just stick to your guns there like a real French Canadian boy the way I brought you up to respect decency—listen, Ti Jean, you'll never be sorry if you always follow a clean life. You dont have to believe me, you know." And she'd sit and we'd all eat. At the last minute I'd stand undecided in my room, looking at the little radio I just got and in which I'd just started listening to Glenn Miller and Jimmy Dorsey and romantic songs that tore my heart out . . . *My Reverie, Heart and Soul,* Bob Eberle, Ray Eberle, all the blue sighing America was racked up behind me in the night that was all mine and the glory of the tenderness of the trembling kiss of Maggie and all love as only teenagers know it and like perfect blue ballrooms. I wrung my hands Shakespeareanly at my closet door; crossing the bathroom to grab a towel my eyes misted from sudden romantic notions of myself sweeping Maggie off a pink dancefloor onto a pier with a moon shining, into a slick convertible, a close kiss long and sincere (just a little to the right).

I'd just started shaving; one night my sister had surprised me combing my hair making a little tuck in my crown for a wave—"Oh boy, look at the Romeo!" It was surprising; two months before I'd been a boy, coming home from fall football practice in iron dusks wrapped in my jacket and earmuff cap, bent, offnights I'd spot pins at the alley with twelve-year-old boys, at three cents a string—20 strings, 60 cents, usually I made that or a buck— Just a boy, I'd only recently cried because I lost my hat while playing in a WPA League basketball game won at the last second by a sensational toss by Billy Artaud almost rivaling the time at the Boy's Club tie-score with one second to go against a Greek team tigerishly named I made a one-hand last-whistle jump shot out of the scrambling pack from about the foul line and the ball hung in the basket a horrid second for everybody to see, bagged, the game over, Zagg and his tricks—an inborn showman—ever-lasting hero. The hat now forgotten.

"By Ma," kissing my mother on the cheek, starting off for school, she herself worked part time in the shoe factory with her grave sense of life sitting grim and tireless at the skiving machine holding stubborn shoe leathers to a blade, her finger-tips blackened, years on end of it from fourteen on, other girls like her up and down the machines—the whole family working, 1939 was a tail-end Depression year about to be overshadowed by events in Poland.

I got my lunch, prepared the night before by Ma, slices of bread and butter; nothing was more delicious than these slices at noon after four hours almost interesting sunny class-room absorbed in personalities of teachers like Joe Maple with his eloquent statements in English 3 or old Mrs. McGillicuddy the astronomy (inseparable)—bread and butter and delicious hot mashed potatoes, nothing else, at the roaring basement tables my lunch cost 10¢ a day— The pièce de résistance was my magnificent chocolate-covered ice cream stick, every one in school 95% licked on them greedily every noon, on benches, in the huge cellar halls, on the sidewalks—recess— I'd sometimes in my grace like the grace that got me Maggie get thick ice cream almost an inch wide, by some mistake in the ice cream factory with rich unbelievable thick chocolate layer that also by mistake was larded and curled right on— by same industrial perchance, I'd get feeble anemic sticks a half-inch, already half melted, paper-thin chocolate falling on the sidewalk of Kirk Street as we'd Harry McCarthy, Lousy, Billy Artaud and me lick our sticks ceremoniously greedy in the winter sun my mind a million miles from romance— So I'd bring my bread and butter lunch, to be stuffed quickly in my homeroom desk—kiss Mother—and take off, on foot, to stride as fast as I could, like everybody else, down Moody past the posts of Textile to the great bridge to Moody tene-ments and down the hill into the city, gray, prosperous puffing in the morn. And along the way the soldiers'd fall in, G.J. off Riverside going to his business course in Lowell High where he learned typing and bookkeeping and made fantasies around the luscious girls who were going to be sexy secretaries, he'd begun wearing necktie and suit, he'd say "Zagg that Miss Gordon is going to take that expression of cool indifference off her face one of these days and let her panties slip on the floor for me, mark my words—and it'll be in one of those empty rooms one of these afternoons"—but instead of actual sexual conquests he'd wind up at two in the afternoon with his books in the Rialto B movie—alone, faced by the reality of Franchot Tone and Bruce Cabot and Alice Faye and Don Ameche grinning smiling at Tyrone etc. and old men and old women living on relief wide-eyed in the show. Too, Lousy'd come angling to my walk from Riverside; then, incredibly, Billy Artaud'd overtake us all from the rear striding madly down from the upper outskirt hill of Moody and just as we reached the canal downtown we'd see all of us that Iddyboy was way ahead and was already leaning out of his freshman homeroom window dutifully obeying the teacher's request to open window—"Eeediboy!" he'd yell, and disappear in, he was the most willing student in LHS and had the lowest marks and otherwise he would have been able to play football and would have killed everybody broken Malden guards in half with one clip of his granite elbow— Open homeroom window in Lowell, rose morn and birds upon the Boott Mill canal— Later it was going to be the open window morn at Columbia University the pigeonshit on the sill of Mark Van Doren and the Shakespeare of drunken sleeps under an Avon apple tree, ah—

Down Moody we'd sweep, primish, young, mad. Crossing us like a streamlet were the Bartlett Junior High School kids taking the riverbank route to the White Bridge and Wannalancitt Street which'd been our route for "How many years Mouse? Remember the winter it was so cold they had frostbites in the Principal's office with doctors?—"

"And the time we had that snowball war on Wannalancitt—"

"The crazy guys come to school with bikes, no kiddin Louse they had more trouble going up that hill from side to side than if they'd walk—"

"I used to walk home every noon me and Eddy Desmond wrapped in each other's arms falling on the ground—he was the laziest guy in the world, he didnt want to go to school in the afternoon, he wanted me to throw him in the river, I had to carry him—sleepy, he was like my cat, crazy—"

"Ah the old days!" Mouse'd pout black and brooding. "All I ask is a chance in this ga-dam world to earn a decent living and support my mother and see that all her needs are answered—"

"Where's Scotty workin now?"

"Didnt you hear?—out in Chelmsford, they're building ι big war airplane base, Scotty and all the old WPA bums go out and dig up trees and cut em down and clear the ground— he's making a million dollars a week—he gets up at four o'clock in the morning—Fuggen Scotcho—I love Scotcho— Dont catch *him* going to no high school and no business school courses, Kid Faro wants his money *now*—"

We came to the bridge. The water trickle between the jagged canyons of rock below, the pools of ice formed, rosy matin on the froth of little rapids, cold—far off, the bunga- lows of Centreville, and the snowy hump meadow, and hints of New Hampshire forests deep in where big men in mackin- aws now with axes and boots and cigarettes and laughs drove old Reos through rutted dirt strips among pinestumps, to the house, the shack, the dream of wild New England in our hearts—

"You're quiet, Zagg—that damn Maggie Cassidy's got you boy, s'got you boy!"

"Dont let no broad get you, Zagg—love aint worth it— what's love, *nothin*." G.J. was against it. Not Lousy.

"No, love is *great* Mouse—something to think about—go to church and pray Zagg You Babe! Marry her! Screw her! Zeet? Have a good one for me!"

"Zagg," advised Gus seriously, "screw her then leave her take it from an old seadog,—women are no good, forever 'tis written in the stars— Ah!" turning away, black—"Kick em in the pants, put em in their place— There's enough misery in this world, laugh, cry, sing, tomorrow is nothing— Dont let her get you down, Zagguth."

"I wont, Mouso."

"Zeet! Look here comes Billy Artaud—already for another

day rubbing his hands together—" Sure enough Billy Artaud who lived with his mother and every morning didnt rise from his bed but leaped out grinning came up rubbing his hands, you could hear the cold wiry sound of his zeal across the street.

"Hey, you guys, wait up— Let the chess champion walk!"

"*You're* the chess champion? Ho ho."

"What?—"

"With my bombarding tactics I can beat you all—"

"Zeet? Look at his books!"

—Wrangling, goofing, we stride without physical pause to school past Saint Jean Baptiste Church ponderous Chartres Cathredal of the slums, past gas stations, tenements, Vinny Bergeracs— ("Fuggen Vinny's still sleepin . . . they wouldnt even take him in vocational school . . . all this morning he'll read Thrilling True Love stories and eat them Drake's Devil Cakes with the white cream in the middle . . . he never eats food, he lives on cakes. . . . Ah ga-dammit I know we played hooky yesterday but my soul cries out for Vinny this gray sad morning."

"We better be careful—two days in a row?"

"Did you hear him yestiddy?—he said he was going to get sexmad now and stick his head in the toilet bowl!")—past the City Hall, the library in back with already some old bums gathering smoking butts at the door of the newspaper room waiting for nine o'clock opening time—past Prince Street ("Zowie, only last summer think of the games we had there, Zagg, the homeruns, the triples, the great Scotch pitching shutouts—life is so *big*!")—("life my dear Lousy is immerelensum!")—past the YMCA, the canal bridge, the entrance street to the great cotton mills with all up down the morning-rosy cobbles the tight serried Colonial doors of a mid-nineteenth century housing block for textile workers celebrated in some of Dickens' memoirs, the sad crapulous look of old red-brick sagging doorfronts and almost a century of work in the mills, gloom in the night.

And we came then mixing into the hundreds of students milling around the high school sidewalks and lawns waiting for the first bell which would be not heard outside but announced from within in a rumbling desperate-faced flying rumor so that sometimes when I was nightmarishly late I hurried all alone across the great deserted spaces only minutes ago scene of hundredfold gabbings now mopped out clean all the principals cubby-holed inside the silent high school windows in the morning's first classes, a mortifying great space of guilts, many times dreamed, sidewalk, grass. "I'm going back to school," dreams the old invalid in his innocent pillow, blind of time.

XII

The class filed into school at 7:50 A.M., generally things rammed and slammed for the last time in strange antenna'd moments when nobody was saying a word and the edge of the bench was cutting my elbow as I leaned my head on it trying to catch some sleep—in the afternoon I really slept, with great success in homeroom study after one o'clock when not spitballs but love notes were thrown around—late in the school day— Sun morning was orange fire in the unwashed windows, making way for day blue gold as birds whistled in trees, an old man leaned on the canal rail with his pipe in his mouth, and the canal flowed— All whorly and whirlpools and dense and tragic and to be seen from half a hundred windows of the north side of the high school building, the new one and the old for freshmen. Gigantic, the drownings in that canal would bloat a book, bloat a page, imaginary, dream'd in that clock hour of the rosy jongling lip of kid days in stylish sweaters. Lousy was in his class, all was right with the world. He abhorred and grinned on his end of a bench in the flaming sun atmospheres of the southwest windows, which in the winter received pale tropical flame from old northeast—the eraser's set out, the personal face-type's got his desk, he hangles and grows frowzy, somebody's got to set him right, the yawning day's just begun. Magazines, peeking at them a minute in his desk box, the lid up—"Oh there in the hall goes Mr. Nedick the English teacher with the over-sized pants—Mrs. Faherty the freshman grade or 9th grade teacher of Shakespearean rhymes'll come among us, there she is, the big important tack-tock of her biglady high heels," Joycean imaginings fill all our minds as we sit there goofily self-enduring the morning, waiting for the grave to lean our heads in, not knowing. In the cobbles by the factory by the canal I understand future dreams. I'll have them later on of the redbrick mills beyond vacant canals in blue morning, the loss brow-banging, done with— My birds will twitter on the branch of other things.

Eyes of pretty brunettes, blondes and redheads of the Lowell Prime are all around me. A new day in school, every-body wide-awake looking everywhere; today 17,000 notes will be delivered from shivering hand to hand in this ecstatic mortality. I can already see Stendhalian plots forming in the frowns of pretty girls, "Today I'll keep that damn Beechly awful innerested in a little idee of mine"—like Date-with-Judies self-communing monologues—"bring my brother into it and then everything'll be set." Others not plotting, waiting, dreaming the enormous sad dream of high school deaths you die at sixteen.

"Lissen, Jim, tell Bob I didnt *mean*—he knows it!"

"Sure, I told you I would!"

Running for vice-president of the sophomore class, pinning photos to crucial letters, rounding up a gang, trying to get something on Annie Kloos. They're all talking anxiously their plots, across the aisles, up and down the benches; the hubbub is so fantastic uproar momentous, weird, like sudden roars of Friday Afternoon California High School Football Games over quiet bungalow roofs, like teenagers at a roller derby, the teacher even is amazed and tries to hide behind the New York *Times* bought on Kearney Square at the only place where you can get them. The whole class invincible, the teacher'll get the authority at exactly the time but better not interfere before overtime starts—"Gonna be golly—" "well gee—" "Hey—" "What you say there!" "Hi!" "Dotty?—didnt I tell you that dress would look *divine*?"

"You didnt miss a trick, honey, I was perfect."

"The girls were wild about it, all of them. You shoulda heard Freda Ann come on! Yerr!"

"Freda Ann?" primping her hair very significantly. "Tell Freda Ann she can go along her own way I can get along without her comments—"

"Oh along along. Down in the hall's my brother Jimmy. He's got that little dumb Jones kid with him?" They join and peek, lip to ear. "See Duluoz up there? He's bringing a note from Mag-gie Cassidy."

"Who? *Mag-gie Cassi-dy?*" And they double and squeal and laugh and everybody turns to look, what are they laughing about, teacher's about to slap for order—the girls are laughing. My ears burn. I turn my dreamy inattention on everybody, thinking about my hot date pie with whipped cream last Sunday—the girls are looking into my blue windows for romance.

"Hmm. Isnt he dreamy?"

"I dont know. He looks sleepy all the time."

"That's the way I like—"

"Oh get away—how do you know how you like?"

"Wouldnt you like to know? Ask—"

"Ask *who?*"

"Ask who went with Freda Ann to the Girl Officers' Ball last Thursday and found themselves all tangled up, with Lala Duvalle and her gang of cutthroats and fingernail scratchers and you know who and know what else? I'm— Oh, here's the silence."

Blam, blam, the old teacher bangs her ruler and stands, very matronly, like an old busdriver, surveying the class for absences and then she makes a note and a few quibblings then from next room walks in Mr. Grass for some special news and everybody bends an ear as they whisper up front, a spitball sails funnily in the bright nice sun, and on comes the day. The bell. We all rush off to our first classes. Ah inconceivably lost the corridors of that long school, those long courses, the hours and semesters I missed, I played hooky two times a week on the average— Guilt. I never got over it— Classes in English . . . reading the very solid poetry of Edwin Arlington Robinson, Robert Frost and Emily Dickinson: a name I never knew to reckon with Shakespeare's. Wonderful classes in some kind of pre-science fiction astronomy, with an old lady with a long stick demonstrating moons at the blackboard. A class in physics, here we were blearily lost trying to spell the word barometer on our gray blue-lined examination paper let alone Galileo. A course in this, that, hundreds of beautiful intelligent young people hung on pursuits of pure mental interest and social jawbones, all they gotta do is get up in the morning, school takes care of the rest of their day, taxpayers support.

Some of them preferred rides to the country in tragic rumble seats, we never saw them again, they were swallowed in reform schools and marriage.

It being winter, I wore my football sweater letter "L"—to show off—it was huge, uncomfortable, too hot, I hung braced in its horrible corset of wool for hours on end day after day. Finally I settled to just my own blue home sweater buttoned down in front.

XIII

The second class was the Spanish one where I found the notes from Maggie, two a week. I read it right away:

> Well I suppose you thought I would never write a note this week. Well I had a swell time in Boston Saturday with my mother and sister but I said to myself when I saw my little silly sister isnt she a little flirt. I dont know what she will be like when she grows up. Well what have you been up to since I saw you. My brother and June that were married in April were here last night. How is school? Roy Walters is at the Commodore Tuesday and I am going. Glenn Miller is coming later on. Did you go to the diner after you left me Sunday? Well I havent any more to say now so
>
> So-Long MAGGIE.

Even if I was supposed to see her that night I still had a long way to go—after school it was track, till 6, 7 P.M. when it was my custom to walk home one mile with stiff legs. Track was in a low vast building across the street, with steel beams bare in the ceiling, great basketball floors six of them, then drill floor of the High School Regiments and sometimes several indoor football drills and some rainy day March baseball practice and big track meets with crowds sitting in bleachers around. Before going there I hung out at the empty halls, classrooms—sometimes met Pauline Cole under the clock which I'd done every day in December but now it was January. "There you are!" She gave out with a big smile, eyes big, moist, beautifully blue, full big lips over great white teeth, very affectionate—it was all I could do—"Where you been keepin yourself hey." Liking her, liking life too, I had to stand there assuming for myself all the gloomy guilts of the soul, out the other end of which my life flowed crying emptying in the dark anyway—weeping for what had been supposed— nothing within me to right the wronged, no hope of hope, blear, all sincerity crowded out by world-crowded actual people and events and the slack watery weakness of my own mean resolution—hung—dead—low.

Heirs leap screeching from doctors' laps while the old and the poor die on, and who's to bend over their bed and comfort.

"Oh I have to go to track in a minute—"

"Hey can I see you Saturday night against Worcester?—of course I'm coming anyhow, I'm only asking your permission so you'll talk to me."

O Wounded Wolfe! (That's what I thought I was, with the reading of a few books later)— At night I closed my eyes and saw my bones threading the mud of my grave. My eyelashes like an old maid being her most carefully concealed false: "Oh you're coming to a meet?—I bet I'll fall at the start and you wont think I can run."

"Oh dont worry I read about it in the papers, big-shot." Poking me—pinching me—"I'll be watching yerr, hey—" Then suddenly sadly getting to her girlish point, "I been missin ya."

"I been missin *you*."

"How could you!—not with Maggie Cassidy ya havent!"

"Do you know her?"

"No."

"Then how can you say that."

"Oh, I got spies. Not that I care. You know I go with
Jimmy McGuire lately. Oh he's nice. Hey you'd like him.
He'd make a nice friend for you. He reminds me of you. That
nice kid you know, your friend from Pawtucketville . . .
Lousy?—a little bit like him too. You all have the same eyes.
But Jimmy's Irish, like me."

I'd stand like a precious being, listening.

"So I get along all right dont you worry I wont knit socks
over *you* . . . hey did you hear me sing at the rehearsal for
the Paint n Powder show? Know what I sang?"

"What?"

"Remember the night last December we went skating, that
pond of yours out by Dracut and comin home in the freezing
night with the moon and the frost you kissed me?"

"*Heart and Soul*."

"That's what I'm goin to sing—" Corridors of time
stretched ahead of her, songs, sadnesses, some day she'd sing
for Artie Shaw, some day little gangs of colored people would
gather around her microphone in Roseland Ballroom and call
her the white Billy—the roommates of her hard-knock singing
days would go on to be movie stars— Now at sixteen she
sang *Heart and Soul* and had little affairs with bashful sentimental boys of Lowell and pushed them and said "Hey". . . .

"I'll get you back Mr. Duluoz not that I want you but you'll
come crawling, that Maggie Cassidy's only trying to take you
away from me to get into the act she wants to have a high
school football and track all around athlete if she cant come to
high school herself because she was too dumb to graduate
from Junior Hi— Hey Pauline Cole is that nice!" She pushed
me, then pulled me to her. "This is the last time I'll meet you
under our clock." It was a big boxlike clock hanging from
the wall of the school, donated by some old class when the
yellowbricks were new—we'd had our first trembling meeting
under it— When she sang *Heart and Soul* in the cold night
snow of fields it was the melting of our hearts we thought
forever— The clock was our big symbol.

"Well I'll see you *some* time."

"Not under this clock, kid."

I'd walk home alone, two hours to kill before track practice, up Moody in the wake of all the others long home and already changed for backlot yellings; Iddyboy had led the parade a long time ago with his books and eager eediboy stride ("How there boy?")—old drunks in the Silver Star and other Moody saloons watching the parade of kids— Now it was two—sad walk up through the slums, up the hill, over the bridge into the bright keen cottages and hills of Pawtucketville, perdu, perdu. Far on the Rosemont basin were the afternoon skaters in their blue; over their heads the dream of clouds long sobbed for and lost.

I climbed the stairs to my home on the fourth floor over the Textile Lunch—nobody in, gray dismal light filtering through the curtains— In gloom I take out my Ritz crackers peanut butter and milk from the pantry with its neat newspaper lining—no housewife of the Plastic Fifties had less dust— Then, kitchen table, the light from the north window, gloom views of grief-stricken birch on hills beyond the white raw roofs—my chess set and book. The book from the library; Scotch Gambit, Queen's Gambit, scholarly treatises on the combination of openings, the glistening chess pieces palpable to dramatize defeats— It was how I'd become interested in old classical-looking library books, tomes, chess critiques some of them falling apart and from the darkest shelf in the Lowell Public Library, found there by me in my overshoes at closing time—

I pondered a problem.

The green electric clock in the family since 1933 traveled its poor purring little second-hand around and around the elevated yellow numbers and dots—the paint chipping was leaving them half black, half lost—time herself rolling electrically or otherwise was eating at paints, dust slowly gathering on the hour-hand in the works inside, in the corners of the Duluoz closets— The second-hand kisses the minute-hand sixty times an hour 24 hours a day and still we swallow in hope of life.

Maggie was far away from my thoughts, it was my rest hour—I went to the windows, looked out; looked in the mirror; sad pantomimes, faces; lay in the bed, everything unutterably gloomy, yawning, slow to come—when it would come I wouldnt know the difference. In the bleak, birds squeak. I flexed my current muscles at the mirror's flat unbending blind blare— On the radio dull booming statics half obliterated lowly songs of the time— Down on Gardner Street old Monsieur Gagnon spat and walked on— The vultures were feeding on all our chimneys, *tempus*. I stopped at the phosphorescent crucifix of Jesus and inwardly prayed to sorrow and suffer as He and so be saved. Then I walked downtown again to track, nothing gained.

The high school street was empty. A late winter afternoon pinkbleak light had fallen over it now, it had been reflected in Pauline's sad eyes— Sagging old snowbanks, a black tree, weak sister sun on the side of an old building—the keen speechless winter blue beginning to appear over eastern eve roofs as the western ones pulse to the rose of distant dayfire dimming off the low cloudbanks. The last clerk's stacking sales slips in Bon Marche's. Dusk bird bulleted to his darknesses. I hurried to the indoor track, where the runners drummed on boards in a dark inside tragedy of their own. Coach Joe Garrity stood bleakly clocking his new 600-yard hope who in gladiator doom pumped and pulled elastic legs to expectation. Little kids threw final meaningless socks at the farthest baskets as Joe hollered to clear the gym, echoing. I ran into the lockers to jump into my track shorts and tightfitting slipper sneakers. The gun barked the first 30-yard heat, the runners shot from tilted fingertips and dug the planks away to go. I made preliminary warm-up runs around hollow clamoring board banks. Cold, goose-pimples on my arms, dust in the dumb gym.

"All right Jack," said Coach Garrity in his low calm voice, carrying across the planks like a mesmerist's, "let's see you try that new arm motion—I think that's been stoppin you for sure."

In inconceivable goofiness of my own mad mind I'd been for almost a month imitating the way Jimmy Dibbick ran, he was a distance runner, none too good, but had a way of pulling himself as he ran, hands far out fingertips stretched pointing pull-pumping like that into air reaching—a screwy style that I imitated just for fun; however in the dash, in which I was Number One man on the team beating at that time even Johnny Kazarakis who in another year beat everybody in the Eastern high schools of the United States but wasnt developed yet—the reach style was bad for my dash, I usually made 3.8 seconds in the 30, now I was retarded to 4 flat and getting beat by all kinds of kids like Louis Morin who was fifteen years old and wasnt even on the team yet just wore tennis sneakers of his own—"Run like you used to do," said Joe, "forget your arms, just run, think of your feet, *run, go,*—whatsamatter you got woman troubles?" he grinned cheerlessly but with a wise humor gained from the fact that he lived no life of recognition and ease, the best track coach in Massachusetts he nevertheless worked at some desk job all day in City Hall and had a handful of responsibility small-paying him. "Come on Jack, run—you're my only sprinter this year."

In the low hurdles among these kids I couldnt beat, I flew ahead; in Boston Garden roaring with all the high schools of New England I ran meek thirds behind longlegged ghosts two of them from Newton and everybody from Brockton, from Peabody, Framingham, Quincy and Weymouth, from Somerville, Waltham, Malden, Lynn, Chelsea—from the bird, endless.

I got down on the line with a group of others, spat on the planks, dug my sneakers in, balanced, trembling, shot off expecting Joe's gun and had to walk back sheepish— Now he held the gun up, we teetered, wondered, aimed eyes down the boards— BRAM! Off we go, I kick myself out with my right arm I let the arms pump themselves crosswise over my chest and run headlong falling for the line furious. They clock me in 3.7, I win by two yards blamming into the big mat against the finish wall, glad.

"There," says Joe, "didja ever hit 3.7 before?"

"No!"

"They musta made a mistake timing. But you got it now, pump those arms natural. All right! Hurdles!"

We put up the low hurdles, wood, some of them need new nails. We line up, blam, off we go—I've got every step figured, by the time we reach the first hurdle my left leg is ready to go over, I do so, slapping it down fast on the other side, *stepping,* the right leg horizontal folded to fly, arms swinging the move. Between first and second hurdles I jump and sprint and stretch and bound the necessary five strides and go over again, this time alone, the others are behind—I go down to the tape 35 yards two hurdles in 4.7.

The 300 was my nemesis; it meant running as fast as I could for almost a minute— 39 seconds or so—a terrible grueling grind of legs, bone, muscle, wind and flailing poor legs lungs—it also meant gnashing smashing bumps with the others around the first turn, sometimes a guy'd go flying off the bank flat on his ass on the floor full of slivers it was so rough, foaming-at-the-mouth Emil Ladeau used to give me huge whomps on the first bank and especially the last when panting sickfaced we stretched that last twenty yards to die at the tape— I'd beat Emil but I told Joe I didnt want to run that thing any more—he conceded to my sensitivity but insisted I run in the 300-yard relays (with Melis, Mickey McNeal, Kazarakis)—we had the best 300-yard relay in the state and even beat St. John's Prep older collegians in the Boston finals— So every afternoon I'd have to run the bloody 300 usually in a relay race, just to the clock, against another little kid twenty yards behind me and no footballing on the banks— Sometimes girls would come and watch their boyfriends in track practice, Maggie'd never have dreamed it she was so gloomy and lost in herself.

Pretty soon it'll be time for the 600—the 1000—broad jump—shot put—then home we go—for supper—then the phone—and Maggie's voice. Aftersupper Lowell talking to me—"Can I come tonight?"

"I told you Wednesday."

"That's too far away—"

"You're *cray*-zee."

—as lonely glooms fall enfolding all the warm organic rooftops of living Lowell—

XIV

After the last six o'clock shot put, the ball in the fingers delicately against the neck cradled, the kick, the hop, the twist of waist, the push up and out of the ball and far—this was fun—I'd go in to showers and re-dress to again for the third time in my busy crazy high day stride Moody Street determined, young, and wild—a mile home. In winter darkness, the Baghdad Arabian keenblue deepness of the piercing lovely January winter's dusk—it used to tear my heart out, one stabbing soft star was in the middle of the magicalest blue, throbbing like love—I saw Maggie's black hair in this night— In the shelves of Orion her eye shades, borrowed, gleamed a dark and proud vellum somber power brooding rich bracelets of the moon rose from our snow, and surrounded the mystery. Smoke whipped from clean chimneys of Lowell. Now at Worthen, Prince and other old milltown streets as my feet shot me past I saw the redbrick faded into something cold and rose—unspeeched—throatchoking— My father's ghost in a gray felt hat walked the dirty snows—*"Ti Jean t'en rappelle quand Papa travailla pour le Citizen?— pour L'Etoile?"* (Remember when your father worked for the Citizen, for the Star?)—I hoped my father'd be home that week end—I wished he could give me advice for Maggie— and in the grim mill alleys of ink blue and lost solstice rose the moseyed shades aside moaning my name, big, shadowy, lost—I shot past the Library now brown-windowed for scholars of the winter eve, the reading room bums, the children's library roundshelved fairytaled and sweet—the profound bloodred bricks of the old Episcopalian church, the brown lawn, the jag of snow, the sign announcing speeches— Then the Royal Theater, crazy movies, Ken Maynard, Bob Steele, the French Canadian tenements seen up side streets, the gay winter North—remnant Christmas bulbs— Then Ah the bridge, the sigh of waters, the soothe big roar low wind coming in from Chelmsford, from Dracut, from the north—the orange iron implacable dusk skies pinpointing the steeples, and roofs in a still gloom, the iron arbrous brows of old hills far off—everything engraved and glided upon the eve and that frozen still. . . My shoes clomped the bridge boards. My nose snuffled. A long and tiresome day and far from finished.

I passed the Textile Lunch windows, saw the bent fishy eaters through steam panes, and turned smartly into my gloomy rank doorway—736 Moody Street—dank—up four flights in eternity. In.

"Bon, Ti Jean est arrivez!" my mother said.

"Bon!" my father said, he was home, there was his face peeking around the kitchen door with a big Oriental grin— At table, my mother's loaded it with food, steamings, goodies, he's been feasting for an hour—I rush up and kiss his sad rough face.

"By golly I got here just in time to see you run against Worcester Satty night!"

"That's right!"

"Now you'll have to show me what you can do boy!"

"I will!"

"Eat! Look at the spread your mother's got here."

"I'll wash!"

"Hurry!"

I wash, come in combed, start eating; Pa's peeling his apple with his scout knife. "Well, I'm all through at Andover— Might as well tell you now— They're layin off, their rush season— I can try Rolfe's here in Lowell—"

"Ben oui!" my mother in French. "It's much better you

stay home!"——her tearful way of arguing and always her
arguments are sweet.

"Okay, okay," laughing—"I'll try my best. Well my little
tyke, how are you my boy! Say, maybe I can get a job at
McGuire's where Nin is— Say, what's this I hear about you
going around mooning over some little Irish girl— Bet she's
a beauty, hey? Well you're too young for that. Ha ha ha. Well
dammit, I'm home again."

"Home *agin!*"—Ma.

"Hey Pa I'll play you a game of football with the board—
Whattaya say?"

"I was thinking of going down to the Club and bowling
a few strings—"

"Well okay, *one* game—and I'll go bowl you a game!"

"It's a deal!"—laughing, coughing on his cigar, bending
quickly with huge red-faced excitement to scratch his ankle.

"Okay," says my mother proud and flushed and la-la'ing
to have her old man home again, "you do that and I'll clear
the table right away and make a nice fresh pot of coffee—aye?"

And in from the joyous cold night of the North come Lousy,
Billy Artaud and Iddyboy, there are big jokes and laughs,
and we choose sides, toss coins, pick teams and play a game.
In the windows is slow frost, the lamplights below are in a
cold and lonely black but quick figures breathing fog pass
swiftly beneath them to definite eager destinations—

Not knowing that I dont deserve life without praising God
I sneak off from the kitchen for a quick quiet phone call in
the dark parlor—calling Maggie— Her little sister Janie
answers. Maggie comes to the phone with a simple tired-
sounding "Hi."

"Hi—Wednesday night I'm comin over huh?"

"I *told* you."

"What are you doing tonight?"

"Oh nothing. I'm bored to tears. Roy and his girl are pl—
that are gettin married in August are playin cards. My father
just left to go to work, they gave him a short call, you shoulda
seen him run out the door—he forgot his railroad watch on
the dresser— He'll be hoppin mad!"

"*My* father's home."

"I'd like to meet your father sometime."

"You'll like him."

"What'd you do all day?—not that it's important . . ."

"I do the same thing every day—walk, school, walk back for a nap, walk back for track—"

"Spendin all your time talking to Pauline Cole under the clock?"

"Sometimes." I didnt hide it or anything. "Doesnt matter."

"Just friends, huh?"

In the way she said "huh?" I saw her whole body and lips and wanted to clup her a mad one she'd never forget.

"Hey—"

"What?"

"If you're bored to tears I'll come over tonight!"

"Okay."

"But I havent got time" (surprised I was). "But I will."

"No. You said you didnt have time."

"Yes I do."

"You said you dint."

"See you in an hour."

"Never mind . . ."

"Hah? I'll be right over. Hey."

To my father and friends riotously laughing in the kitchen: "Hey, I think I'll go see . . . Maggie Cassidy . . . that girl I know . . . she . . . we just . . . have to help her brother with his homework—"

"Aw," said my father looking up with frank stunned eyes, very blue eyes, "it's my first night home, you said we'd go bowling— We'll choose sides with the boys—"

"Zeet? Me and your Pop against you and Iddyboy!" cried Lousy in eager glee squeezing himself, then, to me, low, looking over his shoulder, for the benefit of everybody, "Maggie Cassidy that was? Ah Zagg you Babe that aint right cheatin on Pauline Cole! Hee hee! Hey Mister Duluoz we call Jack Zagg-you-Babe now— Hear that," grabbing me by the neck and making a frown, "now he's cheatin on Moe Cole— Let's drown him in the water, throw him in the snow—"

"Eeedyboy!" echoed Iddyboy with shining eyes showing me his huge fist. "I going to fix you Jack and knock you through the fence!" We made wrestler faces at each other.

Impatiently my mother: "Stay here, stay home Jean—"

Rubbing his hands wirily Billy Artaud: "He knows when he's beat! Doesnt wanta accept that challenge bowling— Let him go!" he finally yelled above all the others triumphantly as a commotion in the kitchen rose making little spiderwebs of the corner ceiling wave. "That leaves four of us, *we'll* have a bowling party—and Missiz Duluoz can keep the score!"

This raised roars of noise and laughing. I had a chance to go. All in life, prime, youngjoy days, riches of sixteen, I sneaked off to the lazy unresponsive girl three miles across town by the tragic-flowing dark sad Concord.

I took the bus—at the last minute avoiding my father's eyes—telling myself "I'll see him tomorrow for gosh sakes—" Ride the bus, guiltish, depressed, looking down, always the dross and dirty loss spine ribbing down life's poor gold and it so short and sweet.

It was a Monday night.

XV

From Pawtucketville to South Lowell the route by bus encompassed the city—down Moody, to Kearney Square below the high school, the fleets of buses, the people huddled waiting against doorfronts of soda parlors, 5 & 10s, drugstores— The sad traffic crunching in from winter, out to winter— The bleak blue raw feel of the wind from the woods cityfying by the few sad lights— There I changed to the South Lowell bus— It would show up always catching at my throat—the mere name of it as the busdriver'd rolled it in the window enough to make my heart beat—I'd look at other people's faces to see if they saw the magic— The ride itself grew grimmer— From the Square out up Central, to Back Central, to the outlying dark long streets of the town where dim frost sits the night by howling-wind garbage pails in cold moonlight— Out along the Concord where factories enlisted its famous flow—out beyond even them—to a dark highway where Massachusetts Street under a brown dumb streetlamp spoked in, small, mean, old, full of my love and the name of it— There I'd get off the bus, among trees, by the river, and dodge the mudholes, seven cottages down on the right to her rambling old unfenced brown-windowed house over-topped by clacking skeletal trees of the sudden from-Boston sea winds blown over wilderness, railyards and hoar— Each house meant my heart beat faster as it passed my rapid step. Her actual house, the actual light that actually upon her was bestowing and around her bathing, mote by mote made rare gold, dear magic, was the commotion hysterical light of wonder— Shadows on her porch? Voices in the street, in the yard? Not a sound, but the dull Victorian wind moaning New England by the river in the winter night—I'd stop in the street outside her house. One figure within—her mother—gloomy pawing in the kitchen, turning sadly in life, putting away her sweet dishes that some day they'd pack away with guilt and sorrow and say "I never knew, I never knew!"—The dumb, the spittling mankind crawing in his groin to make nothing.

Where is Maggie? O wind, songs have ye in her name? Plucked her did ye from midnight blasted milkyard winds and made her renown ring in stone and brick and ice? Hard implacable bridges of iron cross her milk of brows? God bent from his steel arc welded her a hammer of honey and of balm?

The rutted mud of hardrock Time . . . was it wetted, springified, greened, blossomied for me to grow in nameless bloodied lutey naming of her? Wood on cold trees would her coffin bare? Keys of stone rippled by icy streaks would ope my needy warm interiors and make her eat the soft sin of me? No iron bend or melt to make my rocky travail ease—I was all alone, my fate was banged behind an iron door, I'd come like butter looking for Hot Metals to love, I'd raise my feeble orgone bones and let them be rove and split the half and goop the big sad eyes to see it and say nothing. The laurel wreath is made of iron, and thorns of nails; acid spit, impossible mountains, and incomprehensible satires of blank humanity—congeal, cark, sink and seal my blood—

"*There* you are. What are you standing out in the road for? What'd ya come for?"

"Didnt we decide on the phone?"

"Oh . . . maybe you did."

This made me mad and I didnt say anything; now she was in her element.

"What are you so quiet about, Jacky boy?"

"You oughta know. Dont call me Jacky Boy. Why were you on the porch. I didnt see you!"

"I saw you comin down the street. All the way from the bus."

"It's cold out."

"I'm wrapped in my coat snug. Come on in with me."

"In your coat."

Laugh. "Silly. In the house. Nobody home. My mother's goin to Mrs. O'Garra tonight to hear the Firestone Hour, some singer."

"I thought you didnt want me to come. Now you're glad."

"How do y'know?"

"When you squeeze my hand like that."

"Sometimes you get me. Sometimes I cant stand how I love you."

"Hah?"

"Jacky!" And she was on me, all of her, thrown socko into me all huddled to my frame, clung, kissing me wild and deep and hot—desperate—it would never have happened on a regular Wednesday or Saturday night planned date—I closed my eyes, felt faint, lost, heartbroken, salt-sunk drowned.

In my ear, warm, hot lips, whisperings, "I love you Jacky. Why do you make me so mad! Oh you make me so mad! Oh I love you so! Oh I wanta kiss you! Oh you damn fool I want you to take me. I'm yours dont you know? — all, all yours—you're a fool Jacky— Oh poor Jacky— Oh kiss me— *hard*—save me!—I need you!" Not even inside the house yet. In there, by the hissing radiator, on the couch, we practically did everything there is to do but I never touched her in the prime focal points, precious trembling places, breasts, the moist star of her thighs, even her legs—I avoided it to please her— Her body was like fire, packed soft and round in a soft dress, young—firm-soft, rich—a big mistake—her lips burned all over my face. We didnt know where we were, what to do. And dark moved the Concord in the winter night.

"I'm glad I came!" I told myself jubilantly. "If Pa could see this or feel this he'd *know* now, he wouldnt be disappointed— Lousy too!—Ma!—I'm gonna marry Maggie, I'm gonna tell Ma!" I pulled her yielding yearning waist, it popped her pelvis bone right into mine, I gritted my teeth in the memory of the future—

"I'm goin to the Rex Saturday night," she said, pouting in the dark as I licked her lower lip with my fingertip then threw my hand on the floor off the couch and she was suddenly stroking my profile. ("You look like you're cut out of rock.")

"I'll meet you there."

"I wish you were older."

"Why?"

"You'd know more what to do with me—"

"If—"

"No! You dont know how. I love you too much. What's the use? Oh hell—I love you so! But I hate you! Oh go home! Kiss me! Lie on top of me, crush me—" Kisses— "Jacky I wrote you a big note today and tore it up—too much in it—"

"I read the one—"

"I finally sent that one—I wanted you to marry me in my first note— I know you're too young, I'm robbing the high school cradle."

"Ah—"

"You have no trade— You have a career ahead of you—"

"No no—"

"—be a brakeman on the railroad, we'll live in a little house by the tracks, play the 920 Club, have babies— I'll paint my kitchen chairs red—I'll paint the walls of our bedroom deep dark green or sumpin—I'll kiss you to wake up in the morning—"

"Oh Maggie that's what I want!" (Maggie Cassidy? I thought wildly. Maggie Cassidy! Maggie Cassidy!)

"No!" Slapping me on the face, pushing it—angry, pouting, rolling away, sitting up to roundabout her dress again straight. "Hear me? No!"

I'd wrestle her to the bottom of the dark couch re-twisting her dresses slips belts and girdly toot pots both of us panting, sweating, burning— Hours passed, it was midnight, my day was not done— Reverently my hair was falling in her eyes.

"Oh Jack it's too late."

"I dont wanta go."

"You gotta go."

"Ah okay."

"I dont want you to go— I love you to kiss me— Dont let that Pauline Cole steal you away from me. Dont make faces like that I'll get up and walk away— Jacky—I love you I love you I love you—" She kept saying it into my mouth— through my teeth, bit my lip— There were tears of joy in her eyes, on her cheeks; her warm body smelled ambrosial brew in the profound struggle we waged sinking in pillows, bliss, madness, night—hours on end—

"You better go home, dear— You gotta go to school tomorrer— You'll never get up."

"Okay Maggie."

"Say you love me when you wake up in the morning, to yourself—"

"How could I . . . otherwise . . . do . . ."

"Call me tomorrer night—come Friday—"

"W—"

"I mean Wednesday! Kiss me! Hold me! I love you I always will and no one else ever ever—I never was so much in love—never again—you damn Canook you—"

"I cant leave."

"Leave. Dont let nobody tell you nothin about me."

"Nobody *does!*"

"If they do . . ."

"If they did I wouldnt lissen—Maggie that house by the railroad tracks, the red chairs . . . I . . . I . . . cant— dont want to do anything else with anybody else—ever— I'll tell—I'll —we'll— Ah Maggie."

She'd cradle my broken head in her all-healing lap that beat like a heart; my eyes hot would feel the soothe fingertips of cool, the joy, the stroke and barely-touch, the feminine sweet lost bemused inward-biting far-thinking deep earth

river-mad April caress—the brooding river in her unfathom-
able springtime thoughts— The dark flowing enriched silty
heart— Irish as peat, dark as Kilkenny night, sorcerous as elf,
red-lipped as red-rubied morn on the Irish Sea on the east
coast as I have seen it, promising as the thatched roofs and
green swards there bringing tears to my eyes to be an Irishman too and lost and sunk inside her forever—her brother,
husband, lover, raper, owner, friend, father, son, grabber,
kisser, keener, swain, sneaker-upper, sleeper-with, feeler, railroad brakeman in red house of red babycribs and the joyous
wash Saturday morning in the glad ragged yard—

I walked home in the dead of Lowell night—three miles,
no buses—the dark ground, roads, cemeteries, streets, construction ditches, millyards— The billion winter stars hugeing
overhead like frozen beads frozen suns all packed and inter-
allied in one rich united universe of showery light, beating,
beating, like great hearts in the non-understandable bowl void
black.

To which nevertheless I offered up all my songs and long-
walk sighs and sayings, as if they could hear me, know, care.

XVI

Walking home the last mile as all Lowell snored I imagined
myself a far traveler looking for a place to sleep—"Well,
pretty soon I'll have to turn in at one of these houses and go
to bed, I cant go on much further"—and I'd clack along on
the crunchy snows and grits of sidewalks, past moonlight-
whitened wash-hung courts of Moody tenements, past taxicab
stands with a one red light in night, past hamburger lunchcarts with inscrutable shadows munching within in smoke and
heat obscured by vapors of the written glass— For the sixth
time in the day I'd come to the great bridge a hundred feet
over the river and see down there the tiny milky rivulets of
icy Time gurgling in the rockjags, the reflection of starry

paradises in profound black pools, the squawk of strange birds eating mist— Clack went the trees of Riverside as I hushed and nose pinched stumbled on home—"I guess I'll have to turn in this house here—no, the next one— Well, I guess I'll take the fifth one— That's what— I'll just walk in and go right to sleep cause the whole world has invited me to sleep in their house so it doesnt matter what house I go to—"

And I'd turn into 736 Moody and go upstairs and go in the door left unlocked by my family and hear my father's profound snore in their bedroom and go to my spectral room with the big bed and *Jack Jump Over the Candlestick* on the wall and say to myself, "Well, this is a nice place, I think I'll sleep in this bed, these people seem nice"—and with strange self-induced whacky but deeply comfortable wonder I'd undress and go to bed and look in the dark at darkness— and fall asleep in the lap of warm life there.

And in the morning my eyes wouldnt unglue, at breakfast I'd decide to play hooky again, go to Vinny's and take a nap. All the winter world goldened and shined white—

XVII

Vinny's was the big scene of suicide hookies, we'd have wild parties all day screaming—"Come on G.J., play hooky with me today" I'd say at the corner of Riverside and he would and so would Lousy.

"Zagg, you cant talk me out of it!"

Sometimes Scotty'd come, and one time Skunk, and finally with Vinny we began passing up the sprawlings and eatings and yelling with the radio in his house when sometimes we'd have big fights and knock down curtains and it was a job to clean up for the millworking mother—talking about girls instead, listening to Harry James, writing screwy letters to everybody— We began hitting the Club de Paisan poolhall which was a shack in the Aiken Street dump behind the tenements of Little Canada— Here an old ninety-year-old man with perfect bowed legs stood by a pot-belly stove with an old French Canadian red Indian handkerchief to his nose and watched us (red eyes) tossing nickles on the torn pool table for who gets the break. The wind howled and moaned at the hinges; it was huge snow storms we'd pass there, the great gale of snows would whip past the plate-glass windows in one horizontal wild line from Canada coming, from the Sweeps of Baffin Bay—and we were alone in the Club. Nobody else would think of going to such a beat old shack—it was for local winos of Cheever and the river bank probably to in the evening come in with stinking pipes humble old guys spitting in planks—*Le Club de Paisan*—Club of Oldfashioned Peasants— Vinny screeched and danced around on the loose old boards through which the blizzard cold seeped but the stove held out, the old man stoked it, stocked it and kicked it, he knew how to make a fire like he knew how to eat.

"Hey Pop!" they'd call him. Scotty and I, respectful, called him *"L'Pere"* and he always knew the weather. For years of our lost numb childhoods he'd been sitting in wooden tenement lazy afternoon doorways of Moody and Lilley on the Lowell Fellaheen French Day—babies had yodeled, his old ears had heard generations come and go, croaking. Every game we played we threw him a nickle. "Okay my break Scot!"

"Ah go on—that nickle was leaning—"

"Kick him, you babe, kick him—"

They overturn a chair and a bucket, the old man doesn't even bat an eyelash. Our glory's all wild in the gray storm of shacks and dumps outside—our histories weighted down in the middle with unbelievable freights of moment by moment drowsy life hours that our mothers have carried on their eyelashes since our inceptions from their aprons and the first heroic events of infancy. Beautiful Vinny's glory lay in his eyes, health, screams. "If you guys dont stop shaking that table the way you have been doing I'll be ga-dammed for about ask Mouse a halfa fuggen hour I'm gonnna get my boxing gloves and my rubbers and load em full of bolts and screws and swing from the floor as hard as I can with all my weight and kick myself in the ass if I dont brain both of you flat on

the floor, like cows' shining azzoles, dead." And we saw
that he was going to do it if we didnt stop shaking the table.
Scotty didnt even have to mention anything, we saw flashes
of murder in his somber thunderstorm eyes. Lousy was a streak
of terrible lightning if something should suddenly happen, you
wouldnt see him and the air wouldnt split—suave litotical
transsubstantiations of a thrush—I was a self-satisfied dreaming bull supine on the bench or lost in thought shooting at the
table—eying my Coca-Cola. G.J.'s Greekly rage was buried
in his kind politeness and in his humor and goodness:— he'd
have slit the Sicilian from top to bottom in other Mediter-
raneas, showing but yellow of his eyes.

XVIII

Meanwhile my father was walking along the redbrick walls
of commercial Lowell, in the blizzard, looking for a job. He
walked into the dark dank printing plant—Rolfe's.

"Say Jim, how've you been, I want to know if you've got
an opening here for a good linotyper with years of experience—"

"Emil! Great Jesus, Emil!"

"Hi Jim."

"Where in the hell you been? Hey Charley, look, Emil—
Crazy Emil—what you been doin in Andover I hear—"

"Oh yeah, workin well framblin and dandlin around lookin
for something to do— Still got a wife, y'know, and two kids,
Jacky's in high school running with the track team this
winter— Say, I see old Cogan aint here any more."

"No, he died last April."

"Ya dont say-y. . . Well I'll be damned. *He* was over
seventy wasnt he?"—both in dark, satisfied agreement—"Well
poor old Cogan many's the time I saw him pushing and rushing that old wagon around, you'd think a man could work his
life out just workin—"

"That's right, Emil—" Quick muse—"In fact Emil—" (and now the job's sewed up because Rolfe hasnt got anybody else he knows in New England he'd rather have right now than Emil Duluoz and with the rush season on) "—last Saturday night I worked for the *Tele,* they called me up 'bout six o'clock, their regular man was sick and layin off so I said 'Okay' and I went up and boy I melted lead and turned out more galleys a ten-ton truck and it was about six o'clock in the morning when I finished and the back of my neck, and my feet numb from sitting all night—"

"I know Jim— Only last week it was old fartface come up to me and wanted me to go to a show with him then a game over to Bill Wilson's room in the hotel down there see this is all in Lawrence he'd drive me from Andover we had— Oh we saw a lot of nice gals dancing there ya know, hoopsidoo, that Gem Club, on Hollis Street, we had a few beers, I said to Bill 'I gotta finish this copy if you dont mind Bill looks to me like it'll take me to well nigh near midnight'—"

Meanwhile a kid is waiting with papers in his hand for the two old bucks the boss and the big fat man to stop talking but they wont—

Emil, a half-hour later, steps out into the snow, coughs hugely, cigar-a-mouth, and minces off like Babe Ruth or W. C. Fields with the same pout and little short steps but also with a leering pathetical grin looking at everybody and digging all the streets of Lowell with his eyes.

"Oh for krissakes, there goes that old Charley McConnell he's had that damn Model-T Ford ever since I got mine in 1929 and that was at Lakeview for the picnic there and even then he'd have that same look of pitiful defeat in his face, still and all he's made out all right from what I hear— That job in City Hall pays him fairly well and certainly hasnt killed him and he's got a house in the Highlands— *I* never had anything against McConnell"—(scoffing with himself, coughing) —"Well it's all in the way the rain barrel rolls over I guess, they'll spill em out one by one to the hole in the ground out by Edson's Cemetery and we'll take no more trips to Boston that way. . . . The years, the years, that I've seen . . . eat . . . the faces . . . of respectable . . . and disrespectful people

. . . in this town . . . they cant . . . tell me. . . . I dont know who's heir to Heaven, hell, riches, gold and all the immense uncounted cash registers and poorpot pissplots of every grave from here to the Roman diosee and back by golly I've seen and heard it all. When they put me away they better not spend too much money, *I* wont appreciate it from my bed of clay— *They'd* better learn that now. Ha ha ha ha! What a town when you come to think of it—*Lowell*—" He heaved a sigh. "Well it's where my little woman hung her curtains, I guess. The sucker was in the kitchen sittin by the radio, name of Emil. I guess the old lady had it coming to her, to inherit a beast and at the same time I guess she didnt do too bad with the pieces of—grass—I was able to lay around her picnic. My wife Angy— Okay. *God*, tell me if anything goes wrong and you dont want me to go on that way. I'm just tryna please. If I cant please the lion the angel and the lamb all at the same time neither. Thank you God, and get those Democrats outa there before this country goes to hell!"

By now he'd be talking out loud to himself and cutting through the snow head bent, teeth gricked to the sleet, hatbrim down, coat whitening, in the wonderful mysterious hours of an ordinary day in ordinary life in ordinary cold blue life.

Rushing from the Club de Paisan at one o'clock, the day's school over, with G.J. and the gang striding, I'd run into my father rounding the corner of the Moody Street Bridge right in the howl-shroud of the gale itself blowing over the city's bridges, and on across the snowy boards we'd bowl home, the gang in front, Pa and I in back, jawing and jabbering.

"Goin to track practice at four—"

"I'll be there for the opening scene Satty night— Say, how 'bout goin down together?"

"Sure. We'll ride down with Louis Morin and Emil Ladeau in the bus—"

"Ah Ti Jean, I'm glad ta see ya makin good on the track team, it makes my old heart proud by golly. I got a job at Rolfe's this afternoon—looks like I'll be around awhile— Old Gloomy Puss—well I'll have my upsets, but pay no attention to me. I'll be ranting about the government, about the way America has changed since I was a boy. Dont pay it any atten-

68

tion, kiddo—but maybe when you grow older you'll understand my feelings."

"Yeah, Pa."

"Whattaya think of that—ha ha ha—"

"Say Pa!"

"What kiddo?" turning to me eagerly with laughter and shining eyes.

"Did you know who finally beat that Whitney colt down in Florida."

"Yeah, I know, I had one-fifty across the board on him in the club, the bum— Yeah, k—Ti J—Jack—" (stammering to find my name) "yeah kiddo," seriously, far away, broodingly squeezing my arm, realizing I'm just a child. "Yeah me boy—yeah sonny—my kid—" and in his eyes a mysterious mist, dense with tears, springing from the secret earth of his being and always dark, unknown, come of itself, like there is no reason for a river.

"It'll come, Jack—" and in his countenance you saw he meant just death— "What'll be with it? Maybe you gotta know a lot of people in Heaven to make life succeed. It'll come. You dont have to know a soul to know what I know—to expect what I'm expecting—to feel yourself alive and dying in your chest every minute of the livelong day— When you're young you wanta cry, when you're old you wanta die. But that's too deep for you now, *Ti Mon Pousse*" (Little My Thumb).

XIX

Wednesday night came slowly.

"Sit here, by me."

It's Maggie, solemn, her legs crossed, hands folded on her lap, on the couch, in the parlor, fullblast overhead lights, her cousin is going to show us how his magic trick works. It's some kid thing out of a kit book, I'm bored (like by television), but Maggie is dead serious and skeptical and watching every move Tommy makes because as she says "He's such a devil, you gotta watch him, he'll play the *meanest* tricks and tease ya, he's almost a sneak"—Tommy the handsome popular boy cousin that all the Cassidy girls love and look up to and roar and laugh in parlors and kitchens as he performs and does headstands of activity, a good kid, shining eyes, his hair falling in them, full of glee, the little kids already sent to bed are peeking from the top of the stairs where the wallpaper is lit a dim rose by the nightlamp— So I watch Maggie watch Tommy—out of the corner of my eye. Tonight she's more beautiful than ever, she has a little white rose or flower of some kind in her hair, to the left, her hair comes down on both sides of her brow almost over the corners of her eyes, her lips pursed (chewing gum) to watch and doubt. She has a lace collar, very neat, she went to church that afternoon and to Mrs. O'Garra down Chelmsford Road to get that cakemix for the party. She has a crucifix on her dress breast; lace ends on her short sleeves; little bracelets on both wrists; hands crossed, sweet white fingers I eye with immortal longing to hold in mine and have to wait—fingers I know well, cold slightly, moving, nudging a little as she laughs but primly stay folded in her hands—her legs crossed show sweet knees, no stockings, the well-formed calf below, the hint of snowy legs, the little dress pathetically draping off this ladylike arrangement of herself. Her hair hangs, black and heavy, soft, smooth, curly, to her back—the white flesh and the sullen unbelieving river eyes more beautiful than the eyes of all the sun-eyed blondes of MGM, Scandinavia and the western world— The milk of the brow, the pear of the face, the solid silky proud erect neck of the young girl—I take her all in for the hundredth time that night.

"Oh *Tommy*—stop fooling with it and let's see the trick!" she cries, turning exasperated away.

"Yes!" cries Bessy Jones, and little Janie and the mother Cassidy seated with us partly reading the paper and Maggie's brother Roy the railroad brakeman like his father is standing in the door with a loose smile, eating a sandwich, his hands black-in with grime of his job, his teeth pearly white, in his dark eyes the same Irish contemptuous disbelief of tricks and games and yet the same greedy avid interest—so that he too yelled out now "Ah Tom you bull thrower do that red handkerchief one again— This one's bull, I seen what you did—"

I smile to show that I'm interested in everything but in the brown wallpapered parlor of eternity my heart only beats for her so sweet just a pace away, my life.

"Hey," turning to me the drowning devouring scrutinizing coverage of black merry sad eyes in their incredible snow cameo skin, "you didnt see him that time, you were lookin at the floor."

"Lookin at the floor?" laughed the comedian magician. "All my work is going for fraught! Watch this Roy!"

"Yeah."

"Do it!" screeched Maggie.

"Maggie!"—the mother—"dont yell so! Ye'll have the neighbors think we drown cats in here, Luke McGarrity and his upsidedown clay pipe if ever I saw him in this picture in this magazine!" and her matronly big body shaking slowly with laughter. In my bleakness I even accepted the fact Maggie might look like her mother some day, big and fat.

"Come on, you, J-a-c-k! You missed it again! Let me show you a trick I did last year for Bessy's uncle the night he walked out and tripped on the milk can and Ma's chair that was painted was on the porch and he fell on it and broke it— Lookout!" jumping up from the pose so sweet, to run around the room chasing her cousin, like a little eager flushed girl now, a minute ago a portrait of a lady in a cameo ring, with crucifix.

Later—on the porch alone—before going in—necking furiously because Bessy was still inside giggling with Jimmy McFee— "Oh go home! Go home! Go home!" she pulled at me angrily as I held her laughing in my arms, I'd said something that irritated her—her flashes of indignation, poutings, rougeings in nature, of cheek, the lovely frown and forewarning and return of her white smile—

"Okay I'll go"—but I come back again, start kidding her and kissing her again, overdo everything, and she gets mad again but really mad this time and that makes me sore and we pout and look away—"I'll see ya Monday afternoon, ah?"

"Hmf—" (she'd wanted me to see her Saturday night but that was the track meet night and I'd end up at midnight with my Pop in some soda fountain downtown talking with all the guys about the meet and who the high scorer was—big eager-teeth guys with newspapers in cafeterias of the night, Lowell style, a small city well famed for its great cafeteria and soda-fountain devotees, as evidenced and publicized extensively in the local paper in a column written by James G. Santos who'd once worked with my Pa in small newspaper days and was a distant cousin also to G.J.)—Maggie would have to reason me out of a Rex Ballroom dance on that night because not I'd be weary from the races and overly hung-up with my father but I'd be so late to the dance it wouldnt be worth the price of admission—not wanting Maggie to think me a cheapskate I never mention this—and she thinks I really want to sneak out with Pauline Cole like a real smalltown hotshot maybe in fast cars at 1 A.M. on black tar tragedies out by Lakeview—"Dont come then."

"It's better—I'll be 11:30 before I'm even out of the showers," I plead.

"Bloodworth'll be at the Rex."

"Charley?" I was surprised; Charley was an old football team friend who'd only met Maggie accidentally when I ran into him accidentally at a dance one night— His open interest in Maggie I didnt take seriously, she always flirted— He in fact discussed her with me seriously.

"M.C.," he called her, initials, "old M.C.'ll be mad if she knows you didnt show up to track practice the other day, son, Bill—" (he also called me Bill, for Bill Demon)—"us demons and them demonettes is got to stick together"—some talk out of a Popeye cartoon running every night in the Lowell *Sun* the local paper "so us demons is got to watch out for the demonettes, M.C. Number Two" (he took such a vast interest in my affairs he called Moe Cole M.C. Number Two, and the initials fitted—all in the joy mornings of high school life here's these wild complexities happening our minds exploding)—

"It's okay Charley—you take over M.C. Number Two and I'll meet you in Heaven." We joked about it; once he took me to his house and showed me his scrapbook full of pasted pictures of baseball stars of 1920's and 1930's with incredibly old stars whose bones are long interred in crumbling files in the archives of red sun sinking in the Ninth Inning with Nobody On— Seriously, with bleak youngkid dis-knowledge of the incredible ruin of the years and the death they have wreaked on the flesh and jawbones of men including baseball stars, he'd in his scrapbook of 1939 stick the old wan visages of Cincinnati left fielders of the Depression years who just made it from the minors (JOHNNY DEERING wasnt even a jockey yet), names of old players, Dusty Cooke, Whitey Moore—Kiki Cuyler—Johnny Cooney—Heinie Manush—lost forever the still figure in right center with a tanned taut expression on solid legs waiting for the crack of the bat as a little shrill creamy whistle splits the atmosphere stadium hush, the bottomless thapping dull plop of the ball in the catcher's mitt and right after it the umpire's *ump-euoo!* And the guy that's been ya-yagging all afternoon from third base box again says "Ya-yag!" with strange forlorn little voice through cupped hands at the batter with bat back tense and an airplane drones—which I'd see and hear all sadly white-flour pasted in his book of books on his parlor rug in the Highlands. Then we'd rush over to Timmy Clancy's house to play Benny Goodman Artie Shaw records, Clancy'd be the catcher on the spring Lowell High School team and in time President of the United States the way he was politicking the school, the city, had once been Junior Day Mayor of Lowell with big picture of him officiating at a desk, his name I'd seen with awe in Lowell High School baseball boxscores the year before —all of which was shouting talk in record-playing afternoons and new fresh life excitements of the inevitable High School Springtime in America. I liked Bloodworth and in the spring we were going to play outfield together on that Lowell team, he whose name for years (*Bloodworth*) had mystified me when I saw it in Lowell High and Lowell Twi League boxscore— admired him and he was going to show me how to hit a curve when the first green bedsprings of turf began to show among the brown scrags of Lowell Highlands grass (out in left with the football lines still showing in)— I liked the way he'd say

"Oh that guy can *belt* em a mile, seventeen triples last year Bill! And wait'll you see Taffy Truman pitch *this* year, he's been great but this is his year!" Everything was opening up, Taffy Truman was a stylish southpaw with a gape in his front teeth and an incredibly suave draped body, just the way a pitcher should look, Lefty Grove in a loose suit—and he was good, Boston in the National League was after him— Bloodworth's interest in Maggie seemed to me over my head and not serious because I wouldnt notice them and I trusted her to love only me. So she was going to meet him Saturday while I ran in track.

"I'll take M.C. Number One home and take good care of her," Charley'd wink at me—he had a faintly hooked nose and a funny pointed jaw and also separations in the front teeth and a glamorous looseness that made him sensationally look like a center fielder, Bloodworth cf, leadoff man—fast, he cracked electrifying singles into right with one arc-y swing of his southpaw bat . . . made of some paler ash than the others. Ash was the color of his hair too.

"Okay Bill, I'll take M.C. Number One home and see no guys follow her in cars and try to pick her up," and here'd turn away snuffing into himself as if apparently he was really making a joke and pulling my leg or talking the way he always did but with so mock a seriousness I believed and trusted and looked at him like the lamb—hate is older than love. I had no objection to acting like a lamb because my mother'd told me so many stories about my little brother died at nine who was so lamby, Gerard, would rescue mice from traps and bring them back to health in little cardboard box hospitals that were also cathedrals of holy reverence to which his little face with the soft fall of melancholy hair, over melancholy eyes, turned, impossibly hoping—he made everybody cry when he died, terribly from within. O Russia! Saints in America too!

"Then go home," says Maggie, "I dont care if I don't see you till Sunday."

"Sunday I'll be early—"

"Ah!—" waving her hand bitterly, and then suddenly becoming unaccountably tender and sad. "Ah Jack—sometimes I get so tired . . ."

"Of?—"

"Ah never mind." Looking away, with a little pain expression on the corner of her loose, dull smile of heavy womanness ... too much to carry ... the freight of her tired, head-nodding understandings of everything that was going on—a woman looks at a river with an expression not-to-be-named. Her rippling mysterious moods, philosophic, rich, faintly bestial like the torture of skulls and breasts of cats, like the drowning of idiots which is what we've come to expect of our spring now, hand loose doubting on hip balanced with head tossing just a little darklashed lowered disbelief and nay, loose ugly grin of self-satisfied womanly idiocy-flesh, curl of travesty-cruelty, I'd want to rip her mouth out and murder her, sudden interior welling-up of tenderness profound, paining, dark, forming milky frown on forehead, raising moons by the conjuration-fingers up from the bottom of the well which is the womb, nature, black sod, time, death, birth. "Ah go home—Jack—let me sleep. I'm gonna sleep tonight."

"No Maggie, I dont wanta leave when you feel this way—"

"Yes you do—I dont feel any particular way."

"Yes you do—"

"Particular feeling? Just because I just happen sick and tired—of this—and that—what I expect—what *you* expect—I just wanta quit and go home—"

"You are home. There's your door."

Looking at it with a rich frown and a fnuf, "Sure. Home. Okay. Sleep."

"Arent you home?"

"Dream it some other time, so what if it's my home I dont have to get all overexcited about it—"

"I wasn't—"

"You never nothing. Oh Jack—" (pain in her cry)—"go home—stay—do something—I cant *stand* it hangin around day after day not knowing what to do with myself and whether I should get married or not or just—blah—nothing—Oh fer *kri*-sakes, aint you gonna go yet!" (as I'm grabbing her to kiss her)— "Leave me alone!"

Pushing my hand off.

I turn around and walk off into the night.

Four houses down, my neck burning and strangling, in the still winter star solitude she says, distinctly, "Ha ha," and I hear her going in the house, the click of the door, the "Ha ha" not laughed but spoken signifies not only she's not through with me but it worked to get rid of me tonight.

I cant face my own conclusions.

I drag along in wonder, hatred, stunned, realizing it's nothing; I go by the cemetery so bemused with these witchery-tortures of whether this, that, Maggie, I dont notice the ghosts, the tombstones, it's just the backdrop now to my anxious hunchings over knuckles.

Three miles home again I walk, in midwinter midnight, this time not fast, or joyous, but dispirited with nowhere to go and nothing in back—all the night does at the end of a street is increase its distance—

Yet in the morning I wake up reconciled with the fact not only she'll make some kind of apology but I ought to laugh and shake it off and shake her off and she'll climb on again.

My mother sees the palings in my thoughts, advises me— "Stop breaking your head on all kindsa junk—concentrate on your track and school, never mind Gus Poulo and your gang they got nothing to do but hang around you got lots of things, see them later, and never mind that Maggie Cassidy—see her this spring or this summer—dont rush things and dont rush around with every-thing and every-body— Take some advice from you old la-dy, aye?" And she'd wink, and pat my head, and reassure me. "I'm not crazy me." Stopped in the middle of the kitchen floor, my mother, with a kind of ribbon in her coalblack hair, rosy cheeks on both sides of her big blue eyes, her hands joined together at her lean rest on the back of the chair just loosely and for a second, looking at me seriously, primly, grave understanding of the prime things pressed down in her lips, and a twinkle in her eyes, "Mama'll always did show you how to get things done and everything will be all right, I got you for Saturday night guess what?"

"What? *Quoi?*"

"A nice pair of new shoes, when you go to the track and change to your sneakers there wont be nobody be able to say you got old shoes, *tes vielles son pu bonne*" she'd announce

76

and sneak in in an entirely different authoritative almost greedy-sneering believing tone, as a shoe worker she was talking about the condition of a pair of shoes—"so I got you a nice new pair of Thom McAns, didnt cost much."

"Aw Ma *tu depense tout ton argent!*" (Aw Ma you spend all your money).

"*Voyons, ta besoin d'une paire de bottine, ton père itou, fouaire n'achetez avant l'moi est fini lui itou—weyondonc—*" (Look, you need a pair of shoes, your father too, have to buy him some before the month's out too—look here!)—angry such a thing should not be realized, going off into the parlor to straighten out a lace armrest on the sofa while we're talking over my breakfast.

"Ah Ma, I love you" I say to myself, and I dont know how to say it to her out loud but I know she knows I love her anyway.

"So *mange*, eat, forget it—a pair of shoes aint no silverware china bazaar, ah?" And nods, and winks. I sit in the firm eternity there.

I kneel at my bed at night to pray, instead my head falls on the blanket and I just goof with my eyes crushed down. I try to pray in the winter night, moveless.

"Make my skull, my nose, soften, melt; just make me one piece knowing—"

XX

I went to the indoor racetrack that Saturday evening, Pa was with me, rode the bus down jabbing blah blah blah "Well so I said to so and so"—

"Hey Pa, *t'en rappelle tu quand qu'on faisa les lions*— Hey Pa remember when we made the lions, I was four years old, on Bridge Street, and you'd sit me on your knees imitating the noises of animals! Remember? and Ti Nin?"

"*Pauvre* Ti Nin," said my father; talk to him, it would

start him, gather in him, "it's a damn shame the way that poor little girl has found troubles—!"

"—and we'd listen together, you made lions."

"It was fun, I was amusing myself with my little kids," he'd say way off brooding darkly, over lost youth, mistaken rooms, weird troubles and strange gossipy rumors and stiff unpleasant unhappiness of bleary people in parlors, remembering himself with pride and pity. The bus went downtown.

I explained my track to him, so he'd understand the night's races better; he understood that 3.7 was my best time and that night there was a Negro on the Worcester North team who was supposed to be like a lightning eagle in the sprints; I was afraid I was going to be beaten in my city that night by a Negro, just like the young boxers around the corner at the Crescent and the Rex Ballroom when they put the chairs and the ring in the floor of the cold dancers. My father said— "Go as fast as you can, beat the bastard: they're supposed to run like damn streaks! antelopes of Africa!"

"Hey Pa—and Pauline Cole's gonna be there."

"Oh— That's your other girl? Little Pauline, yeh, I like that little one me— Too bad you dont get along with her, she must be just as good as your little Maggie Papoopy there the other side of the river—"

"They're different!"

"Aw, well you're already startin to have trouble with women!"

"Well, what do you want me to do."

Hand up. "Don't ask *me*! Ask your mother—ask the old curé—ask the askers—*I* dont know—I dont pretend to know —I'm just trying to get along in the world— You'll all have to work with me. You'll see that it's gonna be pretty damn bad, *Comprends?*" loud, in French, like an uncle calling the idiot from the corner making clear to me meanings that can never be recorded in the English language.

Together, heads bent forward with the bus, we rode downtown. He wore a felt hat, I had an earmuff hunting cap; it was a cold night.

The crowd was swarming around the dark street outside the brilliantly lit Annex, it was like some great church service suddenly let out and they were all coming to the track meet, an old church a block away, huge trees, redbrick factory annexes, the back of a bank, the glow of midtown Kearney Square red and vague over the backs of tar roofs and neon signs beyond. The football coach from some little suburban town would be there, talking in the door with the owner of a sporting goods store, or old soda-fountain habitué with long memories of track records from 1915 (like in German Europe); my father and I, bashful, would push through the crowds; my father'd be looking everywhere to see somebody he knew, grinning, and wouldnt see anybody. The mysterious inside, with people standing around the great door to the Annex and the track, beyond them were the boards of the banked turns, like circus props huge and dusty. Ticket takers. Little nameless kids jumping around. "I'll go sit in the stands while I can still get a seat," Pop said. "I'll wave at you when you come out."

"I'll *see you*—" But Pop thinks I said "be seeing you" and is already waddling off through the crowds inside, he walks around the banks, onto the floor, to his plank seat; others are standing in the middle of the track in topcoats jawing. Young kids have already started running around in shorts, when they get older than fourteen or fifteen they'll be getting big hood suits with long running ski pants with the school's colors on them; the older boys are inside leisurely changing. The great mysterious Negro flyer is hidden in the opponents' showers somewhere—like a great lion beast I can feel his stalking presence—like a thonged whip the surly tawny tail is flashing at the level floor, the growl, the teeth, no greeting in the V's and W's of his Vow—the rumbling roar of other lions even further down below— My imagination had been fed on circuses and unclean magazines; I looked everywhere like a goof as I hurried to my track shoes.

Others were there—Johnny Lisle—Dibbick who ran so funny, the track team captain—smells of liniment, towels—

"Hey there Jack waddayasay boy?" Johnny Lisle out of the corner of his mouth. "Think we'll win the 300 tonight?"

"Hope I dont have to run it." It was like the railroad local, it was hard work.

"Melis'll run it tonight—and Mickey Maguire—and Kazarakis."

"Krise, they cant be beat."

"Joe was asking me to run it second man but I dont know that route—you know, I'm a 1000-yard runner, I dont wanta wear myself out and get my *♯: ! shins all cracked out—"

"I knew I'd have to run it," I said out loud, really complaining, but Johnny didnt hear me as just then a panic seized us all and we knew there was no more time to talk, in twenty seconds we were all bundling in our running hoods and parka pants and stepping out mincingly on little tiny toe-dancer sneakers with hard rubber bottoms to catch the wood of the indoor planks—nail shoes were for moderner high schools with all-cork tracks. In these tight sneakers you could really streak, they were light.

I saw Pauline at the door. She never looked more glamorous, great moist eyes of grueling blue were mooning right at me like swimming seas, at her age it had all the men turning quick furtive felt hats to see her twice. All I had to do was stand there like a post and let her go. She leaned on the wall wriggling before me, with hands back clasped, I just smiled, she made love speeches.

"Hey. I bet you'll be watching for me behind the forty-yard line, huh? I'll wave. You wave back at me."

"Okay."

"Dont say that I didnt come here to see you because I dont love ya, see?"—in closer.

"What?"

"I didnt think you'd catch it the first time—I'll get even with you if you grrr with me." She was clenching her teeth and fists at me. All the time she never took her eyes off me; she was in love with something, probably me, probably love. I grieved inside that I had to give up her for Maggie. But I couldnt have Mary and Magdalene both so I had to decide my mind. And I didnt want to be a boor and do the wrong thing hurting Pauline—if boor is strong enough, gross enough. So I looked solemnly at her and said nothing and started out to my race. Her sympathies were with me. "What a funny rat!" she also must have thought—"Never comes and admits nothing." Like Faust.

XXI

The Worcester men were out, jogging the banks in blue run suits that looked ominous and alien among our red and gray homey suits—and suddenly there he was, the Negro Flyer, long and thin floating on ghost feet in the far corner of the Annex, picking up, laying down his delicate feet with experimental restraint as though when he'd be ready he'd fly like an arrow and all you'd see is the flashing white socks, the reptilian head stuck out forward to the run. Hurdles was his speciality. I was a sunk ghost of a trackman. But, for all his great streaking in wild track meets of indoor New England brightlight night he wasnt going to reckon on Jack the white boy, sixteen, hands clasped behind him in a newspaper photo with white kid trunks and white undershirt when early at fifteen I was too young to get a regular track suit, ears sticking out, raw, hair piled inky mass on square Keltic head, neck line ramrod holding head up, broad pillared neck with base in collarbone muscles and on each side slope-muscled shoulders down to big arms, legs piano thick just above the white socks— Eyes hard and steely in a sentimental Mona Lisaing face— jawbone iron new. Like Mickey Mantle at nineteen. Another kind of speed and need.

The first event was the 30-yard dash. I saw with satisfaction the Negro star wasnt in my heat, which I won from a bunch of kids, breezy. In his heat I saw him win by yards, fast and low on his feet, when he reached he clawed for the finish line and not just dull air. The big moment of the final heat came. We didnt even look at each other at the starting line, he too bashful for me, I too bewildered for him, it was like warriors of two nations. In his eyes there was a sure glow of venom tiger eyes in an honest rockboned face, so your exotic is just a farmer, he goes to church as well as you, his fathers, brothers as well as you—honesties— The Canuck Fellaheen Indian and the Fellaheen Negro face to face in a battle of spears before they hit the long grass, contesting territories that howl around. Pauline was watching very closely, I could see her leaning elbows on knee in the stands with an intent smile digging the whole drama of the track meet and everybody there. In the middle of the track were the officials, with watches, switch lists, we were making our moves by the clock right on schedule with the Lowell *Sun* reporter's list of events:

30 YARD DASH——*1st (Time: 3.8)—Duluoz (Lowell), Smith (WC) 2nd Heat (Time: 3.7)—Lewis (WC), Kazarakis (Lowell) Final Heat* —

This was coming up, he had done 3.7 in his heat, I 3.8 in mine, which meant the difference of a yard, there was no doubt of his tremendous speed. His hands and arms hung loosely and muscular with great black veins. He was going to play beating drums to my wild alto.

We got down on the line, shivering in a sudden cold gust of air from the street; we tested our spit in the planks, kicked at it with dug-in sneakers, stuck the sneaker in and got down to crawl but on thumb and forefingers level. Bent testing knees, teetered and balanced to feel. Spectators saw the madness of racers—human runners like Greeks of Sparta—the Socratic silences falling over the crowd as the starter raises his gun in the air. To my utter amazement I saw out of the corner of my eye the colored boy laid out almost flat on the floor in a low slung fantastic starting position, something impossibly modern and submarining and subterranean like bop, like the new gesture of a generation. It was in imitation of the great Ben Johnson who ran 60 yards in 6 seconds flat, this kid from the slums of Worcester was mad to imitate him who'd inconceivably broken the world's record by 2/10ths of a second, fabulous ghost streak Negro of Columbia in the late

Thirties. Later on in life I'd see American Negro boys imitating Charley Parker and calling themselves Bird on street corners and it would be the same thing, and son to, this gesture of the early bop generation as I immeasurably understood it seeing it the first time. We teetered on thoughtful fingers just on the verge of exploding into fact, bang, the crash from the thought of running to the running itself, the kick-off to the dash. My friend—whose name was some forgotten-by-me Negro name of inconceivable anonymity and humility— John Henry Lewis was his name—he shot off ahead of the gun and we all flew off in a false start and held up when the gun cracked us to return, he ahead— We reorganized ourselves for the mental anguish of another start. I got down, saw him on my left low and lightly-hung to fly off the floor —and just as I predicted in my own mind the absolute certainty that the starter would shoot he shot but I was already gone. I was flying, luckily legally just barely beat the gun— no one knew but myself and the starter and the starter was Joe Garrity who knew a jump-the-gun when it was illegal and was inflexible (wouldnt cheat) in his knowledge, pity, and sense of duty. I flew ahead of my Negro, my Jim, eyes half closed so as not to see the horror of his black skin at my breast, and hit the tape well ahead but just barely beginning to sense his catching up as he too late gathered a stunned momentum and knew that he was beaten anyway and by the mind. The others were not altogether out—John Kazarakis who was just coming into his own in realization of what a great athlete he really was hung on John Lewis' shirt behind by some half-inch behind me by a foot and also closing in. But my muscular headlong rush beat the thin speed demons just the same and by sheer will. It was like the way I'd once seen Billy Carr run so fast he stumbled in his run and kept somehow in the air and regained his feet and literally threw himself across the air against the finish-line tape all muscles and white power, 3.5, beating great college sprinters in his high school years . . . Billy Carr that went to Notre Dame, whose glamour in Lowell was some rich and hidden thing in the dense tree mansions of Andover Street in the winter night of golden home lights, lovely girls of summer and finishing

schools strolling under laceries of branch in streetlamp sorrows
by bushes, driveways, iron fences, bandana under pouting
lip . . .

My win over John Lewis was received with applause and
by myself with awe—as I bounced off the mattress against
the wall I looked furtively at John and caught his whites of
eye conceding me the race. He even shook his head and said
something to me himself like "Man you" or "Damn" and we
laughed together as we walked back.

They were putting up the hurdles for the 35, bustles, talk,
the reporters typed their results:

30-YARD DASH——Final Heat (*Time*: *3.7*)—*Duluoz*
       (*Lowell*), *Lewis* (*WC*), *Kazarakis*
       (*Lowell*)

Pauline waved; Pa gave me the okay sign. I'd overcome
the ghost. "Ah," I thought, "Ma's gonna be glad—she'll see
that I run and work hard and I'm gettin to my hand. She'll
say to herself, 'Bon, Ti Jean's doing his business, his homework too.'—I'll be able to sit home in the chair not sayin a
word all day Sunday— It's at home we win." And I saw my
father with joy. "Look at his big happy smile—he's talkin to
the men near him— The enemies of my father!—they're far,
not near tonight—their mystery doesnt tear my teeth out
tonight—the fact that we dont know their face, their place,
the savage extent of their indifference to us— We'll bury em
a deep one before midnight." My thoughts ran like fallen stars.
I saw in my eye in the middle of all the world the dark corners
on the floor in my house where my cats, my migs hid, where
I'd put my crazy face in rainy afternoons of no-school when I
really dreamed immortality, the health of my blood and
family, the frightening mystery too. I believed in the planks
of the little corner; I knew that the earth, the streets, the floors
and shadows of life were holy— like a Host—gray, dirty Host
of interesting reality (like the bridge at Orleans) of great smoke
of men and things, where I'd find myself an honor so great
that my father with his old coats, humble hat, would look at
me in another heavened life like you look at a man and we'd

speak rare things—"Ti Nin'll read it in the paper, my sister
—she'll show it to her friends— Lousy'll read it tomorrow
morning when he gets up to go to church—Scotty—G.J.—
Vinny—"

"And Maggie—"

"I beat the speedy *Neigre* from Worcester—and him, he'll
go back to Worcester—maybe if not to tell to *know* that in
Lowell the guys from the alleys and rock streets run like
demons, let the name of Lowell make a noise in their hearts
after this—that in the world where the name is Lowell the
boys brothers and mad hurl themselves howling in this mortal
ocean . . . brothers, boys, wolves of the North." (These
thoughts were all in French, almost untranslatable.)

I could see all the rooftops of Lowell and Worcester in my
victory, my ideas, sensations. They'd put a poet in my craw.
I was ecstatically insane in my innocence. I knew joys not by
name but that they crossed my clotting breast of hot blood
and disappeared unnamed, unknown, uncommunicated with
the thoughts of others but arranged in the same manner and
therefore like the thoughts of the Negro, intent, normal. It
was later they dropped us radar machines in the sky to derange
the senses. Let's hear no more about the excesses of Rimbaud!
I cried remembering the beautiful faces of life that night.

The 35-yard hurdles I also won flying at the start ahead
of Lewis by that white-flashing split second—I skimmed over
the hurdles in a mad anxiety, level with the race I dug floors
away, aimed down the line. I was more surprised than anybody
and John Henry Lewis. And for the first time I hit 4.6 I even
began to wonder if I'd suddenly become a really great runner.

XXII

The track floor was being laid out with broad-jump mats,
high-jump poles, the big shotputters are standing around
agreeing and determining the layout of the jump area so they

can start warming up right away—Ernie Sanderman who later became a round-the-world magician seaman on luxurious passenger ships of the blue sea was our best broadjumper—stood, on his takeoff board, and swung his arms back together and wailed out heaving his tortured neck into the annezvoidathema of the wild Annex, reaching for his landing place of both feet he'd jump ten feet, clear across a narrow livingroom, with big feet flapping to the mark. I also participated in this event, jumped 9 feet and 5, 6 or 7 inches, made points for the team, but always losing to Ernie and usually the visiting champ too and finishing third—

The last event I led off, Kazakaris anchor, the 300-yard hated relay, with bull-knecked Fullback Melis and Irish curly locks Mickey Maguire from Belvedere, zooming around the track like streamliners and the Worcester men in their blue regalia flying a half-foot behind in closepacked races of serious interest, when I was off and underway nothing gave me a bigger boot than the 300-yard run, it was frantic, you had to kill yourself, the guys were screaming on all sides, in the Annex, "Run!" and we'd be hollowly echoing with hard feet on wood bank board turns making a roar coming off just on the inside on the smooth basketball floor into the inside line without now any further booming noise, just cat feet sprinting, all the mothers of Lowell should have come to see their sons show their fathers how they can run—into the woods, into the thieveries and wood piles, into the hysterical idiot streakfoot madness of mankind—

I took off frightened, the guy with me was a white boy from Worcester, I let him shoulder me out of the first turn as we raced with the relay sticks—this was a courtesy on my part. We boomed around the boards—came off, both of us, sleekly, skinly, padding up our court, interested audiences watching interested racers, the whole corps of newspapermen now alert with heads up from their typewriters or from the sidelines, a few, dull, immediate cries of opening-lap audiences. "Bang!" the gun had said, the gunpowder was just spreading in the air—we was off.

My Pop was standing at his bench plank, just bent to watch, tense, his whole body toned to hold up watchful on the quivering hard legs with which he used to play basketball in YMCAs of pre-World War I—

"Okay Jean"—under his breath—"Go on!" He was afraid because I'd given the kid the first bank I'd given up my show. No. I leisurely followed him around the far turn, and as we came into the homestretch of the first of two laps I just passed him with a sneaky quiet sprint he hardly heard and flew ahead of him bent for that first turn again, for the tilt of the boards, and flashed by the line of watchers, the kid was heard to curse, he pictured himself taking off after me—I was already boastfully in the back stretch and halfway along it and had done my booming and my soft-off-step and all things of that nature and was in a straight line for the last turn, no sound, streaking across the kitchen, bent for the last boards—ghosting in—turning with the world on the revolving banks like a funhouse barrel and now very tired and hurting all over and my heart dying from so much pain in lungs, legs— The kid from Worcester overtook nothing, but lost spaces of breeze between us, hopelessly mawkfaced lost and discouraged, almost embarrassed to shame. I run up and assume the handout pose with the relay stick and give it to Melis with a 10-yard lead and he's off running his two laps while the next Worcester kid still waits, mincing nervously on a hot potato—Maguire and Kazarakis complete the race like invisible bullets and it's a farce, no contest, and relays are always sad.

—Won races, leaving other boys embarrassed to shame— Shame . . . that key to immortality in the Lord's grave . . . that key to courage . . . that key heart. "Lord, Lord, *Mon Doux, Mon Doux*" (Canadian boy's pronunciation of *Mon Dieu*, My God) I'm saying to myself. "What's gonna happen!"—won races, was applauded, laurel-wreathed, smiled, patted, understood, taken in—took showers, shouted —combed—was young, youthful, was the key—"Hey McKeever!" echoing now loud bang in the locker room glooms. "Hee hee hee didja take a big ass plunge off that 600 fight! Hee hyah ha—whatta batt-ed . . . Jeeheever, ole Jeeheever sure missed tonight!"

"Kelly? I told Kelly, stop throwing it will ya?"

"Oodja see Smack make that line?"

"Hey, know what happened tonight—"

"Where?"

"Keith's—"

"What?"

"Basketball game—they took on Lowell—"

"What score?"

"63-64."

"Jeez!"

"You shoulda seen Tsotakos—you know, Steve's brother—"

"You mean Samaras?'

"No!—not Odysseus, the guy with the red-shirt brother!"

"Spaneas?"

"No!"

"Oh yeah!"

"He's the greatest—they never had a basketball player like him— Nobody talks about him"—(some little kid with thin hands falling under the sleeves of his coat weighing 98 pounds and a class officer and sometime team manager and only fourteen years old bringing back reports from other parts of Lowell in the eventful exciting Saturday night). My father's standing there laughing and getting his kicks from all these funny children and looking around fondly to find me. I'm just putting on my shirt, comb in my head, making a Hitler mustache at Jimmy Jeeheever with it.

"A great night!" yells an enthusiast from that world-packed Lowell door. "Jimmy Foxx never hit more homers than you guys tonight!"

"Joe Garrity," announces somebody, and here comes our track coach in a shabby sad overcoat sad glinting Harry Truman eyes behind glasses and hands hopelessly folded into his coatpockets and says "Well boys, you did pretty well, you did pretty well. . . . We scored 55 points. . . ." He wants to tell us a thousand things but he's waiting for the reporters and enthusiasts to leave, Joe is very secretive about his track team and his quiet matter-of-fact grave relations with each of his boys and all of them in group. "I'm glad about that win, Johnny. I think you're going to make your name in Boston Garden before spring." Half grin, half joke, kids laughing—

"Gee coach, thanks"—Johnny Lisle, who was liked by Joe particularly because he was an Irish boy and close to his heart. Melis — Kazarakis — Duluoz — Sanderman — Hetka — Norbert — Marviles — Malesnik — Morin — Maraski — and seven Irishmen Joyce McDuff Dibbick Lisle Goulding Maguire, he had international national problems to deal with. My father, far from rushing up to the coach to be seen with him, hides in a corner wearing an appreciative smile as he secretly digs Joe the Coach in his real soul and mentally pictures him in City Hall and realizes what Joe is like—and likes him—

"Yah—I can see him at his old desk—like my Uncle Bob who was that railyard clerk in *Nashué* (Nashua)—trying to get along with things as best he can— No different than me— Didnt I know some brother of his long time ago on the old *Citizen*? or was it Dowd's out on Memorial Road— Wal— And whattaya know, Jacky went and beat that *Neigre*—ha ha ha—when I saw him there I was sure he was too fast for him, but he did it! he did it! Ha ha ha, little tyke, I remember him when he was three feet high and used to crawl on the floor pushing up boxes to me and bringing me toys—two feet high—*Ti Pousse!* Ha ha— Say, that *Neigre* was built, he was sleek—I was damn glad to see my boy beat *him*— that proves he's an athlete—those *Neigres* are the fastest runners in the world—in the jungles of Africa even right now they're running like mad after wild pigs, with spears— You see it in the Olympics, the great Negro athletes there that Jesse not Jesse James Jesse Jones that Jesse Owens flying— the international flavor of the world—"

Pauline is waiting for me at the door, Pa joins her as soon as he finds her.

"Well by God—Pauline—I didnt know *where* you were— I'da sat with you!"

"Why didnt that damn Jack tell me you were here—Hey!" They loved each other, she always had a joke for him, he for her— Their eyes shined as I rushed out of the showers to join them. It was social, provincial, glad, sad; it was ecstasy in the heart. We felt vibrations of love laughing and yelling in the laughing yelling crowds pouring out and milling around;

Saturday night is dense and tragic in all America from Rocky Mount on up, San Luis on over, Killdeer on down, Lowell on in.

"Jack! There you are! Dad," whispering in his ear, "tell that lout we's got a date of our own and we dont want him around tonight."

"Okay keed," my father'd say, puffing on the cigar in a strenuous acting pose, "we'll see if we cant fix him up with Cleopatra next week and make up to him for it." In his jests serious.

"All right, Mark Antony. Or wasnt your name Mark Antonio and you came rovin over here to steal this British baron from my castle?"

"Nah!—we'll shoot him tonight in the stagecoach—Dont worry about nothing keed. Let's go to Paige's and have an ice cream soda."

And off we fly, into the bright dry night, stars above the redbrick snows are keen and clear, knives drop from them— the big sinewy trees with their claws deep under the pavements are stuck so high in the sky they are like lost silver in the Up, people walk among streetlamps passing massive trunk bases of something living and never pay it a thought— We join the flow of the sidewalks leading downtown—to the Lobster Cot—Merrimack Street—the Strand—the whole dense almost riotous inwards of the city aglow for the Saturday night in that time only fifteen years ago when not everybody had cars and people walked to shop and from buses to shows, not everything was locked-in strange behind tin walls with anxious eyes looking out to deserted sidewalks of modern America now— Pauline, Pa and I could not have laughed and experienced excitement and jumped so joyously as we did that night if we'd been in some automobile grimly buried three in a front seat haggling over traffics in the window of the television set of Time—instead we loped on foot over snowbanks, to dry shoveled sidewalks of downtown, to busy revolving doors of wild midnight sodas.

"Come on Jack, you're falling behind. Let's have some fun tonight!" Pauline was yelling in the street, punching me, playing with me.

"Okay."

Whispering in my ear: "Hey, did I enjoy your legs tonight! I didnt know you had legs like that! Gee, can I come and visit you when you have a bachelor apartment? Hey!"

"Say," my father an idea, "how 'bout a nice snack in Chin Lee's?—some chop suey or something?"

"No let's just have an ice cream!"

"Where? In the B.C. or Paige's?"

"Oh anywhere— Gee, I dont wanta get fat Mister Duluoz."

"Aw wont hurt ya—I been fat for thirty years and I'm still here— Wont bother ya."

"Look at Mrs. Madison and her son— You know them Jack, they live next door to me. That little kid always peeking at us?"

"And the dog in the yard with the gray fence?"

"Say"—my Pop—"you two little kids sound to me like you'd make a fine little couple— Why is it ya dont step out together"—laughing in his sleeve— secretly serious.

Pauline "Oh we *used* to go steady, Mr. Duluoz." Her eyes misting suddenly.

"Well why dont you now? Just because *Ti Pousse* is supposed to have some sweetie in another part of the county? —pay no attention to him, listen to his old man, psst," whispering in her ear, out of which they explode laughing, and the joke's on me but I tingle all over with joy to be known and loved by them and agree with my father.

Yet suddenly I remember Maggie. She's at the Rex a stone's throw for me over the neons of Kearney Square and all the dark heads of night and there she is, dancing, with Bloodworth, in the inexpressibly sad musical rose of sunset and moonlight serenades, all I have to do is walk over there, sweep aside the curtain, see all the dancers, look for her form, all I have to do is look—

But I cant leave Pa and Pauline except under some pretext, pretense. We go to the soda fountain, people from the meet are there, also people from the show at Keith's Strand or Merrimack Square, people from events of social importance to be mentioned in the next day, you can see their expensive cars out on the Square, and sometimes right on it (pre-

1942)— My Pa is shabby, crack-toothed, dark and humble in his big coat, he looks around and sees a few people he remembers, sneers, or laughs, according to his feelings— Pauline and I delicately eat our sundaes—because of the tremendous suppressed excitement to fall down on them devouring with big spoons— Just a little hometown scene on a Saturday night —in Kinston on Queen Street they're driving up and down sadly the Southerners, or walking, looking in at bleak hardware hay and grain stores, out at the colored section there's a mob chattering in front of chickenshacks and taxi stands— In Watsonville California it's the gloomy mid field and section hands of Mexico strolling, arms sometimes around each other, father and son or friend and friend, in the sad California night of white raw fog, the Filipino poolhalls, the town green at the bank— In Dickinson North Dakota on Saturday night in the winter it's the howling blizzard, the stalled buses out of town, the wild warm food and pool tables in great restaurant-lunchrooms of the night with pictures of old lost ranchers and outlaws decorating all the walls— The Arctic loneliness snowdust swirling on a rill of sage—outside town, the lost lean fence, the snow moon's fury—Lowell, the soda fountain, the girl, the father, the boy—the local yokels all around the local yokels—

"Okay keed," says my father, "and say, do you want to go home alone with Pauline now or are you coming home or what?"

"I'll go with her—" I have my big Maggie schemes—I wink at my father, false. He finds it amusing.

"See you tomorrow keed. Hey, say there goes Gene Plouffe anyway—I'll go along with him in the bus home."

Then, later, I also get rid of Pauline on some other pretense, concerning time, I hardly have room in my raining heart to see and hear what I have to—I'm lost, bumping in the Square crowds. We mill at the bus, I see her "home" to her home bus in front of Brockelman's— Then, in a dream, I rush to the Rex.

It's midnight. The last dance is playing. It's the lights-out dance. Nobody at the ticket office. I rush in, look. It's dark. I see Bessy Jones, I hear mournful saxophones, the feet are shuffling. Last, late sitters in brooding overcoats up in the balcony.

"Hey Bess!"

"What?"

"Where's Maggie?"

"She left at eleven— Bloodworth's still here— She got peeved and went home—alone—"

"She's not here?" I cry hearing the anguish of my own voice.

"No—she left!"

"Oh"—and I cant dance with her, I cant surmount the mountain dream of this night, I'll have to go to bed with the leftover pain of another day. "Maggie, Maggie," I think— It only faintly dawns on me that she got mad at Bloodworth—

And when Bessy Jones yells "Jack, it's because she loves you," I know that. It's something else is wrong, and sad and sick— "Where's my Maggie?" I cry with myself. "I'll walk out there now. But she'll never let me in. Three miles. She wont care. Cold. What'll I do? Night."

The music is so beautiful and sad I droop to hear it standing thinking lost in my Saturday night tragedy— Around me all the faint blue angels of romance are flying with the polkadot spotlight, the music is heartbroken and yearns for young close hearts, lips of girls in their teens, lost impossible chorus girls of eternity dancing slowly in our minds to the mad ruined tambourine of love and hope— I see I want to hug my Greatshadow Maggie to myself for all time. Love's all lost. I walk out, to the music, to discouraged sidewalks, disaffected doors, unfriendly winds, growling buses, harsh eyes, indifferent lights, phantom griefs of life in the Lowell streets. I go home again—I have no way of crying, or of asking.

Meanwhile Maggie's across town crying in her bed, everything is totally unhappy in the grave of things.

I go to bed with horror on my wings. In my pillow is sad comforts. Like my mother says, "*On essaye a s'y prendre, pi sa travaille pas*" (We try to manage, and it turns out shit).

XXIII

Morning is when the slackened sleep faces of the children of God must be righted, rubbed and waked up. . . .

All that day Sunday I mourn in my room, in the parlor with the papers, Lousy comes to see me and sympathizes with my face making long drawn glooms on his own ("In your old town there is nothing much to talk about except the old saying, 'Dead'," he said actually) but only in between excited reports of everything that's meanwhile been happening —"Zagg—guess what? Mouse and Scotty got real mad the other night and had a big wrestling match at Vinny's, they almost wrecked the stove, Scotty almost killed him— We played basketball with the North Common Panthers Saturday afternoon when you was resting?—I let em have it, you babe— Seven basket two fouls—sixteen points—I just showed them one of my one-hand side shots, zeet? See M.C. last night at the track meet? I was with my mother'n father at my uncle's— I had a nice girl to talk to, you babe— I said I was gonna bite her ear off— She said *eek*!— Hee hee— Barney McGillicuddy O'Toole was hot Satty, eleven points himself, one a long set shot from midcourt, but that team wont be the same, Zagg, till you play again—"

"I will now—I'm through with all this love shit"—

"Kid Belgium Yanny scored two points by God!"

"*Who?*"

"G.J. That's the new name I gave him. Call me 'Sam.' That's my new name. Kindhearted Belgium they also call me. Was M.C. at the meet?"

"Pauline yeah."

"I see her my study periods. Jean," using my French name, "she could even knock out Joe Louis just by lookin at him."

"I know,"—sadly.

"Damn! We shoulda never gone to that damn Rex New Year's Eve! Everything changed since then! Even me!"

"Take it easy, Kid Sal Slavos Len!"

"Well ga-dammit I'm mad!" jumping off the bed with the sudden furious funny small-eyed rage of a mad cat. "Eh? *Mad!* Hey Zagg?"

"Kill em, Sal, dont let em get you down."

"I'll bury em a mile deep!" Lousy swung at the air. "King of the Tits!"

The rest of the gang filed into my room, my mother'd let them in from the front; it was gray Sunday, symphonies on the radio, papers on the floor, Pop snoring in his chair, roast beef in the oven.

"Good old Belgium!" yelled Vinny embracing Lousy. "Scot, show Zagg your contract. He made out a contract to make us promise to help him buy that car next summer."

"Beware if not signed—Signed, the Unknown, that's what it says, Zagg," put in Gus who also was gloomy this day, green, quiet, musing.

Lousy had his fists up before him. "Fight? Fight?"

"The contract?" chuckled Scotty showing his cunning gold tooth. "We will discuss the deal under a few liquidoriums."

With a cat's furious rage raining sweats Lousy was still dancing shadowboxing.

G.J. looked up. "Did you bring that paper Vinny?"

"No—the storm stopped me, I threw it away." Snow outside.

"Lookout!"

G.J. jumped up suddenly with his knife, and placed it in Vinny's back. "The bastid! He'll get shithouse and kill us all!" screamed Vinny.

"Just like Billy Artaud—you know what he said the other night, 'Sorry Mouse I cant help you clean up the Silver Moon saloon gang Depernac's gangsters because my left vertebral artebral is injured'— Wattaguy!"

"This spring every one of you guys is gonna lose his head, I'm gonna pitch and bean you with my new high hard one— Opening day, March!"

Scotty: —(musing aloud) "It'll be wind like a bastid out and it'll be pretty hard to judge those balls that first afternoon and maybe the sun'll be shining and the only thing that'll be wrong is that wind—"

"Sure!"

"Zagg"—Gus solemn—"when I bean you the first time you'll be staggering and reeling at the plate and I'm going to bean you again!—a broken heap they'll see you Pitou Plouffe and the gang groveling to your home in sunset—easy prey to my more blinding than ever speedball and loping curve—" In actuality Gus's pitching was the biggest hilarious in the gang, he had so little control one time he threw a pitch over the backstop and we never found the ball again as it probably rolled down the hill to the river—

We tried to continue and expand these conversations; at suppertime they left. Grayness covered Lowell, the jokes were said, the goofs done— Something was like loss on mute snow banks in the streets; and here in the long dark of late day you'd see the little kids coming back from Sunday afternoon movies tripping from double features at the Royal and the Crown— Sunday night came with one wink of streetlamps— I mooned in the club watching bowlers—I walked in the sad finished-up streets of human time.

Monday morning we blearily blearyfaced met and proceeded to school as usual— Heartbrokenly I could hear the song *I'm Afraid the Masquerade is Over* darkening in my ear as we crossed the windy bridge— All the joy was gone from my anticipation of days—

But in the Spanish class, lo!—a note from Maggie.

I tore it open, slow and thoughtful, shaky.

Dear Jack,
    I am writing this Saturday night after the dance. I feel very blue and let me explain. Bessy came over to me, Bloodworth introduced her to Edna. And you know how I like Edna and her smug ways. She said Pauline was with you at the track meet. Well I flew right off the handle. Edna and Pauline are friends and they would stop at nothing to get you away from me. You made me so jealous I dont know what I said or did all I know is that I wanted to get out of there but the girls wouldnt come home with me. If you have to talk with Pauline please dont let any of my friends see you because it always gets back to me. I cant seem to get over my jealousy it must have been born in me. And of course there is another side to

the story. In my jealousy I do things that hurt you and that is the last thing I want to do. I cant seem to understand that you can go out with any girls you want to without me having to interfere. I realize now how selfish I have been. Jack you will have to forgive me please. I think it is because I like you so much. I will try and remember that it is your privilege to go out and do as you please. I'll be jealous of course but I have to get over it sometime. Some day you might find in me the qualities you admire most in a girl and a selfish one at that. I know you have every reason not to answer but, you always let me get away with too much and I knew it. I just had to write and tell you I felt so sorry about the other night.

With all my love

MAGGIE

Please forgive me

Write soon—tear this up.

That night I was there at eight o'clock, immediately after supper and on the fastest bus, the gloomy air had turned warm, something had broken and mushroomed in the wet winter earth of Lowell, ice was cracking on the Concord, winds blew with a greeny freight of hope over excited trees—it seemed the earth was being reborn— Maggie ran into my arms at the door, we hid in it in the dark silent and tight held, kissing, waiting, listening—"Poor Jacky, you'll never have anything but trouble with a damn fool like me."

"No I wont."

"I got sore at Bloodworth the other night. Did you see him? Today? At school? Can you tell him I'm sorry?"

"Sure—sure—"

Hiding her face in my sweater "I've been feeling awful anyway— My uncle died, I saw him in his coffin. Ah—it's so . . . people tell me I'm bored, I shouldnt hang around the house thinking about boys—about *you*—*you*," kissing me poutingly—"I dont even wanta *leave* the house—if all they've got is coffins, dead— How could I work I dont even wanta live. Oh my—I was so skeered—"

"What?"

"My *uncle*— They buried him Friday morning, they dropped rocks on him and his flowers—I was feeling bad about you anyway—but that's not what was wrong—but I cant tell you—explain you—"

"Nevermind."

She sat staring on my lap for hours, silent, in the dark parlor—I understood everything, held myself in, waited.

XXIV

And that Saturday night when I met her at the Rex, as our usual arrangement, they were playing *The Masquerade Is Over* when she came in with Bessy from the cold—ineffably beautiful as never before, with dew drops in her black hair like little stars in her eyes, and rosiness effulging from sweet laughs tinklin one after another— She was feeling good again, beautiful and unwinnable again forever—like the dark rose.

Her coat smelling of winter and joy, in my arms. Her coquettish looks everywhere—impulsive quick looks at me to laugh, comment, or criticize, and straighten my tie. Suddenly throwing her arms around my neck and pulling up her eyes to my face, her own, seized like a sob to squeeze me, plead love out of me, own and posses me greedily, whispering in my ear— Cold wiggling nervous hands in mine, the sudden grip and fear, the vast sadness all around her like wings— "Poor Maggie!" I thought—looking for something to say— and there is nothing to say—or if you said it—it would fall like a strange wet tree from your mouth—like the pattern of black veins in the earth of her uncle's and all uncles' graves— non-sayable—non-ownable—split.

Side by side we stared at the dance, the two of us dumb and darkened. Adult love torn in barely grown-up ribs.

XXV

Maggie by the river—"Poor Jack," sometimes she laughs, and fondles my neck, looks deep into my eyes rich and snug—her voice voluptuously breaking on a laugh, low—her teeth like little pearls in those red gates of her lips, the rich red gates of summer's fat, April's scar— "Poor Jack"—and now the smile has faded from the dimples, only the light of the smile flashes in her eye—"I dont think you know what you're doing."

"I wouldnt be suss-prised—"

"If you knew what you were doing you wouldnt be here."

"Didnt I say so."

"No—you didnt say so-o——" rolling her eyes drunkenly at me, making me drunk, passing her cold palm over my cheek in a sudden caress so tender the winds of May would understand and the winds of March wait back for, and the soothe "oo" of her lips making some silent little blow word to me, like "oo" or "You"—

My eye'd fall looking right in hers—I wanted her to see the windows of my secret. She accepted it—she didn't accept it—she wasnt decided—she was young—she was cautious— she was moody—she wanted to reach something in me and hadnt done it yet—and maybe that was enough for her, to know—"Jack's a dope."

"I'd never have anything with him— He'll never be a hard-worker like we see, like men, around, Pa, Roy—he's not our kind— He's strange. Hey Bessy, dont ya think Jack is kinda strange?"

Bessy: "N-a-w ? ?—How should *I* know!"

"Well—" Maggie humphin with herself—"I dont know, I must say," turning to camp at teacups, "I rally daont knaow." On the radio, record programs. Pillows all over. If I could have played hooky in *that* parlor. Sunny drapes— morning.

"So ya made up with Jack, huh?"

"Yeah." Rich-throated, like the modiste that's older than

the other, like you see great old women in San Francisco bleak wood tenements sitting all day with their parrots and old cronies talking about when they owned all the whore-houses of Hawaii or complaining about their first husbands. "Yeah. I dont think he'd think much of me."

"Why?"

"I dunno. I told you he was kinda funny."

"Ah you're crazy."

"I guess I yam."

If I'd laugh, and throw love teeth in her face, the big grin of accepting rapportive joy, she'd have just a twinge of sus-picion of my motives—which would deepen—all night—till the bottomless sorrows of the dark—all my dark walks back from her house—all our misunderstandings—all her schemes, dreams—floop—all gone.

XXVI

My birthday party was coming up but I wasnt supposed to know about it—all planned by my sister, to be had in a little cottage up the Pawtucketville hill near the church, her girl-friend's house. It was all supposed to be hidden from me. Presents were bought—little Emersonette radio so auspicious then but later to be little radiator radio of my father's dull flops in cheap hotels in the years to come of his wandering work— Baseball glove, supposed to be mark and symbol of the coming baseball season and all of us to play ball, bought for my birthday by Bloodworth probably—neckties— Every-body was invited by my sister: —Maggie, Bloodworth, Lousy, Iddyboy, a few of her friends, my parents, girls from the neighborhood the boys would bring with them— I wasnt supposed to know about it but I did.

Bloodworth told me.

One night our friendship deepened immensely and sensa-tionally in front of the Giant Store, across from the Silk Mills, the canal, in front of Boys' Club, we'd been talking since practice where he came sometimes to see me run and now aimlessly walking to continue talk had reached the compromise split-up of "I go home this way you go home that way"—to supper— It was already dark, cold winter, the streetlamps of the street bright like diamonds in cold howly grit winds, unpleasant— We hung there just talking— And about Maggie, baseball, everything— To keep warm we just suddenly began playing imaginary catch from about five feet from each other showing our also demonstrative technique styles of catch and throw, the leisurely windup, the throw— "Big leaguers always lob the ball easy" said Charley "you go to Fenway Park and you see the guys before game time just pitching it in easy not one guy throwing to snap and it looks like no effort at all but they can throw the ball far with the same easy lob, from years of easy lobbing— This means 'Dont throw your arm out' "—

"Charley, you shoulda been a big leaguer."

"I'm gonna be—I hope—I'd sure love it— Taff'll make it—Taff will—"

In histories of their own in the Lowell Highlands Bloodworth and Taffy Truman had bent their heads together over their tremendous personalities and hope, ambitions, reading papers over each other's shoulders, rushing to games, broadcasts, known each other's most personal impossible interior hang-up pose core like they'd know their own or the marks of their own wounds— In coldwind nights stalked in jackets talking, like Scotchmen in an Edinburgh of the New World — Both of them worked on the railroad in Billerica, and their fathers too—

"Taff will make it—big leagues—I aint worried, Bill— Here's the way *I* wind up and throw—"

"Here's how my crazy pal G.J. Rigopoulos?—pitches, he's the craziest guy in the world" I yelled to him across the winds and showed him, the Bob Feller exaggerated windup of almost falling back to the ground to throw, long leg up.

On Moody Street we're pitching the invisible game the week of my birthday party, now we were imitating a great battery, I was squatted down with imaginary catcher's mitt, we had ghost batters up and whole innings to play. "Two and O, two on, weary Charley Bloodworth pitching a crucial ninth—peppery sensational Jack Duluoz behind plate—here's the pitch—I think you should know they're gonna throw a party for ya—your sister—"

"Who? *me?*"

"Yeah, boy. Maybe you'd drop dead from excitement or shock or something, I dont know—I dont like surprises myself—so when March twelfth comes just take it easy and you'll see— Your sister and M.C. Number One've been talking on the phone for weeks. You got lots of nice presents boy—including one I aint gonna tell you about—"

My mother and father were deeply involved in the big party too, it was arranged for cakes, for a newspaper reporter to be there, games. I didnt look forward to it because of the immensity of everything. I half guessed that I would have to act surprised and as if I didnt know when everybody'd yell "Happy Birthday!" I bit my lips . . . proud.

XXVII

The big night came.

Everybody was off to the party to await my arrival. I sat alone in the kitchen waiting for Iddyboy to come—"eediboy, come on, my brother Jimmy want to see you about something!" Jimmy Bissonette, the man of the house where the shindig was about to bang—friends of my sister— Outside a huge blizzard has started, by midnight it will have paralyzed Lowell and be making history 20 inches deep, vast, prophetic. How sad and funny that my parents are hiding with fun hats and our own house is empty— I have all the lights out, wait by the window among empty window shades, dark lost coats— I'm all dressed to go in my high school football sweater with the "38" on it for 1938 and a great sewn-in "L" for "Lowell"

a little football sewn in redly in the gray thread of the "L"—
an undershirt beneath, no collar—I want to have my picture
taken by the photographers they'll call from the local papers,
I foreknow— Everybody else will wear coats, vests, ties—I'm
going to look like an absurd child whose gray dream of vanity
even love cannot penetrate.

I look out the window at the tremendous storm gathering.
Through it, eager gleeful big good Iddyboy's plodding
gravely to the plan—I see him in specky sweeps across the
Gershom arc lamp rounding the corner, bent, his shoes leave
little idiotness dots in snow, goodness tramps in the ghost and
glee of it—my chest stabs deep sweet transcendent pain to see
it, him, the snow, the night—across these furying murks thirty
persons are hiding to scream me Happy Birthday, Maggie
among them— Iddyboy rolling along in the slanty glooms, his
big sleeky grin in sleet, teeth shining small separate gleams,
rosy, glad, shadows in his rugged ruddy hardbone nose—an
old pro guard of beef and iron slung low to murder when
smash-football breaks the ruddy turfs—his busty knuckle knob
of fists inbent in stiff sartorial partygoing gloves— "Bash I
boo!" he says—he reaches out a snap punch and bashes the
picket fence clean off the base—says "Grargh" and goes *vlup*
and pelts his picket off—as oft he'd under cold midnight
streetlamps, dared me to try it, *pow!*—life in the nailed-in
picketposts holds stiff, my knuckles burn, I try two more times,
"Hard! sharp! ye boy!"—some oldwood frozenness cracks,
the picket flies off—we range along the fence casting tooth
after tooth out of it, *crack,* Old Man Plouffe who lived across
from our favorite parkfence a strange old idler who'd all he
do is open windows in the middle of the Lowell Night and
admonish the boys *"Allez-vous-en mes maudits vandales!"*
with his stocking cap and rheumy rosy eyes alone in his brown
house by forlorn coffin strips velvet and spittoons he'd hear the
crack of our pickets at 2 A.M.— Iddyboy's dark leer at the
thought of it— "Hoo Gee!" yelled Iddyboy the night the
French Canadian Mayor won the Lowell election, Arsenault
O golden name, Iddyboy in political excitement leaped up
from our fifteen-year-old pinochle game when my parents
were out in the dense Lowell night and crammed his fist

through the plaster of the kitchen wall, a prodigious wallop enough to kill Jack Dempsey gloveless like that—the plaster caved in on the other side in the radio mahogany table room —when my mother came home horrified she was convinced he was a maniac and worse— "He put his fist through it? His boot!" Knuckle marks were sunk in the deep wall. "How did he do that! I tell you they're all crazy the Bissonettes— they've got the damndest men in that family—the father—" Iddyboy, calmed down now—momentarily stops at the wood fence below, I see him turn anxious haggardness four flights up in the soft spit snow to see—"What? No light? Jacky aint dey? Where's that damn He Thee Boy! I'm gonna break that neck! Argh"— He plunges across the street and under my sight at the tenement doors, powerful, silently sore, I hear him barge in the halls, Iddyboy is swimming up to me in the gloom of a dream so huge I see there is no end to it, to me, to him, to Maggie, to life, to wife, to world—

"Kid you big Marine!"—our greetings at the door.

"Come on boy, my brother Jimmy wants to see something about you—"

"What?"

"Oh"—trying to look unconcerned, with heavy tragic eyes falling—"he's nothing, you babe. Come!"

He explodes laughing "Hee!" He squeezes my knee, we sit facing, hard iron racks enclose my knee as we sleek teeth at each other in the continuation of the Eediboy Marines burlying down the planks of the bridge— I feel like saying "I know about the party, Ye Boy" but I dont want to disappoint his big believing heart— We look at each other, old friends. "Come on you lad. Hat! Coat! Less go!"

We bend to the blizzard, go up Moody— Suddenly the moon wheels pale in a crack of penetrative clouds— "Look, the moon!" I cry—"Iddyboy you still believe that man in the moon with the basket of twigs?"

"Those black shapes not eyes! Not a basket of twigs, a *bundle!*—It's wood—*du bois*—Your eye dont believe what you see? It's you moon, kiddo Ti Janny, all the hopeful people knows that!"

"Pourquoi un homme dans la lune? Weyondonc!" (Why a man in the moon? Come on!)

"Ey, ey," ominous to stop, leaning hand on knee, "don't talk like that—it's true *weyondonc*. You're afraid you? You's crazy? Ah? *Tu crais pas?* You dont believe? On your birthday? Dont you do believe?" Iddyboy who in church on Sundays stood straight as a post in front pews of Sainte Jeanne d'Arc turning bulging red faces when loud noises disturbed the silent priest in his silent altar—Iddyboy wanted no pretense in this world.

"It's not true all that!"—firm atheistic adolescent denials I make.

"Non non non! A man in the moon needs that bundle of wood!" he says angrily—shudders hugely in his mighty chest— "Ah gee-boy!"—simple-minded, without alteration sprung from the blood of the pure paisans of the North, the noises issuing from his throat the refined gutturals of an eloquence to tell—"Me I believe in *Le Bon Dieu*, Jacky"—palm up—"He bless me, make me, save me—" He takes my arm, friendly— "Hey!" he yells suddenly remembering the swishy sissy girl of Gersham Avenue who flew along the kiddie sidewalks of dust red ridden dusk flapping his behind with one dainty wink at the hole in the sky, Iddyboy says, "I'm So So Su Su that kid there we see flashipott arouns— I'm a sissy boy too!" and he wiggles off with his powerful butt like iron cannons in coat storms and minces with his nail of a finger in the cold night— He comes back, puts his arm around me again, laughs, conducts me up the street and to the party believing in me—says, loud so you can hear two blocks up, "Argh, we are *good* friends, ey?"—he shakes me, makes me see love in Heaven, makes me ope my stupidness and innocence eyes—his cheeks rich, red, hotnecked to go and sleek up the world through his happy teeth—"See, you babe?"

XXVIII

We climb the steps of the little bungalow, there's just a kitchen light inside, we go in, Jimmy his older brother is smiling at us from the middle of the linoleum— There's a kitchen, livingroom, diningroom, one extra bedroom made up by the childless young couple into a rumpus type room— Strange silence—

"Take off your coat and rubbers Jack," they both instruct me. I do so.

Out of the rumpus room comes a great shriek of voices "Happy Birthday ! ! !" My father bursts out, followed by my mother from another room, Bloodworth and Maggie from another, my sister Nin behind, Jimmy's wife Jeannette, Lousy, Taffy Truman, Ed Eno, others—a swim of faces in my eternity—the house roars. "Wheee!" fiendishly shouting Jimmy is opening a quart of whisky, pushing it at me—I take a burning swig to roars— A great cake emerges, with candles— The opening festivities—I blow them out— Cheers! We're standing yelling eating cake in the kitchen—

"Give the guest of honor a big piece there! Put some weight on him for next fall!"—laughter, a girl's screech of delight from beyond, I've had no time to say hello to Ma or Pa or Maggie in the crowd excitement, the too-much world— I see Iddyboy trying to be social like in movies the cake in his big paw laughing with Martha Alberge his girl and he lets out a big explosive Phnu! of laughter that kicks in his big battering-ram belly and blasts up his throat and out comes spewing a streamer of snivel all over the cake—nobody sees, he falls, kneels on the floor, holds his belly laughing— His fantastic brother Jimmy is screaming excitedly some dirty joke, my father is doing the same thing near the stove, the house-top shivers maniacally in the great now-howling swept-over blizzard, heat beats at the windows, I grab Maggie by the waist, I yell— Door opens, fresh arrivers—red shouting faces turn to it as new people fall in. Roars of approval, applauses, raisings of bottles—"Oh Ti Jean," my Ma is shouting in my ear, "there was supposed to be millions of your school friends here tonight!—Ti Nin fixed you a grand party—not half of em came—you shoulda seen the list she made with Maggie—"

"Maggie too?"

"Sure! Oh Jacky"—mournfully gripping me, flushed, her best cotton dress, white ribbon in her hair, she adjusts my T-shirt under the huge hot idiotboy sweater, "it's an awful storm, the radio's saying it's the biggest in years—" Then gleefully: "Sssst gimme a big kiss and hug, and hey shh dont tell nobody but here's a five spot I'm slippin you, aye?— *tiens*—that's for your seventeenth birthday take in a good show and a big spree on ice cream, invite Maggie to come with you— Ah pet?"

"Boo hoo hee ha ha!" Jimmy Bisonette let out his mad maniac laugh you could hear three blocks away soaring over the blabbers and hubbubings, I stared in amazement, they'd told me this man many a night in wild Lowell afterhours'd challenge anyman to have a bigger one than he had and show how he could shove seven or eight or nine or ten quarters off a table with his piece, all amid roaring laughters of wildparty Canadians of lake cottage clubs in crazy lurid summer with ivy blue moon on the lake or winter when the piano music, smoke, shouting and leaping took place behind bleak shutters and pale reeds creak in stiff ice (the unused divingboard)—to bets, screeches, Tolstoyan hurrahs and huzzahs of revel night —Jimmy insane for girls—on strong squat legs he rushed with wildsweat joy around the wooden bars of Moody, in clubs, at spectral orange houseparties with telegraph wires outside the bay window (Ford Street, Cheever Street)—his ears stuck out—he raced anxiously—his feet rapidly scissored fast little steps—you'd see just the proud raised head the bursting gargling eediboy joy then the longwaist body underneath pumped along by whirring feet . . . spats sometimes, lost Saturday nights of French Canadian ecstasy—

And there's my father, in the press he's only roared, coughed, shouted his own partying words from behind knotted groups of the kitchen—he's in his big new brown suit, his face is dark and almost brick red, his collar wilting, necktie raggedly hopelessly rattysnarled and twisted at his tortured sweaty neck— "Ha ha dont give me that stuff Maggie!" arms around her squeezing her, patting her behind "I know you never showed them the way to wear a bathingsuit I sure am sure you should of!" (Huge cough)—the which Maggie weathers unblinking like detonations— At the windows watchers Aw and OO the storm—

"Gonna be a pippin."

"Look at those big thick flakes falling straight down. Sure sign."

"Yeah with a high wind comin up always means a big whopper—"

"Well let's have a little song someone!—Hey Jimmy sing em your horse song your dirty song!"

"A high school party! Take it easy! Moo hoo hoo hwee ha ha!"

Vinny, G.J., Scotty show up, in big coats, scarfs, with girls, late—the storm— Friends of the family pour in whooping, snow flakes, bottles—the party's wild. Charley Bloodworth's three buddies Red Moran, Hal Quinn and Taffy Truman from the Highlands grimly sit in a corner, the French Canadians yell in French, the boys hear it with rat-tat-tat disbelief, composts and rim-posts, jabberous, impossible—my father yelling "Okay let's talk English so we can chat with Bloody and the boys here—buncha ballplayers you know—say Red, wasnt your father the old Jim Hogan that had that meat market up on whattayacallit Square off Westford Street, you know the one I mean—"

"No," shouting back, "no Mister Duluoz it's an old relative of ours had that store—Luke Moran not Hogan—"

"I remember him—had that little store a few years earlier near West Street—old Maria was his wife—he had jews harps hanging on his wall— Years we traded there. Centreville."

"I don't know who that is—" Red's skeptical. "No—"

They cant come to an understanding who Red's father is— Taffy Truman the great young pitcher sits, hands loosely joined, waits.

Beside him Harold Quinn the hero of Bloodworth's breed and hill, I'd seen him calf-bulgant on second base in dusty

Twi League eves on South Common, the crack of the bat, ball skitters in rough patch grass of second base, Harold Quinn's stepped over and scooped it up with an authoritative glove, has swept it off to first quickly beginning a double play, hustles back to his keystone sack, taps it with a cleated foot, waits, the runner slides to him in field dust clouds, he clombs up the low throw in his glove for the downward unassuming putout tap on the fellow's shoulder, pulls back his left foot turnaway from kicking spikes, spits silently between teeth as the dust starts spreading, his little spit spurt hangs in midair, falling into the dust, the man is OUT— Beside him Red Moran bends forward in his chair holding a small strawhat toy from the rattles of the party—

Bang, crash, all my Lowell raving wild.

XXIX

Heat generates to the ceiling. Vapor in the windows. The wild windows of other houses and Saturday night parties shining the spilling molten hot gold of real life. I'm sweating, the big athletic sweater is killing me, making me hot, wetfaced, sad at my own party. In the kitchen the older folks are already half in the bag, rounds of nips, drinking songs; in the rumpus the youngsters start a post office game with gleeful couples running into the cold dark blizzard windowed unheated parlor to neck. Maggie is the star. Bloodworth, Moran, Quinn, Truman, Lousy even, everybody's rushing her in and out of the parlor for passionate kisses—my face burns with jealousy. I rush her in when the spin-bottle points at us—

"You're kissin Bloodworth like mad tonight."

"Aint we sposed to, dope? That's the rules."

"Yeah but he enjoys it—you enjoy it—"

"So?"

"So—I feel—" I grab her, shivering; she fights out. "Never mind."

"Old jealous. Let's go back—"

"Why right away?"

"Cause—I'm cold in here— Lissen! They're laughin!"
And she rushes back into the heated rooms, I follow emptily
reaching. Alternately cold and hot, the next time we hit the
parlor she flies into my arms and bites my lips and I feel tears
in my ears, wet— "Oh Jack, love me tonight! All those fellers
are after me!—that Jimmy felt me up—"

"Dont let em!"

"Oh you lunkhead—" Hugging herself at the whited windows. "Look the blizzard has put a sheet of snow on the
pane— God I wonder if my father had to go out and work
in this muck—I oughta call home— Maybe Roy's car'll be
stuck—" In my arms, curled, brooding.— "Did you hear
about one of the Clancy triplets dying gee it was one of those
things a sore throat and she died within a day—I could tell
you a lot about it but it's really heartbreaking so let's forget
about it—"

"You always follow the bad news around South Lowell
always always."

"I'm just so skeered somethin'll happen to my family—
Did you hear about Eddie Coledana too? You know Eddie
he's in the hospital a freight elevator fell from the fourth
floor in the Suffolk Knitting Mills Company where he was a
weaver, something went wrong, the elevator was falling the
freight in it fell on top of him isnt that awful? Oh why do I
think of it now at your party?"

"Maggie—Maggie—"

"How's the kid?"—in my ear—"Love of my life—"

"Am I, honest?—what would I have done if you hadnt
come to my party—"

"Are you mad?"

"No—nah."

"—that's the question before the house. Oh," sighing, "I
guess I'm just a scatterbrain." Voluptuously gloomy in my
hopeless arms. I'm afraid to say any more to bore her. Wild,
everybody talking to me, through human mazes all night I
try to struggle to her—knowing that I'm losing her now—

Lousy has me by the arm trying to cheer me up; he's beginning to see; I feel his love for me, man to man, boy to boy, "Aw Jack, easy you babe, easy—you know dont you that I'm still saying that was the best dinner I ever had up your house Sunday, ah?—why it even beats the hamburgers you made last summer— Just for me! You goodhearted Jack! I came in the house, you woke up, you put a half-pounda butter in the frying pan, big pats of meat, zzzt, big smokes, onions, katchup—zeet? The greatest cook in the world!"

Together we watch Maggie rushing off into the parlor with Bloodworth, Red Moran pulling her the other way—I feel like sawing those boys through a crack in the Scotch wood of the Irish Revolutionary doorjamb—

"It's all right, Zagg, she's a young foolish girl having a big time—I didnt kiss her I laughed—I *laughed!* Hee hee! Just a girl, Zagg, just a girl. Next week we down our parafanelyers for a little training, right?—*baseball*! Things are dishing out! Iddyboy our faithful pal will be catcher, Kid Babe Sam me on third base—just like as always, nothing changes you babe!"

"Demand your rights!" yells Scotty joining us, in the middle of the room we stand wound-in-arms touching heads.

"Scot on third—G.J. the magnificent on the mound—a great season of funny games!—All's well!"

Gus joins us—"Zagg I dont wanta say anything but Maggie Cassidy just sat on my hand and wouldnt get off, I tell you I was never so embarrassed in all my life I swear on my mother's name—and she wouldnt budge! And that huge Emil Blooah your father he sure does look at a girl's ass when she walks away but all the time when she's sittin on his lap he's tweaking her chin and saying jokes you know? Zagg what could he do?—he'd kill a girl just by laying on top of her— You shoulda seen how huge his eyes popped! I was scared for Maggie. I warn you Zagg, Frank Merriwell your arch foe has slipped me a couple bucks not to tell you this—"

Lousy: "When this party is over, my friendlies, I'm goin home, you know how the bed feels." In my ear whispering: "Pauline's deeply in love with you, Jack, no shit! She's been raving about you every time I see why even yesterday in my spare as I came in the room she ask me if I wasnt gonna do my homework, I said of it— Boy I never touched my books for the rest of the period. Asking questions here and there— She even said I laugh like you, I talk like you, the same motions. She said if you ever get fatter she is too. Honest Jack she's even talking about the future. She's going to marry you and everything you possibly can think of. I'm not supposed to say this according to what she says. She asks me a lot of questions. She asks me if you have any other girlfriends. She dont mention Maggie. To make it look good on her side I said 'No' in a slow voice—I wish I had a whole day to myself so I could tell you all what she says. Listen you sneakin rat what did you tell Pauline that first Sunday you went up her house—last November after the game— Dont say nothing face to face? Well I know different, she says to me 'Oh I know something about you,' she said, 'you should be ashamed—' Give the full details— Ah? confess what you said!" I'd told her about Lousy and I demonstrating that first kiss. "So long you sneaking Belgium Babe! I'm going to dream up some black angels in my nice white pillow now you babe— What a storm for sleep!"

"Zagg," said G.J. philosophically and brotherly arms around me in the roar, "remember our fights in the hall? You'd call me from outside—'Yanny!'—innocently I'd come down like a normal human being but you were hiding in the dark, eyes gleaming, breathing heavily, pouncing on me— Yesterday I saw everything different, the time you twisted my arm and it cracked I shot a left hook to your body, you wavered under the impact but came back fast with a right cross to the jaw— I retaliated with a sharp left and jab to the groin and boy did you groan—weaving and dodging I came in fast for the kill—shooting four lefts and seven rights I brought you down to your knees, then faster than an eye wink I went for my iron and conked you over the head. A surprised look came over your face, you tried to clamber to your knees —which was your downfall—lifting all strength I swung my john high over my head and bringing it down hard on your dome I felled you like an ox— Ah what a life!" suddenly gloomy. "Happiness'll disappear, bitter grouchy and dont care will come back ever in this ga-dam world. But what the krise if it makes God happy then there's no harm in it— All our dreams, Zagg, childhood together—things like the fights in the hall—Now you're grown up, your Ma fixed you a big birthday party, your girl's here, your father, your friends— Yes dont kid yourself Jack, there is still some kind people left in this world— You may some day be ashamed but dont ever be ashamed of me, what we've known together, us, in our screwy talks and adventures—look at Lousy, good old Belgium going home to sleep—in a minute he'll be headin up Riverside in the blizzard as a thousand times I seen him from my kitchen window and cursed that the world was black, all's right with the world and Lousy self-satisfied and holdin himself in is going to his well-deserved rest—there you have it, Zagg."

Scotty all combed, suited, smilefaced: "You babe if you cant be good be careful—heh heh heh! Till Saturday at 5 P.M. I'm workin now and especially Friday night till 11 P.M. —Vinny got kilt the other day when he hit a hole with Zaza's bike his leg got scratches and four fingers and I think personally he's puttin some on— See him? He's gonna get a big job in Lawrence now carryin huge bundles of cloth on his shoulders from morning till night— But this summer we'll all be together again and have a jaloppy this time and go swimmin after games—"

"I hope so, Scot." Later, by woodstoves, we'd grimly add it all up, together a thousand miles apart.

Firmly he places his arm around me, smiles.

I close my eyes, I see little Puddinhead Bunky De-Beck in his infant wear big sunflower lace sitting in his cookiebox in Saturday night color-section cartoons "Fagan youse is a Viper" he complains to big bedeardoed huge hunkey Chaplin Fagan with big bum's lips replying "Why is I a Viper, Bunky?" as he climbs out the window with a mask in the sad red print— Maggie's dancing wildly, I sit gooping—

Across the party my Ma comes running gleefully hunching her shoulders biting her tongue to throw long embraces around me, wants to show everybody how much she loves her boy, yells "Hey there Jacky what you say Mama's gonna come and give you a big kiss!" smack!

The photographers come, everybody's screaming instructions—sweatingly two group photos are arranged— In the first one I stand between Ma and Pa, Bloodworth Truman and Moran sit to the left representing fellow high school athletes gravely and with glints in their eyes, Jim with arms around his buddies, Jimmy Bissonette sits to the right with his wife Jeannette, hosts— Jimmy is simpering up his face into the camera about to burst goo gool gee ha ha his crashing laughter, all excited in a tightfitting French roué coat like the European coats of pornographic picture heroes performing grave feats in dreary rooms with undressed women—happy crazy nose, tittly-lips, immense pride in the occasion of the night. Behind him stands my father, arm around me, his white fingers on my shoulder are obscured by the white wallpaper, he's glad, big vest, tight coat, all night he's been fevering and shouting in the party and "kidding the hell out of little Maggie ha ha ha"—now in the photo, coughing seriously, he's all flushfaced, proud, holding me close so the world can see his love of his son in the newspaper, with the same simplicity and believingness that Jimmy is holding his joy-face up to the devourous worlds— My father is like a Gogol hero of old Russia in a house. "Go ahead snap that birdie there, we've all got our best smiles—come on Jacky, *smile,* he never smiles that boy of mine dammit when he was five years old I used to come home he'd be sitting by himself on the porch one time he even tied ropes around himself, gloomy little cuss, I'd say 'What you thinkin about there sonny? What for you dont smile you worry your old folks that have given life to you and dont know just how to make up to you for what's at best a gloomy enough world I admit—' "

"Hold still everybody!"

"Ahem!" my father clears his throat, enormously earnest— Flup, the picture's taken— I havent even smiled in the picture, I look like a moronic boy with a strange pinched (by sweat and camera shadows) drawn goofy peaky witless face, my arms hang down joining my hands over my fly so I look like an unnamably abnormal beast of a boy groping dully his vain dreams of glory in a livingroom with big parties around—looking like Pimple Tom of the swill piles, sadfaced, droopy, but everybody sentimentally arranged around me to protect the "LETTER ATHLETE HONORED" as the picture caption says.

Suddenly in the other photo ("Thank God!" I thought seeing it the next day in the Lowell *Evening Leader*) I'm a Greek athlete hero with curly black locks, ivory white face, definite clear gray newspaper eyes, noble youth neck, powerful hands locked separate like regardant lions on the hopeless lap—instead of having Maggie in my grip for the photo like laughing happy fiancees we sit across the table from little presents disposed thereon (radio, baseball glove, ties)—still I dont crack a smile, have a grave vain look inwardly musing on the camera to show that I have special honors reserved for me in the echoey hall and dark corridor of this infinity, this telepathic bleak, this mig, instead of bursting into big laughs like Iddyboy is doing in the back stand-up row arms around Martha Alberge and Louise Giroux—going "HEE!" in a thundering boom cry and gloat of huge Iddyboy lifeloving girlhugging fencecrashing hungry satisfaction that has the photographer's hair leap up. Maggie, for her part, is a study of grave disrespect for the camera, wants nothing to do with it (like me) but has a stronger attitude, doubts while I pout, purses her lips while I stared wide-eyed at the world—for also my eyes grayly shine in the paper and show definite interest in the camera which at first is unnoticeable, like surprise— In Maggie there's disgust undisguised. She wears a crucifix and primly has no further word with world in camera.

XXX

The party ends, rides back home are arranged, taxis called—hoots across the snow, snowballs popping in the growl of spitting snow, cars racing motors to start, *vrroom*—no room. "Can we pile in back?"

"Nieh? I don knowa."

"Aint dee no room?"

"Beh sure! Come ah—"

"Bouee!"

Little teapots take their time.

"Good night Angelique— Good night—"

Calls across the snow—Moody Street a half-block down is a jostle of trucks beating chains, hoots, shovelers, the big blizzard has got men out working— "Hey I'm gonna get me some money," the old boys say down on Middlesex Street Lowell skid row and hop over on sore alcoholic feet to the City Hall or wherever to work for the City. Iddyboy mentioned it as the party broke up.

It had been a huge success—I had nothing to do with that part of it. The buses were running grace to God so most folks go home that way, Maggie who lives three miles away across all the city and out, has to take a cab— We get one down at Marie's all night stand across from where I live. I look up and see the dark windows of our tenement. Now that the party is over everything has the flavor of a dream well accomplished, like having a tooth pulled. Maggie: "This is one time you're not taking me to South Lowell and walking back to Pawtucketville."

"Why not?"

"Not even you could walk in this storm . . . ten inches of snow." Such Sicilian shifts my lamb of love: —I could walk in this storm as well as Colonel North Pole Blake of the Greenland Armadas and had done so to Pine Brook out in the Dracut woods, in the night, in big blizzards, carrying a long stick and planting it down so's not to step into streams entire, or well holes— I'd stood in the forests of night listening to the kissing of the flakes and the twigs of winter, the little sleet spitting like electric particles anticipatory and clicking, in wet gooey gum boughs—

"Yes I could walk in this storm—but I wont tonight, I havent got my overshoes except upstairs and boy am I sleepy wow—it's three o'clock in the morning!"

"Me too. Gee what a party."

"Did you like it?"

"Sure."

"How'd you like my father?"

"He was funny."

"Wasnt he? And we had a pretty good time. Gee some of the guys in there had a good time—"

"That aint the point," said Maggie pointedly.

"What?"

"It was in honor of you. You should appreciate it."

"I *do* appreciate it!"

"Nobody'll believe you if you talk like that."

"Well *you* understand. . . ."

"Yah," said Maggie, almost sneering, "that's because I'm just like you—" Moving her jaws in the history of our love, half tough-looking in the doorway, half hunching over— I'm standing beside her proud, some of the boys in the Textile Lunch across the street can see I got a pip of a brunette waiting for a cab with me—I'm not old enough to chew my nails about not being able to go home with her and lay her. I'm chumpily looking at the upstairs windows of other tenements across the way, Maggie is primping her hair in her little mirror; a sad red ball light hangs in the ceiling of the Taxi tenement porch. Desolate shufflers come up Moody swallowed in the windy fall, athwarted by blazing flakes across the arc streetlamp glow. I kiss Maggie—she throws herself right up to me, loose, little, young, all I have to do is mention the word kissing and she'll play kissing games. I was beginning to sense her sexuality now and it was too late.

Across the street came part of our party, Textile Lunch for hamburgers and coffee, they piled in, you saw a flash of the jukebox, the counterman tattooed forearms on the counter crazy-faced yelling *"Oy la gagne des beaux matoux!"* (Oy the ga-dam tomcats!) at Pa and the older friends half drunkenly jawing into the steamy vapors of the diner, wet, tired, not hungry, gloomily surveying and sneering at everything—but exploding into laughs, big necessary hassel jovialities and shows of neighing concern and sudden good feeling tender and glad— The counterman makes a slight slur in the corner of his mouth when turning to cook the order.

Across, through vapor windows and fly snow, they could

have seen Maggie and me, up, side by side, in a doorway, standing bystanders suddenly turning into kissers and again resuming bystanders for stamping taxiwaiting tendencies.

"Your party was all right, I believe they couldnt a give you a better one—"

"Yeah—not the point— I mean—were you glad to see me tonight?"

"I *had* to see you tonight—"

"I know that but just to see me ha ha just kiddin ya—you'll be all right. After some sleep and you get home you'll be fine—"

"Jacky!" She's thrown herself, arms firm around my neck, loins into mine, but back arched as she leans back to throw her richness vision into mine—"I want to go home to a house to sleep with you and be married."

I drooped to think about it—I had no idea what I should do—"Huh?" I pictured my mother saying Maggie was "too impatient," others talking about it, the sweet future of it with Maggie and I getting home late at night tired from a party, and going up dark steps along rosy wallpaper to the dim velvet darkness of the room upstairs where we take off our coats of winter and put on pajamas and in between in the middle of both garments the nudities of bouncing bed. A bouncing baby boy with Christmas in his eyes. In the crib, in the rose dark, he with little poof pout sleeps his little thoughts away. You couldnt disturb him with rattles of talk and angels with sabers drumming up the brown moth-swarming vision of the Drape, soon enough they'd part, ascendant swimming Heaven *blazing* universal snow particles of the truth—Maggie's baby in the reality—mine, my son, in the snowing world—my house of brown—Maggie's river making muds more fragrant in the spring.

She went home in the cab, it was driven by a friend of mine whose face I'd seen in a thousand Fellaheen dusks of this village in our dirtstreet boyhood, Ned, Fred, he was a nice kid, he made some joke about something as they rolled off sadly big red taillight vaporing exhaust in grim winter conditions and flopped chains off into distance and South Lowell, source of my arrow.

XXXI

Little paradises take their time. Little parties end.

My father was only beginning to raise hell in the diner, I went in for some tail end to my day, but only yawn a few times in the greenish light and scarfed three hamburgers with ketchup and raw onions while everybody carried on the music and the roar of a good old Saturday or Blizzard night in New England, at dawn bottles were opened, shiftings of parties took place, on Gershom Avenue at gray six o'clock when only the old ghosts of Pawtucketville walk wending their white way in black veils to church, there was heard from inside the tenements deep a sudden shrieking high laugh from some old gal in some roundtable black iron range kitchen and windows rattling black little boy cant sleep in his pillow, will be bleary for the blizzard in the morning— Me too I'll go to sleep now and make that black angel in the pillow void open—the world is not void open— "Go ahead Jacky me boy," my father even said rolling down off some big laugh with Ned Layne the wrestler who was part owner of the lunchcart, "go to bed if that's what you wanta do, and all you been doing is yawning, too much excitement for the kiddos tonight"—and Ned Layne would die in the war—nobody'd wrestled in the right arena around there—my sister's friend, the little chum of my sister's girlhood who was going to marry him was barking up a wrong tree in the serious reality of the open world. The tree that was with root of these realities had already threaded knuckly fingers in the bleak.

"Okay Pa, I'm going to bed."

"Did you like your party?"

"*Oui.*"

"Good— Dont tell anybody if they ask ya that I had a coupla drinks at the house, I dont wanta be obliged to kid laws." Before coming home to supper every night my father used to have his two or three shots of whisky in the Club across the way, it was the great time when I could see him head from there to the barbershop straight across the street, the long spacious handling of the scene of this with him inside strawhat hung up in summers' nights as I'm racing along on sneakers where we lived two blocks down, I was two years younger, see him unbelievingly rich in the shop with a magazine and a white barber shroud and the man knee-ing to his work as he shaves. "Good night kiddo, and if you wanta marry Maggie you'll never pick a prettier girl, she's Irish as the day is long and a damn good little scout as far as I can see."

XXXII

"It's a warm coat I have," says Bloodworth walking in the cold north red dusks of March in Massachusetts near the New Hampshire line, "but it's not a warm coat tonight," making a sour joke and sullen, and suddenly I realize he's a great old skeptic who's thought deeply on the weather and uses it in his speech or has such horrid findings swear with it. "Christ, pretty soon the thaw'll be out."

XXXIII

April came. It joined with March in forming mud in the woods, long flying streamers of flags pennoned from the circus flagpole Post-No-Bills advertisements of May. Summer'd reach into the corners of spring and mop em all dry—the essential cricket would crawl from his rock. My birthday party was over, I grew more fond of Maggie now as she grew less fond of me, or surer. The season had swung on some invisible pivot of its own.

Thing was—Maggie wanted me to be more firm and binding in my contractual marriages of mate and heart with her —she wanted me to stop acting like a schoolboy and get ready to be busy in the world, make headways for her and our brood, and breed. Spring rank suggested this in breezes of prim river that now I began to enjoy as the iced ruts in Maggie's Massachusetts Street began to uncongeal, crystal, crack, and swim—"Frick frack" would wave the goodlooking hoodlum on the corner of Aiken and Moody Street and still your May'd come. "Damfool" will be the lark saying on a branch and I know that juices and syrup sops would pulse come throbbing springtime— "Never know would ye the wood was damp on the bottom" would be saying the old champions out in pine fields. I'd walk all over Lowell aweing and ooing my measures to the brain. Doves too coo. The wind like harp'll blow blah blah over Lowell.

Now I'm going to find out how my love for Maggie fares. Not too well.

I had no "Maggie what shall I do?" to ask myself and like a schoolboy finally decided that to hell with her my Ritz crackers and peanut putter would disappear. I pouted like a big baby over the thought of losing my home and going off into unknown suicides of weddings and honeymoons— "Honey," Maggie says, "it's okay, just go on going to school I dont wanta stop you or interfere with your career, you know what to do better than I do. You know, maybe you wouldnt be so practical to live with." It's a warmish late March night; I'm through the blazing moon the March witches are racing their shrouds and brooms, whippets come after, yapping across the bleak, the leaves dont fly they're mashed underfoot, a seething wet beast is rolling its back in the earth, you're about to realize King Baron of the sweet mountains was not going to be coronated in this Kingdom pine sap— I saw blue birds trembling on wet black boughs, "flute!!"

Fluting spring was racing through the corridors and ritual alleys of my sacred brain in holy life and making me wake and resurge to the business of being and becoming a man. I drew deep breaths, cut shortcut quicksteps over the loose crunch cinders of the back-of-Textile dumpside river-viewing

gravel drive—the tremendous views of Lowell from this ball
perch of night, the countless sad tragic waters down there,
over shapes of dead bushes and rat-inhabited wrecks of Reos
Chandlers Pee Pee Poo machines of long ago, and the bad
sand, stinking of sewage—this I could smell in spring to-
nights coming back from Maggie, spring'd send the stale
fender with its sweet rot swills caked underneath and I'd
know—this would be mixed with sweet breath river's voice
Awing at me over the lake of the bend— From Lakeview
clear I could literally smell the pinecones getting ready for
dry gladsummers on the ground, the azaleas were ballooning
again Mrs. Faterty's garden, Rattigan's saloon next door
would only send suds and breezy foam smells in the coming
months—you couldnt mistake spring from the mop handles
ratata-ing on porches of ladies— "There's my Pa now,"
Maggie is saying soon, as she walks down from the corner
where the South Lowell stores and bars were and passed the
joint where Mr. Cassidy's downing his boilermakers before
going home to sleep. "So I said 'We'll reach in get six, kick
one, kick two, kick em right in the lead then we'll spot to
clear and shove the rest!'—'What?' he sez to me 'I cant understand all that in one sitting—' 'Well for krissakes' I said
'you're gettin paid same as I am aintcha? And I been railing
around here for seventeen years aint I? So you expect me to
stop here and explain that to you again. Just keep your mouth
shut and your eyes open—you'll learn—'" Maggie walks by
hearing this speech and smiles, goes home to tell her mother—
Dark laughter. Out comes a little kid on the porch, and the
moon. Among the brown Fellaheen lights of life I'm hurrying,
off the bus at the cemetery corner and right down through a
railroad overpass and big scrabbly lamplit plaza of two roads
converging roughly and across that the pitch into that black
barrel of Massachusetts Street South Lowell Night which has
trellises, clinging vines, curly locks.

Spring blows in my nose, in my airy brain— The call of
the railroad train is howdah'd on the horizon. Bending her
head to me— "So you really dont want to get mixed up with
someone like me— You may think so now but I dont think
. . . it'll . . . work . . . out. . . ." I couldnt believe her, just

hung around to neck some more. Unbelievably grim my view of life and the cemetery, Maggie thinks I'm just a lost thought dope trying to remember what he was going to say. I have three separate things to attend to in the arrangement of my mind with the tumblers falling and falling into place and the safe door opening slowly so slowly it was a lifetime—besides seeing she wouldnt love me now, I spent my time haggling over whether I should go see her or not. She just sat around and didnt care.

These teeth I also threw into the balmy redolent wind. Hands in pockets I trudged to the ghost. In the same way I'd trudge the streets of Chicago in the night a few years later. Same way you see slanters coming through a storm from or to work, war, whorehouse door—

Everything went on as usual in the city itself—except that it was always changing, like me—though the chagrin of the reddy dusk up on Paddy McGillicuddy's street in the Acre up on the hill was mighty the same every time—and something eternal brooded in the sad red chimneys of the mills, ah these heavenward Empire knobs of a great civilization in a valley. The Kingdom of Lowell was bounded and tended thereto, from the paisans of the caucus out in (Michikokus) Methu-*enn* (Methuen),—?$Z&&!!*!—on out.

"You dont love me," she'd say with my lips in her throat. Okay, I said nothing. I had a lot of sawdust to work on in my new kewpie doll. Sometimes, like my little sister used to do, I'd pretend to be asleep when Maggie said mad things. I didnt know what to do.

XXXIV

One night—impossibly sad how came my shadow—seeking the balm and ruby of her arms, lips—we had a date, had arranged it on the telephone. For weeks I'd been finding it harder and harder to get dates, she had developed another

crush—Roger Rousseau, who used to play shortstop for the
Kimballs in the Lowell Twi League at the same time his own
unbelievable father with paunch and glasses played third base
beside him and stooped to delicately lift his grounders off the
grass without having to squat— They lived in the country,
were probably rich barons of this Kingdom Lowell with
medieval wall guards in their apple orchard stonewall— Ran
a dairy— Bloodworth had, with his attentiveness, closeness
to me, smooth grace and warm sincere elegance filled her
March hare months—but now we had to deal with the villains
of May.

Roger R. was coming around more and more. Fewer times
she'd let me come and see him try to come in—there was a
swing in the loamous backyard, she and Roger sat in it, I'd
never Her little sisters looked at me differently; her mother
looked more pained; the old man just went to work and had
no idea who I was. Bessy Jones was away more. The baseball
was coming in: I'd made a new friendship, with Ole Larsen
the pitcher, for the season, and because he lived on Bessy's
street in a wood window wall a pebble's throw from her rickety
washline and they'd in the green pale slur of youngling grass
exchange comments over the Tom Sawyer unwhitewashed
fence . . . "Gee Maggie's giving Jack a hard time—"

"Yeah?" Larsen was 6 foot 4, blond, had shown interest
in Maggie but in the long dark histories of her neighborhood
he'd always laughed at her and never ever took to be serious—
Something Maggie mourned, she liked him— He was like-
able— "Well let him concentrate on baseball with me, we're
gonna have a great team this year." He believed in us—
sincere respect for our friendship— "You gotta learn to hit
that curve—"

The first day of Lowell High School practice I ran with
Freddy O'Higgins in deep left as the coach Rusty Whitewood
belted out a fungo ball that Freddy wasnt gonna make but
I was going to show that I could catch it, to Ole who was
standing beside the coach telling him about me and chatting
in general, I was all unknown in baseball, I ran over the soft
new grass clods and slanted and got behind and beyond
O'Higgins in his own left field (from my center) and tapped

the ground till that ball from high heaven came slowing down and hugening for the ground arc over my head—I reached the backhand glove and got it running away from the plate . . . I brought it down almost stumbling, tucking it in my belly, O'Higgins was not sure what I had just done behind him, I heard Larsen Whoop! at the fungo bat— Beautiful catch, beautiful spring—but I kept missing those curve balls at the plate. When Ole pitched batting practice he made sure to see I'd get just high hard easy easies that I could belt to left— curves had me flailing silent plop tragedies, foot in the bucket —fast balls I turned into new fast balls going the other way and pulled and soaring—sometimes I'd hit 420-foot marks mentioned by everyone and when we came to play in the fenced-in park I hit homeruns regularly in over center-field fence in batting practice but the real game, the serious pitch, the chewing pitcher, the razzing catcher, the crafty ball spinning in—"You're out!" the bat pulling my wrists out as I squat after it benumbed.

Larsen and I were buddies—I made catches for him—we were goin to defeat Maggie. "Give her nothin! Let her worry! Let her call you up! Dont mind her—pay no attentions—you got ball to play, boy! She'll come around again!" Ole gave me advice. We rushed out to Shedd Park after the third bell in drowsy late April afternoons and clutched our gloves and spikes; it was heartbreaking because it was so close to South Lowell, I'd look over the trees above the cinder track for L.H.S. outdoor track, beyond the last tennis courts, in the grieving birch, the first roofs of Maggie's neighborhood Lowell— Then at night, after supper, I'd come along the river —well she got tired of all that. Finally the night we had a date, she broke it herself and just wandered off to talk to Roger R. in the bushes by the railroad bridge—in the sexy sand—
It was too much for me, my heart broke.

XXXV

"You're a sissy," I thought. "Here's the girl you love that you saw in the chorus line of the Keith's Theater in 1927 or 28 when you were five or six and you fell in love with her thighs, her dark eyes—the angel of tinsel God'd dropped you from them wings—Maggie—hit on the skull, dont let her give you that sass." But— "She's the only—"

"Pay no attention to it!" my father said leaving to work out of town again in his death-diving night . . . in seven years he'd be no more. . . . The sun would shine on his nose no more— "You're too young for that stuff. Get other interests in life!" We're standing waiting for the bus on Moody Street, we've been to the show before he leaves town, the Merrimack Square where as of yore the rainy Rin-tin-tin darkness the Fu Manchu balconies the spats of actors but now we'd seen the new crackling movie of the moment—"It wasnt any too good," my father's saying with a complete dedicated sneer. "They try to pass the thing off, you know— Well aside from that, kiddo, dont repent so. You make mistakes and break your spirit worryin about it. You're the only one worried! Oh I know *cette maudite vie ennuyante est impossible*" (this ga-dam boring life is impossible). "I know it! What can we do? Just say, I'll be thinking all the time there's nothing but darkness and death, but I'd bet I've got to be busy with the wife and kids— All right—they cant make any better rafts than that!" He squeezed my arm, I saw the sad curl of his lips, the frank serious blue eyes in the big red face, the big-man grin about to asthmatically wheeze him coughing into a big laugh, and a bending down— For in the end Ti Jean was abandoned to his doom—and I stood and realized it. "I can do nothing in this— Say, now that track is over are you gonna make baseball your main sport? Well—I wont be here to see it, dammit. Ah," A brokendown sigh, "something was damn well supposed to happen that damn well didnt—"

"Where?"

Another sigh: "I dont know. . . . Maybe I thought we'd be closer this year—I dont know. Not only shows—trips, talks —we didnt do much—never do— Ah dammit son it's a terrible thing not being able to help you but you do understand dont you God's left us all alone in our own skins to fare better or worse—hah? So—you say where."—Another sigh. "I dont know."—"*Pauvre* Ti Jean, we got troubles eh?" Shake of head on around and back.

XXXVI

I was sitting on the slope of that park in back of G.J.'s house, an evening in May, 6:30, not yet dark, still light for some time, Scotcho is with us pitching little pebbles—at petals of May— My love, my sick sense, of Maggie Cassidy had grown into a tumultuous continuous sorrow in my noisy head. The dreams, fantasie vagaries, wild drownings of the mind, as in real life I continued to go to school, hot spring mornings now outdoors, practically summer and no more school and I graduate from Lowell High.

In the winter track meets at Boston Garden in the Seaboard Relays I'd run a mad race against Jimmy Spindros of Lowell and others running for St. John Prep, wherever that was; *The Chief* they called Spindros, whose great hawk nose had made him stand in bleak fogs of old football games helmet under arm as captain of the Lowell team—long, tall, strong Greek champion of them all who died in the huge glooms of Iwo Jima. On the cork track of Boston Garden I in my little nail spikes took off with the same luck-jump off the imminent gun bang and flew around the banked turn in my own white lane as fast as I'd ever run in any 30-yard dash and got inside them (the three college runners) on the turn-in lane, probably illegal, behind me I heard them streaking right in my neck but I am flying and hold myself ready to bank into the far turn and wail right around on those nails throwing popcorks at the generation and coming off the board turn to hand my stick to Mickey Maguire who well cognizant of my love affair with Maggie had gone out and eaten big talkative hamburgers with Kazarakis and me in the big Boston night, we all talked of our current girls and problems and endured the harsh neons of that city in 1939 enjoying Greek out-of-the-way lunchcarts near North Station where huge meatloaves were served to us as sandwiches between bread, we'd eat contests— I've never run so fast in all my life, Kazarakis is going to get the stick last and run the gun lap, the final lap—as soon as Joe Melis bullnecked huge battling the runners with his football hips on banked turns would—whoo!—come roaring in—Kazarakis was going to really grab the stick from his hand, and elongate his long waist for a sudden play of long legs and though not tall 5:9 streak away thin and small but powerful and somehow big and wham after the first turn with his stick, groove into it, whir the great legs underneath his motionless waist, you didnt see his arms, overtake and fly forward of college sprinters— we won—but not because I finished my lap ahead of Spindros or St. John's, he came around the last turn momentum-ing into his man and passed Indian Chief Warrior bounding strides past me and handed the stick to his own second man— I fumbled and broke up in the stretch lost between the stick and the run— Mickey Maguire had to sail off and pound and fly his way around the mad track with a good eight-yard loss of lead—Kaz, the three of them made it up— Some kind of defeat in that kind of Maggie Cassidy must have brought me down— I'd reached my peak of love and fabulous success for a night or two—when? One night by the radiator in March she'd started huffing and puffing against me unmistakably, it was my turn to be a man—and I didnt know what to do, no idea in my dull crowded-up-with-worlds brain that she wanted me that night; no knowledge of what that is.

Her arms tight around me, her lips biting and foaming in the ocean of my face, her loins harping against mine in a big song of passion, love, joy, the winds of madness had with March run riot through her right through me we were ready for the fecund join with spring—and be man and wife in the

Universal reality—I even already pictured my little red window house by the railroad tracks—for us—in muddy walks under brown lamps down Massachusetts Street on soft spring nights, when I know all the guys of Lowell are running after trucks of excitement, the chicks are making riddles from a hay-rack with pendant breasts, the whole American night's a-ranked around the horizon.

I'm sitting in the grass of the park with G.J., I'm dreaming straight ahead of me.

Life is sweet, inside of a big cave.

"I'm goin over to see Maggie," I tell Gus—looking under the big trees out at Lowell over the field across Riverside Street—over its waving weeds we could see two miles away rooftops of Christian Hill shining red in the sun, the Kingdom was more beautiful than ever, my Baghdad Fellaheen rooftops up and down little Pawtucketville were creaming into rose for me— I was the beloved youth—blade of grass in my mouth, lying in the slope after supper, seeing—letting the winds of evenin ripple hugely in the trees above, at home, *patria*, land of birth. No idea some day our Kingdom would be overrun by vaster Kingdoms invisible like superhiways through the dump.

"Dont bother with her Zagg," G.J. is saying, "I wouldnt lose myself over no broad, let em all go jump in the lake— my ambition in life is to find some way to achieve *peace*. I am I suppose an old Greek philosopher or something Zagg but I'm serious when I say, screw it— Maggie's been doin nothin but playing you woods, if everything you tell me is true—she's done nothing but give you griefs you big babe greek—all of us know it, Lousy, him and Pauline told me, I was hurrying back from Lowell Commercial College and there they were on the corner of Central and Merrimack with Pauline just went in and bought a new dress in Kresge's across the street up there and I was supposed to help them but anyhow—help them with—I say, fooey on it!"

Leaning over to palm up his hand earnestly, on an elbow —Lousy's spittin silently over an evening blade which doesnt even budge as he zeets one—but lifts wavering boles as he zeets through his teeth softly, like a man whittling a stick at nightfall, a man closing his snap knife on a wood barrel and you hear it across the breeze at nightfall— I thought G.J. was all wrong, I knew better than he did. I said to myself "Well G.J. doesnt know—we—my family—what I'm like— he cant judge even though she's been so mean and me passing up Pauline Cole just to be—*he* doesnt know what he's talking about fuggen G.J." My Ma and Pa'd often told me not to hang around with G.J. For some reason they were afraid of him, "*Yé mauva*" (he's vicious).

"What you mean he's vicious?— He's just like us in the gang—he's all right—"

"*Non*. We know all about him and his vices—he talks about it all the time on the corner—Papa heard about it—what he done with little girls—"

"He doesnt have any little girls!"

"He does *too*! He says he's got a fourteen-year-old girl— He goes around making dirty speech like that, why do you bother with him!"

"G.J. doesnt understand that about me," I reflected, "My— everything I have to put up with and learn and see—and Maggie loves me."

I looked into the soft sky and the moon was coming out pale and cradled in the early blue, and I was convinced that Maggie loved me.

"Dont believe me then," says Mouse. "They'll deal you every kind of pitch they can think of Zagg to get a penny out of you—dont worry I know women I saw everything in my own house with relatives plus in-laws and big fights among Greeks of standing in this community of Lowell—you dont know the half of it, Zagg," Spitting—not like Lousy for eve calms, but for expression, sproosh. "They can take their lousy ga-dam mills down there on that dirty old river dump and stick right up their ass for what I care, Zagg—I'm leaving this Lowell," jerking his thumb at it, "maybe *you're* not but *I* am"—looking at me seething with rage, retribution in his popping eyes—G.J. was growing up his own way.

"Okay Mouse."

"Where you goin now?"

"To Maggie's."

He just waved his hand. "Get in her pants for me, Zagg."

I laugh through my nose and started off. I saw G.J. move his palmed hand—blessing good-by—okay.

I roamed off, negotiated whole Lowells walking down the main arterial mainline vein of Lowell, Moody Street now Textile Avenue, sweeping down on clacking shoes to go find my gory-dowry. "G.J.'s wrong as day."

Night night. Impatient to wait for the bus, I hit Kearney Square on foot a minute ahead of it and jump into the South Lowell bus for roaring wailing rides with the great driver dumping all his passengers most of em in the last streets now just has to bang through out of town tar construction trolley torn-up sewage under outlying streets and blast along just missing holes, posts, fences, to the car barns outside town now turned slick redecorated garage—eying his watch, timetable, his wild interests in time coinciding with mine as I leap off the bus at Massachusetts Street just underpass and be sent skittering on little feet as he continues his roaring journey, goes up the road blinking big red lights— The void of the universe surrounds the lonesome walker— I negotiate along the banks of the Concord, actually just walking in the middle of the street and seeing it through little bungalows, back orchards, abrupt little river down to the little shore, nothing big about the Concord but full of acorns—

Maggie's not down at the end of the street with her dress flapping and us singing *Deep Purple* as in the lonesome romance winter when we'd melted together under frozen stars —now molten faced stars of easy summer were blearing on our cold love—no more bad cars passing us on good roads— "Jacky," she'd said, "– — — ——," untranslatable love words to keep secret if you can remember em at all—

"But now she aint standing in no road," I'm telling myself, hurrying up, the light that made G.J. and I see as we talked about her now faded in the west where she was hidden—

"I think she went down through that broken fence, Jack down that lane—the kids are swimming or talking about swimming tonight." This is Maggie's kid sister, smiling bashfully at me; in a year they'd be saying she had crushes on me, others, but right now still a little girl and writhing around a post to play hopple dee skotch with Jamie ma mop, appata pippity pappety poo—

XXXVII

After that it was just a question of getting on with the ambitions that my family and I had decided for my life so, I went to New York with my mother and we saw Rolfe Firney at Columbia who'd written after my old high school football coach Tam Keating had touted or scouted me to his old friend of the Boston dog races Lu Libble, Lu Libble the big Columbia coach, both of them in the "ribbon committees" of the great crazy dog racing night of electrified rabbits in the huge darknesses near Suffolk Downs with its giant gas tank so huge that I keep seeing it by dog tracks and by the sea in my life— I was going to make my pipesmoking golden-windowed dormitory studies in this great university of the world. I was so proud that when Boston College and Coach Francis Fahey later of Notre Dame tried to get me the following summer I didnt change my mind but stuck to my idea of New York, Columbia, Horace Mann prep school, despite the fact that my poor father wanted me to go to Boston College because it would secure his recent new job in Lowell in a printing plant that did all the jobwork for Boston College, Emil Duluoz once more popular and solid—nevertheless both my Ma and I had minds set on Columbia— The additional details were that of a "football talent search," another story—

Rolfe Firney received us politely, showed us the athletic offices where the faces of the gentlemen seemed to me immensely and richly and beautifully important, men with white hair, grave, grand, all well-dressed, opulent, courteous. I proudly brought my mother to see all this before she returned to Lowell. She'd traveled to New York to arrange for my room and board with her stepmother in Brooklyn where I was going to live while attending Horace Mann prep thereby riding the subway every morning from Brooklyn-of-the-red-heart all the way to Broadway and 242nd Street a total insane twenty miles—I liked it though, because people are interesting in the subway when you're seventeen and you've never savored the big city. I was a really contented kid to see myself at last among the great mountains of glittering buildings. Horace Mann School was built in ivied Tom Brown gray granite on top of a cliff of solid rock—behind it was a beautiful field of green grass—a gym with vines— You saw the immortal clouds of the Bronx floating in the Indian sky and dont tell me it isn't an Indian sky. Below the cliff toward Yonkers lay the vast Van Cortlandt Park for the beautiful decathlon athletes stretching their white aristocratic legs in fields of shubbery and foliage Jews and Italians of a new heroism of another sort of Kingdom Lowell.

Superstitious of midnight the first night we slept at my grandmother's in Brooklyn I lay awake for hours listening for the creak of the ghosts of New York in the house, hearing faintly sounds on the Brooklyn street like lovers late in summer city night giggling in each other's necks by the moon of shipping; it was an altogether different Lowell, and so all opening-out into the big megaphone hole of the world from those Rudy Vallee lips of Merrimack Square and Maine that I knew that it was getting lost like a marble ball rolling down eternity in a bowling alley opening out to darkness down to infinity rockets cells telepathic shock tape.

I lay in bed thinking I was going to be a big hero of New York with rosy features and white teeth—an idiomaniac post-Iddyboy incarnation of the American Super Dream Winner, Go Getter, Wheel,—and white snowy scarf and big topcoat with corsaged girls in tow and no teetotaller I but big journalistic champion of off Times Square (like The Little Theater) as I had seen newspaper tragedists in B movies talking over beers in stale barrooms of neon winking Manhattan night hatbrims lowered like Marc Brandel or Clellon Holmes heroes brown taverns thru the pane glass written Bar & Grille you see the blackracked giant Neon Sign of the Owner of The Paper—Cigar Mouth Mann, grandson of Horace, hardhittin tough jesuitical editor, mainline artist, phlegm screamer of silver blary screens of the Rialto all the times that winter between Maggie and High School I'd played hooky in but now I'm in New York viewing the real thing from a scared bed in Brooklyn, seventeen. Gulp. "G. B. Mannpram, Pub. of the Manhattan Manner Post Evening Star," planes are flying in with serum, and I'm sitting in the bar heroically brooding over the way I just smashed the waterfront gang and G.B.'ll give me a raise (I see G.J. raising his leg to burp, "All right J.D., the job is yours, b-r-up, and dont cut me out of any of that offshore oil of yours"—) and I head for my penthouse, bored with the loose overcoats, shroudy hatbrims of big alcoholic newspaper new york and change casually into evening clothes (dinner jacket with velvet lapel glossy like London fires in a grate, which shine on it making vellum pools of rich wine-bottomless substance on my wealthy breast), and say hello to my wife, idly—

Through her balcony window you can see New York skyline in the starry night lace-dim behind sheer curtains, the sherry and the cocktails are ready, we can hear a piano tinkling from the Gershwins upstairs, and our fire crackles.

Oh how our fire crackles—how lovely the swan of her throat—I lie bedded in black night sending up white puffs of dialogue balloons for my gold encarvened dreams— Dear Angel Gabriel broods over me, listening. (Logs from old Adirondack in the penthouse, my hunting gun is there, early Jack London rich Frisco heroes of the penthouse have invaded New York via Lowell Mass. the viaduct from landing beaches and cold pines of the St. Lawrence River, over the *mer* the Breton fisher boys are snarling up the nets with salt cracked hand and have to do it all over again—) My whirls of world-seeing race around the room, I gulp to see vast mothers of light swarming around and to hear my brother tree in no more wilderness outside in Brooklyn scratch a fence in a little Brooklyn August breeze. My dream has in it a wife beautiful beyond belief, not Maggie, some gorgeous new blonde gold sexpot of starry perfection with lovely lace neck, soft long skin, inturned mouth top—I pictured the gorgeous Gene Tierney—and the voice that went with it, Kitty Kallen, Helen

O'Connell, a young beautiful American girl getting excited in your arms—

Next day, in any case and aside from the validity of these dreams, my mother and I strolled arm in arm across the grass of the Horace Mann field—bleachers, goalposts, the English Gothic roofs, the headmaster's own rose-covered cottage made of stone—a Kingdom military fort overlooking other worlds —already at seventeen I'd formed the idea to some day draw maps and write the history of another world in another geography of another Africa, another planet of Africas, Spains, pains, shores, swords—I had little knowledge of the world I lived in.

It was a rich school for young Jews ranging from age of eight all the way to sixteen, eight forms in all, you could see them arriving now at the school in limousines with their parents to give it the once over. It was high, warm, beautiful. "O Ti Jean how nice it'll be in this little paradise! Oh boy! *Now* it's making sense!" my mother said decisively. "Now we've got something to be proud of—you're going to be a real little man in this place, it's not just old regular school-teachers or one of those dirty old places your father went to in Providence one time and always talked about it and now he wants you to do like him—*non,* go here, and go to Columbia, that's the best idee." In her head my mother saw herself living in New York walking in the big lights of the great exciting world and the great shows, rivers, seas, restaurants, Jack Dempsey, Ziegfield Follies, Ludwig Baumanns in Brooklyn and the great stores of Fifth Avenue in New York— Aready, in my little childhood, she'd brought me to New York to see the subways, Coney Island, the Roxy—I'd at age five slept in the tragic subway of buried people shaking from side to side in the black air of the night.

I had a scholarship at Horace Mann, paying most of my tuition; the rest was up to me, my father, my mother; I helped get a lot of publicity for the school in the newspapers in the fall—there were 10,12 other guys like myself—"ringers" from high schools everywhere—bruisers, we murdered everybody except Blair (0-6), it was a scandal—the bruisers, they too'd had their loves, tempestuousnesses and sadnesses of sixteen.

"Now you're all set," said my mother as we walked among the beautiful clean halls, "we're gonna buy you a nice new coat to look nice in this little place that's so *cute*!" My mother was positive in her secret heart that I was to become a big executive of insurance companies. Just like when I made my First Confession, I was a little angel of pure future.

XXXVIII

She went back, everybody exchanged huge letters— To prepare myself I fixed my room at my grandmother's with dusty old books from the cellar— I seriously sat in the flagstone yard of little flowers and woodfence sometimes with a drink like ginger ale and read *Lust for Life* the life of Van Gogh I'd found in a bin and watched the great buildings of Brooklyn in the afternoon: the sweetish smell of soot and other smells like steam of a great coffee urn beneath the pavements—sitting in the swing—at night the buildings shining—the far train of great howls on the profound horizon—fear grabbing me— and with good reason.

I started football practice but sometimes played hooky to see shows all alone on Times Square, drank huge milkshakes for 5¢ impossibly aerated like cotton you drank illusion of liquid like the taste of New York— I took long walks in Harlem with hands clasped behind my back, staring at everything with great interest in roaring September dusks, no idea of the fearful complexities that would arise later in my mind about "Harlem" and blackskinned people— I got letters from G.J., Scot, Lousy and the Vinny—G.J. writing:

All fooling aside though Zagg, I just cant seem to get used to the idea of you being away. Sometimes I come out of Parent's Market and say "Well I guess I'll go up to Jack's and listen to the 920 Club," then I remember you're away. In one way, I'm glad you're in New York though Zagg, because down here it's worse than the Sahara Desert. By that I mean it's dead. Same old thing day in and day out. It's monotony at its highest. I'm going to school as a P.G. this year Zagg, or at least if I dont change my mind I'm going. My Ma promised me she would try her hardest to send me to college if I did. The way things are now it's a very faint possibility, but I'm hoping for the best. That's about all Jack except dont forget to give your Mother my best regards. [He thought she was still in New York with me.] And here's hoping you have the best of luck in everything.

Your Pal
Gus

Scotty in his brown house kitchen sat down at his mother's round table by the stove and wrote: "Hi Zagguth ye babe: Well I'm—" and talked about his work—"so when I go on days again or better still—" and then talked about Lousy in a way that made me see it had rained on a lot of things since Maggie'd spurned me in sweet Lowell, a bleary new barrel was filling, and all would drown in it—

By the way Lousy left Machinist and is now looking for a job as a foundry man. He's wacky. He ought to stick to Machinist but Zagg did you ever see a guy so bashful to ask for a job. This morning I learned that the Diamond Tool needed a man for a telephone job. I went and got Lousy and when we got down to see the boss you know big office Lousy wanted to turn back, because he was afraid the job was to be nights *when he didnt even know, Zagg,* so I had to make believe I needed a job and Kid Sam followed me in then we filled out the same old application and Belgium never let out a word. I'm telling you Jack he's got to talk his way into a job and if he acts this way he'll be a goner. I'll have to bang it into his head. Well I'll hear from you yet Jack and, you also from me so I'll say good night now as it is approaching the second hour of the Thursday and in about 15 hours I get $29.92 for my last weeks' pleasure. Your pal, SCOTTY, Write Soon.

Iddyboy, from Connecticutt where he'd gone to work: "He thee boy!"—

Vinny wrote like he talked straight from the scene—

He tried it everyway he could, after we got through with her she still wanted more, Zagg please believe me I never seen a woman so hot in all of my life, a female rabbit and you know her very well. B.G. is her initials and she lives next door to me I dont want to write her last name down on paper but you know who I mean. Lousy and Scot were gone to show the unlucky stiffs. Well that's all in a lifetime I guess. Albert Lauzon still goes to the Social Club at half past 4 in the afternoon so he can be sure to be there when the joint opens up good old Belgium— [Lousy'd started to shoot pool in earnest in green night]. Well you old screwball I guess that's all for this time answer soon,

Vinny
Turn Over
Other side

p.s. Hope that you get lots of tail during the time you will be out there my saying is "there's nothing like a very good fresh piece of meat to refreshen yourself," so "F—— my Lad F—— until you have had your fill then f—— some more

You F——face You
Shasspere

F—— EVERYBODY
Have pity on the next girl you take on."

XXXIX

I went through the football season with a bang, there were big explosions of fiesta on the fields of folly and autumnal golden screaming glory—and the 7th of November all of a sudden when I was established and already vexed, mixed, blest, guffawing in the immense things of my new life, new gangs, new New Year's Eves—when on little envelopes for memo I'd write "Keresky job" or "Garden City Defense" (study of the opposing team's diagram) or "$5 Lab fee" or "write math formulas in subway"—and had about fifty crazy screaming friends who climbed the steep hill from the subway to the palace of the school in the red mornings always haunted by new birds—voila—bang—comes a letter from Maggie, and on the back of the envelope (in words as dreamy as an old touch-down before dead men) it says: "Maggie Cassidy, 41 Mas-sachusetts Street, Lowell Mass."

Jack,
    Right off I am going to tell you who it is, it's Maggie. Just in case you want to tear this letter up.
    It must seem funny to you, to have me writing to you. But that's beside the point. I am writing to find out how you are and how you like school. What is the name of the place anyhow.
    Jack wont you try to forgive me for all I have done to you. I suppose you are laughing at me *but I am serious* really.
    About 2 weeks ago I met your mother and sister downtown. I just spoke I would have stopped and talked if we had been going together at the time, but I felt ashamed, if they had even asked me if I wrote to you I wouldnt know what to say.
    Jack cant we make up I am so terribly sorry for all I have done.
    I dont know how it is but some of the fellows you know have been trying to date me up as soon as they found out we broke up such as Chet Rave and some I would much rather not mentioning. I like Chet but not to go out with. He told me your address after much teasing. Bloodworth has been askin for you also.
    Well Jack so long if you dont answer I will know you dont forgive me

                                                    MAGGIE

In the study class, thinking, but also seeing the funny face of Hunk Guidry our center on the team, I passed him the note to read, to show him I had girls, he said no. He wrote on the envelope: "Some shit! You're a heartbreaker just a Casanova."
    I wrote to Maggie a little later.

XL

I invited her to the spring prom. After a few preliminary letters, and I'd learned all about the way things went with their big program of dances.

In November I went home, hitch hiking with my madcap friends Ray Olmsted and John Miller; John Miller, Jonathan actually, a horn-rimmed genius-knobbed hero of the New York Central Park West thickcarpet, his sister played piano, at dinner his lawyer father'd say "*Mens sana in corpore sano—*" "A healthy mind in a healthy body"—which was one of my proudest sayings about myself and coming from an aged lawyer— Ray Olmsted was the tall good-looking Tyrone Pemberbroke of American Love Magazines, handsome, a flat hat, a pipe— They didnt get along with each other, they were separate friends of mine; we had lost adventures on an old New England road, hasseled through New Haven, proceeded to Worcester—dark roads of early hitch hiking with a turkey dinner at the end of the string.

Night. From wild subsequent events with mixups of my gang of Lowell and the New York smart boys such as Lousy breaking a huge windowpane on Moody Street from nothing but sheer glee that Olmsted and Jonathan Miller were so mad —in other words I had brought the gang the cream of the wild Horace Mann world then, looking briskly, I'd dodged out and cut down to see Maggie at an appointed-by-phone time and she hit me from the side with kisses as I half turned away from too much the moment I saw her and we started bending back big kisses to the carpet floor and lurching and pushing in big climax kisses of movie magazines' photos—the seriousness, the long Latin study over lips, the furtive over-the-shoulder peeking at the paranoiac world— But Maggie had tears, and wept her little dimple chin under my bent neck me with my hair hanging low like a French beast now looking into his wild Parisian woman for the lifetime of love —we're about to learn the great lay of life pun blunt. But we dont have time, it's an exciting night everything's happening not only to you but to everyone because of to you!—we're glowing, rich, sick to happiness, I look at her with such love, she with hers, I didnt see any prettier lovers in the sunflower prairies of Kansas when larks squawk in thrashing sunset trees and the old hobo hoes out his sad old can a beans from the pack and bends to eat them cold.

We loved each other.

Therefore no immortal love blood was exchanged between us that night, we understood each other with tearful eyes. I would see her Christmas—soft sweet time.

XLI

I ran home from school and arrived the 21st of December—many things behind, many in front of me. In church I gazed at the old rosary beads of my First Communion given to me by my Aunt Anna of Maine— The golden crucifix now darkened but terribly beautiful the little tortured image, the fists, the little muscles—*Inri* inscribed always like the mark of the mute—the feet nailed on little blocks of yellow metal in my hand— I looked up high, the roof of the church, it's an afternoon service, a great big high school church service, gray dark Sainte Jeanne d'Arc basement, former Mayor Archambault is attending and the priest will mention him— Next to me, front, sits a beautiful honey-colored girl, Diane de Castignac of Pawtucketville, I dream of forcing her to some kind of anteroom to wrestle and moan with her, back of the altar, she has nothing on underneath, I force myself on her and finally surprise her by really getting her and completing the job—charming, juicy— When the church service is over I'll file out with everyone else and there she'll be by the door in the aisle, I'll brush my lips on the sleeve of her coat, she'll say "You'd better!" (we've already made an appointment for later)— Out on the church porch instead of going down the

steps in the Lowell real rainy alley gloom I go over the
balcony, bump Ernie Malo's head with my foot, he says
"Ouch" and oldlady-crazy guy kitchen houses in back, scup-
pers, board fences, garbage gangs of Brooklyn, I climb and
come somehow to the tremendous sea, iron purples brood on
its fantastic scape, clean, clear, I rush down the sand, the
waves of dawn are enormous, our boat is to the right waiting,
I'm going two years before the mast to that desolated spectral
North Pole— The purple clouds the gigantic waves—I jump
in and dash around scared—the cannons are booming over the
surf— Morning and new seas.

"But dont nettle the rose," said the beautiful Visage of
the Virgin Mary as I stared at it.

As though She'd never come to me, but could only come
to women and men of final Last Quartets of life not raw me's.
But I pray. For the success of all my things.

I'd already been to the redbrick hotels of midtown New
York in 1939 and had my first sex with a red-headed older
girl a professional whore— I'd gone around boasting about it
like all the other maniacs in the school, had gulped in the bed
waiting, she came down the hall on sharp heelclacks, I waited
with a pounding heart, the door opened, this perfectly built
Hollywood beauty piled in with her wealth of heavy breasts—
I was terrified— I'd even told Maggie about it but not directly,
hinting at it in letters in some way that she caught on— She
was just as awed as I was.

So I'm in church worrying about sins, syphilis, girl of my
heart and dreams—home from school—neat combed, big
coated, I nod politely as Mme. Chavart nods politely at me,
I'm getting to be a big grown-up man of Lowell . . . with
histories of events in New York, awed news, futures—
enemies imaginary and none otherwise—

New Year's Eve Maggie wants me to do to her what I did
to "them girls in New York"—

"Aw Maggie I cant do that to you!" I say, thinking it too
sinful bigcity to do it to her and not realizing my arms are
broken on a dumb idea. But Maggie is frightened too, she
"shouldnt a said it!" she thinks—we're on the porch, in the
wintry cold of Jan. 1, 1940— I have also been drummed with

142

the idea that if I want to marry Maggie it's better to wait.

At home I tell my mother that I love her and want to marry her; time to go back to New York is near, no more walks to Maggie's three miles down the cold sidewalk—I'll have to go back to my books, friends, huge Metropolitan interests in everybody— It makes me cry.

"Okay Ti Jean—I know you love her— You've got to finish school to fix and prepare yourself for your times— She'll help you if she loves you—if not, she doesnt love you. You see that? Your studies will count in the end—by that time she'll realize everything. Tell her what I said—I'm not interfering in your affairs. You dont have to tell her if you dont wanta— But take it easy— Dont hurry, girls nowadays invent all kinds of troubles— Little Maggie seems okay—go—go see her, tell her good-by— Try to arrange for her to come like you say to your little dance in New York. . . ."

My father was gone by then.

I saw Maggie, said good-by, we looked tearfully at each other and she with new woman eyes deeper than and showing through her own eyes amazing me and making me feel on some wheel of nature.

XLII

Everything is perfect; I get invitation cards. They are big cards with gold paint, and RSVPs chrome tipped like the Chrysler Building. I send one to Maggie.

At the last minute, she wrote me: "Jack, Well I guess I'm in for a swell time Friday or should I say this week end. Call me up at my aunt's before you come over so I will be sure to be ready. And by the way I am wearing a pink gown with blue assesories. You know what if you can get me a wrist corsage get it if not it's O K" (no signature).

Ah, terribly sad the look of her writing on envelopes. In the dust of my black books I saw the moons of death. "Wow,"

I told myself, "is it true I want a woman?—" I felt sick, "Ruin all my—"

XLIII

From sweet Lowell Maggie came to sour New York in a rosy gown.

Corpse ridden Hudson rounded about the Glitter Isle of dark New York America as we raced to the April Prom in a taxi cab across Central Park. The preparations, events, all enormous— She'd come with her mother, stayed with her aunt, was staying the night of the Prom at Jonathan Miller's family's rich apartment, arrangements I had made in earlier attempts to save as much money as possible and probably suggested by Jonathan in the first place as in his brief profound friendship with me he directed my affairs and influenced my mind.

Now we raced across town in a cab—I was all dressed in white tie and tails. During that winter the uncle of Gene Mackstoll a London Man About Town Sam Friedman: "Here you are, Jack"—giving me the suit from his closet as nephew Gene grins "you ought to wear it for the Spring Prom. Take it. It's yours. Here." He gave me other things— To make myself handsome for the Prom I'd got a sunlamp sun tan in the Hotel Pennsylvania with a shave for about two dollars, like a Cary Grant I wanted to walk into the barbershop clacking on heels head stiff courteous and cosmopolitan and have myself led to a chair saying something tremendously witty—or and with a feeling of rich security—instead it was a lonely walk among empty mirrors along the backs of empty barber chairs with an at-attention towel-wristed barber waiting at each one and I chose none in particular and was pulled up by no Ricardo Riduardo to my authority chair. The lamp burned and gave me a terrible lobster red face for the ball.

Maggie has put on the best thing she has—a pink gown.

A little rose in her hair—the perfection of her moonlight magic Irish sorcery suddenly seeming out of place in Manhattan, like Ireland in the Atlantis World— Trees of her Massachusetts Street home I saw in her eyes. All week just because G.J. had jokingly written "My hand still burning from having been sat on by the perfectly rounded buttocks of M.C."—this made her so valuable I wanted her to sit on the hand of my hope—I held her tight; felt suddenly protective in this big cab crossing the glittering Manhattans.

"Well, Maggie," addressing her through all her troubles getting down from Lowell and everything ready, "there it is —New York." Beside us, Jonathan, himself bemused on the skyscrapers with those seventeen-year-old intellectual first thoughts weighing him in and everything to me inconceivably glamorous because of his addition to the scene—

"Hump—t'aint much to *be* in—looks nice," says Maggie— her lips curled— I bend down to kiss and hold back, feeling myself too importantly dealing with Maggie's proper reception tonight to be just kissing—the two of us miles apart in social fear, minds wandering to other matters like the ease of pain in the breast that wants out—not as in our sweet river's nights —not as in love—but to little paranoiac wonderments in the complication of gowns, evening clothes, the corsage I had to rush and get—tickets, furlibues—to make you sigh—in brief, we were doomed to an unsuccessful night, I would never know altogether why.

Her little shoulders had freckles, I kissed every one of them —when I could. But my face was burnt from the lamp and I kept wincing and sweating so I worried what Maggie thought of me. She was too busy being snobbed by the wealthy lavishly gowned girls in there who'd not struggled 250 miles from a railroad brakeman's old house by the tracks in day coaches of the railroad with the necessary striven-for free pass the gown in a box—but had had checks for half a thousand dollars waved under their noses by indulgent millionaire fathers who'd said "Go down to Lord & Taylors or someplace and get yourself something real nice impress the boy invited you—" For their shoulder blemishes and freckles they had sorceries of powder, boxes of shield-soft, sweet nascent poofs or puffs to dab all over and the best stuff available—Maggie didnt even know it was done or how to do it or how to know. Snowily they swam around her like swans, her tawny shoulders with touch of pink from last summer's sunburn and freckles of Ireland were bedazzled by priceless necklaces and earrings. Their snowy arms were advantaged and powdered and glittered; her life arms were hung.

I sneaked her down to a little bar downstairs, in the basement of the Hampshire House, Jonathan was with us, for a moment we were like gay people in an Irene Dunne comedy took over a lounge and no one's around and Jonathan officiated to make drinks and we giggled and talked and I thought we were in some wood panel New York of carpeted luxuries and Maggie felt better being alone and snuggled up to me—

Jonathan (in tails, behind bar) "All right, jack, if it's not Tom Collins I shall have to expel you from our haunt, all I can make is an exorcization dont ask for more—" I look proudly at Maggie for her to see these big words. She's looking around skeptically. Her gardenia hangs sadly. My face is on fire, stiffly in white-tie collar I'd bent to a hundred conversations upstairs feeling that as I inclined my nose politely to the speaker's nose it would reflect red on his face a big flush of silly heat—

"Oh fer krissakes Jonathan get it over with!" Maggie's yelling as John tried to joke and goofed— Finally we were discovered by others, the parties floated in, we went upstairs again. A dazzling affair. A horde of young generation in white tie with promflower girls attending a melee, a gathering, in a building, a tower—crowded—rousing applause, speeches, music inside. Greed oozing from the Oos and Aas of false hellos and dreary compliments and presumptive conceited good-bys. Dancing, talking, looking out the window at Central park and the lights of New York—all of it horrible— we were lost—our hands clutched but with empty hopes— just fear—empty chagrin—longfaced party in real life.

XLIV

"Jack let's get out of here, let's go away—" She wanted to go to secret bars, ballrooms, be alone— I thought of Nick's in the Village— But the arrangements had been made for a gay party of cars to go downtown, uptown, places— She sat in a corner sofa, against me, almost crying—"Oh I hate it here—Jacky let's go back home and sit on the porch—I loved you much better with your skates—your earmuff hat—anything but this— You look awful—watsamatter with your face? —I look awful—everything's awful—I knew I shouldnt of come—I guessed it— Something was wrong— My mother wanted me to. She persuaded me. She likes you, Jack. She says I dont appreciate a good boy when I see one— The hell with it— Give me home any time. Jacky," taking my chin and turning my face to her, looking swimmingly, littly into my eyes with her small perfect eyes here lost in the hurrahs, white roars, chandeliers, "if you want to marry me ever dont ever try to have me come to this New York—I couldnt stand it— There's something about it I don't like— Oh let's get outa here— The hell with all these people—"

"They're my friends!"

"Friends?—Pah—" She gave me a scornful look, as though she never saw me before, and surreptitious— "Buncha no good loafers— Some day'll be begging at their backdoors and they wont even give you a crust of bread you know that as well as I do— Friends—for now friends—later it's good-by Jack— You'll be on your own, you'll see— They wont throw shirts at ye when it starts raining in the mountains. And isnt she the huffy puffy one in her dress cut low enough to show her breasts to the lot of us the hussy she must have more sass than my sister Sissy and seventeen others—"

"You're all s's," I said.

"All s's and dont give a shit. There! I wanta leave. Come on. Take me to a burlesque. Take me anywhere."

"But we're supposed to go to the cars after—lots of plans made up by a whole bunch—"

"I like that Knowles playing the piano—he's about the only one I like—and Olmsted—and Hennessy I guess because he's Irish and you dont catch *him* here do you? Humph: I've had my see, my fill of your famous New York. You know what you can do with it. You'll know where to find me from now on, Bub. Home. Good old h o m e . . ." Dizzy, sweet, all the combined ankles of your raving beauties couldnt measure against the atom of Maggie's flesh in the crook of her underarm, all their eyes, diamonds and vices no competition on the keen point of Maggie's Stardust Personal Me.

"I'm not even looking at *any* of these other women—"

"Aw go on—there's that Betty everybody's been telling you about all night— Why dont you go dance with her— She *is* beautiful— You'll make out in New York—crap's paradise—"

"What are you mad—?"

"Oh shut up— Oh Jacky come home have Christmases with me—never mind all this charivary—fancy fanfares for nothing— I'll have a rosary in my hand at least—to remind you— Little snowflakes'll fall on our pretty roof. Why do you want these French windows? What are the towers of Manhattan to you that needs love in my arm every night from work— Can I make you happier with powder on my chest? Do you need a thousand movie shows? Sixteen million people to ride the bus with, hit the stop—I shoulda never let you go away from home—" Rich lips brooded in my deaf ear. "The fog'll fall all over you, Jacky, you'll wait in fields— You'll let me die— you wont come save me— I wont even know where your grave is—remember what you were like, where your house, what your life—you'll die without knowing what happened to my face—my love—my youth— You'll burn yourself out like a moth jumping in a locomotive boiler looking for light—Jacky —and you'll be dead—and lose yourself from yourself—and forget—and sink—and me too—and what is all this then?"

"I dont know—"

"Then come back to our porch of the river the night time the trees and you love stars—I hear the bus on the corner—

where you're getting off—no more, boy, no more— I saw, had
visions and idees of you handsome my husband walking across
the top of the America with your lantern—shadow— I heard
you whistle—songs—you'd always sing coming down Massachusetts—you thought I didnt hear, or I was dumb— You
dont understand the dirt—on the ground. Jacky. Lowell
Jacky Duluoz. Come on home leave here." She saw aces of
spades in her eyes; in hers I saw them glitter and shine.
"Because I'll never come to this New York to live you'll have
to take me at home and as I yam . . . You'll get all lost around
here, I can just see you— You shoulda never left home to
come here I dont care about anybody says about success and
careers—it wont do you no good— You can see it with your
own eyes— And lookit her with her fine and fancy ways, I
bet she's as balmy as the day is long and they have to spend
thousands a dollars on bug doctors for her—you can have em
brother—so long. —Huh," she concluded, through her throat,
which throbbed, and I kissed her and wanted to devour her
every ounce of her mysterious flesh every part hump rill hole
heart that with my fingers I'd never even yet known, the
hungry preciousness of her, the one never to be repeated altar
of her legs, belly, heart, dark hair, she unknowing of this,
unblessed, graceless, dulleyed beautiful. "They can put me
away any time, I'm ready," said Maggie, "but dont let the
birds sing in *this* hole—"

Out of her eyes I saw smoldering *I'd like to rip this damn
dress off and never see it again!*

Later my sister said "Did Maggie wear her hair off the
face?—or in bangs?— She has a small face— Did she wear
rose? That would go good, she's so dark." She wore bangs—
my little bangs of Merrimack.

XLV

Somewhere in the vast jewelry of the Long Island night we
walked, in wind and rain— Sunday night—the week end over

—the drives, cocktail parties, shows, scheduled arrangements, all fulfilled, without fun—her gown long packed back in the box— She pouted as I conducted her sheepishly across those unknown darknesses of the city— Her aunt's house was somewhere across an empty lot, down a street— The gloom of Sunday night—the wind blew her sweet hair against my lips; when I tried to kiss her she turned away, I groped for the lost kiss that would never come back— In the house the aunt had prepared a big Sunday dinner for us and for Mrs. Cassidy who'd sat out the week end and humbly—helping in the kitchen—a trip to Radio City.

"Did I hear Jack say his belly was empty. You feel weak? —come on, here's soup—"

"Well kids did you have fun?"

Maggie: "No!"

"Maggie! aint you got better manners than that."

I helped her off with her coat; she had a cotton dress underneath; her sweet shape made me want to cry.

"Maggie *never* liked Boston or any place," Mrs. Cassidy told me, "pay no attention to her, she's a devil— She likes to wear her old sweaters and shoes and sit in her swing—like me—"

"Me too Mrs. Cassidy—if I didnt have to play football—"

"Come eat!"

A huge roast beef, potatoes, mashed turnips, gravy—the kind Irish lady plying me with double helpings—

After dinner heartbrokenly I sat across the parlor from Maggie and watched her, half sleepy, as they talked—like home, dinners, drowsy in the parlor, the sweet legs of Maggie — Her dark eyes scanned me contemptuously— She'd said her piece—Mrs. Cassidy saw we werent getting along— The big expedition, plans, the big prom, flowers,—all down the drain.

They went back home on Monday morning after a night's sleep, Maggie to her porch, her kid sisters, her swains coming a-visiting down the road, her river, her night—I to my whirlpools of new litter and glitter—standing in the corridor of the school Milton Bloch who later became a songwriter introducing me to Lionel Smart ("Nutso Smart" to the math professor) who later became my great sweet friend of the modern jazz generation, London, New York, the world— "This is Jack Duluoz, he thinks Muggsy Spanier has the greatest band," and Lionel blushing, laughing, "Count, man, Count"—1940—rush to the Savoy, talks on the sidewalks of the American Night with bassplayers and droopy tenormen with huge indifferent eyelids (Lester Young); school paper articles, Glenn Miller at the Paramount, new shoes, graduation day I lie in the grass reading Walt Whitman and my first Hemingway novel and over the campus field I hear their rousing applause and valedictories (I had no white pants)—

Spring in New York, the first smell of woodsmoke on Third Avenue on the first unfrozen night—parks, loves, walks with girls, styles, excitements—New York on the lyrical perfect shelf of America in the Night, the Apple on the Rock, the green blur of Coogan's Bluff over the Polo Grounds firstweek May and Johnny Mize of the St. Louis Cardinals poles a new homerun— Bill Keresky's sister Mickey in black silk slacks in a penthouse, her red lips and rings of sixteen under eyes, soft initial on her breast—Duke records— Wild drives to the Yale campus, around and around Mount Vernon at midnight with hamburgers and girls— Frank Sinatra incredibly glamorous in loose hanging suit singing with Harry James *On a Little Street in Singapore* not only teenage girls digging him but teenage boys who'd heard that sad Artie Shaw clarinet in California on the quiet perfect street in Utrillo— The World's Fair, sad trombones from the shell, over the swans —Pavilions with international flags— Happy Russia— Invasion of France, the great Pow! overseas— French professors under trees— Mad Marty Churchill reaches into subway and knocks man's hat on floor as train pulls out Har Har Har!— we race on El platform— Waking up one Sunday morning in David Knowles' Park Avenue apartment I open up the venetian blinds, see young husband in homburg and spats conducting beautifully dressed wife with baby in carriage through rippling golden suns, beautiful not sad— A *crème de menthe* at the Plaza, *vichyssoise, paté,* candlelight, gorgeous necks— Sunday afternoon in Carnegie Hall.

Spring dusk
            on Fifth Avenue,
      —a bird

Midnight talks over Brooklyn Bridge, freighters arriving
from Montevideo— Wild generations jumping in a jazz joint,
hornrimmed geniuses getting drunk on brews— Columbia
University ahead— Borrowers of binoculars in Mike Hennessy's bedroom looking at the Barnard girls across the green—
   Maggie lost.

XLVI

It was three years later, a cold snowing night, the Lowell
Depot was crowded with late arrivers from Boston clutching
Daily Records, rushing to cars, buses. Across the street the
depot diner did a thriving business, hamburgers sizzled juicily
on the grille, when the counterman with his old Montana face
let go a batter of pancake mix on the dull gleaming fat of
the grille it shot up a sizzlecloud, loud, as doors squeaked
over and the boys off the train came in to eat. The passenger
train, the 6:05 or 6:06 had just left, a freight was rumbling
through Lowell in the winter dusk snow a hundred cars long,
its tail-end caboose was riding after at the Concord River
Bridge in South Lowell near Massachusetts Street—the locomotive was nosing through lumberyards and wholesale
plumbers and gastanks of Lowell downtown back of the mills
and Chelmsford Street, out in the yards on Princeton Boule-
vard the rolling stock was still in the dribbling snow sweeps.
Down Middlesex Street and over the tracks, a few dull gray
battered doorways hid a few Lowell waiters in the storm.
The Blagden restaurant wasnt doing much business, brown
on a corner, a few dull eaters inside, a cafeteria lunchroom.
In back, the Blagden Garage and Parking was almost all done
for the evening rush. The garageman had just wheeled back

a big truck into place, against the partition wall, and squeezed the last Buick against the fleet deep in the far end of the garage, there was not much space left. The garageman was alone, walking back with his car keys, pencil and tickets, thick thighs hurrying—in a half dance. At the big overhead door he whistled to see the storm dropping softly in the alley; above, a gray tenement kitchen window glowed dully—the garageman could hear kids talking. He turned into the small potbelly office with the rolltop desk, threw the ticket tab on the desk among papers and cigarette packs and threw himself in the swivel chair and turned it around and shot his feet to the desk. He reached down and slugged out of a quart of beer. He burped. He picked up the phone.

Dialed. "Hey there, is that you Maggie?"

"Yeah. Jack? Calling agin? I thought you was all through with me—didnt believe it—"

"Yeah! Come on! I'll come pick you up right now— We'll drink beer in the office, play the radio, dance— I'll take you home—a big Buick—"

"What time?"

"Right now!"

"You sound like you changed."

"Sure. Three years makes a difference!"

"Last time I saw you—was after the Prom—you remember —college boy—"

"I aint no college boy now.—I'm goin in the Navy next month."

"You *was* in!"

"Just merchant marine—"

"Well you were better off— But I'll come—"

"Same old Maggie," thought the garageman, Jack Duluoz, calculating, "I'll be over in twenty minutes sharp. Be ready. I've got to bring that Buick right back. This is like stealing a car. And I'm leaving the lot unattended—"

"Okay. I'm ready now."

"Okay baby," said J.D. "see ya" hanging up and leaping to his feet. He took out keys, went out, locked the door of the office, tried it—walked over to the overhead door just to give it a yank, slapped it, strode back deep into the garage to the Buick, and got in.

The car door frumped softly. It clicked open again as he leaped out and put out a few garage lights— In the gloom now he foraged sadly after something. Then slowly the motor started, he backed around, shifting, came front, headlights flashing—lighting up the shadows of the garage— The horn tooted as accidentally he moved his elbow convulsively in search of cigarettes— Looking suspiciously over his shoulder he drove around, through the door, out into the snowy alley— He wore no hat, just a jacket— Only a few months before he'd been a reporter on the Lowell newspaper, he wore the wild look of a man emancipated into the redbrick heap of night from some bank jail and so gleaming and furtive he looked around frantically with a wild head everywhere hearing imaginary noises and seeing traffics and checking to make sure to be ready—incredibly slowly the Buick crawled to the mouth of the alley. The snow thickened. "*Jack o diamonds*," sang Jack, "*Jack o diamonds, you'll be my downfall*," pronouncing it "Jack o doymonds" as in his memory of G.J. Rigopoulos thus singing it New Year's Eve night of 1939 when he'd first met Maggie this girl he was now going to put the boots to as soon as he got her in this Buick late tonight in the garage, deep— "Baby," he said out loud, "I'm sure gonna get you tonight—aint gonna be like it used to be with you—I'm gonna find out about you at last— I've had women since you, and traveled, and been far—the stories I could tell you'd make your little Massachusetts Street sit pale in *this* star—about railroads, and bottles I throwed, and women brought me gin for supper, and old bo's I followed across fields to hear them sing the blues—and moons over Virginia—and birds in the same place in the dry morning—rails leading south, west— dusty places I sat down in—slept in— Things I've known in the morning at office desk, school desk, personal bedroom desk— Romances I had on gravel—on newspapers in parks— on couches of beery fraternities— Dances I've known alone at night windows— Books I've read, new philosophies I've made— Thorstein Veblen, my dear—Sherwood Anderson, sweet—and some man they call Dostoevsky—and North Pole mountains I've climbed— So dont manage me off tonight, I'll slap your wrist, I'll drive you inta rivers, I'll show ya—" As he talked he drew out of the garage driveway into Middlesex Street having waited for three cars to pass and now barely ahead of three others he swung to the right, on over the tracks, looking fearfully into the hole of night each way for engines of the crack, past the depot, diner, Merrimack Hotel—where, he knew, Reno the owner of the Buick was just simply with his woman in a bed and wouldnt come out till morning and if tonight at all much later —At the foot of the steep hill of School Street at Middlesex he swung up with courage trusting he needed no chains in the mad new snowfall—

Traffics flashed around. He ground up the hill, stopping at the rotary momentarily to see, swinging right, giving leeway in the glorietta hobbyhorses to cars from downtown Lowell, swinging around all the way and on down School, driving confidently now, picking up speed, interested in the dangers of real life confronting. Down past the Commodore Ballroom, down past Keith's Academy, and with the black great Common white and blacktraceries on the left on down toward South Lowell and Maggie's house.

XLVII

But it hadnt changed. Sadly the garageman gazed at the warm lights of the house, the rutted road, the dull streetlamps, the dead vines on winter's porch, the shape dear and loving and half hauntingly unclear of some old couch-form against the corner of the porch where so long ago he'd swooned the wine of the moon in other youths and when his youth was young—

Maggie, at the toot of his horn, ran out. He couldnt see her face. She came around to the door of the car. "Dont you wanta come in see my folks?"

"Nah nah come on—"

She came in, frightened, climbing into the machine on her

hands and knees as with the difficult leg-up she tried to throw herself in to sit. "Well there you are—you dont look the same—"

"Why not?" he demanded.

"You look thinner but you're not a kid any more—you're a kid but you look . . . cold hearted er sumpin . . ."

"*Cold* hearted!! Hah!"

"Er sumpin— How about me did I change any?"

He started the car, looking swiftly. "Sure—you're the kind of girl'll always look the same—good—"

"You didnt even look."

He was pushing the car down Massachusetts Street desperately for something to do dodging mudholes black in the snow.

"Yes I did."

They thrashed and fought deep in the Buick deep in the garage at two o'clock in the morning, the sweetness of the girl was hidden from the boy by a thick rubber girdle at which he pulled and yanked, desperately drunk, poised at the gate.

She laughed in his face, he slammed door shut, put out lights, drove her home, drove the car back skittering crazily in the slush, sick, cursing.

11

13

PRIMROSE SQUARE

*A bitter-sweet romantic tale of broken hearts
and second chances in wartime Edinburgh, from
a much-loved Scottish storyteller*

Edinburgh, 1911. When intelligent Elinor Rae
leaves her crowded tenement family home to
become a maid in an exclusive ladies club in the
idyllic Primrose Square, she doesn't look back.
Two years later and Elinor is still in love with the
square, and now also with Stephen Muirhead, her
evening tutor. But it all goes wrong. Elinor's
head is turned by handsome Barry, and when he
signs up to the war effort without thinking of her,
she is devastated and bitterly regrets her mistake.
But has Stephen really put Elinor behind him?

A Selection of Recent Titles by Anne Douglas

CATHERINE'S LAND
AS THE YEARS GO BY
BRIDGE OF HOPE
THE BUTTERFLY GIRLS
GINGER STREET
A HIGHLAND ENGAGEMENT
THE ROAD TO THE SANDS
THE EDINBURGH BRIDE
THE GIRL FROM WISH LANE *
A SONG IN THE AIR *
THE KILT MAKER *
STARLIGHT *
THE MELODY GIRLS *
THE WARDEN'S DAUGHTERS *
PRIMROSE SQUARE *

* *available from Severn House*

PRIMROSE SQUARE

Anne Douglas

Severn House Large Print
London & New York

This first large print edition published 2013
in Great Britain and the USA by
SEVERN HOUSE PUBLISHERS LTD of
19 Cedar Road, Sutton, Surrey, England, SM2 5DA.
First world regular print edition published 2012 by
Severn House Publishers Ltd., London and New York.

British Library Cataloguing in Publication Data

Douglas, Anne, 1930- author.
  Primrose square. -- Large print edition.
  1. Edinburgh (Scotland)--Social conditions--20th
  century--Fiction. 2. World War, 1914-1918--Social
  aspects--Scotland--Edinburgh--Fiction. 3. Love stories.
  4. Large type books.
  I. Title
  823.9'14-dc23

ISBN-13: 9780727896469

Severn House Publishers support the Forest Stewardship Council™
[FSC™], the leading international forest certification organisation. All
our titles that are printed on FSC certified paper carry the FSC logo.

Printed and bound i...
T J International, Pa...

One

On a fine June morning in 1913, two maids were upstairs in the Edinburgh Primrose Club, making beds. Downstairs, country members who'd stayed overnight – all women, for this was a club for women only – were taking breakfast in the dining room facing the square. Porridge, bacon, kidneys, scrambled egg and kedgeree. Oh, yes, Miss Ainslie, the club manageress, provided excellent food, and Mrs Petrie, the tyrant in the kitchen, cooked it. Though upstairs, Mattie MacCall, one of the maids, shaking a billowing sheet, was betting the ladies wouldn't be eating it.

'Och, no, it's too hot, eh? Did you see 'em, Elinor, all going down the stair in thin blouses and skirts? I heard 'em saying it was going to be a scorcher later on today.'

'They're right, then.'

Elinor Rae, helping to spread Mattie's sheet, smiled wryly. Tall, with dark hair and wide-apart dark eyes, she was nineteen years old and striking. Even in her grey uniform dress, with white apron and white cap, there was something unusual about her. An inner strength, perhaps, or energy? Hard to say but, beside her, the blonde, round-faced Mattie, only a year younger, seemed

5

like a child.

'What'll the weather matter to the members, anyway?' Elinor asked, as the two girls finished making the bed, tucking in the top sheet, plumping pillows, smoothing the coverlet. 'If it's hot, what'll they do? Sit in the gardens till lunchtime? 'Tisn't as though they need to do any work.'

'Some do a bit of charity work, I've heard,' said Mattie, dabbing at her moist cheeks with a hankie from her apron pocket.

'I was thinking of working for a living.'

'Oh, well, they needn't do that. They like writing and reading, though. Sit in the Quiet Room at the desks, writing letters, reading books. Makes my head ache to see 'em!'

'Writing and reading,' Elinor repeated. 'Oh, very hard work, eh? And before that, they've to clean out the grates and do the blackleading? Do the dusting and sweeping, scrub the front steps and clean the brass, run upstairs and make the beds?'

'Ah, now you're teasing, Elinor! You know ladies don't do any of that!'

'Because that's what we do. And that's what I call work. What wouldn't I give if I could sit in the Quiet Room and write a few letters and read a nice book?'

'That'd no' be for me. I was never one for reading.'

'I was.' Elinor's face suddenly relaxed and she gave a smile that sent the sunshine to her face. 'I'm sorry, Mattie. I do go on a bit, eh? It's just that it sometimes comes over me, the different lives folks lead. You see it, when you're in

6

service.'

'I know what you mean. But it's the way things are, Elinor, there's no point trying to change 'em.'

Elinor opened her mouth to speak, then closed it again and, giving a last tweak to the bed cover- let, moved to the open window.

'It's so stuffy this morning, I think I'll just push this up a bit. Need some more air.'

'Get on with you!' cried Mattie, laughing. 'Saying it's stuffy! You just want to look out at the square the way you always do.'

'Do I?' asked Elinor softly. 'Well, maybe I do.'

While Mattie, humming to herself, began rub- bing the marble-topped wash stand, Elinor stood, her arms folded, looking down at the square below.

There it was. Primrose Square. The finest, largest square in Edinburgh's West End. A great oasis of greenery, a piece of countryside in the city, where there was rolling grass with trees, flowers in the spring – yes, real primroses – and elegant railings with a gate only to be opened with a key. Tall houses, set back over pavements, muffled the noise of the streets beyond, even from Princes Street, with its trams and carriages, horses, crowds and brand-new motor cars, so that here in the square was peace and calm.

Ever since she'd first seen it, when she'd arrived for her interview two years before, Elinor had never ceased to be struck by that peace. And the space, the overwhelming feeling of green- ness; the solace that wrapped round her. She had no key, she couldn't open the gate and walk

7

within, but she could look, she could feel she was in the country. She could know she wasn't in Friar's Wynd, which was her home.

Today the square, in the midsummer sunshine, was looking particularly beautiful, but the thought of home, her father's rented cobbler's shop in the midst of towering tenements, brought a little cloud to her brow. Hastily pulling up the window to allow more air, she turned aside.

'I'll just brush the carpet,' she called to Mattie. 'And then we can do the dusting before we start on the landing.'

'I'll do the wardrobe,' Mattie answered. 'And miss out the top. Will you look at all that shopping Miss What's-her-name has piled up there?'

'That's something you didn't mention about the members and what they like to do,' Elinor remarked with a laugh. 'Shopping!'

Two

Cleaning the long landing, working as diligently as she always did, Elinor's thoughts returned unwillingly to Friar's Wynd. As she had said to Mattie, she couldn't help but notice the difference between the club members' lives and her own, and had to admit it brought out the envy in her, which was sinful according to the Kirk, but natural in her view. All she wanted to do, really, was even things up, so that if some people could find life easy and comfortable, others didn't have to exist in Friar's Wynd. She'd been lucky; she'd escaped. How many were left behind?

Her mother, Hessie, for one. Cormack, her brother, always known as Corrie, for another. How wonderful it would have been if they could have been with her, if they could all have lived together where there was light and fresh air and something green to see. Even to move to another street of tenements where the houses were not so tall and didn't block the sky would be an improvement. And there were some streets in the old town like that where, even if the tenants were poor, they saw the sun.

But Walter Rae, Elinor's father, who made a precarious living mending shoes in a wee shop in Friar's Wynd, would never move. Why should he? There were pubs to hand, weren't there? What matter if the Wynd had a terrible night-time reputation, with regular fights and drunken bouts? What matter if the buildings towered so high that the sky retreated in despair, and any sunlight that filtered through was so weak it was not like sunlight at all?

Best not to dwell on it, Elinor told herself, polishing a side table with all her strength to relieve her feelings. She would just keep on going home once a week to see her folks, and continue to hope for a miracle.

After all, she'd got away. First to service with a lawyer's family, which had not, to be honest, been a happy experience, but then to the Primrose, where if Mrs Petrie, the cook, was a bit of a dragon, Miss Ainslie was kind and all the other

9

maids were her friends and where she shared a room with only Mattie and Gerda and had the use of a bathroom. Grand! Best of all, outside the house, any time she wanted to see it, was her own piece of countryside – Primrose Square.

As a smile curved her lips at the thought of what could make her happy, Mattie, who had been brushing the stairs, came up to say that she'd just finished in time. Ada and Gerda were clearing away breakfast, the ladies would be coming up any minute – should she and Elinor go for their cup of tea?

'Aye, we'd best get downstairs,' Elinor replied, peeping over the banisters into the hall. 'Miss Denny's at reception and the front door's open. Come on, time to go.'

'Just hope Mrs Petrie's in a good mood,' Mattie murmured, as they clattered down the back stairs, for of course they only rarely used the little passenger lift or the front stairs.

'Talk about wishful thinking,' said Elinor.

And then they were greeting Gerda and Ada, down with their trays from the dining room, all keeping a weather eye on Mrs Petrie, as Vera, her assistant, made the mid-morning tea.

While the Primrose maids gathered in the kitchen, city members of the club were arriving in the front vestibule where, after signing in at Reception, supervised by Miss Denny, the slim young assistant manageress, they drifted off to occupy themselves. Some to the Quiet Room, for the reading and writing that so impressed Mattie; some to the square, to sit in the garden (they all had keys); some to the Drawing Room, to chat, or read the morning papers, before the coffee already brewing in the kitchen would be served.

The house in the square, opened as a ladies' club some years before by an enterprising company, was ideal for its purpose. A joining of two grand houses, once owned by families, as so many of its neighbours still were, it had lent itself well to conversion, with the new electric lighting already fitted, vast and elegant public rooms and good upstairs bedrooms for the country members, as well as attics for the maids and, in the double basement, store rooms, sculleries and Mrs Petrie's kitchen.

And then, of course, it had its access to a garden and a fine position for all that the members might want to visit – galleries, concert rooms, shops of every kind. It was little wonder that the Primrose was very popular with the ladies of Edinburgh and its outlying districts, who had no access to professional clubs and wanted somewhere to meet and talk away from their homes – just as gentlemen did.

Husbands might laugh at the idea of their wives going out 'to their club', but then many of the Primrose members were not married, the younger ones only having to persuade their fathers to pay the subscription, the older ones with financial independence gladly doing as they liked. The true test of success for the club was that there was always a waiting list for those who wanted to join, and no shortage of young women who wanted to work there.

Oh, yes, as a place to work, the Primrose was a

good one. They just had to put up with Mrs Petrie, and even she was not always in a bad mood. Though on that June morning, when Gerda and Ada laid down their trays filled with uneaten breakfast dishes – oh, heavens, wasn't her face like a thunder cloud then?

'Take cover, girls,' Elinor whispered.

Three

Mrs Petrie, less than five feet tall and thin as a stick, was red in the face and practically fizzing with displeasure over those terrible trays. 'Like a firework about to go up,' as ginger-haired, un-ruffled Gerda had once said of her – and every-one always hoped that they wouldn't be around if she ever did.

Today she was bemoaning the waste – of her food, of her time – as she wrung her bony hands over the handsome plated dishes of unwanted food.

'Would you credit it? All that good bacon left, and best kidneys, ma lovely kedgeree and all? When you think about the poor bairns that'd give the world for food, could you no' burst into tears? Och, I could cry like a babby, so I could!'

She didn't, though, only ordered anxious Vera and her kitchen maid, young Sal, to start trans-ferring the uneaten breakfasts to the larder, while pouring herself another cup of tea and fanning herself with an oven cloth.

'Aye, and you lassies'd better hurry up and drink your tea now,' she told the maids sitting round the kitchen table. 'Time's getting on, and there's the morning coffee to do. Vera, just check the pots on the stove, eh? And put some shortbread out and soda scones. See if the folk up the stair will eat my baking!'

Still simmering, but a little calmer, she sat at the head of the table, directing operations. An efficient little woman, long a widow for, unlike many cooks of the day who were given the courtesy title of 'Mrs', Sarah Petrie had once had a husband. It was only after his death that she'd taken up cooking again, and had come to rule over the Primrose kitchen after being appointed by Miss Ainslie, who was said to regard her as a treasure. Well, it was true, she was a very good cook, and if Miss Ainslie knew she had a temper, she never let on. Good cooks were hard to find.

'It isn't the first time the ladies have left stuff when it's hot weather,' Elinor ventured, after a moment. 'Maybe they'd do better with just toast?'

'Toast?' cried Mrs Petrie, her pale green eyes bulging. 'Just give 'em toast? With my reputation to think of? Everybody knows this club's got the best food in the city. It's what Miss Ainslie wants and what I want and all. Where'd you get such a daft idea, Elinor?'

Elinor shrugged. 'Just thought, if it was hot, it'd save the waste.'

'Aye, well that food's no' going to be wasted. You lassies can have it for your dinner. I'll heat

13

up the kedgeree and chop up the bacon, do some more eggs and it'll be fine.'

'Porridge and all?' Gerda asked cheekily, at which Mrs Petrie's cheeks flamed again.

'Any more lip from you, my girl, and that's just what you'll get! No, I'll have to let the porridge go this time, but you just watch your step, eh? I've enough to do without putting up with impertinence!'

'Mrs Petrie,' came a cool, clear voice as a light tap sounded on the kitchen door. 'Sorry to disturb you and the girls – just wanted a word.'

'With me, Miss Ainslie?' asked the cook, as she and the maids scrambled to their feet, but the manageress of the Primrose was shaking her neat dark head.

'With the maids, really. No hurry. Finish your tea, by all means.' She looked around the watching faces. 'Just come to my office before you return to your duties, if you please.'

With a quick smile, she withdrew, leaving the maids to set down their cups with a nervous clatter, while exchanging anxious looks.

'No' means the sack, does it?' Mattie whispered.

'Oh, no!' cried plump Ada, as Gerda's jaw dropped and Elinor's dark eyes flashed.

'Miss Ainslie's hardly going to sack us all, Mattie,' Elinor said quickly. 'We're needed.'

'Everybody can be done without,' Mrs Petrie said cheerfully, then relented. 'Of course Miss Ainslie's no' going to give you the sack, Mattie! She'll just be wanting to ask you to do something. She's always got something she wants folk

14

to do.'

'Does she want you to do something, Mrs Petrie?' Gerda asked.

'That's between her and me,' the cook answered loftily. 'But she knows I've too much to do to get involved with anything outside this kitchen. Now you lassies had better get off to her office, and Sal, you get the cups washed. Vera, you can do the coffee, so's Ada and Gerda can take it up when they've seen Miss Ainslie. I've the soup to start.'

Still looking apprehensive, the maids filed out of the kitchen, some shaking their heads.

'Think Miss Ainslie will want us to do something?' Mattie whispered to Elinor. 'How will we find the time?'

'Couldn't say, but I have the feeling Mrs Petrie knows what's going on.'

'What is? What's going on?'

'Have to wait and see.'

Four

Miss Ainslie's office was at the back of the house with no view of the square, only the rear garden where the maids pegged out clothes not destined for the laundry. For this reason it had no great appeal for Elinor, but she had to agree that it was a fine room all the same. Perhaps once the study of the man of the house when it had been privately owned, it was now furnished with a mahogany desk, bookshelves, filing cupboards and a table for Miss Denny's typewriter. The flowers at the window had probably been provided by Miss Ainslie, and she herself, standing to greet the girls as they trooped nervously in, was pleasantly smiling.

Almost forty years of age, she was slightly built and short, not much taller than Mrs Petrie, and had, some thought, the look of a bird, with a slightly beaked nose and darting brown eyes. She wore a pale blue shirtwaist blouse, on which was pinned a gold watch, and a family signet ring on her right hand, but there was no ring on her left hand for she was neither engaged nor married. Past it now, poor thing, thought some of the maids, though Elinor would have said that Miss Ainslie probably didn't want to marry. Independence would be what she wanted, and what, in fact, she seemed to have.

'Now, girls,' she was saying, closing the door on Ada, the last one in, 'don't look so worried. I'm sure there's no need to be worried about anything I have to say to you.'

A little ripple of sighs ran round the maids as Miss Ainslie returned to stand behind her desk, though whether the sighs were truly of relief was doubtful. The manageress might have very different ideas on what was worrying and what was not, and everyone wanted to hear first just what she had to say before they could relax. Even Elinor, in spite of her confidence, was somewhat apprehensive, and glanced at Gerda to see how she was feeling. A waste of time of course, for

16

Gerda never gave much away.

What happened next came as a surprise, for Miss Ainslie, turning to her desk, took up a large poster and held it high for everyone to see. 'Votes for Women' it read, in uneven capitals, and they all stared.

'You'll have seen posters like this around?' Miss Ainslie asked.

'Aye,' Gerda replied, after a short silence. 'We've seen 'em.'

And of course they had. Unless you'd been living underground for the past few years, you couldn't have missed them. Suffragettes posters they were everywhere, together with reports of women smashing windows, setting fire to post boxes, going to gaol. But why was Miss Ainslie showing this poster to her maids? Was she a suffragette, then? If so, she'd kept it pretty dark. But she must know that that cause could be of no interest to them. Even if some women ever did get the vote, lassies like them never would.

Her keen gaze travelling from face to face, Miss Ainslie laid the poster down.

'I expect some of you, when you see such notices, think the campaign is nothing to do with you? But I've called you together to tell you that you couldn't be more wrong.' She smiled a little. 'So, you see, what I have to say is not about work, or duties, which is why there's no need for any of you to worry.'

Certainly no sack for anyone, then, but an idea was forming of where this could all be leading. Impossible, of course, if true, but they'd have to hear her out. As they looked at her expectantly,

Miss Ainslie, clearing her throat, began to speak again.

'What I want to ask you today is to think about coming to join me – and others – in the struggle for justice. We need you, you see. We need girls like you, who can bring youth and enthusiasm and make men understand we're not just a bunch of older women with bees in our bonnets. What we're striving for is something of fundamental importance to everyone – to choose the people who will decide how this country is governed, to have a say in what should be done. At present, only men have that right, yet there are as many women as men, and it's been proved that women can be just as clever. Think about all the women teachers! The women who are now accepted for training as doctors! Yet they have no vote.'

So, thought the listening girls, they'd been right in their guess of what Miss Ainslie might want them to do. She spoke well, she was convincing, but could she really believe they'd join her? Elinor raised her hand.

'Mind if I ask, Miss Ainslie, but is it true you're a suffragette yourself? We never knew.'

The manageress hesitated a moment. 'I am,' she said at last, her voice firm and strong. 'I may not talk about my interests at the Primrose, but they are very important to me. Some people here might have the wrong idea of what we stand for, and I prefer not to be involved in discussion with club members. I could not be keener, though, to see women get the vote, and I want you girls to be keen, too.'

She leaned forward a little, holding them still

18

with her bright, bird-like gaze.

'Will you consider it, then? Helping us in our fight? It would mean so much.'

A silence fell, the girls shifting uneasily, managing to look away.

'I don't think it's for us,' Elinor said at last.

'Apart from anything else, we're too young,' Gerda added.

'Aye, too young,' voices chimed.

'No, no!' cried Miss Ainslie. 'I have said, it's young people we need. And by the time we get the vote, you will be of age, I promise you, so don't let your youth stop you coming forward. Come to one of our meetings. I have cards with details which I'll pass round. Take one and at least think about hearing what we have to say. Will you all do that?'

'Yes, Miss Ainslie,' they answered readily, accepting the cards she was beginning to hand out. Oh, thank the Lord, they could agree to that and not upset her. Then if she asked them later what they'd decided, they could make up some excuse for not going. Whatever happened, no one had any intention of giving up precious time off for the sake of attending a suffragette meeting. Miss Ainslie was a wonderful lady and a very kind boss, but she really didn't have the faintest idea how much their time off meant to girls in service, or how they liked to spend it. Only Elinor was still studying the card when she and the other maids left Miss Ainslie's office, and it was Elinor she called back.

'I won't keep you, Elinor, but if you don't mind, I'd just like another quick word.'

Of course I don't mind, Elinor thought, but it wouldn't matter if she did, would it? She had to admire Miss Ainslie's manners, though. It was what her staff liked about her, that she was as polite to them as to the club members. Made them feel they'd like to please her, only Elinor knew that that wouldn't include attending her meetings.

'I saw you reading my card,' Miss Ainslie was saying. 'It seemed to me you were more interested in my appeal, perhaps, than some of the others.' She laughed a little. 'I'm not really expecting much of a response – Miss Denny is with me, but I have to tell you I got nowhere with Mrs Petrie or Vera.'

Elinor nodded. 'Mrs Petrie'd never agree, and when she says no, so does Vera. Sal's the same.'

'I know, I know.' The manageress sighed. 'But I have great hopes of you, Elinor. I have the feeling that you understand what we want, even though you said it wasn't for you. But how can you know, unless you give it a try? Unless you come to our meetings, listen to us speak?'

'I'd like the vote, Miss Ainslie, but is there much chance of it for someone like me without property?'

'We want women from every walk of life to think about having the vote,' Miss Ainslie cried fiercely. 'To work for it, shoulder to shoulder, to achieve it together! That's why I'm trying to get you and the other girls here to come to our meetings. See that working for the vote is not just for the privileged. Remember, I also work for my living.'

20

Elinor looked at her doubtfully. 'I don't know,' she said slowly. 'There's all this violence to think about, eh? Look at that lady who threw herself in front of the King's horse the other day. I'd never be keen to get mixed up in that sort of thing, or breaking windows, maybe going to gaol.'

'You would never be asked to do that, I give you my word. I personally am against all militant action, anyway, but as a group, we would never seek to involve you in violence. Look, what do you say then? Will you come to our next meeting?'

'I'll ... I'll think about it.'

'That's all I ask.' A smile lit Miss Ainslie's features. 'I know that when you've considered it, you'll come to a fair decision. You are an intelligent girl, Elinor. I've always known that and I think you'll do well.'

'Thank you, Miss Ainslie.' With some relief, Elinor turned for the door. 'Now I'd better get back to work.'

'Just do what you think best about the meeting. As I say, that's all I ask.'

'What happened to you, then?' Mattie asked when Elinor joined her to begin washing down one of the bathrooms.

'Oh, Miss Ainslie was just trying to make me go to her meeting.'

'You never said you would?'

'Said I'd think about it.'

'That's right, that's good. We don't want to be mixed up in it, eh? My dad thinks all suffragettes should be locked up.'

'Bet mine thinks the same, but he's never said.'

Elinor dipped her sponge into a pail of hot water and began to clean the bathroom tiles.

'Might find out when you go round. You always like to go to Friar's Wynd on your time off, eh?'

'Oh, yes, see the folks.' Elinor rubbed the tiles hard. Hoping for the best, she thought.

Five

Elinor's free evenings came on Fridays, usually from four o'clock to nine – or ten with special permission. Twice a month, she also had Saturday afternoon off, but she preferred to do her shopping then, or maybe go out with Gerda or Mattie, keeping her free evenings for her family.

She had no 'followers', as male admirers were called, they having been strictly forbidden in the lawyer's house where she had first worked, and though permitted at the Primrose, only Ada could claim to have a 'young man'. He was from her home tenement and could often be seen hanging round the area steps waiting for her on her free evenings, much to Mrs Petrie's disapproval. Still, if it was all right with Miss Ainslie, it should be good enough for Mrs Petrie, Ada would declare, usually adding, 'Silly old thing, eh? How'd she ever get married herself if she couldn't have a follower?'

'How will any of us ever get married?' Mattie

would often sigh.

Marriage was not something Elinor cared to think about. Sometimes, when she remembered her mother, she would decide she didn't want it. At other times, she'd look ahead and wonder if she might take it on, supposing she met just the right person. But who knew what was in the future? For the present, she felt she wasn't ready, anyway, to sink her life into someone else's. Och, no, she'd enough to think about. Especially on Fridays, when she returned to Friar's Wynd.

Always, when she had to make her way from the pleasant West End to the other side of the city where the Wynd crossed from the High Street into the Cowgate, a certain gloom descended. It was not just that the journey by tram seemed so long and noisy, or that when she reached her stop she met the dark buildings of her childhood again and the sunlight began to fade – no, it was much more the uncertainty of how things would be at home.

All depended on her father's moods. If he was in a good mood, you could relax and breathe again. If not, you just had to weather the storm. It always died down, he always got over whatever had spiralled him into a temper, but they all walked on eggshells until they knew how things would go.

Mind, there were plenty of fathers worse than Walter Rae. He was not a brutal man, and though his children had had their ears boxed when they'd misbehaved, he didn't go in for beating his family. Elinor and Corrie could be grateful for that, then, as their mother certainly was, but the

23

truth was his dominance over them didn't leave much room for gratitude. And when you were wondering when the next flare-up was coming, when the eyes would be flashing and the voice rising, you couldn't do much except keep your head down and hope you weren't the target.

Sometimes, Elinor would compare her dad with Mrs Petrie, but tyrant though Mrs Petrie was, it didn't really matter. She wasn't family, was she?

On that first Friday afternoon after Miss Ainslie's talk, Elinor made her way home as usual. The day was hot with no prospect yet of cooling, and as she left the tram and began to walk down the Wynd between the dark cliffs of tenements on either side, she felt stifled, as though there was no air. She had taken off her jacket, but the collar of her blouse was too high, seeming to grip her throat, and she undid the top button, breathing hard, then pushed back her straw hat from her glistening brow.

If only women didn't have to wear such long skirts! She could feel the warm dust from the pavement rising up her stockinged legs as she walked, and the mad thought crossed her mind – what would happen if girls like her just suddenly cut their skirts off right up to the knees? Och, they'd be locked up, so they would. But think of the relief!

Stepping round a group of children chalking the pavement, she paused as someone called her name and turned her head.

'Hallo, Elinor!'

24

It was a fellow waving to her from the other side of the street. He wore paint-stained overalls and his cap on the back of his head showed his curly light-brown hair. Even from a distance, she could see his hazel eyes were bright. 'Just going to your dad's?'

She stood still, trying to remember his name, for she knew him; he'd been in her class at school. Hadn't seen him since then, and he certainly wasn't from the Wynd.

Barry. The name popped out of her memory. Barry Howat. Cheerful laddie, but given to teasing.

'What are you doing round here?' she called, walking on.

'Been doing a wee job in the tenements.' He, too, was walking on, making no effort to cross over to join her. 'Just going home.'

Two boys tore past him, chasing after a can they'd been kicking, and he neatly cut in and kicked it for them, far away up the street.

'Ah, you're too quick!' one told him, running after it, and he laughed.

'That's because I play football, eh? Get some practice in, lads. Elinor, cheerio, then.'

'Goodbye,' she replied, reaching the door of her father's shop, and gave a quick nod as Barry Howat pulled on his cap and disappeared round the corner. A footballer, eh? Where on earth did he play, then? Not that she was interested. Had to think of what awaited her up the stairs in the flat over the shop. Gauge the temperature. See if a storm was on the way.

As she tried the shop door, the bell tinkled and

25

the door opened. So Dad hadn't locked up, That was because he was still there, behind his counter, tall, heavy-shouldered, with the dark eyes she'd inherited from him beneath black brows she had not, and greying black hair clipped short. He wore a baize apron over his collarless flannel shirt and looked as if he hadn't shaved that day, but the good thing – the thing that mattered – was that he was smiling. His mood was good.

A great rush of relief enveloped her, as she smiled back and cried that she was home.

'Can see that.' He set down the piece of leather he'd been shaping and, loosening his apron, came round from the counter. 'Might as well lock up, then, eh? There'll be nobody else in today and your ma'll have the tea ready.'

Hope so, thought Elinor, for meals were always to be ready when Dad wanted them. As she stood watching her father lock his door, breathing in the familiar smells of leather and shoe polish that had always been a part of his shop and indeed of her own life, she quietly crossed her fingers.

Six

When she was a child, Elinor had thought her family very lucky to live over a shop, rather than in one of the tenements of Friar's Wynd. Though wishing they could move out of the Wynd altogether, she still felt that way, for at least in their little flat there wasn't the same sense of being surrounded by people, the constant sound of footsteps on the stairs, the smell of cooking that wasn't theirs.

On the other hand, you couldn't say there was much space to spare over the cobbler's shop. A cramped living room with a kitchen range, a sink, a table and chairs, and a bed in the wall for Corrie. A room for her parents, a cupboard for herself – for it was no bigger than that – and a toilet. No bathroom, of course, so getting washed involved taking it in turns to carry water to the washstand in the one bedroom, and hauling out the hip bath for bathing when other folk weren't around. No wonder Elinor was so happy to be living-in at the Primrose! It would have been worth it, just for the bathroom.

But small though her dad's flat was, there was still the rent to find, for of course he didn't own the property, only leased it from the man he'd worked for as a young man. That was a man

27

who'd given up shoe mending to run a grocery in Newington, saying it was more profitable than cobbling in Friar's Wynd – and heaven knows that could only have been true, for cobbling wasn't profitable at all. How many people could afford to have their shoes mended? How many children didn't have shoes or boots, anyway?

Walter, though, always said they could manage with what he made. Pay the rent, buy the food, as long as Hessie kept up her work, cleaning at Logie's Princes Street store, and 'obliging' various ladies in the New Town. And Hessie did, of course, keep on with her cleaning jobs, and never risked saying they'd manage a lot better if Walt didn't go to the pub so much. Neither of her children blamed her for that.

'Come on, come on, up the stair, then,' Walter Rae was ordering now, as Elinor still lingered, looking down at the shelves behind the counter where pairs of shoes and boots were tied by their laces and labelled with their owners' names. Seemed to her she remembered seeing a good many of these on the shelves before. Were any folk coming in to collect their shoes? Just how much would her dad be short, paying his bills that week? As soon as he'd had his tea, she knew he'd be out to the Dragon, or the Castle, or whichever pub he chose. He'd find the money from somewhere, always did. Probably Hessie's purse, or one of the boxes where she kept funds for this and that.

Maybe I can find a shilling to put in one of Ma's boxes, Elinor was thinking, and would have looked in her own purse if her father hadn't been pushing her upwards.

'Come on, what are you waiting for? I can smell something good. Always does well for you, you know, your ma.'

'Does well for everybody,' Elinor retorted, opening the door to the flat, gladly taking off her hat and looking for her mother.

'Ma, it's me!' she called. 'I'm back.'

'Ah, there you are!' cried Hessie Rae, turning a flushed face from the kitchen range. 'So grand to see you, pet. Sit down now, and rest your feet. It's like an oven outside, eh?'

With her light brown hair and large blue eyes, Hessie, at thirty-nine, still showed something of the pretty girl she had been in her youth, but the brown hair was greying, the blue eyes were shadowed, and only the artificial colour from the heat of the range made her look well.

She and Walter would have made a handsome couple when they wed, though, Elinor sometimes thought, her dad's dark good looks contrasting with the delicate prettiness of his bride, and wished she could have seen a photograph. Probably, at that time, wedding photos were too expensive for most folk and so there was no record of the happy day. And her parents would have been happy then. Of course they would.

'Tea ready?' Walter asked now, washing his hands under the kitchen tap.

'All ready,' Hessie answered quickly. 'I got a nice piece of shin at the butcher's, half price, a bargain, left it simmering all day, and it's that tender, you'd never believe!'

29

'Onions with it?'

'Oh, yes, plenty. And carrots. So I've just the tatties to mash...'

'I'll do that,' Elinor said quickly. 'But where's Corrie?'

'Aye, where is the lad?' Walter asked, pulling out a chair at the kitchen table. 'No' reading again?'

'Studying,' Hessie answered, beginning to look flustered. 'He's been in our room since he got back from work.'

'Studying ... what a piece of nonsense. He's got a damn good job at the tyre factory, what more does he want?'

'He wants to be a draughtsman, you know that – he told us, eh?'

'Well, I think he's wasting his time, let him stick to what he's got.' Walter stood up and gave one of his famous roars. 'Corrie, come on now! We're all waiting for you, what the hell are you playing at?'

'Playing?' asked Corrie, appearing from the back room where his parents slept. 'I've been studying.'

'Now don't you be sharp with me,' his father told him, his eyes flashing. 'You know what I think of you studying. Now sit down and let your mother dish up. We're ready for our tea, if you're not!'

Taking his seat at the table, Corrie said no more. As tall as his father, he had his mother's looks – the wide blue eyes, the light brown hair, and for his height was slender. As he looked across at Elinor passing a filled plate to her

30

father, their eyes met, exchanging messages which required no words, a skill they'd acquired early in childhood, and which had stood them in good stead.

No one spoke as the meal was finished, the dishes cleared and the tea brewed. Then Walter lit a Woodbine and passed one to Corrie, while Hessie, relaxing a little, stirred sugar into her tea and asked Elinor about the Primrose.

'What's been happening this week, then? I always like to hear what you've been up to. Makes a change.'

'Nothing much.' Elinor sipped her tea. 'Except Miss Ainslie called us all together to talk about votes for women.'

A hush fell over the table as Walter took his cigarette from his mouth and leaned forward to stare at his daughter.

'What did you say?'

She looked at him, her heart plummeting.

Oh, Lord, she'd done it now, eh? Why hadn't she remembered what she'd told Mattie, when Mattie had talked of her dad's views on suffragettes? 'Bet mine thinks the same,' she'd said, and sure enough, he was shaping up to sound off about them now, ready to blow like a volcano, and it would all be her fault.

Oh, yes, she'd done it now.

31

Seven

'Elinor, I'm asking you what you just said,' Walter was saying, his voice taking on the husky note that came with his rising temper, his eyes already glowing with fierce dark light. 'About your Miss Ainslie.'

Elinor, returning his stare, managed not to flinch.

'I said she'd been talking to us about votes for women.'

'Saying what?'

'I'll clear the cups,' Hessie murmured, half rising, but Walter waved her down.

'Leave the cups. Let's hear what the lassie has to tell us.'

'What's it to us?' Corrie asked, drawing on his cigarette, not looking at his father.

'What's it to us? I'll tell you what it is to us. In this house, we want nothing to do with women like that, supposed to be wanting votes, and I want to know what this Miss Ainslie's been saying about 'em to my daughter.' Walter leaned forward. 'So – I'm waiting.'

'Dad, all she asked was if we'd think about...' Elinor hesitated, looking down at the table, '...think about going to a meeting.' She slowly raised her eyes again. 'See what the suffragettes

32

had to say.'

'Going to a meeting? Joining 'em, she meant?'

'No, just ... finding out what they believe in.'

'For God's sake, Elinor, we know what they believe in!'

Walter brought his fist down to the table with a crash which made the cups rattle and his family jump like puppets on a string.

'Do we no' hear what they believe in every day of the week?' he bellowed. 'Criminal damage! Setting fire to houses, damaging the King's portrait, blowing up the Royal Observatory! They don't give a tinker's cuss for votes – they just want to cause trouble, get their names in the papers. Why, if they got the vote tomorrow, they wouldn't know what to do with it, they'd have to ask their husbands to tell 'em what to do, that's if they've got husbands, which half of 'em haven't because nobody'd take 'em on!'

'Oh, Dad!' Elinor groaned. 'That's unfair, that's very unfair.'

'Unfair, is it? Well, I'll tell you this, I don't want you having anything to do with the votes for women brigade, and I don't want you to have any more to do with your Miss Ainslie, either. It's clear enough to me that she's a bad influence on you and I want you out of the Primrose Club and out of her way. When you go back tonight, you can hand your notice in.'

'My notice?' Elinor was staring at him with eyes as dark and fiery as his own. 'Dad, what are you talking about? I'm no' leaving the Primrose. It's a grand place to work; I wouldn't leave it for anything.'

'You'll do as I tell you,' he shouted. 'You're no' twenty-one yet, I'm your father and what I say goes. When you go back to the Primrose tonight, you'll give in your notice, or you needn't come back here. You understand? If you stay there, you don't come here.'

Walter sat back in his chair, breathing heavily, and with shaking fingers lit another cigarette.

'Give over looking at me like that, Hessie,' he ordered heavily. 'I won't be disobeyed in my own house. If Elinor wants to see us, she knows what to do.'

'Walt,' Hessie cried, twisting her hands together, while her children beside her sat like stones. 'Walt, you canna ask Elinor to give up her job. She's happy, she's doing well...'

'There's plenty jobs she can do in this city, Hessie. She doesn't have to work for a woman with criminal ideas.'

Criminal ideas. Miss Ainslie. Slowly, Elinor rose to her feet.

'That's it,' she said quietly. 'I don't want to hear any more, Dad. I've put up with you and your tempers long enough. Now, if you want me to go, because I won't leave the Primrose and Miss Ainslie who's been so good to all us girls and is truly against violence, so be it. I'll go.'

As her father sat very still, seemingly so stunned by her daring to answer him back he could think of nothing to say, Hessie began wailing.

'Oh, Elinor, lassie, think what you're saying! You canna give up your home. Your dad would never want you to do that, he never meant that, did you, Walt? Now you just sit down and we'll

34

all be calm—'

'Be calm?' he cried. 'Who's going to be calm? And who the hell are you, Hessie, to say what I want, or what I mean? I've told Elinor what she can do, and if she doesn't want to do it, she can go.'

His voice was shaking, his face scarlet as he leapt to his feet, his cigarette hanging from his lip, and pointed at the door.

'There you are, Elinor, there's the door. You want to be mixed up with suffragettes, you can go out of that and no' come back. And that's my last word.'

'Dad, stop it!' Corrie shouted, jumping to his feet. 'Elinor hasn't even said she wants to be a suffragette. She just wants to keep her job at the Primrose.'

'And I've told her, if she does, she doesn't come back here. I'll no' have my own daughter defying me and don't tell me I don't mean that, Hessie, because I do.'

'And I believe you,' Elinor told him, her voice thickening with emotion. Her gaze went to her mother, who was quietly crying.

'Ma, don't worry, I'll be sure to still see you. I've a few things in your wardrobe, I'll collect them some time. Corrie, keep in touch, eh?'

She turned to her father, who had stubbed out his cigarette and was watching her, breathing fast.

'Goodbye, Dad. Just remember, you made me do this.'

'The key's in the shop door, you can let your- self out,' was all he said, but she could see that his passion was subsiding. Quite likely, in spite of all his roaring, he would be changing his mind soon, but if he did, it would be too late. This time, he'd gone too far.

Going down the stairs, her legs trembling, she could not really believe she was actually leaving home. This was something different from going into service, where you lived away but home was still a part of you, and though she'd always had to worry about how things would be, Elinor knew that she was going to feel like a lost child, not seeing home again.

The key was in the shop door, though, as her dad had said, and all she had to do was open it and step out into the Wynd, where the summer evening was still as light as day and where the air was just as warm as ever. Children were playing, and neighbours standing around, or leaning out of the tenement windows, gossiping. Everything was just the same. Yet changed for ever.

'Ellie!' she heard her mother's voice, calling her by the old pet name she no longer used. 'Ellie, come back, come back!'

'Aye, come back!' echoed Corrie, who was with Hessie, holding her arm. 'You mustn't leave us like this.'

'Oh, Ma – Corrie...'

Elinor ran back to hug them both, tears mixing with her mother's, and feeling Corrie's thin shoulders shaking as he held her.

'I don't want to go, but what can I do? Dad's got no right to stop me working at the Primrose; he's got no right to stop me going to meetings, but if I do, he'll no' let me come home.'

36

'He doesn't mean it,' Hessie sobbed. 'You know what he's like. All blow and thunder, and then it's gone and the sun's out again. Just you come back and he'll no' turn you away, you'll see, eh?'

'No,' Elinor said firmly, withdrawing from her mother's clasp and blowing her nose. 'He's gone too far. I'm taking him at his word, I won't be coming back.'

'Oh, God,' Corrie groaned. 'If only I could stand up to him! If only I didn't let him get away with it – every time – every damn time. You were good, Elinor, giving it to him straight, but I just sat there. What a great Jessie, eh? What a fat lot of use.'

'You have to keep the peace,' she told him. 'There's no point two of us finishing with him, we have to think of Ma.'

'Don't worry about me.' Hessie sighed, wiping her eyes. 'I can manage him better than you folk. I know him, I understand him.'

'Oh, Ma,' Elinor sighed. 'Look, I'm away for the tram. I'll come in and see you at Logie's, eh? We'll arrange a meeting.'

'I'll walk you to the tram,' said Corrie, as Hessie, crying again, turned back to the shop door. 'And then you can fix up to see me some time – if you don't come back.'

'I've said I won't be coming back.' Elinor, taking his arm, shook her head. 'Dad's made up my mind for me. I'm definitely going to Miss Ainslie's meeting now, so that's me the outcast. If that's what he wants, I want it, too.'

And at that the brother and sister, shoulders

drooping, made their way slowly through the warm streets to the tram stop. They didn't speak again until the tram came in sight, when they hugged and said goodbye. There didn't seem anything else to say.

Eight

Sometimes, it seemed, the suffragette groups held outdoor meetings, usually attended by a handful of grown-ups and children, who were not above jeering, but the first meeting Elinor went to was in a large church hall in Newington, an area on Edinburgh's south side. The warm weather had moved away and the evening was chill and wet, but nothing could dampen Miss Ainslie's enthusiasm as she and Elinor made their way to the meeting under glistening umbrellas.

'I'm so glad you agreed to come!' Miss Ainslie told Elinor who, though trying to look confident in her best walking-out jacket and skirt, was still very unsure about this whole venture. 'It's such a shame about the weather, but I know you won't be disappointed. Miss Denny can't be with us, unfortunately, as she has to be at the club when I am not, but she's getting quite keen on our work. After all, why should any woman not want the vote?'

'There is this property qualification, though.'

Miss Ainslie was silent for a moment.

'What I'd like to see,' she said finally, 'is universal suffrage. That means everyone over twenty-one being given the right to vote.'

'And is that what the movement wants, too?'

'Well, I think at present, we're just trying to have the same rights as men. We could campaign later for an extension to the vote.'

'Doesn't seem fair, if you've got to have property to be able to vote.'

'No, I'll admit, it's not fair. Does your own father, for instance, have the vote?'

'No,' Elinor replied shortly, and said no more. She didn't want to discuss her father, as she had not yet told the manageress of his views, or that he had forbidden her to go home while she still worked at the Primrose. In fact, she had told no one, for though there was no hope in her mind that the situation would change, she still wanted only to keep it secret.

'Here we are!' Miss Ainslie cried, as they reached the open door of the meeting place. 'Oh, listen to the chatter – seems we have a good audience in spite of the rain! This way, Elinor.'

Keeping her brave face, Elinor followed Miss Ainslie into the hall. Large and bleak, filled with rows of chairs, it reminded her of school, but on the platform, draped across a table, was a large 'Votes for Women' banner and, instead of pupils, there were crowds of women, not yet taking their seats. Most were well dressed, in fitted jackets, pretty blouses, and large hats – just the sort of ladies you might see any day of the week having tea in Maule's or Logie's department stores.

Others appeared more casual, in tartan stoles and bonnets, or loosely draped shawls and floating print dresses. But all were animated, talking in high, educated voices, smiling, seeming to know everyone around them; all were sure of themselves, very much at ease.

Miss Ainslie was the same. She also knew everyone, greeting them delightedly, to which they responded with cries of 'Jane, how lovely to see you!' and little brushed kisses on her cheek, while Elinor stood apart, thinking she'd known it would be like this and wishing she hadn't come. But then Miss Ainslie suddenly turned and, taking her arm, propelled her forward into a group of interested faces, exclaiming, 'Ladies, may I introduce Miss Rae, who is joining us tonight to hear Mrs Greer? Elinor, I won't try to give you names at this stage, but I know people will want to make you welcome. Everyone, Miss Rae!'

Miss Rae ... Miss Ainslie had called her Miss Rae. At the formality, so unusual for her, Elinor's heart rose and she blushed and smiled, as the ladies bent forward to greet her. She was beginning to make some sort of reply, when a ginger-haired woman appeared on the platform, accompanied by the rector of the church, the only man present, and called for people to take their seats. Mrs Greer, already stepping up from the front of the hall, was ready to speak.

She was a large woman, perhaps in her early forties, wearing a grey two-piece and matching hat over a coil of thick fair hair. Very relaxed in manner, she announced to her audience that she was going to tell them something of the general struggle for the vote in the past. A history lesson, yes, but it would help to make people understand that gaining the vote had never been an easy matter for anyone, which only made the modern woman's fight more difficult.

For instance, did the audience know that you had to go back to 1432 to find the vote first being given to men? That was when Henry VI was on the throne and the voters had to own property worth forty shillings. A fortune, no less, so very few men would qualify. Women, of course, were not even mentioned.

Everyone laughed and settled down to listen as Mrs Greer guided them through the centuries, outlining reforms that prevented abuse of the system, explaining how various Acts had gradually given more men the vote, provided they were householders, and of how women had always been hoping that their turn would come and had always been disappointed. Until here they were in the twentieth century, and activity had never been greater. Mrs Pankhurst had formed a social and political union for women to fight for the vote. Other societies had come into being. Victory was certainly on the way. It had been difficult for men to get the vote at one time; today it was still difficult for women, but they would get there in the end.

'Never give up!' Mrs Greer cried. 'Whatever it costs, work on!' She raised her arm and smiled her beaming smile. 'Always remember, the slogan is – Votes for Women!'

And with that last call, she sat down to

41

prolonged applause, delicately wiping her brow with her handkerchief before rising to take her bow.

'Well, Elinor, what did you make of that?' Miss Ainslie asked, after a few questions had brought the meeting to a close and volunteers were serving tea and biscuits.

'I enjoyed it,' Elinor replied honestly. 'Mrs Greer made it all so clear and interesting; I feel I understand things better.'

'She's certainly an excellent speaker and does so much to help us. Her husband's a lawyer and doesn't approve, but she just steams ahead, anyway.' Miss Ainslie laughed. 'But now you must come and meet more people, Elinor. I think you'll find everyone very friendly.'

'I already have, Miss Ainslie.'

It was true – everyone Elinor met over the tea and biscuits appeared genuinely keen to talk to her, while she in return was intensely pleased to find herself talking quite naturally to them. For the first time she could remember, she was communicating on a level with people who might have been her employers, for though she could talk to Miss Ainslie, it wasn't possible to forget the difference in their positions at the Primrose. Here, there were no differences. She was a young woman who wanted a vote, in conversation with other women who wanted the same, putting forward her views and finding them listened to, which was so remarkable, she found the experience quite heady and exciting. Only a little nagging point of dissent at the back of her mind suggested that in the sort of world she'd like to be

42

in, it shouldn't really have been so remarkable.

Still, when she asked if the violence some suffragettes were using might possibly do the cause harm, it was gratifying that people listened to her and gave considered replies, one agreeing that some folk did believe that.

'But many of us in this group are non-militant and are still grateful that those who aren't have brought our struggle to public notice.'

'And have suffered for it,' another lady put in. 'Their prison experiences have been appalling.'

'Indeed, the militants are truly brave,' someone added, then hastily put a hand on Elinor's arm. 'But don't worry, my dear, you will not be asked to set fire to anything, or put bombs in houses.'

Which was exactly what Miss Ainslie had told her, so that was all right. When they'd left the hall and were on their way to the tram, however, it occurred to Elinor to ask if there was some reason why she would never be asked to do anything violent.

'Is it just because your group is non-militant, or is there some other reason, Miss Ainslie?'

Miss Ainslie hesitated. 'Well, I suppose it's just that people can be treated differently in prison. If someone has – you know – friends in high places – they might do better.'

As understanding dawned, Elinor's dark eyes glittered a little.

'Oh, I see. It's because I wouldn't have friends in high places, so I'd be more at risk?'

'It sounds terrible, I know...'

'No' really. Only to be expected.' Elinor laughed shortly, as their tram came into sight. 'That's what they call the way of the world, eh?'

'Elinor, don't let any of this put you off joining us,' Miss Ainslie said urgently. 'You did really well this evening, talking so easily, meeting so many strangers; I was proud of you. Please, stay with us.'

After a pause, Elinor nodded. 'All right, I'll try another meeting or two, anyway. I do believe in your cause.'

'I'm so glad.'

But as they boarded the tram and took their places on the hard slatted seats, Elinor's thoughts had suddenly drifted home to her family. She did not regret taking the stand she had, yet wished so much it hadn't had to happen. When would she see Ma again? And Corrie? She'd better try to fix up meetings. And Dad? If only he'd been different ... As the days had gone by and she hadn't seen him, the funny thing was, she was almost missing him, too.

Nine

On one of her free Saturday afternoons, Elinor arranged to meet her mother at a little café off the High Street. Though she'd never seen her father, she'd met Corrie once or twice and as the July days passed quickly by had attended another talk for suffragettes in the church hall and two brief outdoor gatherings.

All interesting and enjoyable, even when the children in the streets had to be dissuaded from shouting cheeky messages, but gradually – she didn't even like to admit it – she was beginning to find that some of her early euphoria was fading.

It wasn't that she minded being grateful to the ladies at the meetings who treated her like one of themselves, more that she wished she had been just that. True, she seemed able to hold her own, but while she'd liked to believe at first that there was no gulf between herself and the others, it came to her at last that the gulf was there and couldn't be bridged.

Why not? She'd thought about it a lot, for she felt in her heart she should be the equal of anyone. Where was the difference, then? Background, of course, and education. These women seemed to know so much. They could talk so easily about every subject under the sun, whereas for her and those in her position, the world was so narrow, it was as though they were wearing blinkers and could only see what was around them.

But education could change all that. Could provide opportunities. Help folk to better themselves, if they wanted to, as she did. Only, if you had to leave school early to earn your living, where could you get more education? There had to be a way, Elinor thought, and was determined to find it.

When she met her mother, she wanted to tell her all that was on her mind, but first Hessie seemed to need to talk about her dad.

'He's missing you,' she told Elinor, pouring tea. 'Aye, it's true, I knew he would. Just wishes he could get out of all the trouble he's caused without looking a fool, but canna think of a way. Want some of this teacake?'

Elinor studied her mother. Although she'd dressed up specially for her little jaunt away from Friar's Wynd, she was looking strained, with a new deep line between her brows and the usual shadows beneath her eyes.

'Bet it's no' been easy for you, Ma,' Elinor murmured, taking some of the buttered teacake. 'If Dad's been in a bad mood.'

'He's been all right, that's the funny thing.' Hessie shook her head, on which was perched her best straw hat trimmed with daisies. 'He's more like sad, eh? A bit depressed. Like we all are, Corrie as well.'

'If you're trying to make me feel guilty, it's no use, Ma. Dad's taken his stand, I've taken mine, and there's no going back.'

'But are you really getting mixed up with the ladies wanting the vote, Elinor? If you were to give them up, he'd no' mind if you stayed on at the Primrose, I'm sure.'

'I've been to some meetings.' Elinor drank her tea. 'I do believe in what they're doing, except for the violence, and the group I'm with are against that.'

'So you'll keep on with 'em?' Hessie sighed. 'Seems there's no hope, then.'

'Well, things have changed a bit. It was grand when I first met Miss Ainslie's friends, they were

46

all so nice, treated me the same as if I was one of them. But the truth is, I'm not.'

'You're just as good as anybody, Elinor! The only difference is some folk are better off.'

Elinor passed her mother a plate of cakes and took one herself. 'It isn't just that. I think the biggest difference comes from what's in people's heads. Whether you're educated or not. Now, I had to leave school early—'

'We needed the money, Elinor. When you started working, you were one less mouth to feed. It just wasn't possible to let you do the leaving certificate.'

'I know, I understand, I'm no' blaming anybody. But what's made me think, since I mixed with these new folk, is that I'm never going to better myself unless I get some more education.' Elinor met her mother's eyes with a darkly burning gaze. 'And I mean to do that, Ma. I won't be staying in service for ever.'

'Have you never thought you might one day get wed?'

'Oh, Ma! As though that would be the solution to everything!'

'It might be. Depends on who you marry.'

Mother and daughter exchanged glances, then Hessie looked away.

'Where'll you get this education, then? I mean, you canna go back to school.'

'I'm going to speak to Miss Ainslie about it. There might be evening classes I can do. I've only got limited time off, so I might have to give up her meetings anyway. But she'll understand, she's very kind. Look, I'll get the bill, I've to be

47

away.'

'Oh, lassie,' Hessie murmured, putting her hankie to her eyes. 'It's been grand, eh? Shall we meet again soon? And will you see Corrie again? He was that glad to see you when you met him out of work.'

'Sure I will, and I'll see you, too.' Elinor, rising, adjusted her hat and took out her purse. 'You might say to Dad that I send him good wishes. He won't care, but tell him, anyway.'

'I will, I will. I did say I was going to see you and he never said I shouldn't.'

Elinor shrugged. 'We'd better be grateful for small mercies, then.'

Outside the café, mixing with the tourists heading for the Royal Mile and the sights of historic Edinburgh, she and her mother exchanged hugs and parted to go their different ways, Hessie shedding a tear again, Elinor feeling low. Until she thought again of speaking to Miss Ainslie.

As she had hoped, the manageress was able to tell her just what she needed to know. There were courses for adults available in the city, some begun only last year by the Workers' Educational Association, others organized by various groups, and a few by the council. There would be something to pay, of course, and the WEA would probably charge the least. Miss Ainslie, giving Elinor one of her quick, bird-like glances, raised her eyebrows.

'But what's brought this on, then? I didn't know you were interested in studying, Elinor, though I'm very pleased to hear it.'

Elinor looked down. 'I'm keen to get on,' she said after a pause. 'And I'll need more than I've got to do that.'

'What sort of class would you like to try for?'

'I thought maybe history. Or English – grammar and that.'

Miss Ainslie pursed her lips. 'For a job, you don't think you'd do better with some sort of secretarial skill? Such as typewriting? I believe more and more women are finding jobs in offices these days.'

'Typewriting?' Elinor had never thought of it. Wasn't what she'd had in mind, but might be a quicker way to a better job than studying academic subjects, even though that sort of study was what she felt she needed. 'You think I could be a secretary, Miss Ainslie?'

'Elinor, I think you could be anything you put your mind to. It's such a shame you couldn't have stayed on at school.'

'A shame a lot of folk couldn't do that, Miss Ainslie. But maybe I'll try this typewriting. Where do you think I could find out where to go?'

'Why, you must speak to Mrs Greer at the next meeting. She had a bundle of leaflets she was showing only the other day – she's very keen on bringing education to those who've missed it.'

Mrs Greer? Elinor's eyes widened. And here was I believing I was the only one who cared, she thought, and felt a little guilty.

49

Ten

Mrs Greer was delighted to be able to help Elinor, Miss Ainslie's protégée, as she called her, a word Elinor didn't know, but could guess its meaning.

'You'll find all you need to know in these leaflets I have,' Mrs Greer told her. 'What's available, meeting places, enrolling details, cost and so on. Now, are you going to be able to afford the charge, my dear? I'm sure there are funds available if not.'

'I've got some savings,' Elinor replied quickly, thinking that she'd like to pay her own way, and if she didn't get the new jacket she'd had her eye on, well, too bad. 'But when do these classes start?'

'At the end of August for the WEA, with enrolling two weeks earlier. They're usually held in schools after hours, or a few are at the university. Read through the leaflets and decide what you want to do.' Mrs Greer patted Elinor's shoulder. 'And the best of luck – I really admire your initiative.'

Another word Elinor didn't know. At this rate, she would be spending more time than the club members in the Quiet Room, looking up the dictionaries. Whatever would Mattie say?

Two weeks later, having managed to obtain permission to slip out during the early evening, she made her way to the great gaunt school in Stockbridge where she planned to enrol for the typewriting class.

Heavens, though, the large hall – with its distinctive school smell of chalk, worn shoes, damp clothes and pupils – was crowded out! She'd never thought so many people would be as keen to learn as she was herself. Nothing for it, then, but to join the queue at the desk, where a young woman was booking folk in for the typewriting course, and hope she wouldn't be too long away from the club. In fact, the waiting crowd seemed to melt away just as she reached the desk, and she was about to heave a sigh of relief, when the young woman who'd been taking names rapped out, 'Typewriting is fully booked. This position is closed.'

'Fully booked?' Again, Elinor was taken completely by surprise. 'What do you mean? You can't take me?'

'Of course I can't take you!' the girl cried scornfully, her small blue eyes flashing. 'There are only a limited number of typewriters for the students, and it's first come, first served. You should have got here earlier.'

As she began to gather up papers from her desk and Elinor stood disconsolately watching her, a tall, fair-haired man in a tweed suit came across to the desk.

'What's the trouble, Miss Reynolds?'

'No trouble, Mr Muirhead. This person wanted to take the typewriting class and I've told her it's

51

fully booked. What else can I do?'

The tall man, looking at Elinor, gave her an apologetic smile. 'Sorry about that. I'm afraid the typewriting class is very popular and quickly fills up. Perhaps something else might be of interest? I'm taking another class myself on office management and procedures. How about that?'

'That's got no typewriting,' Miss Reynolds said at once. 'It wouldn't be the same at all.'

'Nevertheless, it is a very useful course,' he retorted, his voice edged enough to make her flush a little.

'Sorry, Mr Muirhead, I'm sure it is. Shall I take this lady across to book in, then? If it's not full?'

'No, I'll take her myself. This way, Miss...?'

'Rae,' Elinor answered. 'And thank you.'

How kind he was, she thought, as he shepherded her through the crowd, his grey eyes so sympathetic. But who was he? He was very well dressed, seemed to be in charge somehow, and the snappy Miss Reynolds had caved in pretty quickly when he'd rebuked her. Why not take his office course, then? It might be just as good as the typewriting.

'My name's Stephen Muirhead,' he told her. 'I'm a course organizer for the WEA, and also a tutor. It's part of my policy to try to find the right course for everyone who wants to learn, which is why I hope my course will be of interest to you.'

'Oh, it is!' she said eagerly. 'I think it might suit me very well. But it might be booked up.'

'Not yet.' He smiled. 'The numbers are good, but it's not quite as popular as typewriting. Mind if I ask, are you an office worker at present, Miss

52

Rae?'

Her colour rose. 'No. I'd like to be, but I'm ... I'm in service. At the Primrose Club.'

'I see. Nice place, I believe.' His expression was the same: he was continuing to smile. 'But you'd like a change?'

'That's right. A change.'

'Well, before you book in, I'll just tell you briefly that the course is designed for people seeking jobs in offices, not necessarily in offices already. So, it will give an idea of the sort of thing they'll need to know, and practice at the different procedures – filing, simple bookkeeping, record keeping and so on.'

Mr Muirhead smiled a little. 'I'm hoping it will help with interviews – everyone's worry.'

'And women are being taken on in offices now?' Elinor asked. 'There are still more men than women in your queue.'

'True, but the fact is single women are being employed more and more.' Mr Muirhead gave a small shrug. 'Although I'm afraid they do earn less than the men.'

'Surprise, surprise,' Elinor responded, and they both laughed, before he saw her take her place in the queue she'd been studying.

'I'll have to leave you now,' he told her, 'but I'll look forward to seeing you again. On the last Thursday in August, seven o'clock at Carlyle High School. That's Fountain Bridge area.'

'Thursday?' she repeated.

'Difficult?'

'It's just that I'll have to try to get Thursday evenings free.'

'I hope you will.'

'Oh, I will.'

As he moved away, looking back once, she had already begun wondering how she was going to manage getting to his class. She would have to hope that Gerda, whose free evenings were Thursdays, would swap with her for Fridays. But supposing she wouldn't? Och, she'd cross that bridge when she came to it. All she knew was that she was determined to get to Mr Muirhead's class, and after she'd booked in and paid her fee, heaved a sigh of relief and put her receipt safely in her bag. She had her place!

Eleven

The following morning when the Primrose maids were having their morning break, Mrs Petrie, passing Elinor her tea, fixed her with a sharp green eye.

'What's all this about you going to night school?' she demanded.

Elinor, turning crimson, swung round in her chair to look at Gerda.

'I asked you no' to say anything!'

'I never did!' Gerda's brown eyes were indignant. 'You asked me to swap free evenings and I said I would, and that's all. Must've been Mattie.'

'Mattie?' Elinor cried. 'I told you in confidence, too!'

'Sorry, Elinor.' Mattie's round face was shame-faced. 'I was just that surprised, you see, and when we were doing staff breakfasts, I was with Mrs Petrie and it sort of slipped out.'

'What's it matter who told me?' Mrs Petrie cried. 'What I want to know is what's it all about? Have you got tired of the Primrose, or what, Elinor? And what's Miss Ainslie say, then, after all she's done for you, eh?'

'I haven't told her yet,' Elinor admitted. 'I will, though, when I ask if it's all right for me to take Gerda's Thursdays. Anyway, she won't mind if I go to night school, it was her idea.'

As Mrs Petrie stared in disbelief, Elinor added quickly, 'And I've only signed up for a class, I'm no' leaving the Primrose, so there's no need to say any more.'

'Don't be telling me what to say or not to say, if you please! What is this course, then? French? German? Arithmetic?' Mrs Petrie laughed short-ly. 'Just who do you lassies think you are?'

'It's office procedures,' Elinor answered coldly. 'If you must know, I tried for typewriting but it was full.'

'Typewriting, eh?' Gerda smiled. 'Sounds good. Mebbe I'll try for it next year, eh?'

'Aye, might be just up our street,' chimed Ada. 'Where'd you go for these classes, then, Elinor?'

'Now you girls can just stop all this!' Mrs Petrie cried. 'Hurry up with your tea and get back to work. Ada, never mind about classes – did you bring the papers down from the Quiet Room? Where's *The Scotsman*, then?'

55

'It's here, Mrs Petrie.'

As Ada hastily gave her yesterday's *Scotsman* from the sheaf of newspapers she had cleared from upstairs, the cook took out her reading glasses.

'Let's see what's happening in this terrible world,' she muttered, unfolding the paper she always claimed. 'That Kaiser fella's always in the news, eh? I never did like Germans. Or any of thae Balkan folk. Always causing trouble.'

'How many Germans has she met?' Gerda asked in a low voice, when they were outside the kitchen. 'Or people from the Balkans, come to that?'

'As though Mrs Petrie needs to know folk before she hates them!' Elinor answered, laughing, and Mattie touched her arm.

'Elinor, I'm truly sorry I told her about your class. Like I said, it slipped out before I could stop it.' Mattie's eyes were woeful. 'Me and my big mouth, eh?'

'It's all right, Mattie. She'd have to find out sometime, anyway – I only wanted to spare all the arguments.' Elinor glanced at the clock in the entrance hall they were moving through on their way to clean inside windows. 'Look, I'll just be five minutes – I want to speak to Miss Ainslie. You get started and I'll follow.'

'Miss A's never going to worry about us changing days off,' Gerda murmured. 'She's easy about things like that.'

But is she going to be so happy about me not going to her suffragette evenings any more? Elinor wondered, as she knocked on Miss Ains-

56

lie's door. Truth is, I have no time now.'

Gerda was right, of course, that the manageress would find no difficulty in giving her permission to the two maids to swap their evenings off. It was only when Elinor had to point out that she could no longer attend the suffragette evenings that she looked a little dismayed.

'Oh, that's a shame, Elinor, when you were doing so well and becoming so helpful to us. Of course, I know you want to go to the class and I'm pleased for you, but couldn't you have spared time for us as well?'

'You've forgotten, I only get one evening off in the week,' Elinor told her quietly, at which Miss Ainslie put a hand to her lip and gave an embarrassed smile.

'Oh, dear, of course you do! What am I thinking of? And I suppose it wouldn't be fair, to give you extra time off, just to help our cause...'

'No, it wouldn't. But I'll still try to go to some of the outdoor meetings on Saturday afternoons.'

'That would be good of you. I know they're precious.' Miss Ainslie sighed. 'If it were up to me, you know, I'd try to get you girls more time off, but the company would never agree. My hands are tied.'

Always were, when it came to asking the folk with the money for anything, Elinor thought, when she was on her way back to join Mattie and Gerda for their window cleaning. Still, you had to be grateful to Miss Ainslie for even thinking of better conditions for her maids. There was no doubt that working at the Primrose was about as good as it could be for girls in service. Would working in an office be any better?

Elinor paused for a moment, swinging her wash leather, frowning a little. It was going to be a lot of work, doing this course. Swotting up on arithmetic, learning different skills, maybe having to do tests and so on. Did she really want to do it?

Yes! came back her eager reply. Oh, yes. Because service at the Primrose was still service, while working in an office would give her a distinct identity that you never had as a maid, as well as perhaps providing a stairway to better things. She would have to leave her beloved gardens, of course, and that would be hard, a real sacrifice, but she'd come back, she'd visit, and they would be in her mind, always. As for the WEA course itself, even if it was hard work, it would be interesting and challenging. And had a good tutor, eh?

At the remembrance of Mr Muirhead, Elinor began to walk on swiftly, surprised to find her face growing warm and probably pink. It was a relief that when she joined the others in their window cleaning, no one took the slightest notice and soon her cheeks were pink anyway, as she rubbed away with her leather, her thoughts free to concentrate on a certain date in August. The last Thursday. Seven o'clock. Carlyle High School.

She'd be there.

Twelve

When the last Thursday in August finally arrived, it was no surprise to Elinor that she was feeling nervous. There was so much pressure. Everyone watching, commenting – especially Mrs Petrie. Oh, dear, oh dear, what were working lassies coming to these days, thinking they could do bookwork the same as educated folk, where would it all end? Et cetera, et cetera. And then there was Mattie, fearing that Elinor wouldn't be able to do the sums required, and Ada asking what good would it all be if she never got into an office, eh? And wouldn't everybody prefer men, anyway?

Only Gerda was supportive, telling Elinor she was doing the right thing and she wished she'd thought of doing something like it herself. Perhaps she still would.

'If I get on all right?' Elinor asked dryly, but Gerda shook her head.

'You'll do well, that's what the others know. They're a wee bit envious, that's all.'

'As though anybody needs to be envious of me!' cried Elinor.

When it was time to go on Thursday evening, she left the Primrose by the area steps, conscious of the eyes watching, aware that she looked her best, even in the blue jacket and skirt she had not been able to afford to replace, but she was nervous. Come on, she told herself, you're looking forward to this, eh? Enjoy it, then.

The evening was still fine, the light still good, though August would soon be September and the northern summer was fading. Having taken a quick look at the gardens of the square to make her feel better, she was hurrying on when she saw ahead the figure of a man approaching. And stopped in her tracks.

It couldn't be, could it? Couldn't be ... her father?

No, he'd never come to the West End, he'd never come to the Primrose. Yet...

'Dad?' she whispered, as the man came nearer and she saw that there was no mistaking her father's tall figure, his way of walking, throwing out his feet as though kicking stones. No mistaking the cap and jacket he was wearing, or the good-looking face, the dark eyes meeting hers.

'Dad,' she repeated. 'What are you doing here?'

He had reached her, was standing close, and she could make nothing of his expression, except that it was not angry, nor did it show any emotion. But then he was there, with her, quite out of his own territory, and there must be some reason for that, so what could it be? Oh, no – no!

Her heart beginning to beat fast, she cried, 'Is it Ma, Dad? Is there something wrong? Is it Corrie? Tell me!'

Suddenly, his features seemed to melt, his eyes soften. He began to shake his head. 'No need to worry, lassie. There's nothing wrong. I just came to see you.'

'But why? You won't say why!'

'Can we no' sit down somewhere?' He looked around, at the fine houses, the gardens with their trees still in full leaf, the railings with their gates, and he smiled briefly. 'This your famous square, then? And everything's locked?'

'Dad, I'm just going out. I'm going to an evening class, it's the first time, and I mustn't be late. I'd no idea you were coming.'

'Spur of the moment, is why. I never even told your ma.' His smile broadened. 'She thinks I'm at the pub.'

'Will you walk with me to Lothian Road?' she asked desperately. 'I've to get the tram there. We could talk on the way.'

Her heart was still pounding, but now with apprehension that her evening was about to crash around her ears. It was the strangest thing in the world that her father had come seeking her, and might be good but then might not, and she felt so confused, she was like some rudderless boat at the mercy of the waves.

'Will you come?' she asked, praying that he would not take offence that she was still going to her class when he had come to see her, that he would not suddenly blow up right there in the middle of the city.

Amazingly, he took her arm. 'Aye, I'll come, Elinor. If we can talk, I want to talk.'

'You'll tell me why you came?'

61

'I should've thought you could guess. Or d'you want me to eat humble pie?'

'Dad, what are you saying?'

She wished now that they weren't joining the crowds waiting to cross the road at Maule's Corner, where Princes Street ended and the two famous churches – St John's and St Cuthbert's – marked the entry to Lothian Road. If only her father hadn't picked tonight of all nights! For there was the tram stop ahead and she must be ready to board when her tram came, or she would be late, and yet she didn't want to board, she wanted to hear what her dad had to say. And try to make herself believe that this was happening.

'I've been thinking I was a wee bit hard on you,' he was muttering, 'that time I told you to go. It's been on my mind – since you went – that I was, well, I was wrong.' He laughed uneasily. 'Got carried away, you see. Well, you know how it is.'

'Aye, I do,' she said eagerly. 'I was maybe too quick, too. Ma said I shouldn't have been so quick, but...'

'No, I told you to go – what else could you do?'

They had reached the tram stop and were standing together, almost fearfully exchanging looks from eyes so alike, trying to make sense of this so strange meeting, the strangest meeting either of them had ever had.

'Do you want me to come back?' Elinor asked at last, in a husky whisper.

'Aye, I do. When you can.'

'Thing is, I've signed up for this course. I've no evenings free in term times.' (Oh, Lord, what

62

would he say?) 'But then there'll be the holidays – and some Saturdays. In fact, I might be able to come this weekend.'

'Come when you can,' he repeated. 'I'll tell your mother you'll come when you can.'

'Dad, she'll be so pleased.'

'I know.' He cleared his throat. 'I sometimes get things right. But what's this course, then?'

'It's learning about office work. I thought I might – you know – try for a different job.'

'Lassies doing office work these days?'

'Seemingly.'

Her tram was looming. She put her hand on his arm. 'Dad, this is me. I'll have to go.'

'I'll see you on, then.'

She kissed his cheek – when had she last done that? – and murmured, self-consciously, 'Dad – thanks.'

He looked away. 'Better join the queue, lassie.'

When the tram halted, she followed people on to the platform, looking back at her father, watching. Neither smiled, but both waved.

'Fares, please,' said the conductor, and she was borne away, her father still watching until the tram was out of sight.

Oblivious to the noise and rattles around her, Elinor was gradually coming to terms with what had happened. Her dad, in one of his good moods, had made the huge effort to seek her out and – yes, incredible though it seemed – had apologized to her. He'd actually got the words out. Admitted he'd made a mistake. Asked her to come back home when she could. Was it possible?

She supposed that, with him, anything was possible. As her mother had said, he could be all blow and thunder one minute, all sunshine the next, and this apologizing to her must be in one of his sunny times, then. On the other hand, she'd never known him cave in to anyone in the family before, and it might just be that when she'd left, she'd given him a shock. She'd stood up to him like no one else had done, and being unused to it, he'd not known how to deal with it. When he'd finally realized that she was not coming back, he'd bitten the bullet and apologized. Because it was true, then, that he'd missed her?

A warm glow consumed her as it came to her that her dad must care for her. Cared for all his family, though he had no idea how to make them happy. Would always want his own way, always be ready to fly off the handle, but deep down, they meant something to him. And understanding that meant something to Elinor.

For a little while, she had quite forgotten where she was going and what for, but when she only recognized her stop at the last minute and scrambled out just in time, it dawned on her with terrible realization that she was going to be late for her first class. She must have missed the tram she'd intended to get, and now she could see from a church clock across the road that it was after seven. The class would already have begun.

Late! When she had wanted to appear so calm and well organized; had wanted to create a good impression on Mr Muirhead and the other students. Late already, when she didn't even

64

know where Carlyle High School was!

Of course, she found it. Found the notice board inside the entrance giving the room number for her class. Arrived at the door, flushed and breathless and, at her light knock, met Mr Muirhead himself. Smiling, thank God.

'Oh, I'm so sorry I'm late!' she burst out, but he only drew her into the classroom.

'That's quite all right. We haven't started yet – I've just been taking a roll call. Come in and find a seat.'

Thirteen

Everyone was looking at her. Or so it felt to Elinor, though with her eyes cast down as she found a seat next to another young woman, she couldn't of course be sure. Aware that Mr Muirhead was waiting for her, she tried to be as quick as possible in slipping off her hat and jacket, which he immediately came forward to hang up, and then, after taking out her exercise book and pencil, managed to snatch a look around her.

The classroom was typical of all the rooms she remembered from her schooldays: long dusty windows, bare boarded floor, maps and posters on the distempered walls, and rows of desks to seat two pupils facing the teacher's table. Squashed into the desks, regardless of height or weight, were twenty or so men and a few women,

65

all young, and none looking at Elinor, as it happened, except the girl next to her who gave her a brief smile. She was rather plain, with freckles and pale blonde hair scraped into a tight bun, and Elinor guessed she'd be very efficient. The sort that could run an office anyway, even without Mr Muirhead's help, but everyone's eyes were on him now, waiting for him to begin.

First, he told them, he'd like to stress the importance now attached to the office in modern times. 'We've moved away from the Scrooge type of office of the past, you see, when you had one clerk scratching away with a quill pen in some old ledger. Now, we have typewriters, telephones, punched card systems, all kinds of modern equipment, and staff trained to use them. Which is where you people will come in.

'It's not just big companies that will need you, because everywhere is recognizing the importance of an efficient office these days. You might find yourself working in some small shop, or maybe a hotel, a college, a school, a department store – all requiring staff who know what to do. To begin with, you may start with junior tasks, such as filing – which is not as easy as ABC, as everyone thinks, but actually quite complex and vital to finding information – but then you'll progress to carrying out other procedures, which we'll cover in this course. Any questions so far?'

Hands shot up all over the room. Could Mr Muirhead outline some of the procedures?

Certainly he could. Keeping checks on stock and supplies, keeping records, particularly of expenditure, paying and checking bills, carrying out simple accounting, liaising with staff and customers, writing reports for senior management – and that was just the start.

At the looks on their faces, Mr Muirhead laughed.

'Obviously, newcomers will not be running offices from the beginning and will receive training anyway, but this course will make sure you know what will be expected of you. If you can show that, you'll be better placed for getting a job.'

'That's all we want,' someone muttered, and there were murmurs of agreement.

Another hand went up from a young man with a shock of red hair at the front of the room.

'You talk about simple accounting – how good have we got to be at arithmetic?'

'To do well in this field, I'd say it's essential to be quite good,' Mr Muirhead told him. 'The job really calls for a logical mind as well as practical skills.'

'Lets out the lassies, eh?' the red-headed man said with a laugh, at which the girls cried, 'Shame!' and the young woman next to Elinor flushed scarlet.

'Please apologize for that remark!' she shouted across the classroom. 'My best subject at school was arithmetic, I'll have you know.'

With a glance at his list of names, Mr Muirhead said curtly, 'Mr MacLean, please do as Miss Cordiner says and apologize for a quite uncalled-for remark.'

'Only bit of fun, Mr Muirhead.'

'I'm waiting, Mr MacLean.'

The red-haired young man stood up, gravely bowed towards Miss Cordiner and said, 'So sorry, no offence meant.'

'I won't say "None taken" as I am offended,' she snapped back. 'But I accept your apology on behalf of the women in this class.'

'May I make it quite clear from the start that no kind of joking offences will be tolerated here,' Mr Muirhead declared. 'Anyone guilty of them will be shown the door. Understood?'

'Understood!' the girls cried, while the men nodded and made a few muttering noises that could be taken as assent.

'Get this all the time at work, eh?' Miss Cordiner whispered to Elinor, her colour gradually fading. 'Men thinking women can't do as well as they can?'

Is that really what I have to look forward to? Elinor wondered. Working only with women, she'd no experience of the sort of prejudice Miss Cordiner was talking about, except, of course, where votes for women were concerned. Yes, there was prejudice for you. She would have liked to ask her desk companion where she worked, except that Mr Muirhead was looking impatient and clearing his throat.

'Could we all settle down now, please, and forget this diversion? For the rest of the time this evening, I'd like to tell you about some of the methods used to keep records and to bring up information when required. It might be helpful if you take down what I put on the board here and we'll go into the detail at the next class.'

Silence fell, except for the squeak of the tutor's

68

chalk on the blackboard and the laboured breathing of some of the men poring over their notebooks. There seemed a good deal to write, a good deal to learn, but as she worked on, Elinor felt she was getting somewhere. Maybe not in the academic field she'd first planned, but on the path to a more rewarding job than being in service. For these were concrete things she was learning, facts that should stand her in good stead, and if it was perhaps too early to be sure of an end – this was, after all, early days – when the bell rang for the end of the evening class, she still put down her pen with a contented sigh.

Fourteen

'Thank you, everyone,' Mr Muirhead called, shaking chalk from his hands after cleaning the board. 'We've made a good start and I look forward to seeing you all next week.'

Miss Cordiner and Elinor, exchanging further smiles, stood up and stretched with the rest of the class.

'Pretty tight fit, these desks,' Miss Cordiner murmured. 'By the way, my name's Brenda.'

'I'm Elinor Rae. Mind if I ask, do you work in an office at the moment?'

Brenda made a face. 'Oh, yes, for my sins, I work in the office of a boys' school. No picnic, I can tell you. The whole place needs sorting out, but my boss is a man who won't let me do anything. I'm desperate to get into some big firm where I can really organize things. How about you?'

'I'm in service at the Primrose Club,' Elinor told her. 'Like you, I'm keen to move on.'

'Don't blame you!'

As they moved to collect their hats and jackets, other girls came up to congratulate Brenda for standing up to 'that' Mr MacLean. 'Cheeky devil,' one was remarking, when the cheeky devil himself joined them, pulling on his coat and grinning.

'No hard feelings?' he asked.

'As long as you behave yourself,' Brenda replied coldly.

'Oh, he will,' called Mr Muirhead, standing in the doorway, rattling his keys. 'That right, Mr MacLean?'

'Scout's honour, Mr Muirhead.'

'On your way, then.'

As the students moved into the corridor and began to depart, Brenda glanced at a little watch she took from her bag. 'Listen,' she said to Elinor, 'there's a café stays open late round here, we could go and have a cup of tea.'

'Oh, I'm sorry, I'd have liked to, but I think I should get back.'

'Maybe next week, eh?'

'Yes, I'll try.'

They were at the outer door to the school when Mr Muirhead caught up with them.

'Enjoy your first class?' he asked cheerfully.

'Apart from Mr MacLean's intervention?'

'I thought you handled that very well,' Brenda replied. 'And, thanks, I did enjoy the class.'

'I did, too,' Elinor told him.

'I'm glad.' He gave her a quick glance. 'Weren't any problems for you, were there? I mean, getting away from the club?'

'Oh, you mean, because I was late?' She blushed. 'No, no problems, it was just my father called to see me unexpectedly.'

He was not to know that saying those words, 'my father called to see me', was a really quite extraordinary experience for her, and only nodded with a smile.

'That's good. Well, I see the caretaker is waiting to boot us out — may I walk with you ladies to the tram?'

'That's all right,' Brenda replied. 'I don't take a tram; I only live up the road.'

They stood in the street in the dusk of the evening, hesitating a moment, until Brenda walked away, calling goodnight over her shoulder, to which the others called, 'See you next week!' Then Mr Muirhead looked down at Elinor.

'If you're on your way back to the Primrose, I believe we'll be taking the same tram. I live in the West End myself, or at least my mother does, and I share her flat.'

'Nice,' she commented.

'Yes, though I'll probably find a place of my own eventually. Just haven't got round to it.'

They walked in companionable silence to the tram stop, where they stood only a moment or two before their tram arrived and they climbed on, Mr Muirhead insisting on paying for Elinor's

71

ticket.

'What's a penny between friends?' he asked lightly over her protests. 'I don't think it'll break the bank.'

As they were shaken along on their short journey, she was aware of his grey eyes often on her face and racked her brains for something interesting to say, only nothing came to mind. Finally, she asked where in the West End his mother lived.

'Shandwick Place. We live over a dress shop.'

'My folks live over a shop, too. Dad's a cobbler; we live over the shop he rents.'

'And where's that?'

She hesitated, looking for his reaction.

'Friar's Wynd,' she said at last, and found no real reaction at all, apart from a polite nod.

'Here we are!' she cried, gladly rising for their stop. 'This is us.'

When they'd left the tram, he said he would see her to the club, looking surprised when she immediately said that that wouldn't be necessary.

'Thanks all the same, Mr Muirhead, but it won't take me a minute to get to the club. I'll be quite all right.'

As though she could possibly risk being seen with him outside the Primrose! There might well be someone looking out, and she could just imagine the questions that would be thrown at her when she got in, after they'd seen her with her handsome escort.

'As you wish, then,' he answered, touching his hat. 'Goodnight, Miss Rae. We'll meet again next week, I hope.'

'Oh, yes, next week – I'll be there! Goodnight, Mr Muirhead.'

Wonderfully relieved, she darted away through the traffic, knowing he was watching until she'd turned at Maule's Corner and was out of his sight. By the time she'd reached the Primrose, she knew he would be home in Shandwick Place, probably telling his mother about his class, probably not mentioning her, just as she would eventually be talking about the class, too, and not mentioning him. Thinking about him, though.

'How did it go?' asked Mattie and Gerda in their attic room, when she was back, taking off her jacket, unpinning her hat. 'Did you enjoy it?'

'Went very well. Yes, I enjoyed it. Met some interesting people.'

'Any men?' asked Mattie.

'The class is nearly all men, as it happens.'

'Aha!' cried Gerda. 'Told you, I might be signing up for night school next year.'

'Me, too,' said Mattie, as Elinor turned aside, smiling a secret smile.

Fifteen

Saturday afternoon found Elinor back at Friar's Wynd, walking with a light step through the children playing the old games she remembered playing herself – peevers, which was a sort of hopscotch, giant steps and baby steps, tig, cock a roosty – how the old days came back! Some of the boys were playing kick the can again. Hadn't that been the game Barry Howat had joined in? Said he played football, and he looked fit enough. But her thoughts were only with what she'd find at home, and how relieved her mother would be to see her.

Her father was still at work in his little shop when she looked in – with a customer, too, so that was promising. Not that Mrs Angus from one of the tenements, wearing a shabby shawl, looked as if she'd be paying out much. Elinor could hear her asking her dad if he could do anything with the ancient boots he was studying. 'All I've got,' she was saying. 'I've had to come out in just ma slippers, look. Now, see what you can do, Mr Rae, and I'll come in Monday. They'll no' be too dear, eh?'

'I'll do what I can,' Walter replied, looking over a pair of half-moon spectacles at Elinor and, to her relief, appearing pleased to see her. 'Off

74

you go, then, Mrs Angus, and I'll see you Monday. Here's my daughter coming home.'

'Wee Ellie?' Mrs Angus exclaimed, turning to look at Elinor with a smile on her worn face. 'Seems no time at all since you were playing peevers wi' Jeanie. Now you're both grown and Jeanie's married. A babbie on the way, and all.'

'Hadn't heard that!' Elinor cried. 'Will you remember me to her, Mrs Angus? Tell her I hope all goes well.'

'I surely will.' Mrs Angus, letting herself out, waved goodbye as Elinor approached her father.

'Here I am, then, Dad. I said I'd come.'

'Aye, and I'm glad to see you. You go on up and see your ma – I'll be up when I shut up shop.'

For a moment, they exchanged long, steady looks, then Elinor hurried up the stairs.

She was, of course, greeted with rapture as Hessie hugged her, then held her at arm's length to look at her, then hugged her again, and burst into tears.

'Now, didn't I tell you your dad was missing you?' she cried. 'Didn't I say he'd come round?'

'Come round in more ways than one,' Elinor answered, laughing, as she released herself and took off her hat. 'Did he tell you he came to the Primrose? Just when I was setting off for evening class, too.'

'Told me when he came back, said everything was fine. You could've knocked me over with a feather. I mean, I knew he wanted to make things up, but I never dreamed he'd go round to your club. That took some doing, for him.'

75

'So, how's he been?' asked Elinor, filling the kettle. 'The way he was when I saw him on Thursday, you'd never think he could be in a bad mood.'

'Aye, that's the way he is.' Hessie shrugged. 'Blew up a bit this morning, to be honest. Found a hole in his sock and you'd have thought it was the end of the world. Then he settled down and was all right again. But tell me about this class you've joined. I want to hear all about it.'

And of course, Hessie wasn't the only one who wanted that. When Elinor had finished giving her the details over a cup of tea, she had to repeat them all over again when Corrie came in, and then yet again when Walter came up, by which time tea was on the table and the atmosphere was the happiest she'd known at home for a long time.

'Seems funny to me, lassies going out to that sort of work,' her father remarked. 'But I suppose it's as good as being in service, as long as you take care and don't get mixed up with any fellas, eh?'

'Why, Walt, Elinor might meet some nice young man with a good job!' Hessie cried. 'She's never likely to meet any at the Primrose Club. They're all women there.'

'Any men on this new course?' Walter asked, and Elinor had to admit that there were.

'But girls as well, Dad, and I sit next to a nice young woman who could be a friend.'

'Elinor can look after herself, anyway,' Corrie put in. 'I think it's grand that she's thought of going to night school. I'm planning to go to a

76

class myself next year.'

'What next?' asked his father, but not too sharply. 'Everybody seems set on going back to school, Hessie. Looks like you and me will have to join something.'

'Dad, you could,' Elinor said seriously. 'The WEA runs all sorts of classes – history, painting – everything. And they don't cost a lot.'

But Hessie shook her head and said she'd never have the time, and Walter said he'd other things to do when he finished work. Everyone knew what those things were, but no one mentioned the Dragon or the Castle. This was a pleasant time they were all enjoying, and no one wanted to spoil it.

'The chap who takes our course actually works for the WEA,' Elinor volunteered, as they cleared the table. 'He's quite important, really, has to organize all the courses.'

'And is he nice?' asked Hessie. 'No' too strict, I mean?'

'No, no, he keeps us all in order but you couldn't call him strict. A very good teacher, as well.'

'That's grand. I'm glad you're meeting all these new people and enjoying yourself.'

'Gives you something to look forward to,' remarked Corrie.

'True,' Elinor agreed, but said no more. What she looked forward to was her own affair.

Sixteen

For the following week's class, Elinor tried so hard to make up for her previous lateness that she arrived too early. At least, that was what she thought, but when she got to the classroom, looking this time as composed as possible, it was to find Mr Muirhead already at his table, surrounded by young women. Even Brenda was there, admiring photographs of various pieces of equipment he was passing round and listening closely with the others to his descriptions – which left Elinor feeling rather taken aback. How foolish! Why shouldn't the other girls be early? She knew it was only the way they were all looking up at the tutor that annoyed her. And that was foolish, too.

Standing in the doorway, she cleared her throat, at which Mr Muirhead looked up and smiled and laid down his photographs.

'Miss Rae! Come in. I've just been showing some pictures of a mechanical calculating machine – that's the Hollerith – and other aids you might find in a large office, but I'll keep them for later, as it's time for class.'

'At least I'm no' late this time,' Elinor murmured, moving to be near Brenda again, who said that the fellows were just arriving.

78

'Sound like a herd of elephants, eh?'

True enough, the heavy footfalls of the young men all coming in together were thunderous, but at the sight of their tutor they hastily quietened down, with even Tam MacLean taking his seat and sending a grin to Brenda, which she, of course, ignored. Everyone seemed keen to listen to Mr Muirhead, who was expanding on some of the items he'd discussed the previous week, relieved perhaps that this time there were no interruptions and no need for threats.

How different evening classes were from classes at school, Elinor realized. Unlike many young pupils, adult students were keen to learn, not only because they'd paid good money for their course, but also because their learning could lead to better things. They were proof, it seemed to her, that she'd been right: education of one sort or another was the key to a better life, and the more she dwelled on it, the more passionate she felt that everyone was entitled to that better life.

When the bell rang for the end of another class, Mr Muirhead looked obviously pleased that it had gone so well. There had been plenty of questions, plenty of interest, from the girls as well as the men, for it was clear enough that they had already determined they weren't going to lag behind, and as Brenda murmured to Elinor, 'Snibs to Tam MacLean, eh?'

'I don't think we'll have any more trouble from him,' Elinor said. 'Though he'll never admit it, even if we do prove him wrong.'

'How about that cup of tea we said we'd have? Can you make it this week?'

79

'Yes, I mentioned it to the manageress and she said it'd be all right.'

'Let's go, then.'

At the outer school door, however, Mr Muirhead appeared, just as before, and asked if Miss Rae was going for her tram. Elinor and Brenda exchanged glances.

'As a matter of fact, we were just going to Rossie's café for a cup of tea,' Brenda told him, at which his face lit up.

'What a good idea! Mind if I join you? We can celebrate the beginning of the course.'

'Yes, please come,' Elinor said quickly.

'Why not?' asked Brenda.

The café, only a few minutes' walk from the high school, struck Elinor as being quite busy for what she thought of as a late hour, though perhaps it wasn't really as late as all that; she was just not used to being out and about after nine o'clock. The pubs would still be open, anyway, and that's where most of the male students from the evening classes would probably be.

Mr Muirhead had just ordered tea and sandwiches for the three of them, however, when the café door opened and several of the male students from the course walked in, led by, of all people, Tam MacLean.

'Well, well, fancy meeting you!' he cried cheerfully, disregarding the frozen looks on the faces of his tutor and Brenda. 'Never expected to see you here.'

'And we never expected to see you!' Brenda retorted. 'Thought you men would be in the pub.'

'Why, we're teetotal, aren't we, lads?' Tam cried, winking, and was all for pulling up a chair, until the men with him made him move elsewhere, obviously not wanting to join their tutor, who just as obviously would rather they didn't.

'What a thing to happen,' Brenda murmured. 'Never thought those lads would want to come in here.'

'It's a popular place after classes,' Mr Muirhead said evenly. We can't expect to keep it to ourselves.'

'Would be Tam MacLean who came, though, wouldn't it?'

'He's no' so bad,' said Elinor. 'He doesn't mean any harm, Brenda.'

'I agree,' the tutor murmured, but Elinor could tell that he wasn't thinking of Tam MacLean, only of his own regret that Tam had seen him in the café. Studying his abstracted face, it seemed to her that he was even better-looking than she'd first thought. His features were so regular, his brows so even, and a lot of women would envy that blond hair of his. No wonder his girl students liked to come in early to talk to him. No wonder she'd wanted to do that herself.

But was there some reason why he didn't want to be seen with her and Brenda? Perhaps tutors were not supposed to meet women students outside class? He's like me, she thought, worrying about being seen by other people, and felt depressed that there would probably be no more meetings with him like this one.

'I think perhaps I should be going,' she said, rising after they'd finished their sandwiches.

'Shall we settle up?'

'Don't worry, this is on me,' Mr Muirhead replied, leaping to his feet, but Brenda shook her head.

'Oh, no, thanks all the same. We like to pay our own way.'

'Look, we are not going to have three bills – that would be ridiculous.'

'All right, you pay, and we'll give you the money,' Elinor offered, at which he groaned and settled the bill, not looking happy at that, or at Tam's cheery call of 'Goodnight' as they made for the door.

'See you next week, eh?' one of the other young men shouted, and with hasty nods, Mr Muirhead, Elinor and Brenda left the café.

'I'm sorry those chaps spoiled things,' Brenda murmured, as she pressed some coins into the tutor's hand. 'But I'll be on my way. Goodnight, then, and thanks.'

'For what? Are you two some of these modern women, then? Not willing to accept a sandwich and a cup of tea from a man?'

'It's the principle of the thing,' she said seriously. 'Not that I'd say this about you, Mr Muirhead, but some men think it makes them seem superior, paying for women.'

'It's more practical than that,' he said quietly. 'Men usually have more money than women.'

'And whose fault is that?' Brenda walked off, waving. 'See you next week, then.'

'Thank God we're on our own,' Mr Muirhead murmured with feeling. 'Miss Cordiner is one tough woman. Let's go for our tram, Miss Rae.'

82

Seventeen

As they made their way to the tram stop again, Mr Muirhead said suddenly, 'Miss Rae – I called you that just now, didn't I? But I was wondering, may I say Elinor? I think you know my name is Stephen.'

She stared at him, amazed. First names – they were for relatives and close friends only. Her family, people at school, people she worked with – those were the only ones who called her Elinor. As for calling him Stephen, she couldn't imagine it.

'Out of class, of course,' he was saying quickly. 'Have to be formal there. But Elinor is such a pretty name, suits you so well.'

'Ma told me she found it in a book of names someone lent her.'

'May I use it, then?'

'If you like.' She was self-conscious, her dark eyes searching the road. 'But here's our tram!'

'And you're not going to argue over the fare, are you?'

'I'll let you win that one,' she said, managing a laugh.

'Know what I wish?' he asked, as they took their seats. 'That you'd let me take you back to the Primrose.'

She shook her head. 'I told you, there's no need.'

'No need, I'd just like to, that's all.'

'I was wondering, though – you seemed upset when Tam MacLean saw us tonight – is it wrong for you to be with us after classes?'

He hesitated. 'There's nothing wrong with tutors having a cup of tea with students in a friendly way.'

'Why did you mind Tam seeing us, then?'

'I suppose I just didn't want his jokes.'

'So, that was all right, then?'

'Yes. What's really frowned on is for a tutor to form a relationship with one of his students. I work for the WEA; I know that that can lead to complications.'

'I expect it could,' she said, suddenly feeling inexplicably low.

'Nothing I've said means I can't take you back to the Primrose,' Stephen said quietly, his eyes, as usual, fixed on her face. 'Why won't you let me?'

'Here's our stop,' she cried, rising from her seat, and as he gave her his hand, his smile was wry.

'We can still talk,' he told her as they left the tram, and in the street, touched her arm as she was turning away.

'Come on, Elinor, what's wrong with my seeing you home?'

'It's a bit like you with Tam,' she said reluctantly. 'Girls I work with might see you, and there'd be questions and teasing. The manageress might no' like it, either.'

'Might not approve? I'm perfectly respectable.'

She laughed. 'Oh, Mr Muirhead – I mean, Stephen – I know you are! No, it's just – well, you understand, eh? How it is?'

'I suppose so.' He sighed deeply, looking through the West End evening crowds towards his own street. 'I wouldn't want you to be embarrassed. We'll just say goodnight, then.'

'Goodnight, Stephen. And thank you.'

'Oh, not for that sandwich, for heaven's sake! But we'll meet again next week, I hope. You are enjoying my class, aren't you?'

'Oh, yes, it's grand. I'm just hoping I can keep up.'

'Of course you can, you're very bright.'

'I was always good at sums at school, but I'm a wee bit worried about the accounts side of things.'

'No need to worry, I'll be there to help.'

They both stood, prolonging the moment of farewell, until Elinor began to move away.

'Goodnight again, Stephen.'

'Goodnight, Elinor.'

She knew he was watching her again as she hurried across the road, and when she turned back at the corner of Maule's department store, she saw that he had not moved. She gave a quick wave and, as he waved back, went on her way, so churned inside with feelings she couldn't face that it was a relief in a way to reach the club and have a problem to solve.

The front door was locked. The area door, she knew, would have been locked by Mrs Petrie some time before, but the main door was not locked until ten. Surely it wasn't as late as that? Yet she knew she was later back this week than last. There was nothing for it but to ring the bell.

'Elinor!' It was Miss Ainslie in the doorway, her face rather serious. 'I've been wondering what had happened to you. Do you know it's almost half past ten? Come in, come in, and I'll lock up again.'

'I'm really sorry, Miss Ainslie,' Elinor said hurriedly, when the manageress had relocked the front door and they were standing in the quiet reception hall. 'I didn't realize it was so late. Some of us went to the café for a cup of tea, that's what took the time. You remember, I did ask if it'd be all right for me to go and you said I could.'

'Yes, on the understanding that you would be back by ten.' Miss Ainslie shook her head. 'But half past ten – that won't do, Elinor. Any country members staying here inform me if they wish to stay out late and that is quite in order, but I am responsible for you and the other staff. I can't have you wandering around after dark, not knowing what time you are coming back.'

'I'm very sorry, Miss Ainslie. I should have checked the time.'

Miss Ainslie's expression softened a little. 'I don't want to be hard on you. I know it isn't easy for you, as you have no watch, but there are clocks around, and I'm afraid I must ask you to be in by ten. We always managed that after the meetings, didn't we?'

Her suffragette meetings, Elinor thought, with a sigh. How much easier things were when she

86

was just attending them.

'I won't be late again,' she promised. 'Goodnight, Miss Ainslie.'

'Goodnight, Elinor.' Miss Ainslie paused. 'And the course you're doing – you're enjoying it?'

'Yes, thanks, I think it's worthwhile.'

'That's good. Well, better get to bed now. Try not to disturb Mattie and Gerda.'

Disturb Mattie and Gerda? They were both awake, waiting for her, looking at her with wide eyes, when she reached their room at the top of the house.

'Hey, what happened to you?' Gerda asked. 'You get lost, or something?'

'Bet you got stick for being late,' Mattie said with a giggle. 'Miss Ainslie would've locked the door, eh?'

'I did get ticked off,' Elinor admitted. 'Some of us just went for a cup of tea at a café near the school.' She took off her hat and jacket and began to take the pins from her hair. 'I've promised to be in by ten next week, so I think I might give the café a miss.'

'Oh, what a shame!' cried Mattie. 'It sounds nice, eh, going out to a café with friends?'

'Might have been.' Elinor, beginning to get ready for bed, gave a shrug.

If there'd been any excitement for her in having Stephen watch her the way he did, it had quite faded away by the time she finally tumbled into bed. What was the point, anyway, in getting excited? There could be no way forward for her where the tutor was concerned, for they were, both of them, surrounded by rules that would keep them apart as surely as a prison fence. Best not to think of him, then.

Easier said than done. She sighed into the darkness, listening to the steady breathing of the other maids, and knew it would be some time before she too could sleep.

Eighteen

When class night came round the following week, Elinor made a special effort to be at the school as early as possible, desperately hoping that she would be able to catch Stephen before all his other women students gathered around him. Her luck was in. When she arrived at the classroom, she found him alone.

'Elinor!' He sprang forward to greet her. 'You're early!'

'I wanted to speak to you.'

'Nothing wrong, is there?'

'No, no, it's just that I was late back last week and Miss Ainslie had to unlock the door for me. She said in future I must be in by ten – that's the rule, you see. Well, it's nine, unless we have special permission, so I couldn't expect her to give me any more time.'

'She's a bit of a stickler for rules, is she?'

'No, it's just that she says she's responsible for us girls, that's all.' Elinor kept glancing at the door, hoping no one else would join them. 'I thought I'd like to tell you, because I won't be going to the café any more. I'd have to keep watching the clock in case I was late again and I couldn't risk that.'

'I suppose not.' Stephen heaved a long, deep sigh. 'That's the end of Rossie's for us, then.'

'Needn't be for you.'

'Oh, don't worry about me. As a matter of fact, I'd just as soon not see Tam MacLean again at the café.'

'I thought you said it was all right for you to be there?'

'Yes, but as we were saying, there could be teasing, and that's not for me. I'm just sorry you're going to miss out.'

She was about to tell him she really didn't mind, when more students burst in and she moved away.

'You're nice and early,' Brenda remarked, when they were at their desks.

'Late back last week, though.'

'You didn't get into trouble?'

'Got told I'd have to be in by ten. Means there's no time for me to come to Rossie's any more.

'Oh, Elinor, that's terrible! What right have they to tell you when to come in?'

'It's usual in service to have to be in by certain times. The manageress feels responsible for us.'

'Responsible!' Brenda snorted. 'You're quite capable of being responsible for yourself, I should've thought. Just tell her you'll be back when you're ready.'

'And start looking for another job?'

Elinor's smile was rueful as Stephen called his class together and began to discuss the financial aspects of office organization, something they might not have to handle themselves for some time, but would need to understand. It was an absorbing lesson, requiring even more concentration than usual, and when the bell rang at the end of the evening, Elinor and Brenda sat back with some relief.

'Sure you don't feel like coming for a cup of tea?' Brenda asked. 'I'm sure there'd be time if we leave quickly.'

But Elinor shook her head. 'I hate having to worry.'

'I've got a watch.'

'Don't tempt me!'

They were putting on their hats and coats when Tam, followed by several young men and the rest of the girls, came up with what was for him a polite smile.

'You lassies coming over to Rossie's?'

'I have to get back,' Elinor said at once.

'Ah, no!' one of the men groaned.

'How about you then, Miss C?' Tam asked Brenda, at which she hesitated, but when one of the girls, a tall, spindly girl named Pearl, took her arm, she agreed that she would come.

'Let's away, then,' said Tam, leading his flock down the corridor, but at the outer door, he paused to look back.

'Sure you don't want to join us?' he asked Elinor, who was lagging behind.

'I have to catch the tram. Mustn't be late.'

'If you say so. Where's Mr Muirhead?'

'Still in the classroom, I think.'

'Och, I get the feeling he's no' keen on being with us anyway. Come on, let's get something to eat – I'm starving.'

As soon as his students had departed, Stephen emerged to join Elinor.

'Wait for me,' he told her. 'I'll just have a word with the caretaker, then we can go.'

At their usual tram stop, the late September air was cold around them, the evening sky already dark. Their mood, too, was dark, as fallen leaves blown by the wind rolled down the street, and they stood close, as though that might help.

'What happened to summer?' Stephen asked.

'Just a memory,' Elinor answered, holding on to her hat.

When their tram came and they were sitting together, she asked him the time and he pulled out his watch.

'Half past nine.'

'You see, there wouldn't have been time to go to the café, would there?'

'I know a little place in the West End where we might have snatched a cup of something.'

'No' worth the worry. I'll just go back to the club.'

'For God's sake!' he cried out. 'Why are things so difficult?'

She had no answer for that.

When they left the tram, he took her arm.

'Still twenty-five minutes to go. What shall we do?'

He gently put his hand against her face. 'I suppose you don't have a key to those gardens in

Primrose Square?'

'A key?' She laughed shakily. 'If only I had. But we couldn't have sat there, Stephen. Just imagine, if anyone looked out of the club and saw us there together, what would they think?'

'To hell with what they'd think.'

'It's no' so easy for me to talk like that.' She shook her head. 'Though I'd like to.'

'We could still go to Princes Street gardens,' he said softly. 'They're not busy at this time of night.'

'It's too late, I'd better go.'

'What am I thinking of, anyway?' he muttered. 'Asking you to walk with me in the gardens. Your father'd be right to knock my head off. Or this Miss Ainslie you talk about. If she's responsible for you, she'd have something to say to me.'

'As Brenda says, I'm responsible for myself!' Elinor cried. 'And I would walk with you in the gardens if I could, but it's too late. I'll have to say goodnight.'

'Look, let's think of a way to meet,' he urged. 'We want to be together, don't we? Promise me you'll think of something.'

'I will, I promise. But now I have to go.'

Once again, she left him, running to Maule's Corner, turning, waving. Once again, he watched her, before walking slowly homewards.

Back at the club, the front door was open and Miss Ainslie was in the hall, greeting Elinor with a smile.

'Well done, Elinor! No problems tonight getting in on time.'

Oh, no problems, Elinor thought on her way upstairs. No problems at all.

In spite of everything, though, her heart was light. It was true that she and Stephen were so fenced round by rules they might never be able to meet. But Stephen wanted to, didn't he? And that was something new. A wonderful man wanting to be with her. An admirer, a follower, something she hadn't even thought she wanted, but now found she wanted very much indeed. She felt like telling everyone, but knew she wouldn't tell a soul, not even Ma. Oh, certainly not Ma, who'd be sure to tell her father, and heaven knew what he would say.

Getting ready for bed, chatting to Mattie and Gerda as usual, her secret stayed firmly that, locked away for herself alone, to take out when she was able, as though it were some precious object to polish and cherish, before closing it up again.

Nineteen

As the year declined towards winter, through cold, bright October and into grey November, neither Stephen nor Elinor solved the problem of how to meet. They had their snatched moments after class when they travelled home on the tram, and their long farewells at Maule's Corner, and did once try the little café Stephen had mentioned. That, however, was a failure, for they barely had time to sit down with coffee before Elinor was asking about the time, and Stephen was groaning.

'Why do you worry so about your manager-ess?' he asked, searching Elinor's face with the grey eyes she so much admired. 'I mean, what's the worst that can happen if you do get back late? She gives you the sack and you find another job? Well, why not?'

'I don't want another job – I mean, in service. Unless I can find something better, I want to stay at the Primrose. It's much better than being in a household; Miss Ainslie is good to us, and ... well, I like the gardens.'

'Even though you've no key?'

'I can still see them.' Elinor was putting on her gloves, getting ready to leave. 'And if you'd ever lived in Friar's Wynd, you'd know what it means to see a garden.'

'I understand,' he said quietly. 'But if you get an office job, you'll have to leave the gardens here.'

'I know, but I won't forget them; I'll still see them when I can.'

He nodded. 'Ah, well, we'd better go.'

Outside, though, on the pavement still filled with passers-by, he made her stop her hurried walk and return his gaze.

'You promised me you'd think of something, but here we are, unable to go for a meal and talk and get to know each other as we should.' He ran a hand over his brow. 'It's getting me down, Elinor. You must feel there's something special between us.'

'Yes,' she whispered, knowing what he said was true, scarcely daring to believe it.

'You feel it, too?'

'I do.'

'And yet, we get nowhere. Look, we can't talk here; I'd better see you on your way.'

It was the following week, when they left the tram that he again suggested they might just walk for a little while in Princes Street Gardens, which were so close to hand and so shadowy that no one would see them. He promised they wouldn't stay long.

'We just need to be alone, don't we?' he whispered urgently. 'I mean, being all the time with other people, it's a form of torture. Yet it seems impossible to get away from them.'

'Let's go to the gardens, then, though there might be people there, too, you know.'

'Not at night, and as I say, if there are people around, they won't see us.' He seemed strung up, on edge, as he took her arm. 'You're sure you're happy about this?'

She nodded, as excited as he, and together they made their way into the West Princes Street Gardens; by day, filled with strolling visitors taking in the park-like atmosphere, looking at the statues of famous Scots, listening to the band, but now, of course, dark and quiet. Not completely empty, though. Elinor was sure there must be other couples around somewhere. She decided not to try to see them.

'The thing is, I feel guilty,' Stephen was murmuring. 'Asking you to walk with me here at this time of night. What would your parents say?'

'I'm a grown-up; I've a right to walk with you if I want to.'

'You know that's not how it is. Girls – they have to be protected.'

'Protected?' Elinor smiled. 'Have you seen the way some folk live in the tenements? Girls there have to learn to protect themselves.'

'Have you had to do that?' he asked quickly, but she shook her head.

'No, I've been lucky.'

'There have been men in your life, though?'

'No. No men.'

'Come, there must have been. Someone who looks like you – you're telling me there've been no admirers?'

'Stephen, when would there have been men in my life? When I left school, I went straight into service where the only man was the lawyer married to my employer and he never even looked at me. Then I moved to a women's club.' In the semi-darkness, Elinor's smile was now gently teasing. 'So, you see, no men.'

'No men.' He drew her slowly into his arms. 'And no kisses?'

'No,' she whispered. 'No kisses.'

He held her close. 'Would you mind if I kissed you now?'

'You're asking?'

It all seemed strange to her, not what she'd expected from this closeness in the darkness of the gardens. Did men usually ask before they kissed a woman? It wasn't what she'd heard. But perhaps men like Stephen did. Men who felt

96

guilty if they walked with a girl and her father didn't know?

'No, I'm not asking!' he suddenly cried, and kissed her on the mouth, holding her shoulders with his hands, making the kiss long and at first gentle, then stronger, until he finally let her go and they stood together, breathing hard.

So this was what kissing meant? This was why men wanted it and girls liked it, Elinor was thinking, for it stirred up so much feeling, so much pleasure. She knew, of course, what it could lead to, although only in theory, for it was true what she'd told Stephen: there had been no men in her life, and certainly no kissing. And certainly not what could follow kissing, either, though she knew about that, too. Had seen the lassies with their bairns, sometimes with wedding rings, sometimes not. So, in a way, she felt herself experienced. But this was her first kiss.

'You minded?' Stephen asked anxiously. 'That I kissed you?'

'No.' She put her fingers to her lip. 'I knew you would.'

'Oh, God, I knew I would, too. Look, I'm sorry.'

'Stephen, there's no need to be sorry. I didn't mind, I liked it, but now I have to go, eh?'

'Yes, of course. Of course, you have to go. The last thing I want is for you to be late.'

They began to hurry from the gardens, hoping, in their moment of intense feeling, that no one would see them, or, at least, would take no notice of them, and no one did. Together, they ran across the road to Maule's Corner, but when

97

Stephen sighed and said he supposed he'd have to let her go on by herself, Elinor told him not to look so glum.

'I've thought of a way we could meet.'

'You don't mean it! How, Elinor, how?'

'Well, you know I've been going home twice a month on free Saturday afternoons? It suddenly came to me that I could see you on one of 'em. I could say I had to go shopping, or something. Then we could meet, have tea, walk somewhere?'

'Oh, that'd be wonderful!' His eyes were shining, his hand in hers, pressing hard. 'Oh, Elinor, what a terrific girl you are! When will it be? When can we meet?'

'I'll tell you at the next class,' she promised, and for a long moment they stood, holding hands, exchanging looks, until she pulled herself free and they both walked fast away, feeling, as their feet touched the old pavement flags, that they were walking on air.

Twenty

'Oh, my, where's the jug, then?' asked Mrs Petrie, fixing her eyes on Elinor coming into the kitchen on a Saturday afternoon two weeks later. Lunch was over and Maisie was toiling over the washing-up, as Vera scrubbed the table and Mrs Petrie herself sat drinking tea by the window.

98

Elinor, in her dark brown winter coat and large fawn hat trimmed with ribbon, stopped and stared.

'What jug, Mrs Petrie? What d'you mean?'

'The cream jug, of course! Don't tell me you've no' seen yourself? You look just like the cat that's been at the cream – is that no' true, Vera? Sal?'

Sal, looking in from the scullery, blushed, nodded and retreated. Vera, setting down her brush, gave a thin smile.

'Aye, you're looking very happy, Elinor.'

'Very pleased with herself, I'd say!' cried Mrs Petrie. 'All this just to see your folks, then?'

'It is my Saturday afternoon off,' Elinor replied smartly. 'I suppose I can look happy if I like?'

'You've looked happy for days, is what I've noticed. Got a secret admirer, then?'

'No!' Elinor cried, a flush staining her cheeks. 'Look, I'm off. See you tonight.'

'Well, don't be late. There's plenty work waiting.'

'No need to tell me.'

Elinor, closing the back door with unnecessary force, ran up the area steps with her brows drawn together and her mouth set in a straight, angry line. Oh, trust Mrs Petrie to try to spoil things, eh? Couldn't let a lassie enjoy her time off without putting her spoke in, doing her best to cause trouble. Well, she wasn't going to spoil this precious afternoon with Stephen, that was for sure. No, no, she must control her feelings, stop frowning, look happy – for she *was* happy, radiantly happy, to be snatching a few hours off with the man who would be waiting for her at Maule's Corner. The nicest man in the world, in Elinor's view. Aye, and probably would be, too, in Mrs Petrie's, if only she could see him.

How wonderful it would have been, if she and everyone else could have seen him, if he need no longer be a secret. But it wasn't possible. At least, not yet. For now, it was best to keep him hidden, safe from comment, disapproval, and maybe envy. Yes, for now, that was the best thing to do.

By the time she arrived at the familiar corner, she had smoothed out her brow and relaxed her lovely mouth, so that when she saw him waiting for her, leaping forward, in fact, to greet her, she had no worries that he would need to ask her what was wrong. For nothing was wrong, everything was amazingly right now that they were together again.

As he took her hands and looked at her with shining grey eyes, she gave a little inward sigh. On that cold day, he was wearing a fine dark overcoat and trilby hat, which he had just replaced after sweeping it off at sight of her, and it seemed to her, as it so often did, a thing of wonder that anyone like him should be waiting for her. Yet mixed with that wonder was a little question. Why shouldn't he wait for her? Why was it the way of the world that it should be so surprising? She knew it was, though, and as they stepped aside from the Saturday shoppers, her question died and her wonder remained.

'Oh, Elinor,' he was whispering, 'I was so afraid you might not come, might not be able to

100

come, I mean. That somebody'd said you could not have the time, or something...'

'Nothing would have stopped me from coming,' she said firmly. 'But tell me, where are we going? I've to be back by six.'

'Six? My poor Cinderella.' He laughed, tucking her arm in his. 'Oh, but I wish you were Cinderella, and then you'd have till midnight. Where are we going? To the station; we're catching a train.'

'A train? Why, Stephen, you know we haven't got time for train journeys!'

'We're only going to Colinton, takes fifteen minutes, or less. There's country there and a nice place for tea, so let's be quick and get the tram to Waverley.'

'I've never been to Colinton,' she told him as they ran for a tram. 'Is there really country there?'

'You bet. Why, it's a village. Not part of the city at all, though they say that'll be coming.'

'I'd love to see it; love to see some real country.' As a tram rolled up and they took their seats, Elinor's smile lit her face. 'Nearest I get to it is the square, but then I love that, too.'

'This'll be different from the square, I promise you. It used to be our favourite day out, to go to Colinton, before my father died.'

'You've never told me about your father.'

'We've had so little chance to talk at all.' His eyes were serious. 'But today, I want to learn all about you.'

Her gaze fell. 'Nothing much to know about me, Stephen.'

101

'Now, why do people always say that?' He leaped up. 'Here we are – here's Waverley. Let's hope we don't have to wait too long for a train.'

They were in luck. As soon as Stephen had bought the tickets and they'd found the platform, their little train came steaming in and they were aboard, Elinor as excited as though she was going to London at least, and Stephen indulgently smiling.

'Don't tell me you haven't been on a train before,' he murmured, as they took their seats in a compartment with only one other passenger, an elderly man reading a newspaper.

'Of course I have!' she cried. 'We did a trip from school to North Berwick, to see the sea.'

'Never went on holiday anywhere?'

She only looked at him, her brows raised, and he coloured a little.

'Sorry, probably wasn't possible.'

'You're right. But this'll be sort of a holiday, eh? Seeing somewhere new? And the country?'

'Wish it could have been longer.'

'I'm lucky it's happening at all.'

Certainly, their journey was short enough, for they'd hardly settled into their seats when they were rising again, and a porter was calling out, 'Colinton!'

'We'll take the lane away from the village,' Stephen told her on the windy little station platform. 'I thought we'd walk a bit first, then come back to the teashop. What do you think?'

'Oh, yes, I want to see some grass and trees. Cows as well!'

'When we came with my dad, we always went

102

to the Dell, where you can see the Water of Leith and the weir, but there are always people there, and we want to be alone, don't we?'

He took her arm, guiding her away from the steep main street of the village towards a lane that wound away into open country, explaining that she would get her chance to see a cow or two in the fields, and horses, too: they would be passing a little farm very soon.

'A farm?' she cried, charmed. 'Oh, Stephen!'

It was all he could do to drag her away from the farm premises when they came to them, for she was exclaiming over the chickens, the milk churns, the tackle lying everywhere, the dogs barking as she looked through the gates, and the farmer's wife at the washing line.

'No, no, Elinor, we can't stop,' he cried desperately. 'We need time alone. You want it, too, don't you? We want to be together.'

'Oh, yes, I want to be with you,' she told him. 'It's just – well, you don't see many farms in Edinburgh, eh?'

'But there are the cows you wanted to see, in that field there. I daresay there'll be horses further on.' He pressed her arm against his side. 'I hope you'll spare me a look, too, from your beautiful eyes.'

She laughed delightedly, until he took her hand and led her into a little copse of trees at the side of the lane, where she became serious, following his mood, which was not just serious, but intense. They didn't speak, just went into each other's arms and stood for a moment. Then began to kiss.

It was wonderfully sweet, that kissing. Elinor

had been expecting it, knew that she wanted it, and responded wholeheartedly. But then it began to dawn on her that Stephen was holding back, that his kisses and caresses could have been much more passionate, much stronger, except that he seemed afraid.

Afraid? He was afraid of her? Or of himself? Her great eyes on his face were filled with more wonder.

'I won't break,' she whispered. 'Don't worry about me.'

'How quick you are!' He shook his head, running his hand over his brow. 'You don't need to be told anything.'

'I want you to kiss me,' she said softly. 'It's why we're here. Why we wanted to be alone.'

'Yes, but I think we should go back now.' He straightened up, putting on his hat which he had thrown aside. 'We'll go and have tea, shall we?'

'You don't want to kiss me any more?'

'Elinor, I want it too much. Look, let's go. We have to think of the time, you know.'

She had to hurry to keep up with him as he strode back down the lane, but by the time they'd passed the farm again, he'd slowed down and seemed calmer. She took his arm.

'I know what kissing can lead to,' she told him. 'Girls like me, where we live, we learn. But it doesn't have to happen, eh? What I'm saying is, there's no need to worry.'

'I do worry, that's the point. Your parents don't know you're with me, do they? What would they say if they knew?'

'Why, they'd understand,' she said uneasily,

wondering if they would. Stephen was not the sort of young man they'd have expected her to get to know, maybe not the sort they'd trust, because of his position as a professional man. Where'd be her hope for a future with him? they'd be asking, and she wouldn't be able to tell them. She wasn't, in any case, thinking about the future.

'Let's leave worrying about them now,' she said quickly. 'Let's just keep on as we are.'

'Meeting in secret?'

'Well ... have you said anything about me to your mother?'

'Not yet. Only because you seem so anxious for other people not to know about us.'

'I thought you were anxious, too,' she said evenly.

He flushed and bit his lip.

'You're remembering what I said, I suppose.'

'About tutors and students? Yes, well, you did say it was frowned on, forming friendships.'

'I know, I know, I did say that. Look, everything will be fine when the course is over at the end of March. Then we won't be tutor and student.' He was relaxing, managing a smile. 'Elinor, we can be just what we want to be.'

'So, for now, like I said, we keep on as we are?'

'For now.' He looked along the narrow village street. 'See, the café's just here. Shall we have tea, then?'

'Oh, yes, please!'

'Are you hungry? I am. Must be this wonderful country air.'

Twenty-One

They were given the last free table in the tea room for, it being Saturday, the café was busy, but it was a table they might have chosen anyway, being in a corner and not too close to any other.

'Now you can tell me more about yourself,' Stephen was beginning with some satisfaction, when a tall young waitress appeared with the menu.

'Scones, teabread, assorted fancies, pound cake,' she reeled off, 'and mince pies.'

'Mince pies?' Elinor repeated. 'It's no' Christmas yet.'

'We always serve mince pies in December,' the waitress said firmly. 'Folk like 'em.'

'May we just have tea and buttered scones?' Stephen asked. 'And cakes afterwards? That all right, Elinor?'

'Oh, yes, grand,' she answered, but as soon as the waitress had gone, she turned to Stephen and groaned.

'Mince pies! I've just remembered, I promised to make some for our do.'

'What "do"?'

'Why, we break up next week, and we all said we'd bring something for our party. You said it was what all the classes did.'

'Oh, God!' He put his hand through his fair hair. 'I did say that, I remember, but it had gone right out of my mind that we'd be breaking for Christmas next week.' He gave an apologetic laugh. 'But you see what you've done to me, Elinor. There's nothing in my head except you.'

'No, no, when you're taking our class, all that's in your head is your work. Teaching us what we should know.'

'I'm glad you think so, or I'd be feeling guilty.'

'No more guilt.'

As the waitress brought their tea and scones and she began to busy herself with the tea things, Elinor shook her head at him, smiling, and he smiled back.

'Come on, now, talk,' he whispered. 'As I keep saying, I want to know all about you.'

'And I keep saying, there's nothing much to say.'

She passed him a scone, took one herself.

'You know my dad mends shoes for a living, and we live in Friar's Wynd. Well, my grand-father was a cobbler, too, and Dad learned his trade from him, but he never had his own shop and neither has Dad. Grandad's dead now. So are all the grandparents. We've very few relatives at all.'

'But you've a brother, you once said?'

'Cormack – we always call him Corrie. He's two years younger than me, works at the tyre factory but wants to be a draughtsman. Thinks he might go to night school.'

'I can give you all the information,' Stephen

said eagerly. 'He sounds just the sort of chap we want to help.'

He covered her hand on the table.

'You sound a very happy family, Elinor.'

She bent her head over her plate. 'Things are better than they were,' she said in a low voice.

'How d'you mean?'

'I don't want to say too much, but Dad – well, he's no' the easiest of men. Still isn't, though Ma says he's mellowed a bit. We're getting on better now.'

Stephen's hand on hers tightened, his eyes sharpening.

'Elinor, he – doesn't...?'

'No, no.' She met his gaze. 'Ma said we were lucky, he's never been one for the belt. Just ... well ... likes his own way. Got a bit of a temper. Like some more tea?'

'Please.' He sat back, sighing. 'Things can be difficult, I know, for some families.'

'Cakes?' asked the waitress, placing a loaded cake stand on the table. 'I can recommend the macaroons.'

'Your turn,' Elinor said quietly, when the girl had gone. 'Let me hear about you.'

'Supposing I say, like you, there's not much to tell?'

'You could tell me about your father, anyway. I'm sorry he died.'

'Yes, it was a tragedy for us. He worked in a bank, thought he might rise to manager.' Stephen passed the cake stand to Elinor. 'Then he caught a chill, it turned to pneumonia, and he never survived the crisis.'

'The crisis?' She shivered. 'I know about that. I've heard of folk in the tenements going through it.'

'Comes after about six days. Everything depends on how the temperature works. If it goes down, you recover.' Stephen shrugged. 'If it keeps going up, you don't. Father didn't.'

'How old were you?' she asked gently.

'Twelve. My sister, Jeannie, was nine. It was hardest for Mother, of course, because she'd to carry on, bringing us up on very little money. She sold the house, moved to a flat, did a wonderful job, managing. An uncle paid for our schooling, I went to university, learned something about business in a city broker's firm, but then when the WEA started up, I got interested. Thought it was just what was needed to help poor folk learn what they'd missed.'

'Like me!' Elinor cried. 'Oh, you've got the right ideas, Stephen!'

'The rest you know. There's really no more to tell. Jeannie married and went to live in Canada; I'm still in Mother's flat, looking round for my own house, working for the WEA.' He leaned forward. 'And very happy to be here with you, Elinor.'

'No' for much longer,' she told him, suddenly rising. 'I can see a clock over there and it's time for me to go. I mustn't be late.'

'I'll get the bill, but don't worry. You'll be back in time, I promise you. Just wish you hadn't always to be watching the clock.'

'Everybody watches the clock, Stephen, if they go to work.'

109

'Not the way you have to watch it, though.' He helped her on with her coat, watched her pull on her gloves, adjust her hat. 'Forever worrying about being late.'

'Nothing I can do about it, is there? If I want to keep my job?'

'Aren't you looking for something better? You're wasted, doing what you do.'

'You really think I could get something different?' Her eyes glinted. 'Because of your course?'

'Because you're you,' he said quietly. 'You have a good brain, Elinor, only you've never had the chance to use it. Like a lot of people, you're held back by circumstances.'

'Exactly what I say, Stephen,' she told him eagerly. 'Folk need chances, they need education. That's what we should work for.'

'I think you're already on your way. Here's the girl – I'll pay the bill.'

In the train moving fast towards Waverley, Elinor, feeling so reassured by what Stephen had said to her, had quite forgotten to think about the time until he told her again that she need have no worries.

'It's as I said, we've plenty of time, you'll be back well before six.'

'It's been a lovely day, Stephen, I'll never forget it.'

'Why, it's going to be the first of many, isn't it?' His smile was uneasy. 'We're not saying goodbye, you know. We'll meet for our "do", won't we?'

'But then there'll be no more classes till January, and on days off, I'll have to see the

110

family. Ma's looking forward to it.'

He lowered his eyes and for some moments was silent, as the train continued on its way. 'How are we going to get through?' he asked at last.

'I don't know. Things are difficult.'

'What about Christmas, then? Surely, we'll meet over Christmas? Or do you have to spend every minute with your family?'

She sat, thinking, as the train began to slow down for its platform at Waverley. 'Maybe Christmas Eve, we could meet? Miss Ainslie always closes the club on Christmas Day and Boxing Day, and we take it in turns to have Christmas Eve off. This year, I'm the lucky one.'

'I'll say!' Stephen cried delightedly. 'That sounds wonderful! Why didn't you tell me about it before?'

'I've only just thought of it. Look, we're stopping. So, what time is it, Stephen?'

'Oh, to hell with the time! Let's look forward to Christmas Eve!'

'Our "do" first,' she reminded him. 'And I've got to think of a way of making the wretched mince pies.'

'One thing I needn't worry about,' he told her with a laugh, as they joined the crowds leaving the station. 'But now I know when we're going to meet again, I don't feel so worried, anyway. Something to look forward to – that's what I like, don't you?'

She didn't reply that things to look forward to had been rather rare in her life until then, only said she'd certainly be looking forward to their next meeting, mince pies or no mince pies. At which he took her hand.

'Elinor, if we weren't in the middle of Princes Street, I'd kiss you. In fact, I might, anyway, and to hell with anyone watching.'

Of course, he didn't, but when they reached Maule's Corner where they must part, she told him, teasingly, that if he was thinking about kissing, he'd better prepare himself for the party next Thursday. There were rumours that some of his students were bringing mistletoe.

'Oh, no!' he groaned. 'Maybe I should be indisposed.'

'No, no, you're our tutor. Besides, you have to bring the lemonade.'

'And you mustn't forget the mince pies.'

'As though I could!'

Their banter was light-hearted, but as she moved away, waving once, Stephen's eyes were so tender on her, she knew she was looking ridiculously happy and had to straighten her smiling mouth as she went down the area steps to the kitchen.

Preparations for dinner were in full swing and Mrs Petrie was stirring pans and shouting orders like the captain of a ship, while Vera and Sal were scuttling about and Mattie and Ada were hurrying away with cutlery for the dining room, Gerda following with the glasses. Now was not the time to ask if she might have some oven space on Thursday, Elinor decided, but when *would* be the right time, she couldn't imagine. At least no one was taking particular notice of her; no one would spot the happiness she was trying to conceal.

As she ran upstairs to change into her uniform, she let herself relax, look the way she felt, and when she studied her face in the bedroom mirror, was pleased with what she saw. True, she didn't know where this special relationship with Stephen would go, but it wasn't yet time to worry about that. Even if it went nowhere, she could enjoy it for now.

Twenty-Two

On the afternoon of the class party, Elinor had a piece of luck. Mrs Petrie graciously agreed that she could have stove time to make her mince pies, as long as she told Miss Ainslie, brought her own mincemeat, and made the time up.

'Ma's given me the mincemeat and I've already spoken to Miss Ainslie,' Elinor replied. 'She said I needn't make the time up.'

'Did she indeed?' Mrs Petrie's eyes snapped. 'I don't know how you lassies do it, but anything you want, you get, eh? Talk about twisting Miss Ainslie round your little finger!'

'Och, she's no' as easy as all that!' Mattie cried. 'She doesn't let us just do as we like, Mrs Petrie.'

'Lets you get away with murder, you mean.' Mrs Petrie sniffed. 'Anyway, Elinor, you can make your pies but you'll have to manage without me. I've to be away to the doctor's about my knee, though he'll just give me more of his horrible ointment, eh?'

'I'm sorry to hear your knee's bad again,' Elinor said with genuine sympathy, though at the same time, her heart was singing. Mrs Petrie to be out? Not hanging over her, watching her every move? That was bliss, that was.

'Don't worry, I'll manage,' she said cheerfully. 'And I'll clear everything up, leave it neat as a pin.'

'You'd better, but Vera's going to keep an eye on you anyway, before she starts the afternoon teas. That right, Vera?'

'Right, Mrs Petrie,' Vera sighed.

As soon as Mrs Petrie had departed for her afternoon appointment and Sal had washed and cleared away the lunch dishes, Elinor and Vera set to work.

'Here's your flour and lard,' Vera announced, clearing space on the table. 'Sugar, if you want to add a wee bit to the mix, and your ma's mince-meat. This is your bowl and rolling pin, your pastry cutters and baking tins – you'll need to grease them first. Now, which oven d'you want to use? The stove, or the gas?'

'Oh, Lordie, which is best?'

'Well, Mrs Petrie hates the gas, but then she's the only one knows how to get the stove just right, eh?'

'Thought you did, Vera!' Elinor cried worriedly. 'I'm counting on you!'

'Afraid it's all guesswork with me. Let's go for the gas, eh? I'll light it for you.'

114

'As long as you don't blow us all up!' Sal called. 'I'm terrified o' that gas, so I am!'

'Come on, it'll be fine.' Vera, striking a match, stooped to light the despised gas oven in the corner. 'There, by the time that's hot, your pies'll be ready to go in, Elinor. You do know how to make pastry, eh?'

'Sure I do!' Elinor retorted, though she wasn't in fact sure at all, not having had much practice. 'You just rub in the fat and add some water, eh?'

'Let's see you do it, then.'

Whether it was beginner's luck or not, Elinor's pastry turned out well. The gas cooker did its job, with Vera keeping an eye on progress, and it wasn't long before Elinor was hanging over a fine collection of cooling mince pies and feeling absurdly pleased with herself.

'Aye, you've done a grand job,' Vera said, shaking a little sugar over the pies. 'Mrs Petrie's eyes'd drop out if she could see these. Thinks nobody can bake but herself, you ken.'

'Must thank you, Vera, for all your help. Couldn't have managed without you.'

'That's all right. We'll just get Sal to do the washing-up, eh? This place looks like it's been in a snowstorm!'

Elinor, however, insisted on clearing up herself, and it was only when all was tidy enough to pass inspection by Mrs Petrie's eagle eye that the maids sank down at the kitchen table for a cup of tea. Sal had run out with the upstairs letters for posting, but would soon be back, and the others would be coming down for their break.

'Wanting to see how you got on,' Vera said with

a laugh. 'Amazed you're baking, eh?'

'So am I! I was regretting ever offering, but now I'm glad I did.'

'Aye, the pies are first rate.' Vera hesitated a moment. 'Did you make 'em to please your young man, then?'

'My young man?' Elinor stared. 'What young man?'

'Why, the young man at this class you go to, of course. Everybody knows you've got one, Elinor.'

'Well, I really don't know how!' Elinor retorted, her face glowing red. 'I've never said I had a young man.'

'Why, you were seen with him, eh? No point denying it.'

'Who? Who saw me?'

'Ada, last Saturday afternoon, at Maule's Corner. It was her time off as well as yours, remember, and she was going to meet her Donald. She said your young man looked ever so nice, quite the gentleman, and seemed so pleased to see you. Then you both ran off, she couldn't see where.'

'Surprised she didn't follow us,' Elinor said coldly. 'Seemingly, we're no' allowed any private life here, with folk spying on us all the time.'

'Ada wasn't spying. She just happened to see you. And there's always somebody to see you, if you don't want to be seen, eh?'

'I suppose so.' Elinor gave a long sigh. 'Oh, I'm sorry, I shouldn't have called Ada a spy. But she needn't have told everybody.'

'She didn't tell everybody. I mean, Miss Ains-

lie doesn't know, and neither does Mrs Petrie.'
Vera grinned. 'You'll be giving thanks for that.
But you know the rest of us are interested, Elinor.
We're pleased for you. It's nice for you to have a
young man. Lord knows, it's what we all want,
eh?'

'It's just that ... well, I don't know what's going
to happen. Whether there's a future for us or not.
I was wanting to keep things quiet until I knew.'

'I'm sorry, then. Maybe we shouldn't have got
to know your secret. But I'm sure there's no need
to worry. Ada said the nice young man looked
really smitten.' Vera stood up and began to gather
their tea things together. 'I'll just get you some
cake boxes to put your pies in – you can bring
'em back tomorrow.'

Twenty-Three

Knowing that all the girls she worked with now
knew about Stephen made more difference to
Elinor even than she might have imagined. It
wasn't just meeting their excited eyes at teatime
that upset her – after all, with Mrs Petrie there,
going on about her new knee ointment, no one
would say anything; she needn't worry about
that. No, what really hurt was the fact that
Stephen was no longer her special secret, but
someone she shared with others. And those
others would all be wondering and guessing how

far her affair might go, which was the last thing she wanted when she didn't even know herself.

As she changed to go to the class, putting on her best shirtwaist blouse in honour of the party, she felt a great searing feeling of regret that this change had come, for whatever Stephen's reaction might be when she told him about it, things could never be quite the same again.

Because of his job, his responsibilities, he hadn't wanted others to know about their association any more than she had, and now that some did know, there would be extra worry for them both. After all, she hadn't yet told her folks that she was seeing her tutor out of class, and at the back of her mind, there was always anxiety over what her dad might say. He might just go back to his old ways and forbid her to see Stephen again. Might even throw her out, as he had done before. And only to think of risking that kind of trouble again made her feel surrounded by a cold, hostile wind.

I'd better tell Ma, she decided, once again hurrying to the class, this time carrying boxes of her precious mince pies under her arm. I'll ask her what she thinks Dad would say. It would be good to tell her, anyway. Never before had Elinor really had secrets from her.

As soon as she entered the high school that last evening of the Christmas term, she sensed the different atmosphere about the place. Everywhere was decorated with children's paper chains and streamers, and the students in the classrooms were all sporting paper hats and laughing and teasing, even though their tutors

118

were desperately trying to keep order on the last festive evening. This was a time to have some fun, obviously.

It was the same in Stephen's room, of course, where Pearl was placing a paper hat on his fair head, while Tam and others, even Brenda, laughed and clapped, and his desk was already piled with a great spread of sandwiches, sausage rolls, small savouries, cakes and bottles of lemonade.

'Heavens, I'm no' late, am I?' Elinor cried, her eyes on Stephen, who was doing his best to seem at ease.

'No, no, come in, we're early, Miss Rae,' he answered, pulling himself away from the students around him and snatching off his paper hat. 'We were just about to begin the lesson.'

'Ah, have a heart, Mr Muirhead!' Tam shouted, taking Elinor's boxes from her arms and opening one to inspect the contents. 'See these grand mince pies Elinor's brought? You canna expect us to have a lesson with all this food driving us crazy!'

'The rule is, we do some work first,' Stephen returned firmly. 'Don't worry, we'll have time to tuck in pretty soon, but now I want you all to take your seats. I'm going to talk more about accounting methods.'

Slowly, but obediently, the class took their places and even made a show of writing in their notebooks as Stephen doggedly continued with his instruction, but there were sighs of relief all round when he finally laid down his chalk, rubbed down the blackboard, and said, with a grin, 'Let the festivities begin, then. Anybody got

119

paper cups for the lemonade? And paper plates for the sandwiches? My word, this is a splendid show you've all put on!'

In dived the students and away went the party food, with everything being admired. Crackers were pulled, hats put on, small contents examined, and under the cover of so much noise and laughter, Stephen was able to approach Elinor and give her a polite smile that didn't match the look in his eyes.

'May I taste one of your mince pies?' he asked. 'I can see they look wonderful.'

'Don't know how I did it, but they've turned out well.'

She picked one out and gave it to him, watching him take a bite and pretend to swoon over its taste, all the time looking at her.

'We'll be taking the tram as usual?' he whispered.

She glanced round, before turning her gaze back to him.

'Hope so. But the others won't be going to the café tonight after all this; they might be on the tram, too.'

'Don't worry, they won't be going home so early.'

'Hey, you two,' said Tam, joining them. 'No more talking, I've got some mistletoe. Don't look like that, Mr Muirhead! What's a kiss at Christmas time?'

'I'm not so sure the WEA plans for kisses in their classes at any time,' Stephen told him. 'And, remember, I have to make sure you're not making a nuisance of yourself to the young

120

women here.'

'Me, a nuisance?' Tam asked with an injured air. 'Why, these lassies expect to be kissed at Christmas parties, Mr Muirhead, just like when they were bairns. But in fact we're all grown-ups, remember.'

'But I'm responsible for you,' Stephen added seriously, then suddenly relaxed and laughed. 'Oh, go on then, take your mistletoe round, but I'll be watching, to see if anyone complains.'

'Watching?' cried Pearl, sliding up to snatch the mistletoe from Tam's hand. 'Why, you'll be joining in, Mr Muirhead, won't you?'

And before he'd had time to make a reply, she'd kissed him on the cheek, then stood back smiling, while Elinor also smiled, if a little painfully, and Tam applauded, grinning.

'Well done, Pearl, you've set the ball rolling. Now, where's Brenda, then?'

'Oh, no, you don't!' Brenda cried, backing away, but when Tam kissed her quite gently on the brow, she only flushed a little and said no more.

'Now, if you've all finished playing around, can we get down to clearing up?' Stephen cried, when the little mistletoe session had come to an end. 'We've been asked to leave everything tidy and I've some bags here for the bottles and paper plates. Any food left, you must take away with you.'

'Are you joking, sir?' John Andrews, one of Tam's friends, asked. 'There's nothing left at all.'

'Except for one sausage roll,' Dickie Rowan, another crony, said, taking it. 'Sorry, folks!'

'At least you won't need to fill up at the café tonight,' Brenda remarked, but Tam said that oh, yes, they would. Why, they wanted nice hot tea, didn't they? They'd only had cold lemonade.

'Sure you don't want something stronger?'

'No, it's the café for us tonight, so's we can all say goodbye till after New Year. Who's coming?'

'Oh, do come tonight,' Pearl urged Elinor. 'You, too, Mr Muirhead.'

But Elinor said she must still get back, and Stephen said he must, too. It had been a wonderful party, though.

'Thanks for being such good students!' he called, as they left the classroom as tidy as possible. 'And a merry Christmas and a happy New Year to you all.'

'The same to you, sir, the same to you!' his students cried, moving out into the cold night. 'See you in 1914!'

'Wonder what that will bring?' Brenda murmured, but no one answered, and after giving Elinor a quick hug, she hurried after the others towards the café, leaving Elinor, with Stephen, to set off for the tram.

Twenty-Four

'Here, let me carry those boxes for you,' Stephen said cheerfully. 'My word, I wish they'd still been full of your mince pies! Went well tonight, didn't it?'

'Very well. They're a nice crowd of folk.'

'They are.' He gave her a quick sideways glance. 'Noticed you were quite popular when the mistletoe came out.'

'So were you. Once the lassies had seen Pearl being cheeky.'

'You didn't kiss me, though.'

'No, and you didn't kiss me.'

'I thought I'd better not. Anyway, we don't need mistletoe to kiss each other, do we?'

As they reached the tram stop and stood together braving the wind, Elinor's great dark eyes searched his face.

'I've something I'd better tell you, Stephen.'

He was instantly alert, though he only said lightly, 'Something good?'

She shook her head. 'The girls at the club know about us. Ada, one of the maids, saw us at Maule's Corner on Saturday.'

'Oh.' He moved her boxes from one arm to the other. 'Well, I suppose it had to happen. It's not the end of the world.'

'You're glad it wasn't somebody from the class?'

'That could have made things difficult.'

'For you. Now they're just difficult for me.'

'They've told your Miss Ainslie?'

'No, but now they know about you, they'll be wondering and asking and teasing – that's what girls are like. Seeing things that aren't there.'

'Here's our tram,' sighed Stephen.

Sitting together, he slid his hand over hers, while holding on to her boxes on his knee with the other.

'Do you think what we have isn't really there, then?'

'No! Of course I don't think that!'

'What then? What do we have?'

'Well, I think we like being with each other. When I'm with you, I'm happy.'

'Exactly how I feel,' he said in a low voice, his eyes never leaving her face. 'The very words I'd have used.'

'Here's our stop,' she whispered. 'Don't let's get carried away.'

'As though we're not already!'

As soon as they'd left the tram, they turned at once for the gardens, walking through the chill air in companionable silence, he still clutching her boxes, she taking his free arm.

'Can't hold you until I get rid of these,' he told her when they halted. 'Mind if I put them on this wet seat?'

'No, but I don't want to sit there.'

'Of course not. Just let's get them out of the way.'

For some time, they stood together, arms around each other, kissing strongly, as the cold seeped into their bones and meant nothing and the night breeze sent old leaves rustling round their feet. Finally, they broke apart and Stephen took Elinor's hand.

'It's wonderful that you're happy to be with me,' he said slowly, his eyes shining in the poor light. 'But the thing is, I feel more guilty than ever. I'm in the wrong, I know I am.'

'Why do you talk like that?' she cried. 'I've said I'm a grown-up, I can meet you this way if I like. Why do you keep calling yourself guilty?'

'Because you're so young, so inexperienced. I'm older than you – I'm twenty-eight. I should know better than to ask you to meet me as we do – snatched meetings, family not knowing. You deserve something better than that.'

'It's difficult for us, Stephen. You have your position to think of, I understand that.'

'But you have yourself to think about too, Elinor. I know you're ambitious. You want to find a better job—'

'I do! I don't want to stay a housemaid for ever.'

'And if it's what you want, I'd like to help you in that. At the end of the course, I might be able to advise on what to look for, put in a word...' He hesitated. 'If it's what you want.'

'I do, I've said.'

'But then, you might like to think about us.'

'Us?'

'Well, we are so happy together, mightn't we ... mightn't there be...' Again, he was hesitating. 'A future – for us both?'

Her lips parted, she held his hand tightly.

A future – for them both? Had he really said that? Did he really think she could be a part of his life? There'd be breakers ahead, if he did. She knew that, if he didn't. There would so obviously be those who'd say she wasn't right – his mother for one, her father for another, each with their different reasons. But if Stephen thought, as she did herself, that she would fit in, well – why not? But it all seemed very far off, their future. She couldn't really picture it.

'I never got as far as thinking about that,' she said huskily, knowing he was waiting for her to speak.

'Perhaps it's not time for you, yet.' Suddenly he moved his hand to touch her cheek. 'As I say, you're very young. You have your whole life before you.'

'What are you saying, Stephen?'

'Oh, God, I don't know!' He kissed her again, with passion. 'Shall we just go on as we are? Until the end of the course? Shall we just be happy together when we can, until then?'

'I'd like that.' Recovering new strength and reaching up, she returned his kiss with equal feeling. 'But listen – what time is it?'

'Oh, Lord, time to go, as usual.' He shook his head. 'If there's one thing I want to do, Elinor, it's to rescue you from the tyranny of the clock.'

At Maule's Corner, they briefly embraced, casting glances round to see if anyone was watching, and spoke of their meeting on Christmas Eve.

'Could we meet for lunch?' asked Stephen.

'If you like. But I'll want to be home for teatime, seeing as it's Christmas Eve.'

He sighed. 'I suppose it's difficult for you, keeping us all happy. You're like one of those conjurors spinning balls in the air.'

'Your mother might want to see you home early, too.'

'True. Well, at least we're meeting for lunch. Would you be happy to go to Colinton again?'

'I'd love it!'

'Doesn't seem such a good idea to meet at this corner now, does it? Shall we say, half past eleven under the clock at Waverley?'

'I'll be there.'

His look on her was long and melting, until he remembered her boxes.

'Oh, see, I still have these. Does it seem a long time ago since you unpacked your mince pies?'

'Years,' she replied, taking them from him.

Miss Ainslie was in the hall again when Elinor slipped in, but it was all right, she wasn't late, and there was no trouble.

'Your party went well?' the manageress asked pleasantly. 'Everyone enjoy your baking?'

'Oh, yes, Miss Ainslie, thanks, and the party was grand. We all had a good time.'

'So glad. You're looking very well, I must say.'

'Am I? Must be because of the party.' Elinor moved hastily away. 'I'll take these boxes down to the kitchen and then get to bed.'

'Goodnight, then, Elinor.'

'Goodnight, Miss Ainslie.'

After replacing the boxes, Elinor climbed the stairs to bed, certain she would have to face more questions, this time from Mattie and Gerda, but for once they were both asleep. Something to be grateful for, even though, as usual, she had no hope of finding sleep herself.

Twenty-Five

The meeting on Christmas Eve might have been a repeat performance of their previous day out at Colinton, except that they were now aware their relationship had taken a step forward. Though nothing could formally be announced until the end of the course, when they would no longer be tutor and pupil, the future had become something they could discuss – even look forward to – and in the meantime, they could continue as they were, enjoying their snatched meetings. Not an ideal arrangement, maybe, but as long as it was temporary, it suited them both.

As for Elinor's idea of telling her mother about Stephen, it seemed the time was not yet right for that. Hessie would almost certainly believe that Walter should be informed, and the more she thought about it, the less Elinor felt like risking it. Maybe it would be best to leave the matter until real decisions were taken? Yes, much the best, she decided, and heaved a great sigh of relief.

After their blissful exchange of kisses in the Colinton woods, lunch at the little café where they had tea before was delicious. Nothing Christmassy, except for the offer of mince pies with the coffee, but a lovely light soup, followed by chicken in white sauce which was as good as anything Mrs Petrie made for the club – praise indeed.

'Oh, that was so nice,' Elinor told Stephen, when the coffee and mince pies arrived. 'A lovely Christmas present, I'd say. Thank you very much.'

'Only thing is, I have a real Christmas present for you. I'll just get it from my coat pocket.'

It was a beautiful silk scarf in autumn colours of copper brown and crimson, perfect for Elinor's dark good looks, and so obviously chosen to please her, it brought the tears to her eyes.

'Stephen, I don't know what to say,' she murmured. 'I've never had anything like this before. It's – well, it's just so lovely, I'll always treasure it.' She smiled and opened her bag. 'I have a wee present for you, too, but I don't know if I dare give it to you, it's so ordinary.'

'Something for me? You shouldn't have spent your money on me, Elinor.'

'Didn't cost much and some of it I did myself.'

She put a package into his hand, which he slowly opened, shaking his head, but when he took out the white linen handkerchiefs each with a hand-sewn monogram of his initials, he smiled.

'Elinor! Did you stitch these for me yourself? They're amazing! Beautiful!'

'Och, they're only handkerchiefs, Stephen.

And any lassie at school could sew initials like that.'

'But these weren't sewn by any lassie at school,' he said seriously. 'These were sewn by you for me, which means I have something to treasure, too.'

'You're meant to use handkerchiefs!' she said, laughing, making him laugh with her, so that people at the next table smiled indulgently and said how nice it was to see young folk so happy. But of course it was Christmas Eve, wasn't it? A magical time.

The magical time for Elinor and Stephen had to come to an end, however, when they reached Waverley Station and had to say goodbye, knowing they would not meet again until the next class in January. Christmas must be spent with their families, and as for Hogmanay – not only did Elinor have to work over the holiday, Stephen had already agreed to accompany his mother to Peebles to visit cousins. There was nothing they could do.

'Couldn't we meet on your free evening?' Stephen asked desperately. 'There must be one in the calendar somewhere.'

'There is, but there'll be so much to do when we open again after Christmas, I've already agreed to work all that week. And the following week Ma's invited some neighbours in – she thought I'd be free.'

'So you are, for her,' Stephen commented gloomily. 'But not for me. Oh, well, roll on January. At least I know you'll be coming to the class. Did I ever tell you what it was like for me, waiting to see if you'd come to the first one?'

'You were waiting for me?'

'Sure I was. As soon as I saw you trying to sign up for the typing, I hoped you'd join my class instead. And when you did, I couldn't wait to see if you'd really come.' He grinned. 'And then, that first evening—'

'I was late!' she cried. 'Oh, Stephen, I never realized – I'd no idea!'

'Just as well.' His eyes went over the crowd of travellers and last-minute shoppers hurrying around them, and his grin faded. 'This is no place to say goodbye, is it? May I see you home, Elinor, just once?'

'To Friar's Wynd?' She gave a little smile. 'Better not. Too many people know me there.'

'I could just come on the tram with you, then.'

'And they all know me on the tram, too. Stephen, they'd put their eyes through you.'

'At least I could see you to the tram? I mean, it's Christmas!'

'All right, as it's Christmas,' she agreed, laughing, and together they made their way to yet another tram stop, where her tram arrived all too soon, and he had to stand, waving, his eyes on her lovely face beneath her large hat, until she was borne away. After a moment, he too turned away, to make his own way home, feeling desolation that his Christmas was in fact already over.

Twenty-Six

Boxing Day arrived, the dreariest day in the year, some thought, and Elinor was one of them. All presents had been exchanged, the Christmas food eaten, the card games played, so what was there to do? Go for a walk round Friar's Wynd in the wintry weather?

Washing up the dishes after their dinner of cold beef and pickles, Elinor sighed and wished again that she might have seen Stephen, but she'd been unable to think of an excuse to leave her family, and he was in the same boat. Now, if they had had a real future all mapped out, if they'd been engaged, for instance, no one would have expected them to stay in all day with their families, but glancing at her father, frowning over an old newspaper, she felt only relief that she wasn't going to have to introduce Stephen to him just yet.

True, her dad had been pretty good over Christmas so far. There'd only been a couple of nervous moments when he'd looked as though he might blow up – one when Corrie had refused to go to the pub with him on Christmas Eve, the other when Hessie hadn't made enough gravy for the Christmas dinner – but he'd simmered down earlier than expected, even enjoying a game of

132

Rummy and not complaining when he lost. Now, though, he was missing his pub outings and his family was treading carefully.

'Just wish there was something to do,' Elinor sighed, seeing Corrie come in wearing his outdoor coat and scarf. 'Where are you off to, then?'

'Football match. Want to come?'

'Football? Me? When have I ever gone to football?'

'Come on, it's only a friendly – couple of local teams. Won't cost anything and you'll get the fresh air.'

'Aye, it's no' a bad idea,' Walter said with sudden interest. 'I might go, eh?' He threw aside his paper. 'Come on, we'll all go.'

'No' me,' Hessie said hastily. 'I'll have your tea ready for when you get back. But you go, Elinor – Corrie's right, you'll get the fresh air and Lord knows you don't get much of that.'

'All right,' Elinor agreed, suddenly deciding that anything would be better than staying in. 'Wait, I'll get my coat and hat.'

Outside, the air was not only fresh but icy cold, with the promise of more sleet, and they had to walk fast to try to keep warm. Luckily, the field at the back of the local school where the match was to be played was not far away, or Elinor might have turned back and even Walter was having doubts.

'I'm no' so sure this was a good idea,' he muttered, pulling his cap down over his brow as they finally took their places in the small crowd of spectators. 'We're likely to freeze to death here, eh?'

133

'Come on, we've got to support our lads,' Corrie told him. 'Western Athletic, eh? The others are Bernard's Academy – it's their field they're playing on.' Screwing up his eyes in the wintry air, he pointed to the players coming on to the pitch. 'I know a couple of chaps there – you might know 'em too, Elinor.'

'Who are they?' asked Elinor, covering her cold nose with her gloved hands and watching the footballers without much interest. 'Why should I know 'em, anyway?'

'They were at school with us. Georgie Howat was in the same class as me, his brother would've been in yours.'

'Barry Howat? Oh, yes, I do remember him. Where is he?'

'He's the one with the curly brown hair, the key man, the centre forward.' Corrie grinned. 'I call him Twinkle-Toes. Just watch his footwork.'

'And what does he do?'

'Scores goals!' her father said, with a laugh. 'Ah, they're off. Now, pay attention, Elinor, try to work out what's happening.'

'Wish I could join in – it'd be warmer running about than standing here.'

Without knowing much of what was going on, Elinor felt she was quite simply being chilled to the bone. She had almost decided to go back when the curly-headed centre forward scored two goals in rapid succession to so much cheering she decided to stay where she was. At least clapping might get her circulation going, she murmured to Corrie, who grinned and said it was now half time. Not so long to go now.

Not so long? The second half seemed interminable, with no more goals, though 'Twinkle-Toes', as Corrie called him, earned his reputation, racing up and down the pitch, doing his best, until the final whistle went with a win for Western Athletic. As their supporters began cheering again, even Elinor joined in, because now they could go home.

'Hang on a minute,' said Corrie, 'let's wait to say a word to the lads, eh? They played well.'

'You mean stay on?' Elinor cried. 'No, I'm frozen, Corrie, I'm going home.'

'We can wait inside the school. They've opened it specially, just for the game. It'll no' take long – Dad, you'll come?'

'Aye, might as well. Be glad to get out o' this cold for a few minutes, anyway.'

Sighing aloud, Elinor watched her breath float in a cloud before her, but resignedly followed Corrie and her father into the lobby of the school, where it was, if not warm, at least not icy. Shouts and laughter from some distance away signalled that the teams were in a changing room, from where, Elinor gave thanks, they soon emerged, looking scrubbed and fresh in their outdoor clothes. Very pleased with themselves, too, in the case of the Western Athletic team, but as people went forward to congratulate them again, Elinor stayed in the background. All she wanted to do was go back home to warmth and tea, but then someone called her name.

'Elinor?'

She turned to see Barry Howat, the hero of the day, smiling at her.

135

'Remember me?'

Oh, yes, she remembered him, not just from school, but from that time she'd seen him in Friar's Wynd, kicking a can for two young laddies. No wonder he'd sent it so far.

'Saw you no' long ago,' she told him. 'Never knew you were such a star.'

'Never knew you were interested in football.'

'Don't know that I am.'

'Don't know if I'm a star.'

He stood watching her and laughing, a slim young man of medium height, not handsome, but with the open, sunny sort of face people found attractive and provided no threat. His hazel eyes were clear, his brow untroubled, and even if she couldn't be sure it was true, it seemed to Elinor that he would be one never to have a care in the world, which she found comforting.

'You just came with Corrie, then?' he asked her.

'And Dad.'

'Oh, yes, from the cobbler's shop, eh? Well, I'm glad you did. What's happening to you these days, then? You got a job?'

'Oh, yes, I'm in service – at the Primrose Club.'

'Posh, eh?'

'It's a fine place. How about you? Still doing house-painting?'

'Afraid so.'

'You'd rather be playing football?'

'You bet.' His eyes were dancing. 'Well, it's been good to see you. Maybe we can meet again, some time?'

At the casually said, friendly words, without

warning, a tide of colour swept up Elinor's face to her brow and she had to look away, making no answer. It was with immense relief that she heard hoarse voices calling Barry back to his fans, and when he said he must go, she only nodded, still too embarrassed to speak.

Why had she reacted in the way she had? There had been no need for her to colour up like that when he hadn't actually asked to meet her, was just being polite, the way people were. And there had certainly been no need to think of Stephen, and yet there he was, in her mind.

It was further relief when her father came up and said they should be going, that it would soon be dark, and why all the chit-chat with Barry Howat, then?

'We were at school together, Dad. I remembered him.'

'Oh, yes? Well, he seems a good lad, eh? A very talented footballer.'

'Good at playing the piano, too,' said Corrie, joining them, as they left the school. 'According to Georgie, he can play anything. All by ear, never from music.'

'They've got a piano?' Elinor asked with interest.

'Aye, seemingly they're a musical family. Parents are dead now, though.'

'I never heard that. How sad!'

'Aye, Bettina – that's the lads' sister – keeps house for 'em.'

Elinor was looking thoughtful. 'You know, I never would have taken Barry to be musical. Just shows how wrong you can be.'

'Och, he's no Beethoven!' Corrie cried. 'Plays in pubs, mainly, sets all the feet tapping.'

'Now you mention it, I've heard him,' Walter remarked. 'Funny thing is, he's no drinker, either. The pints line up and he just hands 'em on.'

'No' everyone's a drinker,' Corrie murmured.

'Well, you certainly aren't!' his father muttered. 'What a killjoy, eh?'

'Barry's thinking of his football. Likes to keep fit.'

'That makes sense,' said Elinor, but no more was said of Barry Howat as the Raes hurried home through the darkening afternoon, looking forward to the heat of the range and the taste of Hessie's Christmas cake.

Twenty-Seven

Slowly, the winter passed and March arrived, with the promise of spring. More than that for Elinor, for the end of March would bring the end of Stephen's course and probable changes to their relationship. Maybe even to her job, for nothing was certain.

She knew she had done well on the course, would be sure to be given a good reference, as Stephen had told her often enough, but whether or not she looked for a new job depended on more than a reference. With the end of the course, she would no longer be Stephen's student, and at their secret meetings, he often said he could hardly wait for that day to come. Nor could Elinor, of course, but for her there was always a little apprehension. How would it all work out? Could she really be so lucky? She tended to put the thought of decision time to the back of her mind.

So wrapped up was she in her own concerns, it came as a shock when Brenda admitted to her and the other girls in the WEA class that she and Tam MacLean were 'walking out' together. Like the rest, Elinor had noticed nothing.

'You and Tam?' she'd cried. 'Why, I'd no idea! You two never got on!'

No one could believe it, but Brenda's rather sheepish expression said it all. Seemingly, they did now 'get on'. Very much so, but Brenda said maybe they wouldn't tell Mr Muirhead. No doubt he wouldn't approve of his students going out together.

'Oh, no doubt,' Elinor had agreed, her spirits sinking, wishing with all her heart that she could tell Brenda the truth about her own relationship with their tutor, but determined all the same not to say a word just yet. She couldn't help rather envying Brenda, though, that everything for her seemed so straightforward.

One morning after tea break, she was surprised to find Miss Denny calling to her from Reception as she passed by. Outside, as she had seen from the upstairs windows, the first daffodils were already flowering in the square and now through the open front door, she could see buds on the

139

magnolias and forsythia and many shrubs she couldn't name. How she wished she could have just stepped out, unlocked the garden gate, smelled the air and walked on the strong fresh grass for a little while! But of course that wasn't possible.

'You wanted me, Miss Denny?' she asked, approaching the desk.

'Yes, there's a letter for you, Elinor. I have it here.'

'A letter?' Elinor was astonished. She never received letters, for who would need to write to her? Something business, was it? To do with her job?

No, the envelope Miss Denny handed over was small and blue, quite cheap-looking, certainly nothing official, and whoever had written her name in large uneven capitals didn't know how to spell it. 'Miss Eleanor Rae,' she read, 'Care of the Primrose Club'.

Well, here was a mystery.

'All right, dear?' Miss Denny asked, turning to attend to a club member who had just arrived.

'Yes, thanks, Miss Denny.'

Elinor walked hurriedly on towards the back corridor she was due to clean, but as soon as she'd checked there was no one about, she opened the letter and took out the one sheet of paper it contained. As she read its signature and few lines of wavering handwriting, her eyes widened and two spots of colour burned on her cheekbones. Hurriedly, she looked round to see if anyone was about, but seeing no one, read the letter again.

'Dear Eleanor,' it ran, following an address in a

140

street in the South Bridge area, 'hope you won't mind me writing to you, but I am doing some work for a firm in the square and I've been looking out for you but never seem to see you. Do you never get time out of that club? If you could come out in your dinner hour, say twelve o'clock, I will be at the far side gate to the gardens. We could have a nice wee chat. Yours ever, Barry.'

Her heart beating fast, Elinor stuffed the letter into her pocket, just as Mattie arrived, carrying a mop and feather dusters.

'You've beaten me to it this morning,' she said breathlessly. 'I've just seen Miss Ainslie and she said, could we be sure to do the picture rails this morning?'

'We always do the picture rails,' Elinor answered absently.

'Aye, but she doesn't know, eh? Just thinks on now and again what we should be doing.' Mattie glanced curiously at Elinor. 'Are you all right, then? You're awful red in the face.'

'Got a headache. Think I might just run out to the chemist's before I come down for dinner. See if they've got anything.'

'I've some wee cashews might help.'

'Thanks, but I'll just check first what they've got. Will you tell Mrs Petrie where I am if she asks?'

'Sure, I'll tell her. And she's sure to ask.'

Sensible Barry, Elinor thought, as she slipped out at twelve o'clock. He knew they would not be so easily seen at the far gate as at the one nearest to the club, and now all she had to hope was that

141

he'd be there, at the far gate, for she hadn't much time.

He was there, dressed in his painter's white overalls, a cap on the back of his head, as he'd worn it when she saw him in the Wynd that time, and she gave a sigh of relief. Until she saw a large van parked quite close, with the name of a painting and decorating firm on its side, and immediately thought his painting colleagues must be about, watching them. Not that they would know her, of course, but she felt so strung up, so uneasy, anyway, it was upsetting.

'Is that your firm's van?' she asked without preamble. 'Are there people you know in there?'

'Ashamed of being seen with me?' he asked, smiling.

'No, of course not, just wondered if they might be watching.'

'There's nobody there, they're all at the back o' the house, having their piece. Thanks for coming, anyway. You got the wee note?'

'Yes, I was so surprised. Why ever did you write to me?'

'Wanted to see you again.'

She gave a little laugh. 'You've taken your time about that.'

'I've thought about you ever since Boxing Day,' he said seriously. 'But I wasn't sure you'd be interested. Then I got taken on to help in this big job here, doing up a house, and it seemed too good to miss the chance of seeing you. So I wrote you that letter.'

'Spelled ma name wrong.'

'Oh, glory, did I? What should it've been?'

142

When she told him, he shook his head.

'That's me, eh? Trying to cut a dash, and I get your name wrong. But it's grand to see you again.' His bright eyes were searching her face. 'I was wondering – maybe you'd like to go out with me? There's a Mary Pickford picture on this week. Thought we might go.'

For a moment, her eyes met his, then fell. When she spoke, her lips were dry.

'I'm very sorry, Barry, I'll have to say no.'

'No?'

'I ... well, I have ... someone.'

'Suppose I'm no' surprised. A girl like you, there'd have to be ... someone.'

She was silent, still not letting her eyes meet his.

'On the other hand, why come out to meet me today?'

As she said nothing, he moved closer to her.

'Must've wanted to see me,' he said softly.

'I think I just wondered ... what it was about.'

'Now you know, would it matter so much? Just going to the pictures?'

'You know it would matter.'

'Aye, I guess so. I was just being hopeful.'

'I couldn't meet you, anyway, Barry. I only get one evening off and that's when I go to evening class.'

'Evening class?' He raised his eyebrows. 'You doing handicrafts, or something?'

'Office management. I want to get a better job.'

'Ah.' He grinned. 'And you've probably got the brains for it. No' like me. All my brains are in my feet. But, look, maybe we could meet after

143

this class, then?'

At the expression on her face, a look of under-standing swam into his eyes. 'That's where he is, eh? This someone? Looks like I've really missed the boat.'

But Elinor was becoming preoccupied with time again.

'I'm sorry, I have to go. I shouldn't really be here, anyway.'

'I'll walk back with you.'

'Better not.' She gave a hasty smile. 'Thanks for asking me out. It was nice to see you.'

'Do you never get an afternoon free? A Saturday, maybe? You could come and see me play again. The team often plays on a Saturday.'

'I do get a Saturday sometimes, but I usually see my folks at home then.'

'Bring 'em with you. Why not? Look, tell me when your next Saturday is and we'll work something out.'

She was beginning to turn away, shaking her head, when he took her hand, pressing it in his own, and she stopped and stood very still. His touch. His hand in hers. She'd never before experienced such a sudden a rush of feeling. It was ridiculous. Crazy. He was only Barry Howat, somebody she'd known at school and who'd never meant a thing. Why, even when she'd seen him playing kick the can in the Wynd that time, she'd felt nothing for him. How had it come about that she felt so much now? Just when she shouldn't be feeling anything at all?

She knew she must go and walked away fast, skirting the railings of the gardens, not looking back, until she reached the area entrance to the club. On the steps down, she paused to straighten her hat and jacket before facing the staff at dinner, but Mrs Petrie's sharp eyes still saw something awry.

'My word, Elinor, what's up with you? You look as though you've got the furies after you – whatever they are.'

As Elinor, taking off her hat, made no reply, Mattie asked sympathetically if she'd found something for her headache.

'They said they had this aspirin stuff, but it's really silly – I forgot my purse.'

'All that rush for nothing!' the cook cried. 'And now you've to be quick with your dinner, time's getting on.'

'It's all right,' Elinor sighed. 'I'm no' very hungry, I'll just have a cup of tea.'

'Hope you're no' sickening for something,' Mattie said, rising to put the kettle on. 'You were that flushed before and now you've lost all your colour.'

'It's to do with that silly class you're going to,' Mrs Petrie declared. 'No wonder you're getting headaches, studying and that. What's it all for, anyway?'

As the maids at the table looked at one another, Elinor knew they were thinking of her 'young man', the one she'd met through the class. And so was she. At least – she hugged the thought to her – she hadn't told Barry when she had the next Saturday afternoon free. He wouldn't come to her home; he wouldn't know when she'd be there.

145

Twenty-Eight

'Guess who was here last week?' her father asked from his shop counter, when Elinor arrived home on Saturday two weeks later.

'Who?' she asked, turning cold.

'Why, that footballer laddie, Barry Howat. Said he was playing football again, asked if we'd like to go.' Walter gave a grin. 'Think he was more interested in you going than us, mind.'

'You told him I wasn't here?'

'What else? I told him I was working and Corrie was out, and your ma wouldn't be going anyway. She came down and had a word with him, though. Said what a nice laddie he was.'

'I certainly don't want to go to another football match,' Elinor announced, as she began to climb the stairs. 'So he needn't come here again.'

'Now, there's no need to be unfriendly. He means no harm. When you see him, try to be nice, eh?'

'When I see him?'

'Aye, I told him you'd be here today. Said he'd be along.'

There was nothing for it but to go on into the flat, where Hessie sprang up, and said she'd put the kettle on.

'Think you might have an admirer calling

146

today, Elinor! Did your dad tell you about Barry Howat coming round? He said he'd come back – wants you to go to the football.'

'Where's Corrie?' Elinor asked, frowning. 'He could go.'

'Gone to the swimming baths with a pal from work. Look, Barry's a good lad. Why'd you no' want to see him play?'

'I've just got no interest in football.'

'You don't have to be interested in football to be interested in the players, Elinor. Or one player in particular.'

'Anybody home?'

Barry Howat was standing in the doorway, Walter behind him, smiling as though he was personally responsible for this appearance, while Barry himself was looking straight at Elinor, his eyes full of appeal.

'Hope you don't mind me barging in, Mrs Rae,' he murmured, turning to Hessie after a moment. 'Mr Rae said it was all right.'

'Of course it is,' Walter said breezily. 'Now you just have a cup of tea while I get back to the shop.'

As he clattered out, Hessie, thrilled, began setting out cups, but Elinor made no move.

'Shouldn't you be going to your match?' she asked, noticing that Barry was wearing a jacket and flannels. He didn't look as though he was on his way anywhere.

'No match today,' he replied cheerfully. 'Other side had to cancel. Messed up their dates, seemingly.'

'What a shame!' cried Hessie. 'Well, you sit

147

yourself down, Mr Howat...'

'Barry, please.'

'Barry, then. You sit down and have some tea – it's freshly made...'

'Thanks very much, Mrs Rae, but if it's all right with you, I was wondering if Elinor and me could go for a walk. It's a grand day.'

'You might ask me, I'm standing right here,' Elinor said coldly.

'Now, now, Barry's just being polite,' Hessie said soothingly. 'I'm sure that'd be lovely, eh, to get out in the sunshine. Elinor, you'd like to go, eh?'

For a moment, she met the appeal in Barry's eyes again, then looked down at the hat she'd just taken off.

'Might as well.' Moving to the mirror, she replaced the hat, as he watched. 'All right, I'm ready. Though I'll have to keep an eye on the time.'

'You both come back here for your tea, eh?' Hessie urged. 'Just like you usually do, Elinor.'

But there was nothing usual about this Saturday afternoon, Elinor knew, as she and Barry, nodding goodbye to her father, went out into the rare sunshine of Friar's Wynd.

'Where shall we go?' Barry asked, putting a felt trilby hat over his thick hair. 'Any ideas?'

'Nowhere much to walk round here,' Elinor muttered.

'Have to take a tram somewhere. Botanic Gardens? The Meadows? All be crowded, of course, on a fine afternoon like this.'

'That's why I like the square. It's never

148

crowded.'

'Canna get in, though, can you? Need a key and I bet you haven't got one.'

She tightened her lips. 'No, I haven't, but I can see the gardens very well.'

He shrugged. 'Look, let's no' waste time, eh? I say we get the tram down Nicholson Street and go walking in the Meadows. Plenty of space there, even if there are folk about.'

'And won't take too long. I have to be home for tea and then get back to the club for six.'

'What a life! No wonder you're looking for another job.'

'We're pretty well treated at the Primrose, to be honest.'

He smiled as they reached the tram stop. 'If you say so.'

Sitting next to him on the tram, Elinor was afraid he would take her hand again but he didn't, just bent his head to hers and whispered that it was good of her to agree to come out with him. He'd had no great hopes.

'I don't know why you still asked me, after what I told you.'

'Thought it was worth a try. Seeing as you came over to meet me in the square.' He added, in a lower tone, 'And you're here now, eh? You agreed to come.'

'It was awkward for me, with Ma listening. I didn't know what to say.'

'Your Ma and Dad know about this someone you've got?'

She stared out of the window at the shops and crowded pavements of Nicholson Street.

'No, they don't.'

'Thought they couldn't, the way they were welcoming me.'

The colour rushed to Elinor's face. 'That's just their way. Doesn't mean anything.'

'Our stop, I think,' he said blandly. 'Melville Drive.'

From the lengthy road that was Melville Drive, they turned into the Meadows, a park made up of two large tracts of land, the east and west sites divided by a long walkway. As Barry had predicted, it was crowded with people, some playing ball games, others running around with children and dogs, or hurrying along the walk that was a short cut to the other side of town. Italian ice-cream men and balloon sellers were doing a good trade, and with the cries of the children, the barking of the dogs, and general atmosphere of holiday mood, Elinor turned to Barry and laughed.

'See what I mean about the square being different?' she asked.

'I see you laughing,' he replied. 'That's the first time today.'

As she immediately grew serious, he took her arm.

'There's an empty seat over there – let's grab it.'

'We're supposed to be walking,' she said, conscious of his arm against hers.

'No, we're just supposed to be together. When a man and a woman go for a walk, they're no' usually thinking of the walking.'

When they had had hastily reached the vacant seat, they sat down, taking off their hats and

150

fanning themselves, smiling in triumph, until Barry's smile faded.

'Now,' he said softly, leaning a little towards her, 'tell me about this man in your life. The one that stops you seeing me. So you say.'

Twenty-Nine

Stephen. He wanted her to tell him about Stephen. How could she, when she felt so bad? For a moment, she closed her eyes, seeing Stephen's handsome face, picturing it twisting, questioning, and it seemed to her that she should go. Just go, without saying a word. End whatever was happening here without another moment of regret...

But when she opened her eyes, she found Barry's gaze on her and made no move.

'I – don't want to talk of him just now,' she said quietly.

'I'd like to know about him.'

'It seems wrong, though.'

'You could say where you met him. I mean, is he in that class you go to?'

'He's the tutor.'

'The tutor? He's in charge? Teaches you?'

'That's right.'

'An educated man, then?'

'Yes, he went to the university here.'

Barry whistled and took out a packet of Woodbines.

'Mind if I smoke? I'm trying to cut down – bad for my game – but I could do with one now.'

'I don't mind. Go ahead.'

'Thing is, I understand why you didn't want to tell your folks.' Blowing smoke, Barry nodded his head. 'You thought they'd no' approve, eh? A university man – he'd never be right, never think you were right, so what's he playing at, they'd be asking? That what you thought?'

'More or less. But there's another thing – tutors aren't supposed to get involved with students, so Stephen said we should wait to tell folk until the course was over. Then we'd be free to do as we liked.'

'Stephen ... I'm glad you said his name.'

'I wish I hadn't.'

'No, it's good. Makes him more real to me.'

'More real? Why would you want that?'

'Because I want to win the battle with him. Canna fight a shadow.'

'Barry, what are you talking about?' Elinor had risen from the bench, her face turning white. 'There's going to be no fighting! No battle!'

'Come on, I don't mean real fighting!'

Barry, laughing, stood up with her and took her hand.

'You know I mean I'm going to try to make you forget him and go out with me.'

'Look, this is all hopeless.' She snatched her hand from him. 'I'm never going out with you, so there's an end to it. Let's go back now.'

'Wait.' Barry ground out his cigarette in the

grass and turned to face her. 'Just hear me out, eh? I'd never try to steal another man's girl if I thought she truly cared for him. Come between two people like that – it'd be the last thing I'd want to do.' He slowly put his hands on her shoulders. 'But I don't think you do care for this Stephen, Elinor. Can you look me in the eye and say you do?'

'You don't know me, Barry. How can you say you know what I feel?'

'I've got the cheek of the devil, but I think I know, all right.'

He was drawing her closer to him, gradually enfolding her, his eyes steady on her face, and she was making no move to pull away, her great eyes returning his gaze as though they would never look away, until he kissed her lips, and then her eyelids closed.

'Why did you come across the square to me?' he whispered, as her eyes flew open and she began to free herself from his arms. 'Why are you here with me now? If you care for him?'

'People will be watching,' she gasped, putting her hand to her mouth. 'Let's go, Barry, let's go.'

'There's no one watching. We needn't go yet.'

But she was already on her way, hurrying from him, as though that would solve everything, knowing it wouldn't, but not looking back. Of course, he caught up easily, stretching out his arm to take hers, but she shook her head.

'No, it's no use, Barry, I couldn't ... I couldn't do what you want. I couldn't hurt him. Don't ask me to.'

'All I'm asking is you do what's right.'

153

As they reached the tram stop, he let go of her arm and they stood together, breathing fast, not speaking until the tram arrived and they could take their seats.

'You have to do what's right for both of you,' Barry murmured then. 'That's only fair.'

'I do care for him,' Elinor declared. 'You're wrong to say I don't.'

'You think you do. But you were just flattered, eh? Carried away that your teacher should've fallen for you. That's all it was, Elinor, I promise you.'

'Talking like that will do no good, Barry. I'm no' listening, anyway.'

'I'll say no more, then,' he said cheerfully. 'But I bet you've heard what I've said. Think about it.'

'You'll come in for your tea?' she asked, when they were back in Friar's Wynd, but he shook his head.

'Please thank your ma, but I'd best get back. Bettina will have something ready.'

She hesitated. 'Your sister looks after you and Georgie very well, I expect. I'm sorry about your mother and father.'

'Aye, it's been hard. Specially when Ma went. Only two years ago.'

'Look, are you sure you won't come in? My folks will be disappointed.'

'Another time, eh?' His hazel eyes sparkled. 'Or won't there be another time?'

She shook her head. 'Goodbye, Barry.'

Though he made no move to kiss her again, she turned quickly into her father's shop anyway, leaving him to touch his hat and walk away.

Without, she noticed, saying 'Goodbye', or indeed anything at all.

All the rest of that day and most of the night, she seemed to feel the strength of Barry's kiss on her lips, so strong, so disturbing, and with that feeling came the memory of his words, moving round and round in her mind, round and round, so that she wanted to put her hands over her ears to shut them out...

'I don't think you do care for this Stephen, Elinor. Can you look me in the eye and say you do? You were just flattered ... carried away that your teacher should've fallen for you ... that's all it was, I promise you...'

In the middle of the night, while Mattie and Gerda slept the sleep of the just, she actually sat up and cried silently into the darkness, 'No, no, no more, please!'

But in the morning, after an uneasy sleep that did no good, she knew what she must do. There were two Thursdays left of the course, and on the first one that came at the end of the coming week, she must speak to Stephen. Not to say that she didn't love him, for she did, in a way; he was so special. So fine a character, so handsome, clever, everything a woman could want. But she knew now that he was not the one for her. She didn't love him as she should, as Barry had already guessed; therefore it wouldn't be fair to pretend that she did. The future they had hoped to plan couldn't happen, and she owed it to Stephen to tell him as soon as possible. Which would be Thursday.

155

But, oh, God, how was she going to get through the days till then? She had said goodbye to Barry, she was quite on her own. How could she face telling Stephen? Watch his face change? Feel the pain of the dagger she had slipped into his heart?

Perhaps he wouldn't be as hurt as she thought. Perhaps she was making too much of what she meant to him. She wasn't vain, she didn't want to think she had the power to hurt him, but her own heart told her that she wasn't making a mistake. Telling him the truth of her feelings was going to wound. And not only him.

As she tried to find the courage to face the next few days, she knew that no one must know, or guess, what she was going through. Secrets, secrets. There had been too many. When all this was over, she vowed never again to have a secret in her life, but just then she couldn't imagine being as free as that.

Thirty

Stephen knew, of course, as lovers do, that there had been a change. Though Elinor had tried to be just as usual at his last-but-one class, she could tell, by his thoughtful look on her whenever she glanced up from her notebook, that he had sensed something was different. She herself was thanking heaven that the session was mainly devoted to revision; for all her thoughts were with the time to come when she would be alone with him, she could never have learned anything new.

At the end of class, when she was putting on her jacket, he managed to catch her eye before being surrounded by other students, and nodded imperceptibly. A sign, she knew, that they would meet as usual on the tram, which was what she wanted, yet sent her heart sinking. Surely someone would notice that her hands were trembling as she adjusted her hat? Surely, she had become very pale? Even Brenda, however, noticed nothing.

'Oh, next week's going to be so exciting, eh?' she whispered to Elinor. 'When we all get our references?'

'What references?'

'Weren't you listening? Didn't you hear Mr Muirhead say he'd be giving references to all who wanted 'em, and of course, we all do!'

'Oh, yes, I remember,' Elinor lied, for her attention had been elsewhere even when Stephen was speaking. 'Thing is, Brenda, it's possible I mightn't be here next week. I might be needed for something at the club.'

'Why, you're never going to miss our last class?' Brenda cried, her eyes wide. 'That'd be awful. We're planning to have a celebration, we are going to take Mr Muirhead out for something to eat, and we thought just for once you'd come as well. And now you say you might not be coming at all?'

'It's no' definite,' Elinor said hurriedly. 'But if I don't appear, I'll be in touch. I've got your address and we'll meet somewhere.'

157

'Oh, yes, that'd be grand, but try to come to class if you can. Mr Muirhead'll be so disappointed if you don't, you know. He's always had a soft spot for you, eh?'

Brenda smiled at Elinor's expression and gave her a quick hug. 'Think we didn't notice? 'Course we did! But here comes Tam, we're away to the café.'

Everyone was on their way, there were waves and goodbyes and cries of 'See you next week', and suddenly Elinor and Stephen were alone and waiting for the tram.

'Thank God,' Stephen said simply. 'Thought this moment would never come.'

His tone was light, but his eyes were anxious. Pretending to look up the road for the tram, she tried not to meet his gaze, and even when the tram arrived, only smiled briefly as they climbed aboard.

'What's wrong?' he asked quietly, sitting close beside her. 'Please don't deny that something is.'

She turned her eyes on him at last. 'I ... have to talk to you, Stephen.'

'I'm listening.'

'Away from the tram.'

'In the gardens, then.'

'Yes.' She glanced out of the window. 'It'll be light, though.'

'Spring is here.' He smiled a little. 'And we prefer the dark.'

Yes, the gardens, even since their last visit, were different now, with daylight still lingering and people still strolling by, or sitting talking on the seats. There would be no kisses that evening, but then there would be none anyway, whatever the light, and a little stab of pain made Elinor catch her breath. There had been such sweet moments with Stephen, she would never deny them; she only wished from the bottom of her heart that she didn't have to say what she had to say.

Thirty-One

'I'm beginning to have a bad feeling about this,' Stephen was murmuring. 'You look so sad. Has something happened to upset you?'

They had stopped beneath trees, away from passers-by, and she turned to face him, bravely holding his gaze again, as he waited for her to speak.

'Stephen, I'm the one who's feeling bad. I ... don't know how I'm going to tell you...'

'Tell me what?'

'That we have to say goodbye. I mean, what we had – it was grand, it was lovely – I'll never forget it – but...'

'But what?' The colour was already leaving his face. 'Elinor, what are you saying?'

With his hands on her shoulders, he held her quite still so that he could search her face with eyes that appeared dark, were not like his eyes at all. It was as though he was becoming a stranger, as though she had made him one, just as she'd made herself a stranger to him.

'What's all this about saying goodbye?' he asked in a low voice. 'What has happened? What's made you talk like this? I thought you were happy with me. I thought we had a future. Elinor, we were making plans, and now it's goodbye?'

'I was happy with you! I was!'

'So what's changed? For God's sake, what's changed? You always knew my feelings for you. If you were happy with me, you must have felt the same for me. You did, didn't you? You cared for me?' His hands on her shoulders grew stronger, he seemed about to shake her, then suddenly let her go. 'So what's happened? Tell me, Elinor. Just tell me!'

'I realized ... it came to me...' She stopped, feeling her voice hoarse, and put her hand to her throat. 'That I don't feel ... as I should. If we're to be together.'

'Don't feel as you should ... what you mean is, you don't love me?' He put his hand to his brow. 'Don't love me as I love you? Is that it?'

'I thought I did,' she said desperately. 'I did think so, Stephen.'

'But you didn't. Maybe you never did.' He laughed shortly. 'Only thought you did. Is that what you're telling me?'

For long moments, they both stood without speaking, each taking in the reality of loss, until a man walking past called 'Good evening!' and they had to reply. When he had gone, they moved further into the trees and Stephen's eyes lost their darkness and began to glitter.

160

'Why did you suddenly come to this conclusion, though?' he asked roughly. 'How did it come to you? Out of the blue? Or is there something you haven't told me?'

She was silent, gazing away from him, desolate that he was beginning to guess the one thing she had wanted to keep from him.

'Have you met someone else?' he pressed. 'Have you? I always thought I was safe. You said you never met any men. Is there someone, Elinor? You must tell me; you owe it to me.'

'I know.' She bent her head, tears welling into her eyes. 'There is someone, then. He isn't my young man, I've only been for one walk with him and I don't know if I'll see ever him again, but...' Her voice trailed off. 'But he's the one I met.'

'And you've fallen in love with him.' Stephen gave a long, shuddering sigh. 'Tell me about him. Let me know about him. Let me know how I've lost.'

'He's someone I knew at school. Then we met again.'

'What does he do?'

'He's a house painter.'

'And what's he like?'

Elinor moved uneasily, unwilling to talk of Barry, but aware she must. 'He's friendly, he's cheerful. He plays the piano.'

'Talented, then?'

'Yes, but his real interest is football. He's very good at football.'

'A footballer?' Stephen gave another short, hard laugh. 'Well, I'd never have stood a chance against him, would I? Without doubt, I was the

161

worst who ever played football at Heriot's. Always the last to be chosen for a team, always dreading match days. Oh, you'll be very happy with a footballer, Elinor!'

'Stephen, I'm so sorry I've hurt you. You don't know how sorry. I never wanted things to be like this, never, you must believe me!'

'You had such high hopes,' he murmured. 'Such a longing to do well, find a better life for yourself. And you could have had it, you know. I don't just mean with me. You could have found a good job, had a career – but you're going to throw it all away, aren't you?'

'No! No, I'm still the same, still want the same. Why, I don't even know if I'll even see this man again.'

'Oh, yes, you will, nothing is clearer than that. You'll see him again and that will be that. Nemesis.' Stephen turned aside. 'Come on, it's growing dark, you're going to be late. I'll walk with you to Maule's Corner.'

Without speaking, they left the gardens and took their last walk together to Maule's Corner, from where they had made in the past so many bittersweet farewells. But this farewell was different.

'Will you be coming next week?' Stephen asked. 'It's the last class, as you know.'

'I don't think so.'

'I'll send you your reference, then. Care of the Club.'

'Oh, don't!' she cried, and burst into tears. 'Don't be nice and reasonable!'

'Nice?' He shook his head. 'Don't worry,

162

Elinor, I'm not being nice. You came to my course, it's fair you should have a testimonial, the same as everyone else. But I have no nice or reasonable feelings for you. I can say I hope all goes well for you, but I'm very glad you aren't coming to my class next week. I really don't want to see you again.'

With that, he touched his hat and left her, walking fast, not looking back, and after a long moment she turned and made her way to the club, walking blindly, not caring if she was late or not, or if anyone saw her tears. In fact, luck was with her. Miss Ainslie had not yet locked up, Mattie and Gerda were busy mending their stockings and took no notice of her, which meant she could slip into the maids' bathroom and put cold water on her eyes. As for the pain of her remorse, she just had to bear it. There was nothing else to do.

Thirty-Two

It took a while for Elinor to get over that last scene with Stephen, but then she'd never expected to escape lightly from what she'd done. Guilt was her burden and must somehow be borne, which meant she would make no move to seek out Barry Howat, and was relieved when he made no effort to see her.

Stephen had said she was in love with Barry, and perhaps she was, but she really tried not to think of him. She felt bad enough, anyway, especially when her reference from Stephen arrived and she saw how good it was. Tears came swiftly to her eyes, but she'd already decided not to use it. Looking for a new job without his blessing – she hadn't the heart. She put it away, together with the lovely silk scarf he had given her, and decided just to keep on working at the club until she felt better.

Mattie asked her once, very sympathetically, what had happened to her young man, now that her classes were finished? He'd looked so nice, Ada had said. Quite the gentleman. They'd all been very pleased for her. Well, except Mrs Petrie, of course, but then she didn't know about him.

'All over,' Elinor replied after a moment or two.

'Oh, no! Oh, Elinor, what a shame! What happened?'

'We just said goodbye. These things happen.'

'He didn't want to pop the question?'

'I didn't want him to.'

'Oh, well, then.' Mattie's look was wary. 'Mebbe you had to say goodbye. There's sure to be someone else, though. Plenty of good fish in the sea, as they say.'

'For you, too.'

'Aye, I'd best cast the net out!' Mattie retorted, laughing merrily, and to Elinor's relief gathered up her dusters and led the way to their next round of cleaning.

Towards the end of April, on one of her Saturday

afternoons at home, Elinor was finishing off doing some sewing for her mother, when Corrie came in, pulling on his jacket.

'Just off,' he announced.

'Where to?' asked Hessie.

'Football. Just another friendly at the school again. Season ends soon.'

Hessie's eyes had brightened.

'Will that nice laddie be playing? Barry, the one who came here?'

'He always plays.'

'Elinor, what say you go with Corrie?' Hessie cried. 'I'm sure that young man is sweet on you. He came seeking you, remember. So, why no' try to see him?'

'I've hemming to finish on this sheet, Ma,' Elinor murmured, keeping her eyes on her work.

'Och, give it here! I can do that any time. Now you put your hat on and go see Barry again. Your dad likes him, you ken, and that means a lot.'

'If you're coming, come on then,' Corrie ordered, glancing at the clock over the range, and Elinor, slowly rising, put aside the sheet she'd been hemming and obediently put on her hat and her blue jacket. Seemed her actions had been taken out of her hands, she told herself, then shook her head. She knew she couldn't say that. She was ready to see Barry Howat again.

'Different weather today from when I came before,' she remarked to Corrie as they walked through the streets in the pleasant spring air. 'Remember how cold it was?'

'Certainly do.' His light blue eyes on her were thoughtful.

165

'Pity Dad couldn't have come as well. He never gets a Saturday afternoon off.'

'Reckon we're better off without him today. Notice his mood? Some customer's annoyed him; he's looking pretty dark.'

'He'll be over it by the time we get back. On the whole, he's been better lately.'

'Plenty of room for improvement. Elinor, mind if I ask you something?'

'Anything you like.'

'Well, I was just wondering why you'd want to come to the football again. Is it just to see Barry Howat?'

Elinor hesitated. 'Ma wants me to see him.'

'Aye, but what do you want?'

'Why these questions?'

'Just interested. Barry's a charmer, all right, but I didn't think he'd be your cup o' tea.'

'I don't know if he is or not. No harm in seeing him play football, though.'

'Main thing is never to get serious. That way, you don't get hurt.'

'You're the expert, eh? When did you take girls out?'

'Hey, I've been out with one or two!'

'And never got serious? I hope not, at your age.'

'Never got serious. Never got hurt.'

'I won't get hurt,' Elinor said tightly, not able to tell Corrie that she was hurt already, because she'd badly wounded someone else.

When they reached the football field, the rival teams were already assembled, and this time Elinor had no difficulty in picking out Barry

Howat. There he was, slim, strong, in dark blue jersey and shorts, his brown hair blowing in the soft breeze of the day, his eyes going round the watching crowd. And spotting her.

She knew he'd seen her, even before he raised his hand, by the way he seemed to stiffen for a second or two, but then as she raised her own hand to wave, he had to turn away. The match was about to begin.

'Think he'll get two goals again?' she asked Corrie, as calmly as possible.

'Could do. He's been doing well lately. Just as long as he watches the ball and no' you.'

'All that matters to him is the game.'

She didn't know if that was true, but she had a feeling that it was.

Certainly, Barry concentrated well enough to score in the first half. Only one goal, but so brilliant, it had Corrie jumping up and down and giving Elinor a full analysis of how it had been done, which didn't mean a lot to her. Much more important was that when the whistle went for half time, Barry came over to speak to her and Corrie.

He was breathing hard, his hair and face dark with sweat, his jersey damp and sticking to his body, but his hazel eyes were shining as they went from Corrie to Elinor, and finally rested on her.

'You came, eh? That's grand, really grand. Never thought I'd see you here.'

'I always watch the team play,' Corrie murmured.

'Aye, but Elinor doesn't. Look, I've got to go but wait for me at the end, eh? Don't go away.'

'We'll wait,' Elinor told him, and watched as he sped off, his feet moving as fast as on the pitch, his energy buzzing like something tangible.

'You're right to call him Twinkle-Toes,' she remarked to Corrie, who said that yes, it was a joke name, but Barry was certainly quick on his feet. Georgie, too, but Elinor already knew that Georgie was but a pale shadow of his brother, always a step behind.

'What's Bettina like?' Elinor asked. 'I don't remember her from school.'

'Well, she's two years older than Barry, so she'd be ahead of you at school. Looks after the lads and does some part-time work as well, I think.'

'Seemingly, they're lucky to have her.'

'Aye, but she's got a young man. What'll they do if she gets wed?' Corrie laughed. 'Might have to learn to cook, eh? Unless they get wed themselves. Men have been known to marry for that very reason.'

Or other reasons, thought Elinor.

In spite of all Barry's efforts, that day his team lost and, at the end of the match, trooped disconsolately off to the school to wash and change and put a brave face on defeat. Elinor and Corrie were fearing the worst from Barry and Georgie, but when they appeared, it seemed they'd already put it behind them. The season wasn't over yet, they declared, and this was only a friendly – they'd do better in the remaining matches, no question.

'Aye, if you make yourself a few more chances!' cried a small, dark-haired young woman

168

wearing a red two-piece and a large red hat. 'Isn't that right, Alfie? They just gave it away, eh?'

'Just gave it away,' a tall, long-faced young man repeated, but Barry punched him lightly on the shoulder and told him to get playing himself, if he was so full of advice.

'Here, Elinor!' he cried. 'Come and meet my sister, Bettina, and her friend, Alfie Daniels. Bettina, Alfie – this is Elinor Rae. Think you know Corrie Rae, eh?'

'Oh, we know Corrie,' Bettina answered, her hazel eyes as bright as Barry's, fastening on Elinor. 'He always comes to the matches, the lovely laddie. But haven't seen you before, Miss Rae. What did you think of this lot then? Och, I was that disappointed!'

'Canna win 'em all,' said Georgie. 'Elinor did see us win when we played here before.'

'Must come again, then. But how d'you come to know Barry, Miss Rae?'

'Oh, please call me Elinor. We were at school together, then met again by accident.'

'Fancy. I was at the same school, but a couple of years ahead. Well, we'd better be on our way. Who's coming back, then?'

'I am,' said Georgie, but Barry was already at Elinor's side.

'I'll walk back with Elinor and Corrie. Don't wait tea for me.'

'Suit yourself.'

As the little group broke up to go their different ways, Bettina said something about maybe seeing Elinor again, but it seemed to Elinor that her manner was not particularly friendly. Of course,

169

she could be imagining it, for why should Barry's sister not be friendly? Perhaps she was a bit of a tartar? Certainly looked as though she might be.

Turning to Barry, she asked if he'd like to come back to have tea at her mother's? He'd be very welcome.

'If you're sure? I mean, it's a bit much, inviting myself.'

'No, it'll be all right. I know she's got ham and cold stuff. There'll be plenty.'

'But aren't you due back at work at six?' Corrie asked Elinor, at which she frowned and said there'd be plenty of time if they hurried.

'Skates on!' Barry said cheerfully. 'And when we've had our tea, I'll take you back to the club, Elinor.'

Thirty-Three

This he did, after a pleasant meal at the flat over the cobbler's shop, during which he charmed Hessie and Walter as easily as though he were a magician, while Corrie looked on without expression and Elinor's dark eyes were wide with wonder. Pleasing her mother was one thing, but her father, that was another! Still, Dad seemed to have got over his bad mood and when Barry and Elinor rose to go, urged Barry to come back and see them any time. Any time, now mind, and he'd be very welcome.

'Thanks very much, Mr Rae, I might take you up on that,' Barry said politely, and after hand-shakes and thanks all round, he and Elinor escaped for the tram.

'You don't know how much it meant to me to see you at the match,' Barry murmured, sitting close. 'Never thought I'd see you again, after the way we parted.'

'I did want to see you, Barry, but I didn't think I could.'

'What happened, then?' He pressed her hand, made her look at him. 'Something changed, eh? Must've done.'

'I don't want to talk about it.'

She met his eyes, saw that they were sym-pathetic, but still looked away. It wouldn't be right, she felt strongly, that she should speak of Stephen to Barry.

'All right, I understand. But try no' to worry too much, eh? If you said goodbye to him, you did the right thing. The right thing for both of you.'

'You think so?'

'Aye, it's obvious. There'd be no point in pre-tending you felt something you didn't. He'd soon have found out, and then you'd have hurt him, anyway.'

'Maybe you're right.'

'I know I'm right!' He squeezed her hand hard. 'But let's cheer up. I can never stay serious for long. Just remember that we've met again and we're happy. Will that bring the smiles back, Elinor?'

'Yes!' she told him, giving one of the wide

171

smiles that could so change her face. 'What a wonderful chap you are, then, for looking on the bright side!'

'That's me,' he said with a grin, rising for their stop. 'We get off here, eh? Means we leave all these people behind.'

'And join more crowds in Princes Street,' she told him, laughing, as they left the tram. 'You're never alone at Maule's Corner.'

'Who's going to Maule's Corner?'

'Well, that's where we can say goodnight,' she said, her smile fading, as she remembered other goodnights. 'But we can cut through to the square instead, if you like.'

'Through this lane here, you mean? Leads to the post office, but what we want is a doorway.'

'A doorway?'

'Don't you know what doorways are for?'

With dancing eyes and a teasing smile, he guided her into the shadows of the post office lane towards the entrance of a shuttered shop.

'This is better,' he whispered. 'It's so damned light these evenings, you feel there's nowhere to go. I mean, if you're poor homeless folk like us.'

'Homeless?'

'With nowhere to say goodnight. But at least it's darker here, and you see, I've found a doorway. Where I can kiss you. And you can kiss me.'

'Barry...'

'What's wrong? Too proud to kiss me here?'

'Someone might see us.'

'If they're walking past, they'll look away. Who cares?'

She said no more, only slid into his arms, let his

mouth find hers, and felt the world was sweet. No longer did any thought of onlookers worry her. No memory of her first kisses with Stephen interrupted her rapture. No one, she felt, could ever stir her as Barry stirred her, could ever open up thc world of love as he did, and when they released each other and exchanged looks, she knew that he'd recognized his power over her.

But he only said, breathing hard, 'Better be getting to your club, sweetheart. You go in the front door, or the back?'

'The area,' she answered huskily. 'But you needn't come with me.'

'What do you mean? I'm seeing you to your door, wherever it is.' Catching her expression, he shook his head. 'Och, you're no' worrying about folks seeing us again? To hell with that. I'm no' skulking round corners for anybody.'

'No, you're not,' she said with sudden decision. 'There's no reason why you shouldn't be seen with me. We're allowed followers, anyway.'

'And I'm a follower!' He laughed and took her arm. 'But don't be late, eh? Or they'll blame me.'

They arranged to meet on her next Thursday evening off, not at Maule's Corner, but at the Scott Monument in Princes Street, and as she waved goodbye to Barry at the top of the area steps, Elinor was already wondering how she would get through the days until then.

But she took comfort, not only in the memory of those doorway kisses, but also in a feeling of intense relief that was just beginning to make itself felt. There need be no more secrets. She need never worry about secrets again. If people saw her with Barry, fine. She'd every right to be with him and no one need object. In fact, her parents liked him, which was the most amazing weight off her mind. Even when she opened the door to the club kitchen and saw Mrs Petrie glowering and everyone running around preparing dinner, she felt as free as a bird. A bird in love! What could be better?

Thirty-Four

The summer weather of 1914 was glorious. Everyone thought so. Everyone said they'd remember it, though when they said that, they didn't know they would have special reason for remembrance. They didn't know it was to be the last summer before the world changed.

The staff at the Primrose admired the sunshine as much as anyone, their problem being that they couldn't spend much time in it. With no access to the gardens of the square, they could only take their tea break in the area, where the views were of the feet of passers-by and where there was certainly no greenery. On the other hand, at least, it was better than sitting in the kitchen, with the range sending out heat and Mrs Petrie's face, bent over her day-old newspaper, getting redder and redder.

'Could you no' use the gas cooker for the lunches?' Gerda had the temerity to ask one day

174

in June, at which Mrs Petrie's face grew redder still, while Vera and Sal shut their eyes, fearing the storm.

'Now, Gerda, don't you be telling me how to do my cooking!' Mrs Petrie exploded. 'I've always cooked on that range and a bit of summer weather's no' going to stop me now.' Folding her newspaper, she adjusted her spectacles, glaring around over the top of them. 'Anyway, seems to me we're all going to have more to worry about than what I cook on, if this paper's anything to go by.'

'How's that, Mrs Petrie?' Mattie asked politely.

'Why, it's all here, read it for yourself. Seemingly all Europe's dying to go to war. There's France and Germany at loggerheads, and Austria and Serbia, and Russia stirring the pot, so that the least little thing might set 'em all off. And then we'll be in trouble, too – so the paper says.'

'Why?' asked Elinor. 'Why should it matter to us if other countries start fighting?'

Mrs Petrie's brow was furrowed. 'I'm no' sure, to be honest, but looks like we'll join in. They're all men in the government and you ken what men are like. Anything for a scrap!'

War. As the maids returned to their duties in the heat of that Scottish summer's day, it didn't seem at all likely. Not that any of them knew anything about war, of course, except that there had been some fighting with the Boers in South Africa, but that was a long time ago and it hadn't affected anybody they knew.

'Och, these papers, they'll say anything, eh?' Ada muttered. 'Just hope they're wrong, anyway.' She stood still, looking down at the pile of starched dining-room tablecloths she was holding. 'Just hope my laddie would never have to go to war.'

'Or yours, Elinor,' Mattie said sympathetically, for of course, like all the staff at the Primrose, she knew about Barry.

Hadn't they all seen him on Thursday evenings, saying goodnight to Elinor at the area gate? Such a cheerful-looking fellow, eh? Not so handsome as the one before him, as Ada reported, but still the sort you wouldn't mind walking out with, that was for sure. Even Mrs Petrie, who'd spotted him once or twice, seemed to approve. What more could anybody ask?

For a moment a shadow crossed Elinor's face, but then she smiled and put her arm round Ada's shoulders.

'Don't worry, it's just like you say, Ada, the papers write rubbish – they only want to sell copies. There isn't going to be any war.'

'I think you're right,' Ada murmured, sniffing a little. 'Why, I've never even heard o' this Serbia! Trust Mrs Petrie to go worrying us all!'

It was Miss Ainslie who explained why Britain might be drawn into a conflict – not that she thought there'd be one, anyway. She had passed Elinor and Mattie taking down curtains for washing from some of the unoccupied bedrooms, and had stopped to ask if the girls were managing all right in the hot weather, her eyes resting mainly on Elinor.

Oh, Lord, she's going to ask me about the

suffragette meetings again, Elinor thought, groaning inwardly, for Miss Ainslie had more than once tried to persuade her to go back to the meetings once her course was over. Even when Elinor had explained that she now had a young man she saw on her free evenings, the manageress had still remained hopeful. Perhaps an occasional evening, Elinor could attend, she'd suggested, not having any idea how Elinor longed to spend every minute of her time with Barry and would never sacrifice an evening with him for a suffragette meeting, however much she believed in the cause.

Before anything could be said about meetings, however, Mattie, after saying they were managing well in the heat, had piped up with a question about the newspapers. Did Miss Ainslie believe what they said? That we might get drawn in to fighting?

'They're only thinking of Belgium,' Miss Ainslie explained. 'You see, if little Belgium were to be involved, we'd have to help out.'

Belgium? The girls exchanged glances. What on earth had Belgium to do with anything?

'We signed a treaty long ago, promising to take care of the Belgians in the event of trouble. So it would be a question of keeping promises.'

'And we'd go to war for that?' cried Elinor. 'Doesn't seem right to me.'

'Don't worry, it won't come to war.' Miss Ainslie's tone was decisive. 'There's not even a real hint of it at present, the papers are just looking for a story. My advice is not to read them. Elinor, may I have a word?'

'I don't like to keep nagging,' Miss Ainslie said in a low voice, as Mattie went out with an armful of curtains, 'but you were such an asset to us, Elinor, I'd very much like to see you back at our meetings. You really don't think you can manage one or two?'

'I'm afraid not, Miss Ainslie. I'd like to, but ... well, I've no time.'

The manageress sighed. 'Time, our enemy. Well, maybe in the future, it might be possible. Don't forget us, anyway.'

'I won't do that, Miss Ainslie.'

'There's one other thing – I was just wondering, this course you did – weren't you going to try for an office job when it ended?'

Elinor lowered her eyes. 'I was, but I haven't done anything about it yet.'

'Because of the young man, I suppose? Well, we must be grateful that this means you'll be staying with us a while longer. Unless, of course, you get married.'

Deep colour rose to Elinor's hair and she turned aside.

'There's no talk of that yet, Miss Ainslie.'

'That's another relief, then.' Miss Ainslie began to move away. 'Well, I must let you get on. I'm glad we've had this little talk, Elinor, but do tell the others not to worry about a war. Why spoil these lovely summer days?'

'What was she on about, then?' Mattie asked, when Elinor joined her. 'The suffragettes again? You were her only taker from here, that's why she canna let you go. Bet she asked about Barry as well, eh?'

'Why should she?' Elinor called down from the stepladder she was standing on to reach more curtains.

'Well, she might be wondering if you're going to get wed.'

'Look, I've only been out with him a few times, there's no talk of marriage.'

'He'd be right for you, though, is what we think. I mean, better than the other one. That'd never have worked, eh?'

As Elinor descended the steps with a load of dusty material, Mattie smiled.

'Why, I bet he never took you to see his ma, did he? That other one? Bet Barry will take you, and pretty quick, too.'

'Barry's mother is dead,' Elinor said quietly, at which Mattie's face grew serious, but not for long.

'That's very sad, but just think, Elinor, you'll have no mother-in-law!'

'How I wish you'd stop talking like that!' Elinor cried, folding curtains with wide sweeping movements and coughing in the dust. 'Why'd you do it, Mattie?'

'Sorry, Elinor.' Mattie's round eyes were woeful. 'It's just that I've got no laddie of my own yet, and I know if I had, I'd be thinking of getting wed all the time.'

Elinor set down her folded curtains and said, after a pause, 'It's all right, Mattie, I understand. I shouldn't have snapped at you.'

But she kept her thoughts on getting wed to herself.

179

Thirty-Five

'I understand,' Elinor had told Mattie. Perhaps too well, for if Mattie would have liked to be thinking about marriage, Elinor actually *was* thinking about it – and after all her reservations! All her hopes just to make something of her life herself. Even when she and Stephen had seemed so close, she realized now that she'd always been wary of the idea of commitment. When he'd talked of their future, she'd seen the snags. Whereas now ... well, things were different.

Different because of Barry. The way she felt about him, it was only natural she should be looking forward to taking the next great step. And she knew he was feeling the same. They were just so happy together, so much at ease, for Barry was himself so easy-going, so good-natured. Having seen at close quarters a father whose moods and tantrums had ruled his family's life, she could hardly believe her luck that someone like Barry who had no moods or tantrums should be hers.

'An absolute tonic to be with,' was how Elinor described him to her mother, who absolutely agreed with her. So fond was she of Barry, she was even happy that Elinor should spend her free time with him, rather than visiting home.

'Och, when you're courting, we don't expect you to spend time with us!' she cried. 'That's the way things go, eh?'

'I don't know that we're exactly courting,' Elinor said. 'I mean, there's nothing been said.'

'There will be,' Hessie told earnestly. 'I can tell by the way he looks at you. Oh, yes, he'll want to be wed; he's just like a lot of men, scared of the idea. End of being fancy-free for them, you see, but they all come to it one day. The only way they can get what they want, eh?'

Suddenly, her look on her daughter sharpened. 'That's why the lassies have to be careful, Elinor. Or you know what can happen.'

'Don't worry, Ma. It won't happen to me.'

'Just remember what I've said, though. And hold out for the wedding ring, eh?'

If only life weren't so difficult, though, Elinor often sighed to herself. If only there didn't have to be worries about making love – 'going all the way', as folk called it. If only no one need have a baby unless they wanted one. Talk about pie in the sky! No point in wishing for the impossible, was there? Just had to take as much pleasure as you could in kissing and caressing and not expect more until you were married. Which was why Elinor's thoughts dwelt on marriage as never before.

And they did have some wonderful times together, she and Barry, on her evenings off, or her free Saturday afternoons. Sometimes going to the cinema to see the silent films where they watched Charlie Chaplin or Mary Pickford, and listened to the piano keeping up with the action, while they sat at the back, holding hands and looking forward to exchanging kisses on the way home.

Or, maybe going for walks in the beautiful weather, in the Meadows or by the Water of Leith, hiding themselves under trees if possible, where they might even lie together, though Elinor was cautious at first about that. Barry had laughed and drawn her down to him, saying it was an old Scottish custom for a couples to lie together still in their clothes, now hadn't she heard of it? No, she hadn't, she'd laughed, she was sure he was making it up, but she'd lain beside him all the same, and had given herself up to delight in being so close.

Sometimes, though, it was all much more tranquil, just having tea in a little cafe, Elinor handling the teapot, Barry watching, then walking slowly back to the Primrose, maybe looking over the railings at the gardens, before saying goodbye on their best behaviour, conscious that some eyes somewhere would be upon them.

How Elinor wished days like these would never end, but in late June Barry suggested something new. A visit to his home with Bettina and Georgie on her next free Saturday afternoon.

'It's time we had a get together,' he told Elinor. 'And you can hear me tinkle the ivories and all.'

'Barry, that'd be perfect! I'd love to talk to Bettina and Georgie and hear you play the piano. It's very kind of Bettina to ask me.'

'Oh, she didn't ask you,' he said carelessly. 'It was my own idea. She'll be glad to see you, though. Georgie, too.'

'You're sure?' Elinor asked doubtfully.

'Sure I'm sure. It's all arranged. You be thinking of what tunes you'd like to hear and I'll play 'em for you.'

'June twenty-seventh is the next Saturday I can take. Shall we make it then?'

'That'll be fine. I'll tell Bettina.'

'She mightn't be free.'

'She will be,' Barry said airily. 'I'll call for you same as usual.'

Thirty-Six

The Howats' flat was in a side street off the South Bridge, not part of a tenement but the ground floor of a small terraced house. From the look of the exterior, no maintenance had been done for some time, but the flat itself was beautifully clean and tidy, something that Barry commented on with a grin.

'Aye, Bettina here keeps the inside as neat as a pin, but seeing as I'm a painter, the outside gets neglected. But then, why should I do the landlord's work for him?'

'Why not, if it makes the place look better?' Bettina cried, after she'd shaken Elinor's hand and thanked her for the little posy she'd brought. 'But getting Barry to do something for me is just impossible!'

'It's the same at home,' Elinor said quickly.

'Our shoes are always last to be mended, though my dad's a cobbler.'

'That right? Well, please take a seat, while I get the tea. Georgie'll be back in a minute, he's just away to the dairy.'

Though she seemed pleasant enough, Elinor felt there was still a certain reserve in Bettina's manner. She had Barry's looks, but as with Georgie, Barry's natural charm was missing, perhaps in Bettina's case to be replaced by strength of character. In other words, she liked her own way, was Elinor's verdict, whose fascinated eyes were now moving round the flat, taking in the shining range and well-brushed matting, the framed country scenes and photographs on the walls, the sofa and chairs with protective covers, the table set for tea with currant loaf already cut and a large ginger cake.

So this was Barry's home? It seemed to be more Bettina's. There was no feel of Barry about it, somehow, except for the old, yellow-keyed piano in the corner, at which he was already seating himself and waving to her to come and sit close by.

'Here goes!' he called. 'The great concert begins. What d'you fancy, then?'

'Oh, Barry, I don't know. I never hear much music.'

'Ah, that's a shame. Our folks used to sing a lot, at the kirk and local concerts, and Bettina sings, too, and plays the piano.' Barry was already running his fingers up and down the keys. 'Georgie and me, we're no singers, but I earn a few bob at the pubs with the piano, and

184

Georgie plays the organ.' Barry laughed. 'At the kirk, of course; we've no organ here. How about if I play you an old favourite – "Shine on Harvest Moon"?'

'That sounds lovely,' Elinor cried, already enraptured. Not since she was at school had she really heard anyone play the piano; certainly no one played anything in Friar's Wynd.

While Bettina moved around in the background and Georgie arrived with a can of milk, Barry played his own selection of popular tunes – some Scottish, some from theatre shows, some from the ragtime music he said were his favourites.

'Ah, listen to this!' he cried. 'This is Scott Joplin's "Maple Leaf"! Hear that rhythm? And here's his "Solace" – you'll like this, Elinor – so romantic, so sad.'

'Almost brings the tears to my eyes,' she told him, at which he switched to 'Pine Apple Rag', quick and snappy, to make her smile, and seemed ready to play for ever, until Bettina cried, 'Tea's ready!'

'One last one,' he told them and finished with Harry Lauder's 'Roamin' in the Gloamin'', a song even Elinor knew, and they all went humming to the table.

'I thought you played really well, Barry,' Elinor told him earnestly. 'You could play anything, I'm sure.'

'Not from music,' Bettina said smartly. 'The trouble with Barry is that he'll never bother to learn anything properly. I mean, Ma offered him piano lessons same as me and Georgie—'

'Aye, a shilling a time with old Mrs Hossack,'

185

Barry put in serenely. 'I told her to save her money.'

'So you just vamp out tunes you've heard and if anyone shows you a piece of music, you canna play it. I don't call that clever!'

Did Bettina really not like Barry? Elinor was wondering, observing her cold expression as she filled up cups and passed the currant bread. If so, she'd be the first person Elinor had met not to respond to his charm. He and Georgie seemed to get on well, though, so perhaps Bettina was just somehow resentful of Barry's sliding through life without doing any of the work she had to do. Must have been hard for her, having to take on her mother's role.

'Can I help you clear away, Bettina?' Elinor asked quickly at the end of the meal when the two brothers moved to sit down and light cigarettes. Must show willing, she thought; must get on the right side of Barry's sister.

'Thanks,' Bettina replied, stacking the tea things on a tray. 'If you come this way, I've a wee scullery out here where I do the dishes and the washing.'

Handing Elinor a tea towel, Bettina gave her a quick glance.

'At least you're one to help,' she murmured. 'No' like some.'

'You mean the laddies?' Elinor smiled. 'They are never keen to do the washing-up.'

'As a matter o' fact, I was thinking of the lassies.'

'What lassies?' Elinor had paused in her drying of a plate, but Bettina was now working fast, setting dishes to drain.

'The ones we've had here,' she replied. 'Barry's lady friends. Never offered to do a thing.'

A cold little feeling trickled down Elinor's spine.

'He's brought other girls here?'

'One or two. Two, to be honest.' Bettina's colour suddenly rose and she put her hand on Elinor's arm. 'Look, I shouldn't have said anything. I said to myself before you came, I'll say nothing, but then I suppose it's all right, eh? I mean, you'd expect somebody like Barry to have had a few lady friends?'

'I suppose so.' Elinor began slowly to continue drying dishes. 'They're in the past, anyway.'

'Sure they are!' Bettina, smiling warmly on Elinor, seemed now to be trying to make amends for her earlier coldness. 'And I think he's more interested in you than the others. You'd probably be good for him, too. Just don't butter him up too much, eh? He thinks enough of himself as it is.'

On the way back to the club, Elinor was subdued, undecided whether or not to mention what Bettina had told her. It had been a blow to hear that Barry had taken other girls home, but then it was true what his sister had said. No one would expect him not to have had other girls before herself. Still, to take them home, as though they were special, as she'd thought herself special, that was what hurt.

'Hey, what's up?' Barry asked as they left the tram and approached the lane where they usually paused to exchange kisses. 'You've been as silent

187

as the grave all the way back. What have I done, then?'

'Nothing.' Elinor's fine eyes rested on him with a considering look. 'It's just that I didn't know you'd taken other girls home.'

'Oh, hell, Bettina's been blabbing, eh?' Barry heaved a long sigh. 'I knew I shouldn't have left you alone with her. Thing is, what's it matter? I've been out with other girls, nothing unusual in that. I've no' been living in a monastery.'

'But taking them home, as though they meant something to you – that's what surprised me.'

'They didn't mean anything to me, that's the point.'

'And I don't either?'

'No, you're different.'

They had reached the lane and left the bright sunshine for its shadows. Barry, taking Elinor into his arms, kissed her swiftly. 'And remember this, sweetheart. Didn't you go out with your tutor fellow before you met me? And have I ever got upset over him?'

'No,' she admitted reluctantly.

'Because he's in the past, like the girls I took home. Let us live for today, eh?'

They made their passionate goodbyes, which gradually soothed Elinor's pain, until they had to make their way to the area gate of the club, where they were, as always, very decorous in saying goodnight.

'See you Thursday?' Barry whispered. 'Just as usual?'

'Just as usual,' she murmured happily.

But the headlines in the Monday morning

188

papers gave the news that was to prevent anything being usual in their lives ever again, even if they didn't know it.

'Archduke Franz Ferdinand and wife Sophie assassinated in Sarajevo!' screamed the banners. 'Heir to the Austro–Hungary throne shot by a Serb!'

What would happen now? asked the editorials. How would France retaliate? Where would Germany stand? And Russia? And Great Britain?

'Why, whatever has it got to do with us?' the maids asked at the Primrose, for nobody seemed to have mentioned Belgium, which Miss Ainslie had said might be important.

On the fourth of August, they were to find out what it had to do with them. On that day, their country was at war.

Thirty-Seven

Seemingly, it all came back to Belgium, after all.

For there it was, in the club's newspapers that the maids rushed up to read before the members arrived – the whole awful list of events that had involved Belgium and their own country in war.

Like a fall of dominos, one event had triggered another, with the Serb's assassination of the Archduke being the start, causing Austria to declare war on Serbia, Russia to declare support for Serbia, Germany to declare war on Russia, then France, and – because they needed to get through it and weren't given permission – Belgium. What could Great Britain do? They had to keep their promises. As the last domino to fall, after a failed ultimatum, they declared war on Germany.

'Oh, Lord,' groaned Gerda, 'it's just like Miss Ainslie told us. We promised to defend Belgium, so there we are.'

'She didn't think there'd be a war, though,' sighed Ada.

'Got it wrong, then. Quick, we'd better get downstairs before anyone catches us reading the members' papers.'

'Aye, what'll Mrs Petrie say if she finds out we've read 'em before her?' asked Mattie, but they all knew that for once they had more to worry about than Mrs Petrie's temper.

Four days had to pass before Elinor could see Barry on Thursday evening. Four days during which war fever seemed to grip the country, a sort of euphoric relief that the talk was over and action lay ahead, and away went hordes of young men to enlist, while flags were waved and people were proud.

Not Elinor and Ada, however, who wondered why anyone should want to go to war and hoped that their young men would not be called up by the government, to go whether they wanted to or not. They'd never be fool enough to volunteer, they were sure of that, and with so many men already enlisting, plus the regular army, perhaps there'd be enough to fight without conscripting any others. Besides, the papers were saying everything would be over by Christmas, which meant they wouldn't be needed anyway.

Thank God Corrie was not rushing off to join up either, Hessie told Elinor. He'd thought about it, but Walt had told him not to be so daft. It was only that some lads at the factory had got together to join up as a 'Pals' unit – friends going together – and Corrie had thought he should go, too. But he'd seen sense in the end and it was to be hoped Barry would feel the same.

'Barry?' Elinor cried. 'Why, he'd never volunteer. He wouldn't want to leave his football!'

'Or you,' Hessie said fondly.

They were to meet at the Scott Monument in Princes Street, walk up to the Old Town to a café for high tea, then maybe go to one of the cinemas. The evening, still full of sunshine, was warm, the air relaxing; maybe they shouldn't go and shut themselves in the darkness, but light was their enemy and the cinema a welcome place to be together and not be seen. First, though, Elinor wanted to hear Barry's ideas on the war.

'What d'you think of it?' she asked, when he came strolling up, a cigarette at his lip. 'This awful war?'

'Had to happen.' He discarded his cigarette and kissed her cheek. 'The Kaiser's wanted it all along, eh?'

'Why, though? Who would want a war?'

'For power, maybe.' Barry shrugged. 'Plenty are pleased about it, anyway. Sort of – clears the air.'

191

'Clears the air? I should think it'd do the opposite.'

'Means we know where we stand.' Barry slipped her arm into his. 'Come on, let's get to the café. I've something to tell you.'

Something to tell her? Afterwards, she'd wondered why she hadn't been more afraid. But he'd been so much his usual self, his eyes bright on hers, his smile easy. Why should she have been afraid?

In the café, they sat opposite each other at a corner table that gave them privacy and ordered their usual – ham and salad for Elinor, sausages and mash for Barry.

'Oh, dear,' Elinor sighed, pointing at the sausages. 'Barry, you should be having salad like me.'

'Rabbit food? No' me. I'm stocking up on ma favourites. They say you only get bully beef in the army.'

'In the army?' Her eyes were wide. 'What's that got to do with you?'

'I've enlisted,' he said calmly. 'I've joined the Royal Scots.'

The silence that followed was not really a silence at all. True, she wasn't saying anything, but in her head were beating all kinds of noises, jangling, terrible noises, as though guns were already firing, and she wondered if she would ever be able to speak again through the mesh of sounds.

'Don't look like that,' Barry was saying, cutting up a sausage. 'It'll no' be for long. All going to be over by Christmas, then I'll be back.'

'Why?' she asked at last, her lips so dry she could scarcely speak. 'Why volunteer?'

'Show willing, eh? For King and country. Got to do your bit.'

'They're no' calling men up. You may never be needed.'

'Och, I want to go! I want to tackle the Kaiser, show him what's what. It'll be better than house-painting any day of the week, I can tell you.'

'You don't mind leaving your football?'

'I'll probably get some football in the army, and besides it'll be there when I get back. And so will you, sweetheart. I tell you, I'll no' be gone long. Now you eat up that green stuff, eh? No waste allowed.'

But she couldn't eat anything and didn't even try. Putting her knife and fork together, she leaned forward to look at Barry, her lips parted, her eyes enormous.

'Barry,' she said softly, 'can we be married before you go?'

Another silence fell, but this time there were no noises in Elinor's head, no fear that she might not speak again, for she was waiting for Barry. He had finished his meal and was looking down at his plate, finally pushing it away and raising his eyes, their look on her as bright as ever.

'Phew!' he said lightly. 'That took me by surprise.'

'Because I shouldn't be asking?'

'No, no. It's just – well, out of the blue. I'd no idea it was in your mind.'

'No idea it was in my mind?' Elinor's face was flushed, her eyes flashing. 'Wasn't it in yours?'

193

'Ah, look...' He reached over the table for her hand but she held it back. 'Look, you know me. You must know I'm no' the marrying kind. I thought you understood.'

'Understood what?'

'Well, that I live for the day. I've said so, eh? I live for the day; I don't plan for the future. I'm no' ready for that and neither are you. Look at the way you didn't want a future with your Stephen.'

'I never said I didn't want a future with you.'

'Never came up, did it? We were enjoying ourselves, weren't we? Just going out together, that's what we had. I'm no' saying I wouldn't want more, but I wouldn't expect it from a girl like you, and I wouldn't want to be married to get it, either, so what we had suited me and I thought suited you and all.'

'It was ... just temporary?' she asked, after a pause.

'Why are we talking as if it's over?'

'Just temporary?' she repeated.

'Well, wouldn't have lasted, nothing does, but it was grand, eh? I was much happier with you than any of the others.'

'Were you?' Elinor turned her head, looking for their waitress. 'Shall we go?'

'Hey, what about some tea? And treacle tart? They've got nice cakes here.'

'Well, you order some tea and treacle tart, then. I have to go.'

'Go where?' For the first time, she saw his sunny expression fade, his eyes sharpen. 'Elinor, you're never leaving me? Come on, I've explained how things are. We can still meet when I come home.'

She was beginning to feel ill, her face tightening with the effort to keep back tears. She knew she must get away, away from Barry, out of the café, and prayed he would not follow. People were staring as she pushed aside her chair and rose from the table. Perhaps she was looking odd – perhaps they were expecting her to faint. She would not faint. No, she would not.

'Goodbye, Barry,' she whispered. 'No, don't come. Pay the girl, eh?'

'Wait!' he cried, as she reached the door. Heard the bell jangle. Was out in the fresh air, taking deep gulps of it. Knew he was behind her, saw the tram. And ran.

Her last sight of him was his strangely puzzled face as she was borne away, tears slowly moving down her face at last, aware that she might never see him again but still unable to wish him luck. As she had put a dagger into Stephen's heart, so had Barry put one into hers; she owed him nothing. All the same, she should have wished him luck. He was going to risk his life; he might never come back.

But she couldn't think of that. Couldn't think now of anything at all. Not even the war, and what it would mean. Soon, she would begin to feel again, she knew it, but as the tram rattled on down the Mound, she felt only numb. Slightly unreal. A single cardboard figure sitting alone, when so often there had been someone with her, holding her hand, looking into her eyes.

But this was how it was going to be. This was her future. It was lucky she still couldn't feel anything about it, and let her drenched eyes rest on her city, looking so beautiful in the dusk of the summer evening, until the tram reached her stop and she had to get down. Brace herself to face the people at the club. Needn't tell them anything yet. Oh, not yet.

Walking slowly, she passed the gardens of the square and paused to look at the green of the grass and the leaves of the trees and shrubs, all so lovely in the soft light of dusk. They had always given her solace. Still did, but she knew she must wait – wait for time to do its work before she could fully take delight again in the gardens. Or anything, for that matter.

Here was the gate to the area, the worn steps down to the back door, and she could hear voices, probably from the girls making cocoa. Faces would be turned to hers. Someone would notice her tears. They would be wondering...

Ah, maybe she would just tell them. She and Barry had parted. He was going to the war, but they had parted anyway. Yes, she would tell them, let herself begin to feel, come alive, however bad it was.

The back door opened, Mattie was on the step, shaking a cloth.

'Why, hello, Elinor!' she cried. 'Want some cocoa?'

Thirty-Eight

Over by Christmas? The war? That was a joke. Though nobody was laughing.

In fact, barely three weeks after war had been declared people had discovered that there was nothing to laugh about in this war, nothing to make it an adventure, or a great lark, or better than going to work. They discovered it the hard way, when news came of the retreat by the British in France after the Battle of Mons, defeated by the Germans at the cost of 1600 men. A further defeat followed, at Le Cateau, where the casualty list was huge. No more euphoria, then, even though recruitment still continued, but at least the volunteers knew now what really lay ahead; they no longer carried false hopes of a speedy victory.

Meanwhile, strange things were happening at home, as people gradually became used to the idea that they were now at war. At first, there had been the problem of panic buying of food, but when that had been resolved, real shortages began to show up, as manufacturers began to switch from goods for the home to equipment for war. Worse for some, even than the shortages, was the sudden disappearance of servants, as women took the places of men, making munitions, working in factories, and saying goodbye with a light heart to domestic work.

'Can't get staff now,' the older lady members at the Primrose complained to Miss Ainslie. 'The girls just don't seem to exist any more.'

Just like some of my staff and our younger members, Miss Ainslie would have commented to Miss Denny, except that Miss Denny had gone to learn to drive an ambulance and would soon be leaving for France. And the younger club members? They, too, had vanished to take up voluntary work, leaving the club an echoing shadow of its former self, while Vera had deserted Mrs Petrie for the munitions factory, along with Gerda.

And when Mrs Petrie demanded how she was going to manage with only wee Sal to help, Miss Ainslie had to tell her gently that only a handful of ladies were requiring meals now, and with no country members staying overnight, the time might soon be coming when even the number of maids that remained might have to be reduced.

'I really don't know what is going to happen,' Miss Ainslie admitted later to Elinor. 'This whole thing is becoming a nightmare.'

'It is,' Elinor agreed, as the manageress gave her a sympathetic glance.

Everyone, of course, knew of Elinor's own private nightmare, though she never spoke of it after her first announcement, and showed little of her inner turmoil in her strong, lovely face. For, of course, her numbness hadn't lasted long. She'd had to suffer, and was still suffering, not only from loss of love, but also a certain humiliation that she should have offered herself as a wife to Barry and been turned down. In a way, she rather hoped that that feeling would crush out her heartache, but it hadn't happened yet.

Nor did she know what had happened to Barry. He had turned up at the club with another note, offering to meet, but she had thrown away the note and had not contacted him. It was lucky, anyway, that he was departing, for her father was all set to seek him out and give him 'what for', which would have been disastrous – for Walter, rather than Barry. Yes, she thanked God that he was away, out of her life, and also that Stephen Muirhead would never know how her affair with him had ended. But what had happened to Stephen himself? She just hoped, wherever he was, that he was safe.

'To tell you the truth,' Miss Ainslie was saying, 'I'm afraid now that the club will have to close. It's what the owners believe.'

'The Primrose? To close?' Elinor's eyes were filled with horror. 'Oh, no, that couldn't happen, Miss Ainslie, it couldn't!'

'I know how you feel. I feel the same. But there's a war on, places are closing all around us. It will only be until things get back to normal.'

The two women exchanged long, sorrowful looks. Back to normal? When would that be? They knew now that trench warfare was becoming established and that battles could rage for weeks on end before being won in no decisive way and with enormous loss of life. There was no point in even talking about peace at this stage.

'When d'you think there might be a decision?'

Elinor asked a little huskily. 'On closing?'

'Fairly soon.'

'Suppose I should be thinking about some war work, anyway,' Elinor murmured after a pause. 'Mattie'd like to go for the munitions, but I'd rather do some sort of nursing. I've done a bit at the Red Cross centre and enjoyed it.'

This was true. Working at the centre on her free Thursday evenings had been the best thing Elinor had found for taking her mind off the man who'd spent other Thursdays with her. In nursing, there simply was no time to think of anything but the work in hand.

'Why, that's excellent, Elinor. If you'd like to have extra hours there, I could give you some time off.' Miss Ainslie gave a tired smile. 'As you know, we're not so busy these days.'

Barely a week later, the blow fell. Miss Ainslie called everyone together to her office for an important announcement.

'No' about the suffragettes this time, eh?' Mattie whispered, and even Elinor smiled.

Everyone knew that the women's suffrage movement had temporarily ceased its activities, with most of its members busy with war work. When things returned to normal, they would resume their quest for the vote, but for the time being, there were other needs to be met.

'What I have to tell you will come as a surprise,' Miss Ainslie was saying now, at which Elinor heaved a deep sigh, believing that she knew what to expect. In fact, she didn't, for she was as surprised as everyone else when the manageress announced in her cool, clear tones that the club had been taken over by the government.

'Requisitioned, as they call it. The Primrose, as we know it, is to close, but will reopen, when conversion is complete, as a small convalescent hospital for soldiers. Some will be recovering from wounds, some from neurasthenia – what's known as shell shock. This will be its role until the end of hostilities.'

Those listening exchanged glances. Requisitioned? That was a long word with an unwelcome meaning. For them, at least, as it was certain they would all be losing their jobs.

'So we'll all be given the sack, Miss Ainslie?' Ada asked, to make matters clear.

'I'm afraid so, but it's quite possible that when the conversion is finished, there'll be jobs going here. For domestic workers, or assistants to the Queen Alexandra's nurses who will be looking after the patients.'

Again, glances were exchanged.

'It's munitions for me,' Mattie said firmly. 'Vera and Gerda say the wages are no' bad and you can do overtime.'

'I've always been in service,' Ada sighed. 'I'm no' keen on factory work.'

'Nor me,' said Sal. 'I'm going to stick to cooking.'

'Ha!' Mrs Petrie exclaimed. 'And where are you going to pass yourself as a cook, may I ask?'

'Miss Ainslie, how long will the conversion take?' Elinor asked quietly. 'I'd like to try for an assistant nursing post.'

'I'm told by the owners that it should be finished by next February. All our furnishings will have to go into store, of course, and temporary fitments will be going up for the wards, but there'll be no need for operating theatres or anything of that sort. The patients here will either be convalescing, or, as I say, shell-shock sufferers.'

Miss Ainslie, clearing her throat, looked from watching face to watching face.

'I'd just like to say, I know it's hard, to lose your jobs, and this has been, I hope, a happy place to work, but perhaps we should think – you know – of the club's new role.'

'How d'you mean?' asked Mrs Pierce. 'It's no' our role, eh? We're leaving.'

'That's true, and we're all upset about it, but at least we can take some comfort knowing that the club's not going to be left empty. It will be providing a place where some of the war casualties can come after treatment, to rest and build up their strength, get used to injuries that can't be healed. That's why I say we should be glad of our club's new purpose. To help those who've fought for us. So many have been killed already, it's good that something's being done for those still alive.'

There was a short silence, during which the maids lowered their eyes, and Mrs Pierce blew her nose.

'Aye, that's true,' she admitted, after a moment. 'You put it very well, Miss Ainslie. I wish there was something I could do, but I think I'll just be taking a wee rest. How about you?'

'Me?' Miss Ainslie smiled. 'I'm following Miss Denny's example – I'm joining the VAD – that's short for Voluntary Aid Detachment.'

'Sort of nursing?' asked Mattie.

'Well, nursing and anything and everything. Serving where you're needed, I suppose.'

'Make a change from working at the Primrose Club,' Mrs Petrie remarked, but Elinor smiled.

'Serving where you're needed? Sounds pretty much like working at the Primrose Club to me.'

Thirty-Nine

It was early March before the transformation of the Primrose Club into a small military hospital was completed. By then, of course, the staff had made their tearful farewells and taken their last tours of the building they knew so well. Exchanged last hugs and promises to keep in touch – and scattered: Miss Ainslie to her VAD training, Mattie to a munitions factory, Sal to the kitchens of one of the hotels still functioning, Mrs Petrie, in spite of her talk of 'resting', to cook for a titled family in the New Town who welcomed her with open arms, they having had no one to cook for them for months.

As for Elinor, as she'd planned, she'd applied for a post as nursing aide at the new hospital and, after an interview with a stern-faced QA nursing sister, had been accepted, while Ada had surprised everybody by announcing that she was finally going to get married. Aye, it was about time, eh? But after her Bob, against all her protests, had put himself in the army and was now due to go to France very soon, they were determined to marry first. A registry office wedding, no fuss, but would everybody come?

Of course they would, and on a cold bright day in February, with Gerda and Vera joining in, the old friends from the Primrose met at the registry office together with the families of the young couple, and threw their confetti and shed a few tears. Afterwards, there was a meal at a nearby café, and then the 'going away', which was only as far as a boarding house off Lothian Road, while the guests thanked Ada's parents and separated.

Not before sighing and exchanging bleak looks, for wartime weddings were not like other weddings. You couldn't necessarily hope for a long and happy married life for the couple, could you? Not with the casualty lists from France and Belgium as long as they were, not with the dreaded telegrams being delivered to relatives every day of the week.

'Bob might be all right,' Mattie said with a brave attempt at optimism. 'I mean, there has to be some who come back.'

'Very true,' Mrs Petrie agreed, but even her sharp eyes were shadowed, and no one else had the heart to say anything. Certainly, there were no looks or questions directed at 'poor' Elinor, whose young man had gone to war but had seemingly made it plain she needn't wait for him. She wouldn't even know what had happened to him, would she, whether he was alive or dead?

No, she didn't know, and tried not to think

204

about it. These days, after all, she was thankful she had other things to occupy her mind, such as the new job she must soon take up at the converted club, which she was already worrying over. That nursing sister had been pretty stiff in the interview, hadn't she? Emphasizing all the difficulties that Elinor, as an unqualified nursing aide, would face, how she must be prepared for any job that came her way – cleaning the sluice, emptying bedpans, helping handicapped soldiers with dressing, shaving, walking, et cetera. And, above all, not minding what she saw.

'The effects of modern warfare are not pretty, Miss Rae, as you will have already discovered with your Red Cross training, but in a hospital such as the Primrose Military, you may find some sights even more distressing. Convalescent the patients might be, but all that means is that they're over their operations. It does not mean that they will be truly recovered and looking as they used to do.'

'I understand,' Elinor had replied. 'And I hope I know what to expect.'

Still unsmiling, the sister accepted her reply, rose, shook her hand and told her she had been successful in her application.

'I think you will do well,' she added grudgingly. 'You're a strong-looking girl and strength is another thing we are looking for. I believe I forgot to mention that.'

What a relief it would be, Elinor thought, after Ada's wedding, to begin her new job and be free of anxiety about it. Since the closure of the club, she'd been living at home and working as a temporary sales assistant at Logie's Department Store, where her mother was still employed as a cleaning lady. There were now plenty of vacancies at the rather grand store, where at one time it had been difficult to get even a foot in the door, and Hessie said she couldn't understand why Elinor didn't just stay there, instead of wanting to work in a hospital where goodness knows what sights she'd have to face. After all, she'd wanted to better herself and working at Logie's was better than being in service, eh? What did she want now, then? What was driving her?'

'I just want to do something to help, Ma. I want to try to repay what the soldiers are doing for the country.'

'That's what Corrie wants to do,' Hessie said worriedly. 'You know he's had one or two of those white feathers pushed in his hand? For no' being in uniform?'

'What, from awful women?' Elinor's face was red with anger. 'They make me so cross! Staying at home in perfect safety and going around accusing young fellows of cowardice.'

'But Corrie thinks they're right, you see. One of these days he's going to run off and join up and your dad'll have a fit. I'm no' joking. I worry about him, the way he goes on over Corrie.'

'We're all worried.' Elinor sighed.

Forty

Working at the new Primrose, though, turned out to be, for Elinor, no worry at all. Wearing a grey uniform dress similar to the QAs but without, of course, their badges of rank or their outdoor scarlet cape, she slid with amazing smoothness into the routine of the converted hospital, able to use what she had learned and quick to learn more. Though it was true there were things to get used to – more upsetting even than she'd imagined – well, she did get used to them and accepted them, knowing it was, after all, worse for the young damaged soldiers than for her. It was their suffering she had to think of, as well as the torment of those without obvious injury at all – the shell-shock cases, the most difficult of any to treat, it was said.

It had helped Elinor that the people she worked with – the doctors, the other nursing aides and the QAs – were pleasant and friendly, with even the matron in charge being welcoming, and Sister Penny, the senior nursing sister who'd interviewed her, quite relaxed in manner, once she'd seen Elinor's willingness to learn. All were intrigued to discover that she had worked at the Primrose when it was a ladies' club, and asked her how she found it now.

'Very different,' she told them with a smile, though in fact it was possible for her to recognize the old Primrose beneath all the partitions and new functions of the rooms she used to know. In a way, it had been a little creepy at first, as though ghosts of her old self and the rest of the staff were still there, moving through the places where they'd once worked, mixing with the shadowy club members long departed to their new activities.

Now, the wide reception hall had been chopped up for doctors' surgeries, the Quiet Room was reserved for treatment by the nurses, the elegant drawing room had become a common room for the men, complete with easy chairs and games tables, and the dining room, where the maids had hurried around, serving Mrs Petrie's delicious meals, now offered very different fare. Mounds of boiled potatoes, great vats of stew, huge solid rice puddings and spotted dick to follow, all prepared by army cooks in a cheerful, easy-going fashion that would have had Mrs P herself hitting the roof. How lucky that she was no longer there!

Upstairs, small wards seemed to have been magically created, although a number of single rooms remained, one of which Elinor recognized as the one she had shared with Gerda and Mattie, where she had spent many a sleepless hour. Except when on night duty, all staff at the new Primrose lived 'out', the QAs in a nurses' home, Elinor and other aides with their families, which suited Elinor well enough.

Though the atmosphere at home could still occasionally be uneasy, Walter Rae had certainly rather mellowed, though Corrie had to tread carefully whenever the progress of the war was mentioned. Casualty lists were just as high, especially as a new front in the Dardanelles had been opened in April, with the British, Australian and New Zealand forces trying to capture Constantinople in an effort to gain a sea route to Russia. They were not to succeed, many men were to die or be injured, and as one QA remarked to Elinor, some would probably end up in places like the Primrose, trying to get their heads back together and face life again, eh?

Elinor was silent, thinking of the closed faces of the shell shocked, their blank eyes fixed on sights others couldn't see and wouldn't want to have seen; horrors no young fellows should have had to see and forever remember.

It was said that these patients would eventually be moved on to specialist hospitals, but at present there was a shortage of such places, and the doctors at the Primrose had to do what they could. There were some senior army men, it seemed, who didn't believe there even was such a thing as shell shock, and that those who claimed to be suffering from it were just trying it on, but Elinor couldn't imagine how anyone looking into the patients' eyes could believe that. Such desolation could not be faked.

Often, seeing the results of war on men, she thought of her brother and his passionate desire to enlist and do his bit. And end up like the patients she helped to nurse? She couldn't bear to think about it. Or that Barry might meet the same fate. Not that she often thought of Barry. More often than not, it was Stephen she found herself thinking about, not even knowing if he had joined up. She thought he probably had – it would be like him to want to help his country – but she had no way of finding out where he was and had no right to know, anyway, after what she'd done.

Still, his fine face came often into her mind and, one strange day in April, she thought she saw him. He was in the entrance hall of the Primrose, his tall, straight figure in khaki uniform standing before a nurse at the small table that had replaced Miss Denny's handsome reception desk. Passing through, on her way to attend to a patient, at the sight of Stephen, Elinor stopped in her tracks, her heart jumping.

'Stephen!' she almost called, but then remembered she had no right to expect him to speak to her. Perhaps he had sensed her presence anyway, for he turned his fair head and looked at her. And – oh, God – it wasn't him, it wasn't Stephen.

So much like him, with the same height and slim build, the same set to the shoulders and the fair hair she'd always said women would envy. But the face wasn't his. A nice face, a pleasant face, but not his, and though she half-smiled and he smiled back, before turning to the nurse who was asking him some question, she felt such a pang of disappointment, she longed just to turn aside, go into the gardens and try to be alone for a moment.

She couldn't, of course, do that, though these days she did have access to keys, for the patients had been given permission to sit in the gardens and it was one of her duties to give them any help needed. To sneak in on her own, off duty, was something she liked to do, hoping no one would notice, but now she must continue on her way, her heart still thumping and crazy questions beginning to form in her mind.

What had she done? Thrown away what had been hers? Which would never be hers again? What madness had come over her? Why had she done it?

Because Barry was exciting, that was why, as she suddenly began to see. He was exciting and he had excited her. Drawn her to him because of the new and strange passion he had caused her to feel, made her forget all that she'd felt for Stephen. But Barry had never intended their relationship to be permanent. He lived and loved for the moment and moved on, while Stephen's love would have been for a lifetime. A lifetime she knew now she would never share.

Walking slowly on, trying to remember where she should be going, she heard a woman's voice say her name and turned her head.

'Elinor! Elinor, is it you? Now, why did you never get in touch?'

'Brenda!' cried Elinor, shaken from her thoughts by the sight of the familiar face. 'Oh, how grand to see you! But why are you here?'

Forty-One

She was looking prettier than Elinor remembered. Pink-cheeked, eyes sparkling, her knot of pale blonde hair looser than before – Brenda had blossomed. And Elinor thought, why, she's happy! That's why she looks so different. Everyone knew that happiness was the best aid to good looks, and Brenda was good-looking now.

'What am I doing here?' she asked, holding Elinor at arm's length and studying her. 'I'm going to be working here, that's what. I've just had an interview to be a nurses' aide and they've taken me on. How about you?'

'I'm already a nurses' aide! Oh, fancy you and me doing the same thing – is that no' strange?'

'I think it's wonderful. I start next week and I'll already have a friend – what could be better? Look, could we talk? I've so much to tell you and you never got in touch.'

'I know, I feel bad.' Elinor gave an apologetic smile. 'Thing is, I have to take a patient down for some treatment now, but I get off early today – five o'clock. Could we meet at that little café in South Queensferry Street?'

'You bet.' Brenda's newly attractive face was wreathed in smiles. 'Elinor, this is a real bonus for me, knowing you'll be here. It'll make such a difference, eh? I don't mind telling you, I'm scared stiff about the new job.'

'I was the same, but there was no need and you'll do well. See you at the café, then.'

After they'd hugged and parted, Elinor, on her way to her patient, glanced back at the reception desk, but the fair-haired soldier was already putting on his cap and leaving. He caught her look and again gave a polite smile, but she had the feeling that he was not to be a patient and that she would not see him again. Not that it mattered, he was not the one she wanted to see, yet she marvelled over how things could work out, how a perfect stranger could show her how she felt. And of course that didn't matter, for there was no point in feeling as she did. It had come too late.

At the West End café, Brenda was already at a table when Elinor arrived, and said she had ordered tea and buttered toast, if that was all right.

'Wonderful, I'm always starving by this time of day.'

'You'll be living at home, eh? Hope you won't be in trouble, being late back?'

'Och, no. Ma knows I'm often kept at work.' Elinor smiled, as the waitress brought their order and Brenda poured their tea. 'Anyway, I didn't want to miss seeing you and hearing all your news.'

'Heavens, can't you see it?' Brenda cried, pointing to the pretty pearl ring on her left hand. 'Tam and I are engaged!'

'Engaged?' Elinor, seizing Brenda's hand to

213

have a closer look at the ring, gave a delighted smile. So that was it? The explanation of Brenda's blossoming? She might have guessed it, yet was still surprised, Tam and Brenda having seemed so far apart at one time. It was easy to see, though, that Brenda was truly happy, and Elinor congratulated her, saying she couldn't be more pleased.

'And it's a lovely ring, Brenda. When did Tam give it to you?'

A slight shadow crossed Brenda's face.

'Before he went to France – just last month. You know he joined the Black Watch? Oh, yes, he must volunteer – nothing I said made any difference – just kept saying he liked a good fight and he'd do his bit against Jerry, et cetera. Then when he had a weekend's leave, he popped the question.' Brenda sipped her tea. 'I told him not to worry about a ring, I didn't need one, but he insisted, borrowed the money from his dad and there we are. Engaged. Bet you never thought you'd see the day.'

'I'm sure you'll both be very happy,' Elinor said earnestly. 'Tam's a bit of a joker, but I've always known he was good-hearted under all the show. It'll be wonderful for you, making a new life with him.'

'Well, first we have to have the wedding – that'll be on Tam's next leave, just something quiet at the kirk. But, thanks to Mr Muirhead, he has a good job to come back to when the war's over – if he comes back, that is.'

'Don't talk like that, Brenda! He will come back, he will!' Elinor had flushed a little. 'How'd you mean, thanks to Mr Muirhead?'

'Well, he gave Tam such a good reference and a note to a paper works manager he knows, that Tam got into the office where they were saying he would do very well. Stephen promised to do something for me, too, but I'd already decided to try for nursing.' Brenda put down her teacup. 'Did you know he'd enlisted?'

'Mr Muirhead? No, I didn't know.'

'Joined the King's Own Scottish Borderers.' Brenda's eyes on Elinor were suddenly curious. 'But what happened between you two?' she asked softly. 'Something did, didn't it?'

'It would never have worked out for us,' Elinor answered after a pause. 'Anyway, I met someone else. And before you say anything, that didn't work out either.'

'Oh, Elinor, I'm so sorry. Look, I won't pry any more. Tell me what it's like to work at the Primrose, then. Are the fellows all right? I mean, not difficult with the nurses?'

'The better they feel, the sooner they start teasing and trying to flirt. But, to be honest, most of them aren't up to taking an interest.' She hesitated a moment. 'I expect they warned you, to be prepared for things you mightn't want to see. I mean, the doctors have done what they can, but some cases – well, they're still pretty bad.'

'It's all right, the sister did warn me, and I know what to expect.' Brenda raised her hand to their waitress. 'I did some voluntary work at the Royal to prepare myself for this job, anyway, and I know it's not going to be easy. But I have to do it, you see – for Tam's sake.'

215

'I understand.' Elinor stood up. 'Look, let me get this; it was my idea...'

'Come on, what's a pot of tea and a bit of toast?' Brenda laughed a little. 'Remember that argument we had with Stephen about paying the bill?'

'I remember,' said Elinor, who remembered everything.

Outside, they hugged, saying how much they were looking forward to working together, then both ran for their trams, still waving goodbye.

All had gone to war, then, Elinor mused, travelling home. All the young men she personally knew – Barry, Tam and Stephen. But not Corrie. He, at least, would not be in danger. Would it do any good to pray for the others? She'd pray, anyway, even for Barry. Thank God, though, she needn't pray for Corrie.

So she believed. Until she reached home and found her mother sobbing and Corrie sitting with his head in his hands.

'He's done it!' her mother cried. 'Oh, I knew he would. Corrie's joined up, Elinor, and your dad's in a terrible mood!'

Forty-Two

Elinor, pulling off her hat and coat, sank into a chair at the table, where the remains of a meal seemed to indicate that the trouble had started in the middle of tea.

'Aye,' said Hessie, catching her glance, 'we said we'd no' wait for you and I'd just dished up a lovely bit of finnan haddie, I was lucky to get it—'

'Ma,' Elinor sighed, 'never mind the finnan haddie.'

'I'm just saying. Well, then Corrie came and sat down and he looks at me and your dad and he says, "I've done it," and your dad says, "Done what?" And Corrie says...'

'I said I'd volunteered,' Corrie burst out, raising his head and staring desolately at Elinor. 'I said I couldn't stick being out of uniform any longer, and I'd signed up for the Royal Scots. That's all I said, and he blew up.'

'Blew up,' Elinor repeated. 'Like he used to do?'

'The same,' Hessie murmured, putting her hankie to her eyes. 'When he's been so much better lately, and all. But he's only thinking of Corrie, you see. He doesn't want him to join up, and be at risk. He says why get killed if you don't

217

have to?'

'As though anybody can talk like that when the country's at war!' Corrie shouted. 'Conscription's coming anyway, so what's the point in hanging about, letting everybody think you're a coward? Plenty have gone from the factory and I want to be gone, too. I want to do my bit, same as other people, only Dad thinks I should do what he tells me and won't listen to anything I say.'

'Well, he heard you today,' Hessie wailed. 'He heard you and we all suffered. We none of us could eat anything, with him shouting and turning red, and then he leaps up and gets his jacket and out he goes, thundering down the stair like a herd of wild animals.'

'Where'd he go?' asked Elinor. 'Don't tell me – the pub?'

'Where else?' asked Corrie. 'At least he's out of our hair, eh? And with any luck he'll be in a better mood when he comes back.'

'Maybe. There's no saying how he'll be, with you still going to war.' Hessie's eyes were darkly brooding. 'The thing is, Corrie, you've never given a thought to me, have you? How it'll be for me, waiting for the telegram? Because that's all mothers do these days, when their sons are fighting. Every day, you see the casualty lists in the paper and you think, will it be today? Will it be tomorrow? One day, your name'll be there, I know it, Corrie, I know it!'

As she dissolved into tears again, Corrie leaped to put his arms round her and Elinor stood by, tears stabbing her own eyes, until Hessie quietly released herself and said she'd clear the table.

218

'It has to be this way, Ma,' Corrie said in a low voice. 'Canna just be left to other folk to win the war for us. Think I'd put you through all this if I didn't believe I had to?'

'No, no. I can see you have to go.' Hessie dried her eyes and began to gather up the plates from the table. 'But it's hard. Elinor, you've had nothing to eat – shall I fry you a bit of fish?'

'No, I'm all right, thanks. I had some tea and toast earlier on with Brenda – you know, she's coming to work at the Primrose, too.'

'Tea and toast'll never keep you going. I'll put the kettle on and make you a sandwich. Corrie, you could do with something, too, seeing as we none of us got our proper meal.'

'When do you have to leave?' Elinor asked Corrie in a whisper, as Hessie filled the kettle. He lowered his eyes.

'Next week. I do feel bad about it, but what can I do? I have to go.'

'I know you do, and Dad probably does, too. He'll come round in the end, you know, he always does.'

'Maybe no' this time.'

Still, with fresh tea and cheese and pickle sandwiches, they all began to feel a little better, though the thought of Walter's return hung over them liked an ominous cloud. Just wish he'd come in and get it over with, Elinor was thinking, when the sound of a fierce rapping on the downstairs shop door made them all jump.

'Someone's knocking!' Hessie cried. 'Corrie, go and see who it is!'

'Mrs Rae, Mrs Rae, are you there?' they could

hear a man's voice calling, as Corrie began to run down the stairs. 'Hessie, hen, are you there?'

'Oh, God, oh, God, that's Josh Pringle's voice!' Hessie, her face paper-white, was following Corrie, with Elinor close behind. 'One of your dad's pals, you ken – something must've happened. Oh, God, what can it be?'

Corrie, already at the front door, was standing back as a small wiry man came stumbling in, his face as white as Hessie's, his scared eyes fixed on her.

'What's wrong, Mr Pringle?' Corrie asked, taking hold of his mother's arm. 'What's happened? Is it Dad?'

'Aye, it's Walt, he's been took ill. We were in the Castle ... had to get Sammy, the barman, to call the ambulance ... they think it's a seizure...'

'A seizure?' Hessie was collapsing against Corrie's shoulder, while Elinor held her hand. 'Oh, no! No!'

'Where've they taken him?' Elinor asked Josh, who was now wiping his brow with the back of his hand; she could smell the alcohol on his breath, though he was sober enough. 'Quick, where do we go? The infirmary?'

'That's right, the Royal. He'll be there by now; they went off in a great hurry.'

'We'll follow, we'll go now,' Corrie said decisively. 'Thanks very much for coming to tell us, Mr Pringle. We appreciate it.'

'Come on, Ma,' Elinor murmured, helping her mother back up the stairs. 'Let's just lock up the flat and go.'

'I feel so bad,' Hessie was whispering. 'This is

what I've always dreaded. His face so red, you ken, he sometimes looked as if he could collapse – oh, but where's Josh? I must thank Josh...'

'Never mind, Hessie,' Josh called as he left them. 'You just tell Walt I'll be in to see him, eh? Tell him, the lads are thinking of him.'

'Let's lock the door and go,' cried Corrie.

Outside in the street, they stood for a moment, considering how best to get to the Royal as quickly as possible.

'A taxi?' Elinor was sorting coins in her purse. 'I've a shilling – that'd be enough, eh?'

'Aye, a taxi,' Hessie gasped. 'A taxi would be best – but where can we find a taxi?'

'No taxis round here,' said Corrie. 'Where'd you find a taxi rank in Friar's Wynd?'

'Tram, then!' cried Hessie, putting her hand to her mouth. 'Hurry, now, hurry! Oh, d'you think your dad'll be all right?'

'Sure he will,' Elinor told her reassuringly while they ran to the tram stop. 'He'll be at the Royal by now and they'll be taking care of him.'

'He'll be in good hands,' Corrie put in. 'Try no' to worry, Ma.'

But of course they were worrying. Elinor, sitting next to her mother in the tram, with Corrie close by, knew their anxiety was natural, yet when their father had led them such a dance, it might have been thought they wouldn't have been so concerned.

There was no doubt, though, that of late he had mellowed.

Look at the way he had come to seek Elinor out at the Primrose and had even apologized, which

221

had seemed so remarkable because it was so rare! But he'd done it and shown such a different side of himself; she'd longed for him to be like that always. Too much to hope for, perhaps, but he'd certainly become easier. Until tonight, when Corrie had defied him, and he'd reverted to his old ways. He had 'blown up', and now was ill, and here they were worrying. Just like any family would, and that seemed right.

Forty-Three

The April evening had gradually darkened by the time they hurried into the Royal Infirmary's main entrance and found Reception, but the great hospital was still filled with noise and activity, not yet ready for night. Elinor, used to the same sort of atmosphere, still found herself as full of dread as Hessie and Corrie, still as strained as though she were like them, with no experience at all. For of course it was true, she too had never known what it was to have someone close in a place like this. What a difference that made!

'Walter Rae?' the woman on duty in Reception repeated, looking down at a ledger on her desk. 'Oh, yes, he came in recently – he's with the doctors at present.'

'Can we see him?' Hessie asked, twisting her hands together. 'I'm Mrs Rae – this is Mr Rae's daughter and his son.'

'I'm afraid you won't be able to see him just now,' the receptionist replied kindly. 'But someone will come to speak to you soon if you wait in the general waiting room. That's just to the right there.'

Having thanked her, they made their way to the room she had indicated where several people were already waiting, staring into space, and took seats on hard wooden chairs. There was a low table in front of them, covered in well-thumbed magazines, but they made no move to read anything, only sat like the others, eyes cast down, waiting in silence.

Time passed. A large wall clock ticked.

'Ma, maybe I could find you a cup of tea?' Corrie whispered at last, but Hessie shook her head. No tea. Silence descended again, suddenly to be broken by a young nurse who opened the door and called someone's name. A man leaped to his feet.

'If you'd like to come this way, please?'

'Oh, yes, yes!'

Away he went, the door closed, and silence again fell.

'Oh, God, canna stand this,' Corrie muttered and, picking up one of the old magazines, was flicking through it when two more people were called, and then another, and suddenly the Raes were alone.

'What's happening?' Hessie wailed. 'They've forgotten us!'

'No, they haven't,' Elinor told her. 'It's just that the doctors must still be with Dad – we'll have to wait till they can tell us anything.'

223

'Oh, but where's that wee nurse, then? I just wish she'd come!'

In fact, it was a doctor who came. A youngish, dark-haired man wearing a crumpled white coat and smelling of disinfectant. He walked with a limp and his expression was grave.

'Mrs Rae?' He looked at Hessie.

'Yes, I'm Mrs Rae.' Hessie's voice was thin and reedy.

'I'm Dr Drewer, one of the doctors who's been attending to your husband, admitted with apoplexy some time ago.'

Apoplexy. The Raes exchanged glances. Now they had a name for Walt's illness, and didn't like it.

'Apoplexy?' Corrie repeated. 'Is that the same as a seizure?'

'A seizure can cover a number of things, but Mr Rae is certainly suffering from apoplexy – what some call a stroke, or in Scotland, a shock.'

'A shock?' Hessie whispered. 'That's what I was afraid of. But how is he, Doctor? How is he?'

'At the moment, he's stable and has been transferred to a side ward, but he's not conscious and we're monitoring him. Tomorrow we'll be carrying out some tests and will be able to give you a better prognosis then. I mean, a better idea of...'

Dr Drewer hesitated and Corrie asked quietly, 'Of his chances?'

'We've every hope he will pull through, but, of course, these cases are difficult at this stage to assess.'

'Can I see him?' asked Hessie. 'Can we all see him?'

Again, the doctor hesitated. 'Just for a moment. Just from the door, perhaps.'

It was terrible to see him, even from the door, his face so heavily purple, his breathing so slow and laboured, his eyes closed. He didn't look like himself – that was what was wrong. Didn't look like the darkly handsome man whose presence ruled them, who could alter everything for everybody by just a change of mood. Now, he seemed ... what was the word Elinor sought? Powerless. Could anyone who looked as he did ever regain power? Or even ordinary feeling?

Both she and Hessie were crying a little as a nurse led them away, and Corrie was very quiet. There was no sign by then of the doctor, and it was the nurse who told them to telephone next morning to see how Walter had got through the night.

'Telephone?' Hessie repeated blankly.

'It's all right, Ma, I'll ring up from the Primrose,' Elinor told her. 'They'll let me use the phone.'

They went out together into the night, walking slowly, eventually finding the stop and catching their tram without seeming to know what they were doing.

'Are you still going to the Primrose tomorrow?' Hessie asked Elinor.

'Well, I'll be needed, I think I should, but I'll come back in the afternoon and then we'll go to the hospital.'

'Depending how he is,' Corrie said with stiff

225

lips. His face, Elinor noted, was mask-like, wiped of all emotion, but somehow she wasn't surprised when they arrived home and he sank into a chair and covered his eyes with his hand.

'This is all my fault,' he muttered. 'I did it, I brought it on. I knew how he felt, he'd been upset before when I said I was going to enlist, and I still went ahead and told him. So, I'm to blame.'

'You are not to blame!' Elinor cried, as Hessie went about making tea, with her lips pursed and her reddened eyes only on the kettle. 'How can you say that? If you want to join up, you've every right. It was Dad who was in the wrong, flying off the handle because you wouldn't do as he said. I don't know if being in a rage had anything to do with what happened, but I do know it had nothing to do with you!'

'Ma doesn't think so,' Corrie said wearily. 'I can tell the way she's looking at me.'

'Ma, that's no' true, is it?' cried Elinor. 'You know Corrie was right to volunteer, just like other men. Their fathers are proud; it was only Dad who got worked up, and he shouldn't have done.'

'He only got worked up because he couldn't face Corrie being in danger,' Hessie said flatly. 'And that's the truth of it. Corrie needn't go to war. There's no conscription.'

'I thought you said you understood, that I had to go,' he said sharply.

'Oh, I don't know what to think,' she cried, her face working with emotion, and burst into tears. 'Look, let's no' quarrel, with your dad lying in the Royal,' she wailed. 'Let's stick together, eh?

I don't want to upset you, Corrie.'

'And I don't want to upset you, Ma.'

Mother and son clung together, while Elinor quietly made the tea and poured it out.

'You're right, Ma,' she said quietly. 'We should stick together. We're going to need all our strength.'

'All our strength,' Hessie agreed, and they drank their tea, holding back the tears, then hugged and prepared to go to their beds, hoping to get through the night somehow.

Forty-Four

Mr Rae had come through the night, Elinor was told when she rang the infirmary next morning, but there was no change in his condition. No change. That meant he had not regained consciousness. When Sister Penny asked with sympathy how her father was, Elinor's look was troubled.

'He hasn't come round yet. That's no' so good, is it?'

'Well, it's disappointing, but it can take time, you know. The doctors will be doing all they can.'

'Oh, yes, I know. But I have the feeling that what's happened to Dad is pretty serious. I mean, I've heard of other people having these attacks and recovering quite quickly – is that no' right?'

'They can, of course, but every attack is different, and patients are different, too.' Sister Penny put her hand on Elinor's shoulder. 'Try not to worry, anyway. See how things are when you go to the Royal this afternoon.'

'Thank you for giving me the time, Sister. I do appreciate it.'

'That's quite all right. You need to be free to see your father and we're all hoping you find some improvement.'

Improvement. They were desperate to find it – Elinor and Hessie, with Corrie, who'd been given an hour or two off to join them at the Royal. Desperate, yet still hopeful, until they stopped at Reception and asked if they could visit Mr Rae.

'Mr Rae?'

As soon as she saw the way the receptionist's eyes slid away, an icy hand seemed to squeeze Elinor's heart and glancing at Corrie she could tell by his face that he was feeling the same. Hessie, however, had noticed nothing and when she was told that Dr Drewer wished to speak to her, she seemed to accept it as something to be expected.

'He'll be telling us what they've found,' she murmured, as they made their way to the waiting room. 'They were going to do some tests, eh? Oh, I do hope your dad's come round by now.'

Even when Dr Drewer asked them to step along to a smaller room where no other people were waiting, she still gave him a quiet look of expectancy, until she saw his face more clearly, when her own face changed.

'Mrs Rae, I am so sorry...'

He had pulled forward a chair and was gently making her sit down. 'So very sorry – there was nothing we could do.'

'What ... what are you saying?' Hessie's eyes were wide. 'Corrie, Elinor – what's he telling me?'

'Oh, Ma,' Elinor whispered, as she and Corrie put their arms around her. 'Ma, Dad's gone.'

'Mr Rae had what we call a massive stroke,' Dr Drewer was saying softly. 'There was never a great deal of hope, but one never knows - sometimes patients rally, sometimes last for weeks – but Mr Rae never recovered consciousness. He slipped away, very peacefully, at five minutes after twelve noon.'

'Peacefully,' Hessie repeated. 'Aye, peaceful at last. Poor Walt, poor Walt. No more working himself up, eh? No more finding things wrong with the world. Your dad's found peace, you bairns. We needn't cry, we needn't cry.'

They did cry, though, when Dr Drewer asked if they'd like to see him and showed them into the side ward where Walter lay, looking, yes, wonderfully peaceful. The high colour in his face was fading fast, his eyes were closed as before, but a lock of dark hair lay over his brow, and he did seem more like the man they knew than when they'd seen him the previous evening. Except for the strange tranquillity which had never been his, even when in a good mood. Always, there'd been movement in his face, his dark eyes showing emotion of some sort – passion, temper, high feeling, anyway. Now, of course, there was

229

nothing. That was what death meant. No more feeling. Only rest.

'There is a minister here if you'd like to speak to him,' a nurse murmured, but they shook their heads. They weren't great kirk-goers. Later, there would be the funeral service to arrange; perhaps they would find consolation talking to the minister then. Now they just wanted a little more time with Walter, until they had to face all that had to be done.

There was so much to be done, after a death; neither Elinor nor Corrie had realized how much. Hessie, though, had had experience.

'Aye, I buried both my parents,' she sighed, sitting at the kitchen table that first evening they were without Walter. 'And a struggle it was, to find the money. Made me decide to put something away for funerals every week, so when your dad's folks went, we'd no' be scratching round, trying to borrow.' She put a hankie to her eyes. 'And now it's your dad's turn, too. I canna bear to think of him, all alone at that undertaker's.'

'Ma, it's best for him to be there,' Elinor told her. 'We couldn't have brought him back here, and the undertakers are taking care of everything.'

'At least I'll be able to give him a good send-off,' Hessie sighed.

'Seems to me an awful thing to spend money on,' Corrie muttered. 'I mean, buying coffins and that. What do the dead care about the way they're buried?'

'Corrie, that's a terrible way to talk!' Hessie cried. 'You want your dad in a pauper's grave?'

'No, it's just that this business of having to pay out to undertakers when folk have so little – seems no' right to me.'

'We've a lot to take care of tomorrow,' Elinor murmured, changing the subject. 'I'm wondering if I can get some time off, to give you a hand, Ma.'

'I'd be glad if you could. There'll be the neighbours round tomorrow, bringing what they can – folk are good like that – but they canna help with all we've to do.' She rested her eyes on Corrie. 'And you'll get to the funeral, eh?'

'You know I will. I don't report to the regiment till the next day.' He sighed. 'And look, we've been through all this. You know I wish I hadn't to go – specially now we've lost Dad – but I've no choice. It's duty.'

'Aye, well, let's say no more. I think I'll just go in the other room – be on my own for a bit.'

As her son and daughter remained at the table, Hessie went quietly into the bedroom she'd shared with Walt and closed the door. Elinor and Corrie exchanged looks.

'What's going to happen to Ma?' Elinor asked, after a moment or two. 'When the shop is let to someone else, they'll want this flat. Where will she go? Where will any of us go?'

Corrie's eyes glazed. He put his hand to his head.

'Oh, God, the shop! I never thought! Dad's gone and Ma'll have to find somewhere else to live. And what's she going to live on?'

231

'We'll have to see how things work out.'

'We know how they'll work out! Somebody'll take the shop and want the flat and Ma'll have to find somewhere to live, without Dad's money or mine!' Corrie stood up and began to pace in agitation about the room.

'Listen, I think Ma will manage,' Elinor told him quickly. 'She's got her cleaning job and might do more hours, and she's got me to help, as well. Try no' to worry. You've enough to think about as it is.'

When Corrie threw himself into a chair, shaking his head, she added hesitantly, 'About Dad, did you ever think we'd miss him so much?'

'Miss him?' Corrie put his hand to his brow. 'I don't mind telling you, there were times when I wished him gone. Maybe you were the same?'

'I never wished him dead. Just, you know, that I could have somebody easier – for a dad.'

'Aye, well, no one could ever say he was easy.'

'But he did care for us, Corrie. I found that out when he came to find me that time. And he was different after that – mostly. I did love him, really.'

'Mostly. I'm no' sure he'd really changed. But the thing is, now he's gone, it's hard to imagine life without him. Funny, eh?'

'I'll miss him,' Elinor said slowly. 'He wasn't a happy man, he knew he shouldn't be as he was. Maybe he was only learning to change when he died.'

'Still had a last row with me.' Corrie fixed Elinor with earnest eyes. 'You say I needn't feel guilty, I still do. I wish it hadn't happened.'

232

'Corrie, it's true, you needn't feel guilty. The real worry now is that you're going away.'

'I'll be coming back.'

'So easy to say!' She waited a moment. 'You're in the same regiment as Barry Howat, you know. I don't want ever to see him again, but I'd be small-minded if I didn't wish him well. You could tell him that.'

'Elinor, I'll be in a different battalion, I'll probably never see him. Hope I don't, to be honest, after the way he treated you.'

'All over now.' Suddenly Elinor's face crumpled and she flung her arms round her brother. 'Oh, Corrie, come back like you said, just come back!'

'I promise you I will,' he said huskily, and when Hessie came out of her room to find them both in tears, the three of them stood together, supporting one another, for quite some time.

Forty-Five

Hessie had been right about the neighbours. Every day, people came over from the tenements, bringing what they could – soup, or pieces of ham, shortbread, if they could afford the butter to make it, scones, jars of pickle, or jam.

'Will you look at this place?' Hessie cried. 'It's like a shop, eh? Still, it'll all come in handy for the funeral tea.'

All arrangements to do with Walter's death had

233

been completed, with Elinor, who had been given some time off, doing most of the work, and now all they had to do was get through the funeral which was to be held at their nearest kirk. The next day, of course, was the day of Corrie's departure, but they were trying not to think of that.

One piece of good luck had relieved the family's minds, for Hessie's future in the flat over the cobbler's shop was assured. The landlord had let the shop to a widow from Nicholson Street, who wanted premises for her dressmaking and alterations business, and did not require the rooms upstairs.

'Oh, what a relief!' Elinor remarked to Corrie. 'That's a huge worry out of the way, especially as he's taken a shilling off the rent, seeing as Ma's a widow now. You'll feel better, eh?'

'Aye, I will. I've been lying awake at nights, wondering what we could do.'

'Me, too,' said Elinor. 'I sometimes wonder if things will ever get back to normal.'

Then she stopped, biting her lip, for things for Corrie were not going to be normal in any foreseeable future.

Still, the funeral went off well, with a good crowd to mourn Walter, and a fine spread laid out afterwards in the cobbler's shop, as Mrs Elder, the dressmaker, had not yet moved in. With enemy ships blockading British shipping, food was in short supply, but it was hard to imagine it, seeing all that the neighbours had managed to find for Hessie, and everyone was very cheerful and full of chat, as was usual at funerals.

How can they seem so happy? Elinor wondered, standing aside from the throng, slim and pale
in her black dress. Yet a moment's thought told
her that no one was really happy, no one had any
reason to seem cheerful except that they wanted
to appear so. Many of the young men from the
tenements were already away to the front, leaving those at home to the kind of anxiety Elinor
and Hessie were already feeling over Corrie. And
then there was the continued anxiety over money,
for if some war work was well paid, most jobs
were not, and there was always the rent to find,
eh? And boots for the bairns'?

She shouldn't be critical, Elinor told herself. At
this time, everybody had something to worry
over. Even the well-to-do had to fear the ring of
the doorbell, the sight of the telegram. How long
did a young officer last at the front? Three weeks,
was it? The thought crossed her mind ... was
Stephen Muirhead an officer? She'd never
thought to ask Brenda, and didn't in any case
want to show the interest in him that was fast
occupying her heart.

After Walter's burial in a Newington cemetery,
she and Hessie spent a quiet evening with Corrie,
their last for some time, trying like the mourners
to appear cheerful, but with less success. It was a
relief, really, when they could go to bed early and
make the morning come more quickly, get the
parting over, as Corrie put it. Soon, it was indeed
over, the hugs and brief kisses given, the promises made to write, and he was away, walking
down Friar's Wynd with a canvas bag on his back

and a last wave to the two women waving back.

'That's him, then,' Hessie sighed, turning in to the cobbler's shop, where no Walt bent now over his customers' shoes. 'Now, there's just you and me, Elinor, and you'll be gone soon, eh?'

'I'll be back tonight, Ma. I'm sorry to leave you, but they've been so good at the Primrose, letting me have the time off, and I know I'm needed.'

'Aye, you get back, pet. I'll be all right, I've plenty to do. And you've your friend to see, eh? She must've started work by now.'

'Brenda, yes, that's true,' said Elinor. 'I wonder how she's been getting on.'

'Very well!' cried Brenda, when Elinor arrived back at the Primrose. 'Wonderfully well. At one time, I'd never have thought I could do something like this, but I love it. I think of Tam and remember I'm doing my bit and then I'm really happy.' She took Elinor's hand. 'But never mind me. How have you been managing? I was so sorry to hear about your father.'

'Thank you. I must admit, it's no' been easy – was such a shock, you see. And then we had to say goodbye to Corrie, my brother, as well. He's joined the Royal Scots.'

'Oh, your poor mother! To lose your dad and then to have your brother going to war. But she still has you, that's something. My dad died years ago and there's just my mother and me at home, so I know how things are.'

'I'll do all I can for Ma. I promised Corrie when he left, I'd see she was all right.' Elinor gave a faint smile. 'But your mother will be gaining a son soon, eh? When you're married to Tam?'

'Yes, when. Oh, I just hope he can get the leave some time. He thinks maybe July, but nothing's sure. You'll come to the wedding, Elinor?'

'Need you ask? There's no' much to look forward to these days, but I'm looking forward to that!'

Who had liked something to look forward to? Elinor's smile faded, as she remembered. Stephen, of course. 'Something to look forward to, that's what I like,' he'd once said, and what he'd been looking forward to was another meeting with her. But there would be no more of those.

'I'd best get on,' she said quietly. 'Always so much to do.'

Good news came at last for Brenda, when Tam's letter arrived giving the dates of his leave in July. Barely a week, but it would be enough for their wedding and time away on honeymoon. He'd have to leave all the planning to her, but who was more efficient than his dear Brenda? 'Yours,' he'd ended, 'with love and desperation to see you again, your own troublemaker, Tam.'

Brenda, in seventh heaven, read the letter to Elinor, whose day was brightened by such hope of happiness. It was like a ray of sunshine in the darkness, but darkness was to descend again when an event occurred that no one could have foreseen.

Forty-Six

News came first to the Primrose from a QA who'd gone out to buy her usual early edition of a newspaper on the morning of May 23rd, and come running back, white-faced.

'A terrible train crash!' she cried, waving her paper. 'The worst ever known – near Gretna Green – and all Royal Scots men – oh, so many killed and injured – it's terrible, terrible!'

Royal Scots men. Elinor's heart stood still. Oh, God. Corrie! Had he been on that train?

'What happened?' people were asking, as she stood with her hands clenched at her sides, fearful to hear details from the QA who had bought the paper. In fact, it was the matron who told them, calling all the staff together to pass on the information she'd been told by telephone the previous evening.

It seemed that the accident had happened at 6.50 a.m. on the morning of the 22nd. Men of the Royal Scots were in a special troop train, travelling to Liverpool to embark for Gallipoli, when their train collided with a local train left where it shouldn't have been by careless signalmen. A goods train and a train of empty coal trucks then hit the two damaged trains and a fire broke out, sending the old-fashioned wooden framed carriages of the troop train up in flames. Of the soldiers involved, 226 were found to be dead and 246 were badly injured, leaving only a handful of men unharmed.

Looking over her reading glasses, the matron paused as a stunned silence followed her words.

'I'm sure you'll agree that nothing could be more tragic or ironic than what happened to those soldiers on their way to Gallipoli. To be killed or injured in their own country before they could even reach their destination abroad is too horrifying to think about, but there are two things I want to say to you now.

'The first is that I know some of you would like to be able to offer your services to help the injured, but as we are so very stretched here, I'm afraid that's just not possible. I'm really sorry – I wish we could have done something.

'The second is that, as you know, we have some patients here who are in a very fragile mental state because of their experiences. It might be as well to withhold news of the accident from them until we can take the time to prepare them. I'm sure I can leave this to your discretion.'

Thanking them for their attention, the matron was turning to go when a QA put up her hand.

'Excuse me, Matron, but have any details been released about which Royal Scots battalion was involved in the accident? My brother is a serving officer with the Eleventh.'

'I'm sorry, I should have made it clear – I know some of you will be anxious about relatives. The men were from the Seventh, known as the Leith

239

Battalion, because so many came from that area.'

Taking off her reading glasses, the matron looked around her listeners and gave a little sigh. It seemed that no one had a special grief for someone lost at Gretna Green, but that didn't mean that their hearts were not going out to those who had died and their families. Plain to see was the shock and sorrow on all the faces of those turning to take up their duties, trying to come to terms with death and destruction, not on some foreign battlefield, but very close to home.

'Not your brother?' Brenda whispered to Elinor.

'No, thank God. I suppose if I'd thought about it, I'd have realized he wouldn't have been ready yet to go out to Gallipoli, but I just heard the words "Royal Scots" and everything turned black. Now I'm thinking of those who died.'

'Me, too. I'm shaking. Let's get on with things and then make some tea, eh?'

'Tea, yes. What would we do without it?'

But as she began her morning's work, Elinor was thinking of someone else she'd almost forgotten. Barry was Royal Scots, too, but not from Leith, which meant he wouldn't have been on the fatal train. Another reason for thanking God, though why God should single out one soldier rather than another to be saved was not something she'd ever worked out or even questioned. All she knew was that even if Corrie meant more to her now than Barry, she still was glad that Barry was safe, too. No doubt Bettina and Georgie would be thinking the same, but she never saw any of the Howat family now, which perhaps was just as well.

And then, she did see Bettina. As it had not been possible for Primrose staff – apart from Matron – to be spared for the funeral of the dead soldiers, Elinor had gone after work to pay her respects at the Rosebank Cemetery, where the men had been buried in a mass grave. As she was leaving to make her way home, she saw Bettina ahead of her, dressed in black, and wondered if she should speak. Might be awkward, she was thinking, when Bettina turned round and the problem was solved.

'Why, it's you, Elinor!' she cried. 'Have you been to the cemetery?'

'Hello, Bettina. Yes, I couldn't go to the funeral, so I went to put a few flowers on the soldiers' grave.'

'I did the same thing.'

The two young women, studying each other, were silent for a moment, then Bettina cleared her throat.

'I was that sorry about ... what happened between you and Barry,' she said, with some nervousness. 'I always said, you were the best lassie he brought home.'

'Water under the bridge,' Elinor answered. 'I was upset at first, but I'm over it now.'

'That's good, I'm glad.'

After another short silence, Elinor asked, 'How are things with you, then?'

Bettina shrugged. 'Well, Alfie's joined the Navy, but we got wed before he left, so I'm Mrs Daniels now.'

'Congratulations – that's very good news.'

241

'Yes and no. What sort of married life is it, when you never see your man? And then ... did you hear what happened to Georgie? Killed at Le Cateau way back at the beginning of the war. This black I'm wearing is for the poor laddies from Leith, but I feel like wearing it all the time, eh? I see you're in black, too.'

'Just for today. My dad died lately, but I have to wear uniform at the Primrose Hospital where I'm working.' Elinor hesitated. 'I'm very sorry to hear about Georgie, very sorry indeed. I hope Barry's all right?'

'Och, he's fine. In Gallipoli, but will be moving to France, he thinks.' Bettina smiled. 'Says he'll be playing the piano in the trenches.'

'Playing the piano?'

'His wee joke. But I bet he does play football in no-man's-land, eh? I can see him, kicking the ball to the Jerries.' Bettina put out her hand and Elinor shook it. 'I've to go for ma tram now. Nice to see you, though. Keep in touch.'

'Yes, we'll do that,' said Elinor, knowing they wouldn't, and went her way, her mind working over Bettina's news. Poor Georgie, then. Always in the shadow of his more talented brother, now not even that. A name on a casualty list, all hopes and prospects gone. Remembered by his sister, though, and perhaps by Barry, too, though he wouldn't be one to dwell on death's sting. He really was just the way he seemed, wasn't he? One who would never have a care in the world, or perhaps would never allow himself to think he had. Certainly he wouldn't be losing any sleep over his broken love affair with herself.

Thank heavens, she was over the pain of losing him. Hadn't lasted long, so her love might never have been as genuine as she'd thought. Perhaps he'd done her a favour, after all, turning her down. The more she thought about what she'd lost – or, more precisely, thrown away – Elinor was ready to believe he had, but knew it wouldn't do her any good. You made mistakes, you paid, that was life's teaching. And she was paying now for what she had done.

Back home with Hessie, however, describing the newly prepared mass grave in the cemetery, Elinor's thoughts moved to the true tragedy of the Gretna Green rail crash. How humble it made her feel, to consider the loss of those young lives and the grief of their families, and compare her own troubles with that sort of loss and suffering. She really should put her worries aside, she decided, and concentrate on doing her work well at the Primrose. Perhaps permit herself to think of the one bright spot on the horizon, which was Brenda's wedding.

Forty-Seven

For days before the wedding, Brenda was so excited, so tensed up, her high spirits spread throughout the Primrose, with everyone wishing her well and keeping their fingers crossed for the bridegroom's safe arrival back home. Though she'd said she would have liked all the staff to see her wed, obviously that wasn't possible and in the end, after a whip-round to buy a crystal salad bowl as a present, Elinor was the only one given permission to attend.

'You'll no' be wanting to wear your black or grey for a wedding,' Hessie told her. 'Come on, your dad'd be happy to see you looking your best. How about that sweet pink dress you made yourself? It's July, it'll be hot.'

'Think it'd do?' Elinor asked doubtfully. 'It's nothing special.'

'If you buy a bit of matching ribbon for your hat, I think it'd be grand. There's a war on; no-body'll be expecting you to be dressing up too much.'

'The pink it is, then,' Elinor agreed and, on a steamy July morning, set off for the kirk near Brenda's home, looking, her mother had said, an absolute picture.

'Oh, it makes me feel good, to see you dressed

like that again,' she'd sighed, pressing a hankie to her eyes as she so often did. 'As though the sad times have gone, though I know they haven't.'

'They'll be gone one day, Ma, so cheer up, and I'll maybe bring you a piece of wedding cake back – if Brenda's managed to find one.'

Joining a group of brightly dressed guests outside the kirk, Elinor for a moment felt, like Hessie, that all the sad times had passed. Everyone seemed so happy and light-hearted, that when the bridegroom arrived, looking so smart in his tunic and kilt, his red hair catching the sunlight, quite a little cheer went up, at which Tam gave his old grin, and catching sight of Elinor, turned from entering the church to give her a great hug.

'My word, Elinor, it's grand to see you! And looking so nice, eh?'

'You're looking good yourself, Tam. I do believe you're slimmer.'

'What, with all the bully beef I eat? Hey, I'd better get going, eh?'

'I'll say,' said John Andrews, one of Tam's friends Elinor remembered and now his best man, wearing similar uniform. 'Don't want the bride to see you still talking when she arrives. Though who could ever stop you talking?'

As Tam and John entered the church to take up their positions, the guests followed, for time was getting on. Any moment now, the bride would arrive, accompanied by an old family friend to 'give her away', and a cousin who was her bridesmaid.

For a wartime wedding, it was traditional and

expensive, Elinor thought, and was certainly not the sort that could be afforded by anyone she knew in Friar's Wynd. But then she'd always guessed that Brenda's family had money, and if Mrs Cordiner wanted to spend it on her only daughter's great day – why not? Listening to the organ, soaking up the atmosphere, Elinor turned to smile when a latecomer slipped into the seat next to hers. And froze. The fair-haired man in officer's uniform who had just arrived was Stephen Muirhead.

She was not imagining him this time. No, this was the real man, visibly shocked at the sight of her. See his sudden pallor, and how, when her dark eyes met his, he instantly looked away. *Why, it's true, he doesn't want to see me; he doesn't even want to be near me.* Should she move? She couldn't, she would have to pass him. In any case, she felt her limbs so heavy, so unwilling to respond, that she was as still as a statue. Thank God, the organ had struck up the wedding march; the guests were on their feet. Brenda must have arrived.

Somehow, Elinor followed the service. Somehow she noted that Brenda looked radiant in the white dress her mother had made for her, that her bridesmaid was sweet in blue, and Tam so proud he couldn't take his eyes off his bride and sounded out all his responses as though he were ringing a joyful bell. While all the time, Stephen was by Elinor's side, his presence burning into her consciousness, so that she was glad to sit down when the register was being signed and the organ played, wishing with all her heart that the

ceremony would end and she could be somewhere else.

It did end, of course, and as soon as the bridal
couple had come down the aisle, Stephen moved
after them and Elinor was able to follow and
mingle with the guests outside.

'Brenda, you look wonderful!' she cried, as
soon as she was able to reach the bride.

'And you, Elinor, you're beautiful!' Brenda
was flushed and smiling as they exchanged hugs.
'Oh, it's so lovely to have you here.'

'I wouldn't have missed it for anything,' Elinor
declared, and after the bride and groom had been
borne away by motor car to a nearby hotel,
followed on foot, in company with Pearl, who
she remembered from Stephen's class. Some way
ahead, she could see Stephen himself, walking
with some people she didn't know. And with all
her heart, she hoped he wouldn't look back.

'Is this no' amazing?' Pearl was asking. 'I
mean, that Tam and Brenda would ever get wed?
Remember how they used to be? Always striking
sparks?'

'That's the way it goes sometimes.'

'Aye, you're right. How about you, Elinor? You
engaged, or anything?'

'No. I'm just working at the Primrose Club
that's now a convalescent hospital.'

'And I'm nursing, too. Training full-time at the
Northern.' Pearl laughed. 'All that office stuff I
swotted up on for Mr Muirhead has quite gone
out of my head! Talking of him, didn't I see him
somewhere around?'

'Yes, he's here,' Elinor replied. 'Think this is

247

the hotel, eh?'

'Oh, very grand! Mrs Cordiner's done Brenda proud, eh? This must be costing a bonny penny. Still, what's money these days? Spend it while you can is my motto!'

Drinks were being served in the hotel's pleasant garden, and as Pearl dived away to speak to some people she knew, Elinor stood alone for a moment, looking round at the cheerful guests, thinking how far removed all this was from anything to do with the war. Was it even in the same world as the battlefields abroad? As the mass grave in Rosebank Cemetery?

But then, as at her dad's funeral, she chided herself for not seeing what lay beyond the happiness of this little interlude. All the young men in uniform, even the bridegroom himself, would soon be returning to France. All those left behind would be suffering. No one here, however cheerful they seemed, was forgetting the war, she could be sure of that.

'Elinor,' came a voice at her side and, turning, she saw Stephen standing with a drink, his grey eyes upon her.

Her own eyes widening, she said nothing.

'Look, I'm sorry I didn't speak when I saw you in the kirk just now,' he began quickly. 'I ... well, I suppose I was just so surprised to see you. Never expected to, though that was stupid, when I knew you were Brenda's friend.'

'That's all right,' she murmured. 'I didn't expect to see you either.'

'I've seen Tam a few times. When he knew I

had some leave, he asked me to come to his wedding.' Stephen hesitated, seeming ill at ease. 'How are you, then?'

'Very well, thanks. I'm still at the Primrose, but it's a hospital now.'

'Oh, yes, I heard. Not married yourself?'

'No.'

'I thought you might be, by now.'

'No, I don't see ... I don't see anyone now.'

'You're not with the footballer?'

'We ... parted.'

'I see.'

'He's in France, with the Royal Scots. My brother's with the Royal Scots, too – he's just joined up. And my father is dead.'

'I'm sorry to hear that.'

'It was very sudden, quite a shock.' Elinor's gaze was still resting bravely on Stephen's unsmiling face. 'How are you, then? I see you're an officer now.'

He shrugged. 'For what it's worth, a captain, yes.' Again, he hesitated. 'Also, I've met someone. A VAD, as a matter of fact. Drives ambulances, very well, too.'

Elinor, lowering her eyes, was concentrating very hard on showing nothing of what his words had meant to her. 'I hope you'll be very happy.'

'Good God, you think anyone can be happy at this time?'

'Brenda and Tam are happy.'

'For now,' he said quietly. 'Seems we're being called in to lunch, so I'll say goodbye. I'm glad we had this talk, Elinor. I believe I was a bit hard on you, the last time we met, wasn't I?'

She shook her head. 'I never thought so, but I'm glad we had a talk, too. Goodbye, Stephen, and good luck.'

He smiled at last and moved away, making no suggestion that they should have lunch together. Later, when she shared a table with Pearl and two of Tam's friends, she saw him sitting with the people he'd walked with earlier. But after the lunch and the speeches were over and the bridal couple had left for a secret destination, there was no sign of him. Not that it mattered. They had made their goodbyes; there was nothing else to say.

Returning slowly to Friar's Wynd, her thanks given to Brenda's mother, her farewells made to Pearl and others, Elinor tried to come to terms with her own particular bad news. She told herself it had been good to see Stephen, to part on better terms than before, and to know that he'd met someone else and was no longer suffering over her own betrayal. Yes, all these things helped her to accept that he had gone from her life, and that she must concentrate on what she had. Work, for instance. Working, especially for others – that was the way to get over heartache. To fill the mind with something else, even if it was easier said than done.

Only after she'd gone to her bed, having given Hessie a full account of the wedding and changed from her pink dress to help with the chores, did she allow her eyes to fill with tears. Tears for her own mistakes. And for what might have been.

Forty-Eight

If Elinor wanted to forget her sorrows in work, there was plenty of it at the Primrose. There were so many new patients arriving in the late summer that Matron was beginning to worry seriously about overcrowding, bemoaning that nobody had ever forecast that there would be so many cases needing help.

Of course, other hospitals were in the same boat, with the specialist unit at the Royal Victoria, for instance, being as full as the Primrose, and the general hospitals all taking their share.

'We must just do what we can,' Matron ordered. 'More hospitals are opening all the time, but for now we must take those who need us and hope that more beds will be released as recoveries are made.'

'Ever hopeful,' one of the QAs sighed later, causing Sister Penny to say sharply that the recovery rate at Primrose was very good. Many soldiers were passing medical boards to return to their duties, even though there were some who had to be invalided out. Either way, beds became available.

'Not so much from the neurasthenics,' someone observed, at which Sister Penny frowned and agreed that curing those patients with mental problems was a much longer process, but even there, the Primrose had its successes, thanks to its excellent doctors – Colonel Shannon, Major Henderson, and Major Brown. On that confident note, the discussion ended.

'I don't mind how hard I work,' Brenda confided to Elinor. 'I'm just so happy, you see.'

At Elinor's dubious look, she smiled and nodded.

'I know what you're thinking, that I must be worrying, too. Well of course I am, but somehow I just feel that Tam will come through. He's not the sort to let things get to him and whatever happens to him, I believe he'll survive.'

'I can see how you might feel that, but I'm so superstitious, I'd never dare to talk about it.'

'You, superstitious? Elinor, I don't believe it. Such a sensible girl, you couldn't be.'

'I never used to be. Always walked under ladders, never threw salt over my shoulder, but since the war, I've become ... well, more afraid, I suppose.'

'For your brother?' Brenda gave Elinor's shoulder a sympathetic pat. 'He'll be all right, I'm sure. Anyway, he's still in England, isn't he?'

'No, in France. We just heard.'

'Oh, well, Tam's been all right in Gallipoli and France so far, and so has Stephen Muirhead. Didn't you see him at the wedding, Elinor? Come through without a scratch! Some lead charmed lives, eh? And I'm hoping Tam'll be the same.'

'Me, too,' Elinor said, moving on to her next duty.

One thing that still gave her pleasure, of course,

252

was her beloved Primrose Square garden, and so far no one had objected to her sliding in without a patient whenever she had a break. Who would care, really? It wasn't as though there were club members around these days, and the doctors and senior nurses had too much to do to spend time keeping watch on her.

It was one lunchtime in late September, when she had let herself into the gardens again, that she was able to see two familiar faces looking in through the railings.

'Ada! Mattie!' she cried, running to open the gate she'd locked. 'Oh, how nice to see you!'

Dear, plump Ada and cheerful young Mattie were almost squeaking with excitement as they all embraced one another, and then stood back to take stock.

'My, Elinor, you're looking well,' Ada remarked. 'What I'd give for your waistline! Bet you can see from mine there's a babby on the way?'

'You're expecting?' cried Elinor. 'Why, Ada, that's wonderful! And so are you looking well – and Mattie.'

'Canna think why I'm looking well,' Mattie sighed. 'This is my afternoon off, but working at that munitions factory's no joke, I can tell you. Money's good, but I sometimes think I'll just get wed. Did you know I was engaged, Elinor? Aye, to a fellow who works at the factory. He's got terrible asthma, poor laddie, so they'll no' take him in the army, which suits me, eh?'

'And Bob's out of it and all,' Ada said with satisfaction. 'Got what they call a Blighty one. You know, a wound that's no' so bad but you

253

have to go home with it. He's lost two fingers on his right hand, so canna fire a gun, and has to do light duties at the depot. Cross about it, too, but I say, for God's sake, be grateful, now you'll see the babby!'

'Vera and Gerda – they all right?' asked Elinor. 'And do you ever hear about wee Sal?'

'Och, they're all fine,' said Mattie. 'Vera's walking out with somebody, and Gerda's got promotion – always the bright one, eh? And Sal's doing well, cooking at that hotel, snibs to Mrs P, eh? But nobody sees her.' She gave Elinor a quick, keen look. 'But how are you, Elinor? You happy working at the Primrose?'

'Yes, very happy. My dad died recently, so I'm doing what I can for Ma, seeing as Corrie's away in France, as well.' Elinor smiled. 'And before you ask, no, I'm no' married or engaged or walking out. Just working.'

'Fancy, and you were always our beauty, eh? Still are, and that's a fact. Somebody'll be along soon.'

'I'm all right as I am. Look, I wish I could ask you two in for a cup of tea, but I'm just on dinner hour and I'll have to go back. Did you just want to come up and look at the old place?'

'Aye, we sometimes meet in Princes Street,' Ada told her, 'and I says to Mattie, let's go and look at the Primrose, eh? But we never thought to see you, Elinor, and in the gardens, too. Do they give you a key now, then?'

'Ssh, only supposed to be when I bring patients.' Elinor hugged both girls again. 'Look, can we all meet some time? I get an afternoon off, too.'

'We'll drop you a card,' said Ada. 'It'd be grand to meet up. Talk about the old days when we all worked here.'

'Seem like a dream,' put in Mattie. 'Think it'll ever be a club again, Elinor?'

'When the war's over, why not? I sometimes get a postcard from Miss Ainslie. She's sure it'll re-open one day.'

'And then she'll start marching for the suffragettes again,' laughed Ada. 'Elinor, we'll hope to see you soon, eh?'

'Aye, and take care – of that babby, too. Bye, Mattie – don't let 'em work you too hard.'

'Bye, Elinor. All the best.'

They waved to one another before Ada and Mattie turned back towards Princes Street and Elinor ran into the Primrose, pleasantly cheered by the meeting with old colleagues. But then she halted, for Brenda was running across the hall, her face so changed that Elinor turned pale.

'Brenda, what is it, what is it?'

'Mother brought a letter round – it was from Tam's commanding officer – he's been wounded, Elinor – at the Battle of Loos – he's coming home to hospital here.'

'Wounded? But he's all right?' Elinor was holding Brenda tightly. 'He must be, if he's able to come home.'

'Yes, but there are no details. The officer didn't give any.' Brenda's eyes were searching Elinor's face. 'Why do you think he didn't? Because Tam's very bad?'

'No, no, I'm sure it's just the way they do

things. You'll be told everything at the hospital. Which one is it?'

'It's in Craigleith, but he won't be there yet. I've phoned and they say they'll let me know when he arrives, but it'll be a few days yet.' Brenda wound her hands together, her eyes spilling tears. 'Elinor, I don't know what to do. Sister Penny says I should go home, come back later, but what can I do at home? Mother's so upset, it will be so terrible – waiting...'

'Why no' stay here, then?' Elinor asked gently. 'You're needed here, it might be best.'

'Stay here? Yes, I think you're right. It'll fill the hours, won't it? To work?'

'It will; always does. Come on, let's see what's to be done.'

As they moved away together, a QA came towards them, her black regulation shoes tapping noisily on the uncarpeted floor.

'Quick, could one of you run up to Corporal MacAdie on the top floor? He's spilled his lunch again, all over his bed. Hands shaking like a ninety-year-old, poor fellow.'

'I'll go,' said Brenda, hurrying to the stairs, while the QA, glancing at Elinor, shook her head.

'Brave, lassie, eh? We've just heard about her Tam – hope he pulls through.'

'He will; he's got great spirit.'

'Need more than spirit to survive the Battle of Loos, from what I've heard. Och, if they'd just put the women in charge, this war'd be over tomorrow!'

'In charge?' Elinor smiled grimly. 'They don't even give us the vote.'

256

Forty-Nine

It was several days before Tam arrived back in Scotland, during which time news filtered through that the Battle of Loos had been one of the worst for British casualties. So many regiments had been involved, so many men, that Elinor and Hessie, thinking of Corrie, were terrified to read the casualty lists. Even when they didn't find his name, they still couldn't be sure he was all right, for many of the dead, it was said, could never be identified. Thank God, a message came at last to say he was safe, which meant Elinor only had to worry about Stephen. And Tam.

Poor Brenda, away to the hospital to be with him – everyone at the Primrose was thinking of her, the happy bride who had so soon become the anxious wife. But at least Tam was alive, and home. That must be good news.

'Just as long as they haven't kept anything from me,' Brenda whispered to Elinor before she left for the hospital. 'I have this awful feeling that something is wrong, something has happened that's worse than a wound.'

'No, no, you mustn't think like that. They'll never give details till they see you, and Tam will be all right, I'm sure of it.'

257

But of course, Elinor wasn't sure of it, which was why the time seemed so long while Brenda was away, for the worry over what she might find was all too real. It seemed as though she would never return, and it was only when Elinor was due to go home and standing on the steps with her coat on that she saw her, coming round the square.

'Brenda, thank heavens!' Elinor hurried to greet her. 'Oh, how is he? How's Tam? Come in and tell us.'

'No, I can't.' Brenda's face was very pale, her blue eyes quite dark. 'I can't come in just yet, Elinor. No, don't ask me. Look, will you come with me to the café? We can talk there.'

As she read the messages Brenda's face was sending, Elinor's heart sank. There had been bad news at the hospital; nothing else could have made Brenda look as she did. But she agreed at once to go with her to the café, where they ordered tea, but nothing to eat, and when it came, Elinor pressed Brenda's cold hand.

'Tell me what's wrong, tell me about Tam.'

Brenda raised her tragic gaze to Elinor's face.

'He's scarcely wounded at all,' she whispered. 'But he's shell-shocked. He can't speak.'

Shell-shocked? Unable to speak? Tam, who had never been known to be lost for a word in his life? Even the thought of it hit Elinor like a blow and for a moment her head almost swam – but then Brenda's devastated face above the teacups brought a reminder of who was really suffering, and she leaned forward.

'What did they say, Brenda? Tell me exactly

what they said.'

After a few moments of hesitation, Brenda, in a low, strained voice, began.

'As soon as I got to the hospital, a nurse took me to an office where an army doctor was waiting. He said he wanted to talk to me before I saw my husband, to explain what had happened.'

With a long sigh, Brenda took off her hat and ran her hand across her brow.

'He told me I must be prepared to find Tam very different from usual, very subdued and not able to talk, but I wasn't to worry, it would pass in time, and when I asked how he'd been wounded, he said Tam had been very lucky. He'd been blown some distance by a mortar bomb, but he'd only had some concussion and minor injuries.'

Brenda stared into her teacup.

'Would you say it was lucky, not to be able to speak?'

'Well, I suppose he just meant he was lucky to survive,' Elinor answered uneasily. 'To be blown up – anything could've happened.'

'Yes, well, then the doctor told me about the shell shock. He called it a neurasthenic problem, and when I told him I worked at the Primrose and knew about that sort of thing, he seemed relieved. He told me again not to worry and that there was a good chance that Tam would recover quite quickly, as many did. Which is not exactly true, is it?'

'We see recoveries all the time at the Primrose, Brenda.'

'Some recoveries, but not many quick ones. Anyway, the doctor said that Tam might be moved from Craigleith. It was converted from the old Poor House in 1914, you know, only as a hospital for the wounded.'

'Not for the shell-shocked, then?'

'Well, seems they see how people progress. If they don't recover quickly, they probably ... move on.'

Perhaps to the Primrose? Elinor wondered, but Brenda didn't suggest it.

'Did they let you see Tam, then?' she asked, after a pause.

'Oh, yes. Took me to his ward. One of those long ones, very clean and tidy. Most of the patients were in bed, but one or two were sitting in chairs. They had blue flannel suits.'

'And Tam? What about Tam?'

'At first, I didn't recognize him. He was in a corner bed, just lying still. They'd cut off some of his hair where there'd been a gash, and that was bandaged. His hands were bandaged, too. When the doctor took me up to him, he looked up and I think he recognized me – there was a look in his eyes – but when he tried to say my name, nothing came.'

Tears were glistening in Brenda's eyes, as she looked up into Elinor's face. 'Oh, it was so awful, Elinor. He was so pale, like a ghost, and he seemed so ... lost. I felt like bursting into tears, but I didn't. I held his hand and the doctor said he'd leave us – a nurse would tell me when to go.'

'Poor Brenda, poor girl, you're being so brave.'

'I don't feel brave at all. You know who the brave ones are.' Brenda sighed and slowly put on her hat. 'When I was leaving, the doctor said again that Tam might have to be moved to a specialist unit. Possibly the Primrose, which would be convenient for me. I didn't tell him that the Primrose is the last place I want Tam to go.'

'The last place?' Elinor stared. 'But why? I think it would be ideal.'

'Oh, no, Elinor, no. I couldn't bear to see him there. With all those poor chaps we nurse? Oh, I couldn't, I couldn't!'

'I don't understand. He can get better at the Primrose, and you'll be there with him. What's wrong with that?'

'So many blank, dead faces,' Brenda muttered. 'No, I don't want him there, and I won't be there myself, anyway. I'm going to give up my job and look after him, that's all I want to do.'

Dabbing at her eyes, Brenda gazed at Elinor with a sudden spark of interest.

'Listen, do you think there's any chance that I could get him into a private nursing home somewhere? I've a bit of money in savings...'

'Brenda, Tam's still in the army. They'd never let him go to a private hospital. As soon as he's better, he'll have to go before a medical board to decide what happens next.' Elinor sighed. 'And wherever he goes, the patients will be the same, so he might as well be in a place you know.'

Again, for some time, Brenda was silent, then she gave a little shrug.

'So be it, then. But it might be like the doctor says, mightn't it? He might get better very quickly and not have to go anywhere at all?'

Except before the medical board, Elinor

261

thought, but only said aloud, 'When can I see him? They did say he could have visitors?'

'Oh, yes. It'll do him good to see people.' Brenda stood up, searching in her purse for money for a tip for the waitress. 'Just don't expect him to look the same.'

'He'll be the same Tam underneath,' Elinor said quietly. 'We just have to find him.'

Fifty

No change. Those were Major Henderson's words to Brenda some weeks after Tam had been moved from Craigleith to the Primrose. As the doctor in charge of his case, the major had worked hard with him ever since his arrival in late October, and at first had had high hopes of his recovery.

'But there it is,' he admitted sadly on that winter afternoon. 'So far, there has been no change in your husband's condition.'

They were in his small consulting room, the place where he and Tam 'conversed', as he put it, with the major asking questions and Tam writing down answers in his notebook. He had not seemed unwilling to do this, but was not, it seemed, good at expressing himself on paper. He had always been a 'talker', as Brenda had told the doctor, never one for sitting down thinking about things, and now, after his traumatic experience at

Loos, all he could write was: 'Nobody understands.'

'At first, that seemed a breakthrough to me,' Major Henderson told Brenda. 'If I could get him to see that other people did understand what he'd been through, that could be the start to his recovery. But when I pointed out that the other patients here had suffered in the war, he only shook his head, and wrote: "Not at Loos".'

'What can be done?' Brenda whispered. 'I sit with him every day, I get him to look at me and tell him he's safe, but all he does is look away.'

The major heaved a sigh. 'We must just keep on digging. I feel sure we'll get there in the end. Tam will become himself again. But it may take longer than we thought.'

When Brenda thanked him and rose to leave, he put his hand on her shoulder.

'The main thing is that he has you. You're his rock, his real support, and I'm very grateful that you're here. One day, you'll see, you'll have your reward. He will come back to you.'

'But the war's not over, is it? If he does recover – won't he have to go back to the front?'

'We'll cross that bridge when we come to it.' The major opened the door for her. 'Let's just get him better first.'

The days passed and Christmas loomed on the horizon. And a very different Christmas it would be, too, everyone knew, from Christmas 1914, when the hope had been that hostilities would soon be over. Why, there'd even been a truce between British and German soldiers in no-man's-land on Christmas Day! Imagine that happening now, after all the battles and the terrible loss of life. People now just lived from day to day, waiting for a breakthrough, for a real truce between nations and peace again. 'Peace and goodwill to all men.' Aye, that was the Christmas message, but in 1915 it sounded hollow.

Every afternoon, as Brenda had told the major, she sat with Tam in the room he shared with another corporal, or maybe walked in the West End or the square.

'He really likes to be in the fresh air,' she said to Elinor, 'and I'm wondering if you could do me a favour? Could you go out with him today? I have to go to the dentist's.'

'Oh, sure I will, Brenda. But poor lassie – have you got toothache?'

'Yes, and I'm terrified. It's shameful, I know, when you think about what Tam and all the others have been through, but when it comes to the dentist, I'm just a coward.'

'No' the only one,' Elinor said with a smile. 'Did you hear how many soldiers had to be seen by the dentist at Craigleith because they'd never dared to go before?'

'Don't tell me. But thanks, Elinor. Wrap up warmly, eh? It's freezing today.'

As soon as lunches were over, Elinor, in her winter coat and an imitation fur hat that had been given to Hessie by an employer long ago, collected Tam from his room and saw to it that he had his greatcoat over his hospital suit of blue flannel, and was wearing his army cap, a khaki

264

scarf and woollen gloves.

'You're so thin these days,' she told him, 'you need plenty of warm clothes.'

He shrugged, then took off his gloves and fished his notebook and pencil from his pocket.

'So you're lumbered with me?' he wrote. 'I'm not very good company.'

'You're the best,' she replied. 'But where would you like to go today?'

'The gardens,' he wrote in reply. 'They are peaceful.'

'My favourite place. Though they might be a bit rugged today.'

As soon as she'd put her key in the gate, the familiar feeling of peace stole over her, cold though the air was and frosted every blade of grass.

'Too cold to sit down,' she murmured. 'I think we'll have to keep walking, Tam.'

She took his arm and they began to walk slowly round the paths, Tam breathing deeply, as though he couldn't get enough of the fresh, clear air, Elinor covertly studying his haunted face below his army cap. It was as though she was with a completely different person from the Tam she used to know in Stephen's class, and again she wished, as she always did, that she had a key to unlock his mind, as she had been able to unlock the gate to the gardens. But weren't they all seeking that? And how likely was it that they'd find it? Though Major Henderson kept telling Brenda it would come, that Tam would get better, Elinor knew how far away recovery might be.

Oh, how cold it was! She felt her face must be

turning blue, and her fingers, even in thick gloves, were probably the same, when suddenly she felt Tam halt beside her, as though jerked by some invisible string.

'What is it?' she asked, as though he could reply, while he kept on staring fixedly ahead at the railings beyond the trees. Then he raised one hand and pointed and, as her eyes followed his lead, she, too, stood very still. It was like a repeat performance of the scene at Brenda's wedding, and just as startling, for the same officer who had slipped into the chair next to hers was the same one standing at the railings, gazing in. Only he was wearing a greatcoat today, of course, and his face was reddened with the chill, but she would have known him anywhere.

'Stephen?' she whispered.

And then she was filled with such a burst of emotion, she almost trembled where she stood, for Tam's mouth was working, his gloved hands were at his lips, as though he would force the words out, and then, in a voice no louder than her own, she heard him say, 'Mr Muirhead?'

And Stephen came running round to the gate and began rattling it and calling, 'Yes, it's me, Tam, it's me! Elinor, you've locked the gate! For God's sake, let me in!'

As soon as she'd opened the gate, he ran to Tam and shook him by the hand, as Tam stood, trembling, just as Elinor was still trembling, and the three of them were gazing at one another in something like awe.

'Stephen, he said your name!' Elinor was crying. 'When he's unable to speak!'

266

'I know, I know, I was told.' Stephen was hanging on to Tam's hands, his grey eyes shining. 'But he said my name, I heard him. Tam, I heard you say my name. Please, please, say it again.'

'Mr Muirhead,' Tam croaked. 'Mr Muirhead. You ... were at ... Loos.'

'Yes, Tam, I was at Loos, just like you. I came to see you after I heard about you from John Andrews. But let's go inside, shall we? Elinor, take us in, will you? This fellow needs to see his doctor!'

'Major Henderson, Major Henderson!' cried Elinor, running ahead. 'Come quickly, Tam can speak!'

And as Brenda, who had just arrived back from the dentist's with a scarf around her mouth, for she had had a tooth extracted, stood transfixed, staring at Tam, he held out his arms to her.

'Brenda,' he said softly. 'Brenda, it's me. I'm back.'

Fifty-One

'One thing's for sure, this is nothing to do with me,' Major Henderson said ruefully. 'You cured yourself, Tam.'

'No, you helped me a lot, sir,' Tam told him earnestly. 'But it was seeing Mr Muirhead – sorry, Captain Muirhead – that did it. If he hadn't come to visit me...'

267

As Tam's strange husky voice trailed away, Brenda pressed his hand, her eyes on his face following its changes, from the blankness she'd so much dreaded to the dear, familiar look of the Tam she used to know.

They were in Colonel Shannon's office, all those wanting to hear how Tam had come to speak again. The doctors, Matron and Sister Penny, with Brenda standing close to Tam in a chair, and Stephen and Elinor squeezed in at the door.

'Do you feel up to telling us what happened?' Colonel Shannon asked Tam quietly. 'It could be of great help to us to know the trigger that brought back your voice.'

'I know, sir, but I can't say exactly why seeing the captain did the trick. All I know is that he was at Loos, he understood what it was like – he'd have seen what I saw – and I needed that, I needed somebody who'd been there like me.'

'But why was this so important to you, Corporal? You'd fought before; you'd had experience of battle. Why was Loos different?'

'Because of the gas, sir. It was the first time we'd used it, and it went wrong. The wind blew it back; it came to our own trenches, and I saw ... I saw the men – I saw 'em trying to get out of the way, I saw 'em gasping, and I knew I'd to get out, too. But then there was this great flash and a terrible pain in my head – I never knew any more till I woke up in the field hospital.'

As Tam's voice failed again, there was a long silence, broken by Major Henderson.

'And when you tried to speak, Tam?'

'I couldn't, sir. I couldn't make the words come. I could just see – I kept on seeing – all those men, and when I came back home, folk kept trying to help, but they couldn't, because they weren't there. They didn't know what it was like.'

Tam's eyes went to Stephen, who was still standing next to Elinor, his hands clasped together, his eyes on Tam.

'But the captain knew,' Tam said in a whisper. 'Captain Muirhead knew. He used to teach me, I was in his class. I knew, when I saw him, that he'd understand. Is that no' right, sir?'

'It's exactly right,' Stephen answered. 'I understand, Tam. But you're not alone, you know; there are others who understand, too. An awful lot of us were at Loos.'

'But they're no' here, sir, and you are. And when I saw you, it was ... wonderful. I felt the words coming back, I felt I'd be strong again.'

Again, silence fell. Brenda gave a little sob and tightened her grip on Tam's hand. Elinor's eyes, too, were moist with tears; she didn't dare to look at Stephen. The colonel stood up, the other doctors with him, and Matron cleared her throat.

'Time for a rest, I'd say,' she told Tam briskly.

'Quite right, as usual, Matron,' Colonel Shannon said with a smile. 'I think Corporal MacLean should return to his room now and have a quiet time. Captain Muirhead, I know you'd planned to visit today but it might be better if you could come in tomorrow, if possible?'

'Certainly, Colonel. I don't have to leave until the day after tomorrow.'

'Good man. Meanwhile, Major Henderson and I will discuss this case and make some notes. I think I can say that it's been extremely interesting.'

'Interesting, he calls it,' Stephen murmured to Elinor, as they watched Sister Penny accompanying Tam and Brenda back to Tam's room. 'It's a bit more than that to Tam.'

'Thank God you were able to visit. If you hadn't, I don't think there'd ever have been a breakthrough.'

'It's strange, though – I never would have thought Tam would react as he did. He always seemed so strong, so tough. But you never can tell how war will affect people.'

'You seem pretty strong yourself.'

'Lucky, you mean. I've had minor wounds but nothing much.' They had come to Tam's door and waited a moment. 'How's your brother, then? He's come through all right?'

'He's been lucky, too. So far.'

'That's good. Well, I'll just say goodbye to Tam, and look in tomorrow.'

'I'll see him later.' Elinor hesitated. 'Do you have to go back to France, then, after this leave? Couldn't you have Christmas here with your mother?'

'No, I have to get back.' Stephen smiled slightly. 'The army doesn't take into account what mothers want.'

And maybe you want to get back, anyway, thought Elinor, to see the lady ambulance driver, but she only returned his smile and wished him well.

'May you stay lucky,' she told him.

'Thank you,' he replied, and did not ask why she was saying goodbye, when he was planning to return to the Primrose the following day. Of course, he didn't know that tomorrow brought her half day and she'd already decided to spend it at home.

Oh, just wait till her mother heard about Tam, then! She'd be so happy for him, thinking how she would have felt if Corrie had been in his situation. And happy for Brenda, too, who'd been so brave, and had looked after him so well. What an amazing day this had been, hadn't it? So terrible to think of the scenes at the battle that folk could not imagine if they hadn't been there, but so wonderful that so far Corrie and Stephen had been spared, and Tam had taken the first steps to being himself again. Wonderful, wonderful day. So why was she still dashing tears from her eyes as the tram rattled her homewards? Best not to ask.

Fifty-Two

Christmas passed. Hogmanay passed. And then it was 1916, and who knew what it would bring? Not the end of the war. No one expected that.

There were two good pieces of news in January. One was that Ada had her baby – a boy she called Robert after his father, but he was to be known as Rob, rather than Bob. Elinor went round to see him, with a matinee jacket she'd knitted, and found herself feeling amazingly cheered by the sight of the new little life, whose clean slate was free from the worries and horrors of a world at war.

'Let's hope by the time he grows up there'll be no more wars,' she murmured to proud Ada.

'Amen to that!' cried his mother. 'But I wouldn't bank on it, Elinor. We're a stupid lot, eh? What could be more stupid than what's happening now?'

The second piece of good news was that Tam had made a full recovery, returning to his old character as though he'd never lost it, and was becoming increasingly restless at what he called his idle life at the Primrose.

'Bring on the medical board,' he told Brenda and Elinor. 'I want out of here.'

'How can you say that, Tam?' Brenda cried. 'After what you've been through, you want to go back to the fighting to suffer it all again?'

'It's my job,' he said seriously. 'I have to go, Brenda; I couldn't live with myself if I didn't.'

The doctors, however, were not so sure that a return to active duty would be the right thing for Tam. Something had happened to him at Loos that might well happen again, for though he felt his old self, underneath there might still be that crack in his mind that had opened up before. All would depend on the opinions of the medical board members, of course, but possibly a spot of pen-pushing at regimental HQ might not come amiss.

'Pen-pushing? Oh, God, you can't mean it!' Tam cried to Major Henderson. 'It'd be like putting me in a cage – I'd never stick it.'

'Just for a time,' the major told him comfortingly. 'Just to see how you go.'

'I know how I'd go,' Tam muttered. 'Straight off my rocker.'

In the end, he got his way. The board pronounced him fit for active duty and in February he returned to France, while Brenda made her own return to full-time work at the Primrose, drooping like a flower out of water, but saying no more.

'What's the point?' she asked Elinor. 'Tam's doing what he wants; there's nothing I can do about it, is there?'

Except pray, they both thought.

They might have taken comfort, as the year moved on, that British forces appeared not to be involved in any major conflicts, if it hadn't been for the terrible battle of Verdun being fought between the French and the Germans across the Channel with tremendous loss of life. The great naval battle of Jutland, for which both sides claimed victory, had lasted only a couple of days, but Verdun, which began in February, showed no signs of ending, even by July. By which time, the British were in action again at a place that was to be remembered for years to come.

'Where did you fight?' men who'd survived the war might be asked, and if they answered, 'the Battle of the Somme', no more need be said, for everyone had heard of the Somme, everyone knew that it was the British version of Verdun, even though French troops were part of it, and went on almost as long. And everyone knew how many had perished. Oh, if you'd survived the Somme, you were a lucky man indeed.

How can we still be lucky? Elinor pondered, reading the casualty lists. How can we expect Corrie to come back, and Tam and Stephen? As with Loos, it seemed almost every regiment was involved; there could be no escape, and nothing was being done by the politicians to end the fighting.

'I feel we're in one great black nightmare,' she said once to Hessie. 'Why isn't someone doing something to bring it to an end?'

'If you're expecting the governments to do something, think again,' her mother said wearily. 'This war never was about anything that matter-ed. Mrs Elder and me were just saying that very thing when she popped up for a cup of tea.'

'It's nice she's turned out to be such a friend,' Elinor commented, who had been pleased to find the new tenant of the downstairs shop so agree-able. 'Could have had some bossy person who'd no' let us call our souls our own.'

'Aye, Freda's really easy-going and such a beautiful needlewoman – her lassie's the same. I'm thinking of getting Freda to make me some-thing, in fact, when I feel like going out again. She doesn't charge much.'

Elinor, studying her mother, gave a smile. 'You all right these days, Ma?' she asked quietly. 'I mean, apart from worrying about Corrie?'

'Aye, maybe I am. I do miss your dad, trouble though he was, but I'll have to admit it's easier, eh?' Hessie's own smile was rueful. 'Doing as you like, it's no' bad.'

'No' bad at all,' Elinor agreed.

It was November before the Battle of the Somme dragged itself to an end, with the loss of thousands of men and a gain of only six miles into German territory. No victory, then, though the French had claimed some degree of success at Verdun, which finished in December.

There was no doubt that 1916 had been a terrible year, even though for Elinor, Hessie, and Brenda there had been good news. Corrie was safe, Tam was safe with no repeat of his breakdown, and Stephen had also come through, if with a bullet in his knee, as Tam had heard. How was he, really? Elinor wondered. Still seeing his lady ambulance driver? Oh, stop it, she told herself. Think of something else. Work, perhaps. Always helped, having to work.

Still, she was cheered, along with her mother, when Corrie arrived home for a short leave in November. He didn't look too bad, either, which they could scarcely believe, knowing the sort of thing he must have experienced.

'Oh, it's just so grand to see you,' Hessie said fondly. 'You're really here, Corrie, and looking so well!'

'How d'you do it?' asked Elinor. 'What's your secret?'

'I switch off,' he answered calmly. 'No' when I'm there, of course, canna switch off then, but when I'm away, I close my mind to it. The way I used to do with Dad sometimes. When he was going on, I used to get worked up, but when he wasn't around, I tried no' to think about how he could be.'

'Fancy,' Hessie commented wonderingly. 'You put the war out of your mind, the way you did with your dad?'

'Ah, I'm no' comparing Dad with the war,' Corrie said hastily. 'I'm just telling you how I learned to switch off.'

'No need for it now,' sighed Hessie.

'Except for the war,' said Elinor.

In December a new patient from Musselburgh's hospital for the limbless arrived at the Primrose.

'Why he's coming here?' Elinor asked a QA when she was making up a bed for him the day he was due. 'Musselburgh's the place for helping amputees.'

'Yes, but this chap lost a leg on the Somme and is severely depressed. The usual story – needs to learn to accept.'

'What a shame.'

'Yes, used to play football, and can't believe that's all gone.'

Pausing with her hands on the sheet she was smoothing, Elinor looked up.

'A footballer?' Her heart was beating fast, which was ridiculous. How many men played football? 'A professional?'

'Don't think so. Just for a local team.'

A local team. Elinor finished making the bed and wondered when the new patient would arrive.

'They're bringing him over by ambulance.

276

He's got crutches but will need one of our wheelchairs. Now, let me see, what's his name?' The nurse consulted a paper and read aloud, 'Corporal Howat, Royal Scots.' And Elinor turned white.

Fifty-Three

She knew she would have to see him some time, but as soon as she saw the ambulance arrive at the front entrance, she felt like flattening herself against a wall and turning invisible. Barry Howat here, at the Primrose? And she would have to help in caring for him? Desperately sorry for him though she was, and feeling guilty that he had fallen from her thoughts, she couldn't imagine how they would get on after the way they'd parted. Of all the things she'd dreaded, this was one she'd never expected to come about, but now that it had, she must somehow face up to it. Find the courage to see Barry again, do what she could to help. It couldn't be much.

Keeping out of the way, she didn't see him taken up in the crazy old lift to the room he was to share with a quiet young man from a Highland regiment. One who gave no trouble, except when he decided to wander, for he never slept. Most patients had problems there.

First, Barry would have to be seen by one of the doctors, an examination arranged, treatment for his depression discussed, then one of the QAs would have a word, and finally a nursing aide would look in, to check he had everything he needed. And that should be me, Elinor decided. Go on – get it over with!

Wearing a blue hospital suit, he was sitting in an armchair by the window, looking out at the light fading over the square. Already street lamps were being lit, for the December afternoon was closing in. His case was by his bed, waiting to be unpacked; a pair of crutches was propped by his chair and in a corner of the room stood a wheelchair.

'Oh, no,' Elinor, at the doorway, whispered to herself. 'Oh, no, there's the wheelchair!'

A memory came to her of Barry flying up and down the field at that first football match where they'd met again, his feet moving so fast it was no wonder Corrie had called him 'Twinkle-Toes'. She felt like crying.

'Hello, Barry,' she said quietly, but he'd already turned his head and was peering through the dusk of his room.

'Who's there?' he asked sharply.

'It's Elinor.'

'Elinor?' He sat up in his chair and as she switched on the light and he saw her standing there, so slim and straight in her grey uniform, her dark eyes so apprehensively fixed on him, he shook his head as though he were dreaming.

'Elinor Rae – here? Still working here? Have I gone back in time, or what?'

She came forward to stand by his chair, looking down at him, and with that closer look, she saw, as with Tam during his illness, that Barry had changed. At one time, she'd believed that nothing would have changed him. As with Tam, he was the sort to take life in his stride, to take whatever came along and still come up smiling. But the war had changed Tam, until his recovery, and it had changed Barry, who had not yet recovered, for though he appeared no older, he somehow seemed like a man who'd endured a lifetime. The hazel eyes were no longer clear, the curly hair had vanished into a flattened army short back and sides, the mouth that had always been ready to smile was now one straight, grim line.

'I still work here,' she told him, 'but it's to help the nurses now – I'm what they call a nurses' aide.'

'Your war work, eh?' He shrugged. 'Glad you can do it. You can see what's happened to me. My war's probably over.'

'Don't say that. You can still do useful work.'

'Spare me all that rehabilitation rubbish.' He straightened himself in his chair. 'Look, what d'you want with me, then? I've seen a doctor, I've seen a nurse, what the hell do I have to see you for? No' planning to wash me, I hope? No' cleaning my teeth? I've still got hands, you know. I've only lost one leg.'

'I just have to check you have all you need,' she answered evenly, trying not to show her dismay at the change in him. 'Unpack your case and so on. Don't worry, I do it for everybody, whether they've got hands or not.'

'Sorry,' he said after a moment. 'That's me these days, eh? Jumping down everybody's

279

throats.'

'It's all right, Barry, I understand.'

'No, Elinor, you don't.' He slumped back. 'Look, you just do what you have to do. But I've got all I need. Musselburgh Limbless gave me the lot. Even a dressing gown. Posh, eh?'

'I'll unpack your case, then.'

As she moved about, putting away his things in his share of the chest of drawers, hanging his outdoor coat and the hospital dressing gown on pegs, she was aware of his eyes following her and was relieved when she'd finished her task.

'How about a cup of tea?' she asked brightly. 'Did the nurse say you'd be all right to come down to join the others? There's tea and cake in the recreation room.'

'She said there'd be somebody to show me where to go. I suppose that'd be you.'

'That's right.' Her eyes slid to his crutches and away again. 'Shall we go, then?'

'I'm no' sure I can face it.'

''Course you can! Everybody's in the same boat here, they'll make you welcome, I promise.'

'Everybody's lost a leg? Doesn't seem likely.' He slowly rose from his chair, balancing on his remaining leg, and for the first time, she saw the material of his hospital suit neatly folded over his missing limb and felt compassion rise like a great lump in her throat.

'I mean, everyone's got some problem, that's all. Now – do you want your crutches, or would it be easier if you took the wheelchair? There's a lift.'

'I know there's a bloody lift.' He tossed his

head, straightened his shoulders. 'Och, let's go for the crutches. They might as well see me at my worst.'

She brought him the crutches and with a heave of his body he settled them under his armpits, turning to her when he was ready, so that she could lead the way, and slowly they made their way together to the lift.

'No' much room in it,' she said with a laugh, when she'd brought it up, but he made no reply.

At one time, he would probably have been like some of the recovering patients, bringing himself as close as he dared to his nurse, and grinning or making silly remarks. 'What are you doing to-night, sweetheart? How about meeting for a fish supper, eh?' But he was like the silent shell-shocked men, who scarcely noticed their attendants, never thought of chatting them up, never wanted a fish supper. Again, Elinor felt great compassion rise for Barry and prayed that some-one could do something to help him. Major Henderson, maybe? But no one could give him back his leg.

There were artificial limbs, of course, but there were so many wounded soldiers needing them now, the waiting lists were lengthy. It was said that since the war, great improvements were being made in manufacture, but what was the good of that if you never got to the top of the list? As they entered the recreation room, Elinor resolved to ask Barry about his prospects for a false leg. It might make all the difference to his attitude.

For new patients, meeting the old ones was

281

always a bit of an ordeal. Like the first day at school, when everybody seemed to know everybody else, except you. Now, the crowd round Brenda at the tea urn all turned to look at Barry humping himself in, and though some smiled, others only turned aside. No one spoke, except for a QA – Sister Warren – who called out, 'Now listen all – this is Barry Howat, just arrived from Musselburgh. Make way and let him sit down.'

'I don't need to sit down,' Barry muttered.

'Yes, you do. How are you going to hold your cup, then?' Pulling forward a chair, Sister Warren made Barry sit down, ordered Elinor to take his crutches and Brenda to give him tea and a piece of slab cake, then rushed out like a whirlwind, which was her way. There was some laughter and one or two men came forward to speak to Barry, asking where he'd lost the leg. 'The Somme? Aye, lot o' fellows lost more than that there, eh?'

'I know that,' Barry snapped. 'I know I should be grateful.'

'Oh, we're all grateful!' someone muttered.

'Barry, do you see what's in the corner?' Elinor whispered a little later. 'A piano. It would be nice if you could play for us.'

'I don't play these days.'

'Why not? You could.'

'True, I don't need two legs to play the piano.'

'I wish you wouldn't be so sharp. I'm only trying to help.'

'Sorry. I told you what I was like. Fact is, I've no interest in playing now. There are no tunes in my head any more.'

'Oh, Barry!'

'Am I allowed to go back to my room? I'm feeling pretty done in.'

'I'll take you back. Give me your cup.'

'You needn't come, I know the way.'

'I'd like to. I want to ask you something.'

After Elinor had returned his cup to Brenda, who gave her a sympathetic smile, they made their slow journey back to Barry's room, where his room mate was lying on his bed, smoking.

'No smoking in the bedrooms, Donald,' Elinor told him. 'You know that very well. Now why aren't you downstairs having tea and cake?'

'No tea and cake,' answered young Donald, who was so thin he looked as though he never had tea and cake.

'Well, say hello to Barry Howat, then – he's just arrived from Musselburgh.'

'Hello, Barry.'

'Hello, Donald.'

Propping his crutches nearby, Barry swung himself on to the bed and lay stretched out, his hazel eyes on Elinor.

'What did you want to speak to me about?'

'I just wanted to ask you if you'd thought about getting an artificial leg.'

'Have I thought about it? Elinor, I think about nothing else. But at the rate they're being supplied, I'll no' get one till about 1935. By which time I'll be a goner.'

'That's nonsense!' Elinor hesitated. 'But we'll talk later. I have to go now. Don't forget, supper's at seven. Donald, you take Barry down, will you?'

'Where are you going, then?' asked Barry,

sitting up.

'Off duty. Early night for me.'

'Will you be in tomorrow?'

'Oh, yes, but you'll be very busy tomorrow. Starting treatment.'

'But you'll be in, though?'

'Yes, I'll be in. Goodnight, Barry. Goodnight, Donald. Someone'll be in to check you're all right, Barry.'

'Aye, there's always someone coming in,' said Donald. 'Frightened we'll disappear if they don't keep opening the door.'

'Goodnight, Elinor,' said Barry quietly. 'And thanks.'

She smiled, and went out, still feeling that lump in her throat, still feeling she might cry, but managing to hold back the tears.

Fifty-Four

Next morning, when she could catch him, Elinor asked Major Henderson if he could spare her a moment.

'I know I shouldn't ask, really – these things are confidential – but I was wondering how you'd found Corporal Howat today? I know him, you see – we were at the same school. That's why I'm interested.'

She knew none of the other doctors would have given her any information at all, but had hopes that the major, who was very sympathetic, would tell her something of Barry's case. He seemed pleased, anyway, to hear that she was someone Barry knew.

'You're a friend of his, Elinor? That could be very useful.' His look was gentle. 'But I'm afraid I can't give you more than general information – these interviews are, as you say, confidential.'

'It's just that I feel so sorry for him, remembering how he used to be.'

'Of course. Well, he is certainly very deeply depressed. Most people are, when they lose a limb, but some cope better than others. Barry is one who can't reconcile himself to a different life from the one he's always known. Football, active interests, independence – these he can't see himself living without. In fact, he told me...' The major suddenly stopped himself. 'I'm sorry, I can't tell you any more. All I'd better say is that it's going to be a long job.'

'Is there anything I can do?'

'Why, yes, I think there might be. If you're a friend, perhaps you could take him out, in his wheelchair? I think he needs to be in the city, see people, feel he's still in the world, even if handicapped. And maybe you could talk to him, too, and persuade him that he still has a useful life to live. Would you be able to do that?'

'Yes, I think I could. I'd like to help, anyway.'

Major Henderson hesitated. 'The only thing is – it sometimes happens – he might become too attached to you. You might have to watch out for that.'

'It wouldn't happen with Barry and me,' Elinor

said tightly. 'I know that for sure.'

'How can you?' he asked, smiling. 'We can never be sure how other people will react.'

'With Barry I just know.'

And at the look in her dark eyes and the tightening of her lips, Major Henderson decided it was better not to press the point.

'It's interesting, though, that you knew him as he used to be,' he murmured. 'We don't often get that sort of insight. What was he like, then?'

She paused, her mouth relaxing into a smile.

'He was one of the most cheerful people you could wish to meet. Everyone knew him for that. Nothing bothered him, everything was easy. Sunny, I think, is the way I'd describe him.'

'Sunny? Good God.' The major bit his lip. 'What the war can do to people ... I can't even recognize him from the man you describe.'

'He played the piano, too. Anything and everything, all by ear. Now he says he hasn't a tune in his head.'

'Ah, Elinor, didn't I tell you, we have a long way to go?'

'You're going to take me out?' Barry asked later. 'In the wheelchair? No thanks, I'm no' parading myself in the streets, looking for sympathy. That's no' going to happen.'

'Who says you're looking for sympathy? You have to have fresh air – this is a way of getting it. And seeing other people.'

'And letting them see me. No, no. It's what some fellows like, I've heard. Everybody fawning and telling 'em they're heroes.' Barry shook

286

his head. 'No' for me, Elinor. Forget it.'

'It's what Major Henderson wants,' she said shortly. 'No point in arguing. Next fine afternoon, we're going.'

He stared, his eyes narrowing. 'Yes, ma'am! As you say, ma'am! Where do I report, then?'

'There's no need to make fun, Barry. I'm simply telling you what Major Henderson said.'

'Ordered, you mean.'

'It was more of a request – something to help you.'

'All right.' He shrugged. 'If I have to, I have to. Next fine afternoon, we go.'

'I think, once we set off, you'll enjoy it. It's nearly Christmas and the shops are all trying to be cheerful.'

When he made no reply, she sighed. Talk about uphill work, she thought, then, remembering his situation, drew on her patience.

'Are they letting you out for Christmas?' she asked lightly. 'They do their best to celebrate here, but a lot of patients try to go home for a couple of days.'

'I suppose I could go to Bettina's, if she'll have me. She visited me in Musselburgh, but we'd nothing much to say. I told her no' to bother coming to the Primrose.'

'She might still want you for Christmas?'

'Well, her Alfie's still in the Navy, risking life and limb, and Georgie's gone, so she thinks I shouldn't be out of the battlefields.'

'Oh, that's a piece of nonsense, Barry! I'm sure she doesn't think any such thing. When you've...'

'Lost a leg? That's no excuse in Bettina's eyes.'

Barry gave a rare grin. 'Och, I'm being a bit hard on her. I expect she'll have me for Christmas dinner, if she's having one. At least it's the ground floor.'

'Ground floor?' Elinor repeated, then blushed. 'Oh, sorry, I see what you mean.'

'Aye, takes me a long time to climb the stair these days.'

'How about we go down to the recreation room for a cup of tea?'

'No need for you to come, Elinor, thanks all the same. I can manage your wee lift myself now.'

And as he moved painfully away on his crutches, it seemed to her that Barry was already doing what he could to hang on to his independence. If only he also could master his depression and accept his injury, too – but, as the major said, to get him to do that looked like being a long job.

Fifty-Five

On the first afternoon Elinor took Barry out, the weather was chill and grey, but the Princes Street shops were filled with light and whatever could be found to sell to bring some cheer to the war-weary public. Certainly, the public was keen enough to go shopping and Elinor found it no easy task steering Barry's wheelchair through the crowds.

'Are you sure I'm no' too heavy for you?' Barry asked, trying to look pleasant as passers-by smiled at him, murmuring such remarks as 'Well done, laddie!' and 'Brave fellow, then.'

'No, no, I'm tall and strong,' Elinor answered, rather regretting her words, as she knew he was the one who wanted to be tall and strong, but deciding it was best to carry on talking. 'I'm afraid there's an awful crowd out today, but Major Henderson thinks it's good for you to mix with folk, you see.'

'He might think that, but all I can see are legs,' Barry returned. 'Everybody's got legs – what good does that do me?'

'You're supposed to be looking at the shops, or the Castle, or something to cheer you up. That's the object.'

'How about a cup of tea, then? It's damned cold in the street and I've got a few bob spending money. I'll treat you.'

'There's a nice little place off George Street,' Elinor told him, glad herself to think of being out of the cold. 'Should be quieter there, too.'

It was remarkable how much better they both felt in a comforting warm atmosphere, with hot tea and mince pies before them and pleasant people around, all legs hidden beneath tables.

'Oh, this is nice,' Elinor murmured, pouring Barry more tea. 'There are still some things to enjoy, aren't there?'

His eyes were resting on her face, rather flushed from the cold, her eyes very bright, and he gave for once a genuine smile.

'Aye, it's some time since I had a mince pie,

I'll agree.'

'I made some mince pies once, for the Christmas party our course had. They were pretty good, too.'

'Your tutor fellow enjoy them?'

Elinor looked down. 'He did, as a matter of fact.'

'What happened to him, then? Let me guess, he's an officer somewhere?'

'In the King's Own Scottish Borderers. Fought in plenty of battles.'

'You don't need to tell me. I've nothing against officers, except the ones who do the planning. This fellow been wounded?'

'Had a bullet in his knee, I believe.'

'And he's all right? Lucky devil.' Barry finished the last crumb of his mince pie. 'You keep in touch?'

'No' really. He's found someone else now. A lady ambulance driver.'

'Oh, yes, I know the sort.'

'They do a very good job, Barry.'

'Sure they do. Everybody does a good job. Never seem to get anywhere, that's the trouble.'

'Mind if I ask you, but how did you get on with the major?' Elinor said after a pause. 'I mean, for your first session?'

'Och, it was just what I expected. Questions and answers and all very nice and friendly. He seems a good chap, but he's never going to get my leg back.'

'The main thing is to be very honest, they say, tell the doctors everything, no' what you think they want to hear.'

'I told him something that made him jump.' Barry took out a packet of Woodbines. 'Can we smoke in here?'

'Most people are. I don't. What did you tell him, Barry?'

'Said when I was looking at the sea at Musselburgh on my first day out after the op, for two pins, I'd have thrown myself in.'

'Barry, you didn't mean it!' Elinor had turned pale. 'You would never do that!'

'Sure I would,' Barry answered carelessly, lighting a cigarette. 'Still might. Why not, if my whole life has changed? I'm just waiting to see how things go.'

'You never told them at Musselburgh?'

'No, but they might have guessed. I'm described as depressed, eh? And I'm here.'

'Major Henderson will never let you do such a terrible thing!' Elinor cried and, leaning across the table, took Barry's hand. 'And neither will I!'

His eyes flashed with pleasurable fire and for a moment she saw again the old Barry, the cheerful, devil-may-care fellow she'd fallen in love with. Though no longer in love, she was deeply compassionate for him, determined to pull him back from the brink of despair, to make him see that life was still worth living. As quickly as it had appeared, the old image faded, yet there was still something of it there, some sign of a spirit that might give him the courage to go on.

'Why, Elinor,' he said quietly, 'you're quite a tonic, eh? I think it should be you doing the major's job.'

'I want to do what I can to help. Listen, if you

291

get your artificial leg, you'll be able to lead a life the same as anyone else. No' kicking a football, but doing plenty of other things, learning new skills and all such as that. Why throw everything away, Barry? Promise me you never will.'

He took his hand from hers, drew on his cigarette.

'Maybe later. Will that do?'

'Have I made you feel any better?'

'You have. This is the best afternoon I've had since I don't know when.'

'I'm glad. Maybe we'd better go back now.'

'I'll get the bill. Now that's something I can do, eh?'

They returned through the darkening streets, where the shoppers were still jostling outside the lighted shops, turned at Maule's Corner and arrived back at the Primrose.

'Easy does it,' said a patient who had also been out for a walk. 'Let me help you up the ramp, eh?'

'Thanks, that's very kind,' Elinor told him, as the young soldier helped her to pull Barry's wheelchair up the ramp on the front steps.

'Any time.'

He touched his cap and ran ahead, but as she and Barry progressed through the hall to the lift, she saw with a sinking heart that a shutter had come down once more over Barry's face. Needing another man to help him had brought it home to him, it seemed, that he was in a wheelchair, and for a moment she thought that all her efforts to cheer him had been wasted, that he was back to what he had been. In the lift, however, his expression lightened and he smiled.

'Elinor, that was grand,' he said quietly. 'When can we go out again?'

Fifty-Six

Another wartime Christmas arrived. That year, Elinor was on duty with Brenda at the Primrose over the holiday, but didn't mind. The atmosphere was relaxed and they enjoyed giving those patients who couldn't spend the day away as good a time as possible. These did not include Barry who had, after all, been invited by Bettina for Christmas dinner, along with her Alfie who had managed to come home on leave from his ship.

'That's put her in a sweeter mood,' Barry informed Elinor. 'Doesn't mind me being out of the war now Alfie's home for a bit.'

'You just do your best to enjoy the day,' Elinor told him, 'and don't make Bettina out to be worse than she is.'

'You're too nice, that's your trouble,' he said with a smile, but was pleased when Bettina herself splashed out on a taxi to collect him and expressed herself delighted with his present of a bottle of scent, chosen on his behalf by Elinor.

'You really seem to get on well with our Barry,' Brenda remarked, after Elinor had waved him off. 'You sure he's not getting too keen?'

'On me? No, that's out of the question.'

'Why? Patients do get attached to medical staff, it's well known.'

'Doctors, maybe, but I'm no doctor.' Elinor hesitated. 'Thing is, I haven't told you this before – was too embarrassed – but he's the one.'

'The one?'

'The one I went out with and it all came to nothing.'

'Elinor!' Brenda's eyes widened. 'How awkward for you, having him here!'

'I thought it would be, but it's been fine. I felt bitter at the time we split up because he didn't want me, but that's all in the past. Now I feel so sorry for him, I just want to help him.'

'Oh, well, that's all right, then. But take care he doesn't see something that's not there.'

'All he wants is to be as he was before. I honestly don't think he's interested in me at all.'

Hessie, though, when Elinor saw her at Hogmanay, wasn't so sure about that.

'I bet he is falling for you, Elinor, when you do so much for him. Canna blame him, eh? Though I blamed him plenty after the way he treated you. Now, I suppose, we've to forgive and forget. Poor laddie, eh?'

'Ma, you're like everybody else, thinking Barry's sweet on me, but it just isn't true. He showed me pretty clearly what he wanted when we split up and it wasn't me.'

'Aye, but things are different now, eh?'

Hessie began setting out her one bottle of port and the remains of her Christmas cake, in preparation for the visit of Mrs Elder, the dressmaker, who was coming round to see the New Year in with her young daughter, Sally.

'But you be careful, eh?' she went on. 'It'd no' be a bed o' roses, married to a fellow who's lost a leg and is feeling blue all the time. You make it clear, you're no' getting involved.'

'Oh, Ma,' Elinor sighed. 'There'll be no marriage, I can promise you.'

'Here they come,' was all her mother said, as the visitors arrived. 'Open the damper of the range, Elinor, let's get a bit of warmth.'

And it was pleasant, sitting together, waiting for the clock to strike twelve and usher in 1917, but Elinor did wonder if things weren't a little boring for seventeen-year-old Sally. Shouldn't she have been out at the Tron Kirk with friends? It was the traditional place to see in the New Year, after all.

'Och, no!' her mother cried. 'She's far too young for that. I'd never have a minute's peace if she was out in the town for Hogmanay.'

'Plenty of lassies my age go to the Tron,' Sally, dark-haired and pretty, said sulkily, but it was plain she knew she'd get nowhere with her mother, who was still looking worried, and said no more.

'Shall I put the drinks out now, to be ready?' Hessie asked. 'There's lemonade for Sally, if she doesn't like port, and we might as well cut the cake.'

As she busied herself pouring drinks and slicing the cake, she sighed a little.

'This is when you think of the missing ones, eh? Walt always liked his dram at Hogmanay.'

And other times, thought Elinor.

'My Keith was the same,' Freda remarked. 'And then there's your Corrie, Hessie. Shame he couldn't have got more leave.'

'Is that him there?' Sally asked, studying a photo of Corrie on the shelf over the range. Wearing his uniform, he'd been taken against the mysterious background of a battleship – the photographer's choice – and was looking very young and rather startled. 'Isn't he handsome?'

'He is,' Hessie said fondly. 'You'll have to meet him when he next comes home.'

'I'd like to,' Sally cried with such enthusiasm that her mother and Hessie exchanged glances. 'Be sure to tell me when he comes.'

'You could write to him, you know,' Elinor suggested. 'Soldiers love getting letters.'

'I don't know him, though.'

'You could be what they call a pen friend. A lot of women write to the soldiers that way.'

'I'm better at sewing than writing,' Sally admitted, with a giggle. 'But I could have a go. Will you tell me where to write?'

'I'll find the address for you now.'

'No, wait,' ordered Hessie. 'Look at the clock. Nearly twelve. Get ready, everybody!'

All four rose, glasses in hand, their eyes on the hands of the old mantel clock, and as the hands moved to twelve and the clock began to strike, Hessie cried, 'To 1917! Happy New Year! May it bring peace to us all.' Her voice trembling a little, she added, 'And bring the laddies safely home.'

'To 1917,' the others echoed, drinking the toast. 'Happy New Year!'

They exchanged hugs and kisses and shed a few tears, as Corrie looked gravely on from his photograph. With them in spirit, his mother and sister said, from wherever he was, at the beginning of another year of war.

Fifty-Seven

After all that had been said about Barry's possible feelings for her, Elinor felt a certain diffidence about seeing him again after New Year, but all was well. She could detect no change in his preoccupation with his own situation, and though she did sometimes find his eyes resting on her, she decided she'd been right and everyone else wrong over his attachment to her.

Which meant their little outings could continue with no worries, except perhaps for the winter weather, which was bitterly cold, sometimes wet, sometimes snowy, but not usually bad enough to keep them in.

'Thank God,' Barry commented, as they set out one February afternoon, muffled to the eyebrows. 'I couldn't stand being indoors any longer. First, there's old Henderson, jawing away, then that nurse giving me exercises, bending me around till I feel like swearing in her ear. When am I going to get away, then, Elinor? When's the sentence up?'

'Depends how soon you get better.'

He twisted round in his wheelchair to look at her.

'They canna do anything for me. I'm never going to get better.'

'Oh, Barry, don't say that! I hate to hear you talk like that, after all we're trying to do.'

She had been pushing him along the paths in the Princes Street gardens, but was beginning to feel numb with the cold and afraid that it was too cold for Barry, having to sit in his chair. Better go back.

'No!' cried Barry. 'No' yet, Elinor. We usually have tea, eh? I canna face going back just yet.'

'It's just so cold...'

'We'll get warm in the café. Come on, if you want to help me, this is the way.'

She gave in, turning his wheelchair to return to Princes Street, crossing over and moving into George Street, the wind all the time cutting through their clothes, turning their noses red and their hands white, until they reached the haven of the café.

'They know us here now,' Barry remarked, as the waitress smiled and took their order. 'Wonder who they think we are? Brother and sister? No, we look too different. A couple of lovers?'

Elinor's head jerked up, but he only grinned.

'No, I expect they realize, you're my nurse and I'm your patient.'

'Did you mean it?' she asked, putting her hands to her face, which was gradually becoming less cold. 'When you said you'd never get better?'

He made no reply, only stirred the tea she gave him.

'Like one of these buns?' she asked.

'Please.'

Still he said nothing, until she'd set the buttered bun on his plate, when he leaned forward and fixed her with his intense gaze.

'I did mean it, Elinor. I'll never get better ... unless you're with me.'

'Me? I don't understand. I'm with you now. Why do you say you won't get better, then?'

'You call pushing me out in a wheelchair being with me? Making my bed? Running the hospital bath? Looking after me, Elinor, that's no' what I want.'

'What do you want?' she asked fearfully.

'I want you to marry me.'

Colour flooded her face and receded, as she desperately drank some tea and tried to think what to say, as he kept on looking at her with those eyes that could seem so dead but were now so much alive.

'I've had time to think in the Primrose, you know,' he continued. 'I've had time to see what a fool I was, back in 1914 when I joined up. You wanted us to marry and I didn't want to be tied down.' He gave a short laugh. 'Tied down? I guess I'm tied down now, all right. Stuck fast, eh? But you were right. We should've married. I see that now, and though I've no right to ask you to take on a cripple—'

'Don't call yourself that!'

'It's the truth, it's what I am.'

'When you get your artificial leg...'

'When! That's so far away, I can forget it. As I say, I've no right to ask you to take me on now,

299

but I'm asking, anyway. I feel you're my only hope. You're all that stands between me and...'

He fell silent, began to eat the currant bun, mechanically chewing, as though it had no taste, and after a moment, Elinor ate hers.

'More tea?' she whispered.

He nodded and she filled his cup. Then their eyes met.

'What do you say?' he asked hoarsely.

What could she say? She was all that stood between him and ... what? What did he mean? The sea at Musselburgh? No, surely he'd got beyond that? He'd realized there was a life for him after his amputation; she'd made him see that, hadn't she? Seemingly not.

'I'll never get better unless you're with me,' he had said.

So what could she say?

'I'll have ... I'll have to think about it.'

'But you're no' turning me down? You'll think about it?'

'I will, I'll think about it.'

A smile lit his face, his eyes shone, and he reached over to press her hand.

'Elinor, you don't know what this means to me. That there's a chance ... Listen, I want to thank you—'

'No, wait, wait till later.' Her eyes went round the tea room away from Barry – she must be brave about this, think it all out carefully.

'Let's get the bill,' she said quickly. 'Let's go back.'

When she'd taken him back to his room, she was relieved to see that Donald, his room mate,

300

was there, lying on his bed, smoking, and had to have his cigarette taken away and another word of reprimand, which meant she and Barry could not speak of what was in their minds. His eyes, of course, were saying plenty, and she was able to meet them and let him understand she'd meant what she said.

'I'm off duty now,' she told him. 'Got to face the cold again – oh, dear!'

'Stay on,' called Donald. 'Have a delicious supper with us.'

'No, I must get home. See you in the morning.'

'In the morning,' Barry repeated. 'Goodnight, then.'

''Night, Elinor,' said Donald.

'Goodnight, goodnight!' She got herself out of the room somehow and ran downstairs to dress for the cold again, to face the winter evening, catch her tram, arrive home at Friar's Wynd, where Hessie was simmering one of her stews.

'Poor lassie, you look frozen, eh? Come by the range – there's *The Scotsman* if you want it. Somebody left it on my tram.'

While her mother put a cup of tea at her elbow, Elinor leafed idly through the paper, then stopped, pierced through the heart. Pierced by something sharp and deadly, though it was only a name, leaping out at her from the announcement page.

'The engagement is announced between Captain Stephen Muirhead, only son of the late Mr Arnold Muirhead and Mrs Edwina Muirhead, of Edinburgh, and Miss Frances Glenner, elder daughter of Mr and Mrs Bertram Glenner, of

Kelso.'

'You all right?' Hessie's voice asked, from a distance. 'No bad news in there, eh?'

'No, no. Just tired, that's all.'

'Drink that tea, then. I'm nearly ready with this stew.'

Very slowly, Elinor drank the tea, then rose to set the table, help her mother serve up the potatoes and carrots to go with the stew, took her place, ate away as though nothing had happened.

Except that she knew now what her answer would be to Barry Howat's proposal.

Fifty-Eight

The following morning, hurrying up the steps to the Primrose, Elinor saw Major Henderson just ahead. He turned to greet her, but in the light of the entrance hall, suddenly showed concern.

'Are you all right, Elinor? Seem a little...'

'Just rather a poor night last night,' she said quickly, knowing there were deep shadows beneath her eyes and that she did indeed look far from well. 'Nothing to worry about.'

'That's a relief.' He laughed. 'Can't afford to have you going on sick leave, you know.'

'I was wondering, could I have a word, Major? There's something I'd like to tell you.'

'Of course. Come into my office.'

Always so polite, he set a chair for her and,

hanging up his greatcoat and hat on a stand, moved to his desk to face her. 'Fire away, then.'

'Well, something's happened you should know about.' She hesitated, keeping her eyes down, then looked up directly into his kindly face. 'Barry Howat has asked me to marry him.'

'Oh, God.' He gave a groan and put his hand to his brow. 'This is my fault, isn't it? I knew something like this could happen and I still asked you to take him out, thinking of him instead of you. I'm sorry, Elinor, I really am.'

'That's all right, sir. It's nothing to do with you.'

'What did you tell him? Did you let him down gently?'

'I ... I said I'd think about it.'

'Think about it? Why, you're not serious! You can't be considering marriage with Barry. He's a sick man, he still has a long way to go...'

'He says he won't get better without me. He says I'm all that stands between him and – I don't know – disaster, I suppose. I can't just say no.'

Major Henderson leaned forward, his face taut and serious. 'Elinor, listen to me, what Barry's doing here is very, very common. It's a form of blackmail used by invalids or people with problems, to get their own way. You must just call his bluff. That's if you don't actually want to marry him. You don't, do you?'

'No, I don't. Not now. Now, it's all over. But you see, I did once. There's something else I should tell you. Barry and me – we were going out together before the war. I really loved him then, and I thought he loved me, but when the war came, he said he didn't want to marry, he wasn't the marrying kind, and he volunteered for the army straight away.'

'When he could, he didn't want to marry you?' The major again put his hand to his brow. 'The truth being that he didn't need you then. So, now, when he does need you, when he's become dependent on you, he feels you should marry him because he can't go on without you. He can. We're here to help him, and once he has his artificial leg, he'll have a totally different outlook. You'll see, I promise you.'

'I daren't risk it, Major.' Elinor stood up. 'I daren't risk saying no. If anything was to happen, I'd never forgive myself.'

'Nothing will happen. We'll see that it doesn't.' Major Henderson came round his desk and took her hand. 'Look, you can't let yourself do this; you can't sacrifice yourself to him. I've seen too many lives ruined to want to let you ruin yours, too. I'll speak to him—'

'No! No, don't say anything. I've thought about it and I'm willing to do what he wants. I mean, he's the one who's really made a sacrifice, the way I see it. Maybe I should do what I can for him.'

'Elinor, there'll be other people in your life. One day, you'll meet someone you really want...'

'No,' she said decisively. 'I'm no' interested in thinking about the future. I'll try to help Barry now.'

For a moment or two Major Henderson gave her a quiet, considering look, then he sighed deeply and went with her to the door.

'If it's what you really want, then go ahead. But perhaps I could suggest that you don't rush into any ceremony? Say it would be best to wait a while, until he is stronger. Will you do that?'

'Yes, I think you're right, that would be best. And I want to thank you, for talking to me, it's been a great help.'

'I wish I could think so. But any time you need to talk to me again, please come to see me. You are good and caring, and I'll be glad to listen.'

She smiled briefly and left him, moving fast upstairs to give Barry her answer, knowing that the longer she waited, the more difficult it would be. Once she'd spoken, once she'd burned her bridges, she would feel better. No going back, then.

'Barry,' she whispered, entering his room, glad to see that he was alone.

'Elinor!' he cried, and held out his arms.

What could she do, but go to him?

Fifty-Nine

Although Major Henderson was duty-bound to inform the colonel and his colleagues of Barry's engagement to Elinor, it was agreed that the news should not become common knowledge.

'God knows what'll happen if the other patients think they can start marrying the nurses,' Colonel Shannon groaned. 'But if some good comes of it for Corporal Howat, I'm prepared not to ask Elinor to leave. We've not had much luck with him and this could be something of a turning point.'

'If there's real improvement, how about sending him down to Queen Mary's at Roehampton?' Major Henderson asked. 'He might not have his new limb, but he could learn new skills and trades there. They've had a lot of success with amputees.'

'And that would solve our problem with him here,' the colonel agreed with enthusiasm, at which the major raised an eyebrow, but thought it best not to say that that had not been his point.

'I really don't know what to make of it all,' Matron said frostily. 'Normally speaking, I couldn't countenance any engagement between a nursing aide and a patient, but it appears they were known to each other before and it does seem likely that Elinor can really help Private Howat. If you're happy about it, Colonel, we'll just have to say that circumstances alter cases and hope the whole thing is resolved very soon.'

'Amen to that,' said Colonel Shannon.

The only person Elinor told, after upsetting Hessie with the news that she was, after all, going to take on Barry, was Brenda, who was of course sworn to secrecy.

'Are you sure you're doing the right thing?' she asked with so much doubt in her voice, it was plain she wasn't at all sure herself.

'I have to do it, Brenda,' Elinor declared. 'Barry's in a very fragile state – if I don't support him, there might be consequences.'

'Honestly, I think that's his look-out. Why should you have to promise to marry him? You could just say you'll be his friend.'

'Wouldn't be enough. I could leave him, you see, I could marry someone else. So he'd think he could never be sure – unless I marry him.'

'At least he's agreed to wait to be wed until he's made some improvement. And if he gets his new leg, maybe he won't need you after all.'

'Oh, that will never happen, Brenda. He'll never let me go, whether he gets his new leg or not. And the waiting lists are still very long.'

Elinor put her hand on Brenda's shoulder.

'But what's the news for you? How's Tam?'

'Waiting for the next big battle. Hasn't come yet, but it will.'

'Barry's sister thinks he's lucky because he's out of it, but I wouldn't say that, the way he is.'

'I wouldn't say anyone is lucky in this war, Elinor.'

Whether he could be considered lucky or not, Barry began very slowly to get better. Though still brooding over his failure to obtain an artificial leg, there was no question any more of his being considered a suicide risk. As the weeks went by, he seemed to be responding to Major Henderson's treatment, and to be willing to consider that there might be life after amputation, but to those who knew of his secret engagement it was clear that he was still dependent on Elinor.

'So, not completely better yet,' Major Henderson told Elinor, as the grip of winter lessened and there was the prospect at last of spring.

'But we are now considering sending him down to Queen Mary's Hospital in Roehampton. He will benefit from being taught new skills there – even a trade – and that's very important for his future. The only thing is, he will have to manage without you while he's there. You think he can do that?'

She looked dubious. 'Maybe not. He might want us to get wed before he goes.'

'Even if you did, you wouldn't be able to join him. And I thought we'd agreed you shouldn't rush into things.'

'He is getting better, Major.'

'Even so.' His gaze was meaningful. 'See how he gets on at Roehampton.'

'There's no way I can put him off for ever,' she said after a pause.

'No, but wait a while longer. As I say, see how things go down there. First, of course, I have to tell him about it – he doesn't even know what we're planning. If you're taking him out this afternoon, I'll tell him when you get back.'

In the event, the major didn't have to tell Barry anything, for when he and Elinor returned from their outing, a letter for Corporal Howat had arrived by the afternoon post.

'What's this?' he wondered, sliding from his wheelchair to the chair by the window in his room, the brown envelope in his hand. 'Looks official, eh?'

'Probably wanting money,' called Donald, laughing.

'They'd be lucky if they got anything out of

me, eh?'

While Elinor moved about, hanging up Barry's coat, tidying the room, he opened the envelope and read its contents. Then he looked up.

'Elinor,' he said, his voice strangely hoarse. 'Guess what?'

'What?'

'They want me to go down to a hospital in Roehampton.'

'For training?' she asked, mystified that he'd had an official letter about something that hadn't been arranged.

'No, not for training! For the fitting of an artificial limb. Oh, God, Elinor, I'm going to get my new leg! I'll be walking again, on two legs, with two feet. My turn's come at last!'

Sixty

It was strange, to be at the Primrose without Barry. Elinor couldn't get used to seeing someone else sharing his room with Donald; kept expecting to find him there, waiting for her to take him out, looking glum if she was late, brightening when they were together.

Suddenly, that was all in the past. Barry was far away, achieving what he wanted, and she was ... well, she had to admit it – free. For now, at least, for of course he would be coming back. Not to the Primrose, but probably the flat he shared with

Bettina, from where he'd probably attend a medical board and some decision would be taken about his future. Even with his new leg, he could not go back to the front, but a job might be found for him at regimental HQ; he might well stay in the army.

She had promised to write to him and had kept her promise, but letters from him were few. One said he was pleased things were going well for him at the hospital with the fitting of his artificial limb, and he would probably be staying on after he'd had his training in the use of it. There was this business of learning a new trade, to fit him for civvy life, seeing as he wouldn't be able to climb ladders in his old job. Hadn't decided yet what it would be, but he'd let her know. Would she please not forget him, anyway? Remember, they'd agreed to be wed one day. As though she could forget it.

A couple of postcards followed, and then a letter saying he'd decided to go for tool making as his new trade and would write more about that later – but no more letters came. No doubt he was too busy, with all that he had to learn at Queen Mary's. Even so, Elinor wasn't pleased and drew her dark brows together, thinking about it. If she meant so much to him, how come he didn't keep in touch?

Then news came of the next big battle everyone had been expecting, and it hardly seemed worth worrying over Barry's failure to write letters. Who could think of anything except the terrible nightmare that was Passchendaele?

All battles were terrible, of course, but the

difference between others and the third battle of Ypres, as Passchendaele was sometimes known, was the mud. After the heaviest rain for thirty years on the Flanders Plain, everything was a quagmire, with mud so deep men and horses could drown in it, guns and tanks were lost, food was too damp to eat.

Although people at home couldn't possibly appreciate what conditions were truly like, the newspapers gave some idea, and news came through, anyway, from injured soldiers who had been sent back for treatment. And the cry went up again – what was it all for? Reaching the Belgian coast and destroying German submarine bases, it was said, in the hope of ending the blockades that were preventing food reaching Britain. But at the end of July, when the battle first began, no one knew if that could be achieved. All anyone knew then was that the casualty lists were as long as ever.

And this time, one of the casualties was Corrie.

There was no telegram, thank God; he wasn't killed, or reported missing, just unable to fight on with an arm that had been shattered, and sent home for a patch-up operation at Craigleith Hospital. Hessie and Elinor, though grateful he was out of the fighting, were constantly worried, fearing that he might lose his arm, become an amputee like Barry, and though he would take it better, they knew what was involved and lived on a knife edge until after the operation. The news then was partly good and partly bad. Good, because Corrie was told he would not lose his

311

arm. Bad, because it would never be completely healed, he would never regain full use of it, and his right hand, too, had been affected.

'Oh, well, could be worse,' he said with a smile and a shrug, when Hessie and Elinor came to visit him in his hospital ward. 'At least I've still got the arm, eh? I reckon I've been lucky to have lasted so long without trouble.'

'This battle must surely be one of the worst you've been in, though,' Elinor commented, and saw, for the first time in her brother's face, the same sort of shutter she had seen descend on the faces of so many wounded men.

'Sorry,' she said hastily. 'I know you don't want to talk about it.'

'Aye, if you don't mind, I won't. Thing is, my method of switching off things I don't want to remember is no' working at the minute. Maybe when time goes by, eh?'

He closed his eyes and Hessie, nodding to Elinor, was rising to leave, saying he should rest, when a nurse brought two more visitors.

'Now, somebody'll have to move,' she said briskly. 'Only two at a bed, if you please.'

'Why, Freda!' cried Hessie, seeing Mrs Elder and Sally advancing towards Corrie's bedside, carrying a bunch of chrysanthemums. 'I never knew you were coming!'

'Sorry, dear, I should've said. I've shut the shop, so we'll no' be staying long, but we wanted to bring your laddie some flowers, and we thought you wouldn't mind.'

'Och, no, we're just going. And my, your flowers are lovely.'

312

'Lovely,' Elinor agreed, smiling at Sally, who was looking flushed and very pretty, as Corrie opened his eyes and gazed at her in surprise.

'I'm Sally Elder,' she said quickly. 'You won't know me – I've only just started working for Ma – but I've seen your photo. I was going to write to you...' Her flush deepened. 'Only I didn't know what you'd think.'

'I can tell you, I'd have thought a letter was grand!'

'Oh, well – wish I'd written, then.' Sally gave a radiant smile. 'Anyway, Ma and me, we got you some flowers.'

'To maybe brighten up the ward,' her mother put in, showing Corrie the chrysanthemums. 'Reckon they should last a while, eh?'

'They're beautiful,' murmured Corrie. 'Thank you very much.'

'I'll find some water for 'em, eh?' Freda suggested, as Hessie and Elinor kissed Corrie's cheek and said they'd be back tomorrow. 'Then I'll away, as the laddie looks like he should sleep.'

'So I'd better go, too,' Sally whispered, but Corrie's head moved on the pillow.

'No, don't go,' he murmured. 'No' just yet.'

'Looks like he's got an admirer, eh?' Hessie whispered to Elinor as they left the ward. 'But Sally's a sweet girl and would make a grand wife. Shirt making, collars and cuffs needing turning, anything like that, she could do – she's wonderful with her needle, just like her ma.'

'Collars and cuffs needing turning?' Elinor laughed. 'Just what's needed in a wife, I'm sure!'

313

'Well, it's true, Elinor. You get a woman who can sew, she'll be handy at everything, is what I say. And a man needs a handy wife.'

'She's very pretty, too. That's what Corrie will notice.'

'Just as long as he's spared,' Hessie said bleakly. 'Think of all the lassies who'll never have husbands, eh?'

She gave Elinor a sharp look as they came out of the hospital into a sunny afternoon, finding the freshness of the air a relief after the hospital atmosphere.

'That'll no' be you, of course, if you go ahead with this idea of marrying Barry. I think you'd be better off on your own.'

So do I, thought Elinor but made no reply, and was glad when Hessie changed the subject by asking after Tam. Had he come through the battle all right?

'So far,' Elinor told her. 'But the battle's going to go on for months. Brenda's just living from day to day.'

'Like most people,' said Hessie.

Only a few days later, Elinor received a card from Barry, saying that he was back in Edinburgh and would be calling at the Primrose the following afternoon.

'Watch out for me, walking in on my two legs,' he wrote. 'I want to see the looks on all the faces. Yours, too, sweetheart, but I want you to come round to the flat, so we can talk. Can't wait to see you. Love, Barry.'

314

Sixty-One

As soon as she saw him, standing in the entrance hall of the Primrose, so straight, so proud, Elinor's eyes stung with tears. She had never really thought of how he would look out of his wheelchair, away from his crutches, but now she realized that his freedom to stand alone had put the clock back, had turned him again into the Barry she once knew.

As members of staff gathered around him, clapping and even cheering, she dashed the tears from her eyes and began clapping with the rest, delighted as they were, to have something to cheer about at last.

'Barry, you are one of our successes,' Major Henderson told him, widely smiling. 'You're proof that if you stick at something, you'll get there, and we're proud of you.'

'Absolutely right,' chimed Colonel Shannon. 'The major is absolutely right. You worked for it, Corporal Howat, and you got it. Bravo!'

'I didn't do it alone, sir,' Barry said firmly. 'And I want to thank everybody here for all their help – especially the major and Elinor here. They were that patient – well, I don't know how they put up with me. And then the folk down at Queen Mary's, they were wonderful. Miracle workers is

315

what they were, but so are you folk here. Deepest thanks to all.' He waved his hand. 'Anybody want to see me walk?'

Everyone stood back as he slowly and stiffly moved down the hall, breathing hard, concentrating on every step, but getting to the far wall before he stopped and turned.

'Well, what d'you think?'

There were cries of 'Well done!' and more clapping, even from Matron, before the staff began slowly returning to work.

'I've got to go,' Elinor whispered to Barry. 'But I must tell you how wonderful it is to see you on your feet, Barry. I'm so proud of you.'

'I've to see Major Henderson now – some formalities to go through before I'm signed out of here – but I'll be at the flat tomorrow afternoon. Is that no' your time off? Maybe you could come round? Bettina will be at work, but I'll put the kettle on.'

'I'll be there,' Elinor promised.

For some time, back at work, she felt quite euphoric over Barry's success, but gradually the feeling faded and she began to worry. Though it was true that she was proud of him, and also true that he seemed his old self, her old feelings for him still had not come back. Heady and exciting, it was never meant to last, as she'd discovered, and would never return.

So, what if tomorrow he told her he wanted to fix a date for their wedding? What would she say? He seemed to be so well, no longer in any danger; maybe there was no need to marry him. Maybe she would be safe, just to say no. Unless

... Unless he'd been relying on their marrying all the time he'd been doing his training? Unless he could still go back to what he'd been, without her support?

No, no, he had his new leg, he would be all right. But the thought still came – supposing he wasn't? How would she ever be able to let him down? All she could do was see what happened tomorrow. And hope.

The first things she saw, when she arrived at the Howats' flat, were Barry's crutches propped against the wall. At her look of surprise, he shrugged.

'Insurance, Elinor. If anything happens to the new leg, where would I be?'

'Oh, I see. But nothing will happen to your leg, will it?'

'I'm a boy scout, I'm prepared. But come on in and let me look at you.'

When she had slipped off her jacket and was putting up her hands to tidy her hair, he took her hands down and studied her so long, she flushed and moved away.

'Pretty as ever,' he declared. 'No, more than pretty. Beautiful, I'd say, is the word for you.'

'Oh, that's enough.' She took a seat. 'No need to flatter me. I thought you wanted to talk.'

'Tea first, talk afterwards. Then, if you're good, I might play for you.'

'Oh, Barry, you're playing the piano again?' As she looked across to the old piano in the corner, Elinor's eyes brightened. 'You're really better, then?'

'I am. Now, you wait there and I'll put the kettle on.'

'Amazing,' Elinor said, laughing. 'I mean, you making tea.'

'I'm a changed man,' said Barry.

With his tea, they had potted meat sandwiches and oatcakes, but no cake, as Bettina had left a message to say she'd no eggs.

'Lucky to have anything, the way things are going,' Elinor commented. 'Food's getting harder and harder to find these days. They say we'll end up with rationing.'

'All because of the U-boats' blockade, but if Haig ever gets to destroy their bases, it'll be a miracle. All that fighting in Flanders'll get nowhere.' Barry took Elinor's hand and led her to the sofa, still protected with its cover. 'But let's leave that, eh?'

Now it comes, she thought. Now will come the wedding talk. As she turned her dark eyes on him, trying to show no apprehension, he lit a cigarette.

'I'll start straight in,' he began, after smoking for a few moments. 'Tell you what's in my mind.'

'I'm all ears,' she said, with a light laugh that sounded false even to her.

But having said he'd begin straight away, Barry seemed to falter, glancing at her and away, then carefully studying his cigarette.

'Go on, then,' she said at last, and he cleared his throat.

'Thing is, when I was down at Queen Mary's, I got to thinking, you know, about us.'

'Yes? What about us?'

318

'Well, maybe I mean you. I got to thinking, maybe what we'd decided was a bit hard on you. All right for me, but maybe it was asking too much of you.'

Elinor, sitting very still, her hands folded on her lap, had begun very slightly to tremble. What was he trying to tell her? She thought she knew, but couldn't be sure. Couldn't hope too soon.

'You're talking about getting wed?' she asked slowly.

'Aye. Getting wed.' He looked at her again, then lowered his eyes. 'When I asked you to marry me, I think I wasn't – you know – myself. I was just so wrapped up in how I felt, I didn't consider you at all.'

'You were ill, Barry. You had to consider yourself.'

'Aye, well I did, eh? I mean, where did I get the damned cheek to ask you to saddle yourself with me? A chap who couldn't even stand up straight at the time? What in God's name ever made you take me on?'

She hesitated, trying to think how best to put it.

'I suppose ... I was afraid – of what might happen.'

'Because I threatened to end it all, if you didn't?' Barry drew on his cigarette. 'They call that blackmail.' He raised his eyes and gave her a long, cautious look. 'Maybe I wouldn't have tried it on, if it hadn't been for ... for remembering you cared for me once. You did, eh?'

She knew he was trying to discover her present feelings. She knew she could tell him.

'I did,' she agreed. 'But that was a long time

319

ago.'

'So, when you said you'd marry me, you didn't feel the same? It was just to help me? Elinor, you were crazy, eh? Why'd you do it? Why'd I let you?'

'I told you, you were ill. I wanted to protect you.'

He sat back, shaking his head. Looked at his cigarette and stubbed it out in one of Bettina's ashtrays.

'Elinor, I don't know what to say. That you'd do that for me – well, I didn't deserve it. You should've just told me what to do. Put up with things the way other fellows do, or go jump in the sea. Why should you sacrifice yourself for me?'

'We were friends. I wanted you to be safe – get better.'

'You were sorry for me, that was it. You were sorry enough to take me on, when you didn't love me. I still canna get over that.'

'You'd made a sacrifice yourself,' she said in a low voice. 'All you men make sacrifices.'

He reached over and took her hand, held it hard.

'Elinor, I meant what I said – I'll be for ever grateful for what you did for me – and what you would've done. I'll never forget it. But there's no need to do any more. You see what I mean?'

'I see what you mean.'

'And you're happy about it?'

'I'm quite happy. We're friends and I'm glad. And glad you're better and have your new leg and everything.' She kissed his cheek and stood up. 'Think I'd better be going, eh? Thanks for

320

the tea.'

'Hey, did I no' say I'd play for you? The piano's in a state – needs a damn good tuning, but come on, I'll give it a go.'

As she had done once before, she stood close, watching as he sat down and touched the keys, which were in truth jangly, but not enough to deter him.

'Just one of my selections,' he said with a grin, beginning to play 'Keep the Home Fires Burning', before moving on to other wartime favourites and popular music-hall songs. Finally, he gave a resounding performance of Scottish reel music and leaped up from his stool as Elinor clapped and clapped.

'Nothing too sad, eh?' he said, seeming as cheerful as she ever remembered him. 'Everybody likes a good tune and it's grand to be able to play again. I'm even earning a few bob at the pubs, just like the old days. That's before I report for duty at HQ, of course.'

'What work will you be doing?'

'Oh, handing out equipment, stores, uniforms – that kind of thing. No paperwork, thank God. And when the war is over, I'm going to try for the tool-making I told you about. Should be all right for that, eh?'

'You'll be all right,' she told him, moving to the door,

'So will you,' he said quietly, following her. 'Somebody's going to snap you up, you know. Somebody who deserves you, and all. You know who I think has a soft spot for you? Major Henderson.'

'Major Henderson? That's a piece of nonsense, if ever I heard one.'

'No, you can sometimes tell about these things, eh? And I know he's no' young – must be thirty-seven if he's a day – but he's a grand chap. No' married, either. He'd be perfect for you, Elinor. If that tutor fellow is really out of things.'

'I told you, he has someone else. In fact, he's engaged.'

'To the lady ambulance driver? Bet that's a mistake.'

We all make mistakes, thought Elinor ruefully.

'I'll walk back with you,' Barry offered after a moment, but she shook her head.

'No, I don't think you should try to do too much at this stage. I'll be all right.'

'And can go faster?' he asked wryly. 'But this isn't goodbye, eh? We'll meet again?'

'Sure we will.'

They knew they might not, but kissed, smiled, and parted, Elinor walking swiftly away, looking back once to wave, and Barry, watching, then turning into the house and closing the door.

Walking home more slowly, Elinor was wondering if it could really be true, that Barry had released her? That she was, in fact, free?

At first, she couldn't believe it, but as she began gradually to accept that he no longer wanted marriage, and that she need worry no more about letting him down, she found her spirits rising. So sweet was the relief, she might almost have felt happy, except that this was not a time for happiness, and she didn't expect it, anyway.

How she wished that Barry had not mentioned Stephen, which she found so painful. And then to talk of Major Henderson in that silly fashion! Now, when she went into work, she wouldn't be able to look him in the face. Though she would have to tell him she was no longer engaged to Barry and knew he'd be relieved. It would be easier all round, if a patient, even an ex-patient, was not marrying one of the hospital workers.

It was Stephen who was still in her mind, however, by the time she reached home. Why ever should Barry believe his engagement to be a mistake? He didn't know one thing about it, and neither did she. Obviously, though, Stephen must be happy. Obviously, he had forgotten whatever he had once felt for her, and she should try to feel the same. As though that were possible.

Might she see him again, though, just once, to know that he was safe? Was that too much to ask? Probably.

Sixty-Two

'Over by Christmas,' they'd said of the war in 1914. But when yet another Christmas rolled round in 1917, no one spoke of an ending. It was as though they'd come to accept that they might always be in a state of war, for there never seemed even a chance of a breakthrough. Why, even the entry of America into the war against Germany had not so far made a difference. No doubt it would, eventually, but for Christmas 1917, hope of any change was in short supply.

Still, efforts were occasionally made to try to appear festive. At the Primrose, for instance, it had been decided to hold a party for staff and patients, with dancing in the dining room to a wind-up gramophone, a singsong to the old piano, played by Major Brown, sausage rolls and sandwiches provided by the army cooks. Matron, to everyone's surprise, had contributed a large Christmas cake, without icing, alas, but was said to include brandy – the only alcohol permitted.

'Heavens, don't see us getting drunk on that!' laughed Brenda, who was in wonderfully good spirits with Tam, home on leave, thin but fit, at her side.

'Who needs drink?' he cried, taking her on to the floor for the next dance. 'We're having a grand time, anyway.'

'Oh, it's so wonderful to see Tam looking so well,' Elinor murmured, as Major Henderson joined her in watching the dancing. 'I mean, after all he's been through.'

'He's certainly another of our successes. Somehow, he's found the strength this time to cope with whatever horrors he's seen, and that means a lot to us here.'

'Because you set him on his way, just as you did with Barry.'

'I'm not so sure of that. I think you had more to do with his recovery than I did.'

'Don't forget his new leg,' Elinor remarked with a smile.

'Ah, no, that was a godsend for him, I know. But he's not here tonight, is he? I think he was asked.'

'No, he hasn't come.' She paused for a moment. 'He's really happy, now that he can walk, but maybe, seeing folk dancing – maybe that'd be too much.'

'Yes, it's hard.' The major heaved a sigh. 'But, look, you're not dancing yourself. They've just changed the record. Shall we take the floor?'

The dance was a foxtrot – not something Elinor knew – but the major led well, made it easy for her, and she felt no self-consciousness in dancing with him, having long ago put out of her mind Barry's foolish remarks. Major Henderson was the type to be naturally courteous and thoughtful, and what he felt for her was clearly no more than the same kindly interest he gave everyone. Which was just as well, as she had no wish for anything more.

'Talking of Barry,' he said quietly, as the dance ended and they moved to chairs. 'I'm still so relieved you and he didn't go ahead with wedding plans. Marriages for the wrong reason often end in failure.' He gave a quick shrug. 'Not that I speak from experience. I've never been married, though I was once engaged.'

'I see,' she murmured, though she didn't, and thought it strange that the normally reticent major should now be talking about himself.

'Yes, it was before the war. I was engaged to someone from Reigate – my home town – but she died.' The major looked down. 'Diphtheria.'

'Oh, I'm sorry!'

325

'It's all right; it was a long time ago.'

'Circulate, Major Henderson, circulate!' came a cry from Matron, as she sailed up with Sister Penny in tow. 'There are a number of ladies waiting for partners, and patients waiting for you, Elinor. Come along now – you know Colonel Shannon wants us all to be mixing at this Christmas party!'

With a rueful grin, the major allowed himself to be led away, while Sister Penny steered Elinor in the direction of a group of patients sitting together.

'On the floor now, on the floor!' the sister cried. 'You're all supposed to be enjoying yourselves this evening! Here's Elinor, come to take you, Private MacDuffie, and if I take you, Private Mennie, you others can move around and ask some of those nurses over there. Quickly, now!'

'We're enjoying ourselves here,' Private Mennie muttered, backing away from Sister Penny's outstretched hand, but it was to no avail. As the other patients scattered, he was taken on to the floor, followed by Elinor with Private Mac-Duffie.

'Reckon I'm the lucky one,' he murmured, as they tried to fit their steps to an old-fashioned waltz. 'Getting you to dance with, eh? There's a lot o' fellows keen on you, Elinor.'

She only smiled, trying to avoid his feet. It was true, of course, that patients often thought themselves to be in love with those who cared for them, but such romantic ideas always disappeared at the end of the hospital stay. Only Barry and she had ever got as far as an engagement, and it was no surprise that that, too, had ended when Barry recovered. Oh, what a relief that had been to her! And to Major Henderson, seemingly, but that would only be a sign of his genuine interest in everyone's welfare. What a shame about his fiancée, though. No doubt he would always be faithful to her memory...

'Ouch!' Elinor cried.

'Sorry,' groaned Private MacDuffie. 'Was that your toe?'

'Nae bother,' she said faintly. 'Nae bother at all.'

'Had a good time, then?' her mother asked, when she got home late after the party.

'I did, I really enjoyed it – apart from the odd injury to my toes in the dancing.'

'I bet,' said Corrie, laughing. 'I know what soldiers' feet are like!'

His mother and his sister looked at him fondly, still unused to his being at home, a civilian again, discharged from the army with a right arm and hand that were virtually useless. Though he'd taught himself to write with his left hand, there was no question of a draughtsman's career for him now, or even factory work, and he had found himself a job as a salesman in a gentleman's tailor's in George Street. It wasn't bad, he said; he could make something of it, and it did mean he had wages and could save up to get married to Sally.

There was an engagement that would last, Hessie and Elinor had told each other with pleasure. It would have to be a long one, of

327

course, until they could afford to wed, but they were both so much in love, they'd be sure to get there in the end. Meanwhile, Sally was stitching her trousseau and already discussing her wedding dress with her mother.

Two happy people, Corrie and Sally, Elinor thought as she went to bed. Which meant, then, that some few could be happy in spite of the war? She hoped so. She hoped her brother's marriage would help to salve the pain of his memories, just as perhaps Stephen's would help him to forget. But Elinor couldn't bring herself to dwell on that. Besides, she didn't even know what had happened to him – that was the worst of all.

Sixty-Three

It was the end of January. Too late for the sales, but Elinor was looking round Maule's on her free afternoon, in the hope of finding a bargain, perhaps cheering herself up, for her spirits were low.

'Wish I'd the same time off, so I could've come with you,' Brenda had said, for with Tam back at the front, she too was feeling depressed. Not that looking round the shops would be any solution to that, but at least it would be a change of scene. 'Maybe you'll find a new hat,' she'd added hopefully, at which Elinor had smiled.

'Need more than a new hat, I think, to make me feel better.'

'A ceasefire, then?'

'Aye, that'd do.'

As she'd guessed, wandering round the large department store didn't really help. There was very little that she really wanted, and those things she did want, she couldn't afford. What am I doing here? she asked herself, and was standing at the glove counter, turning over gloves she didn't need, when she heard a lady standing next to her say, 'I'll take this pair, then – would you put them on my account please?'

And the assistant replied, 'Certainly, Mrs Muirhead.'

Muirhead? Elinor stood very still, gloves in her hand, and very slowly turned her head to look at the lady by her side. She was perhaps in her late fifties, a little on the plump side, but well dressed in a dark blue cape and sweeping skirt, with a matching hat over silvery fair hair. Her face was rather long with a fine nose and short upper lip, and the eyes that briefly met Elinor's before returning to the assistant were grey. Fair-haired, grey-eyed, good-looking ... Oh heavens, there was no mistaking it, this was Stephen's mother. Of course, she would shop at Maule's, she just lived in Shandwick Place. It was even surprising that Elinor hadn't seen her before, for she would have known her anywhere. Mrs Muirhead, Stephen's mother. Whatever it cost to her nerves, she must speak to her. Must somehow find out about Stephen. All right, he was engaged – might even now be married – but surely she had a right to know if he was safe?

As Mrs Muirhead finished her transaction and

turned aside holding her little parcel by its string, Elinor bravely took a step forward.

'Excuse me,' she began, huskily. 'Is it ... Mrs Muirhead?'

'Yes, I'm Mrs Muirhead.' The lady's look was of course puzzled. 'May I help you?'

'I hope you won't mind if I speak to you, but I heard your name and I wondered if you were related to Mr Stephen Muirhead.' Elinor's colour was high, her lip trembling. 'I used to be in his evening class, you see, at the WEA.'

'In his class?' Mrs Muirhead was smiling warmly. 'Why, that is so interesting. Stephen is my son, Miss...'

'Rae. My name is Elinor Rae. I work at the Primrose Hospital, helping the nurses, and one of his other students works there, too. We wondered – you know – if he was all right?'

'Oh, yes, thank God. So far, he is safe. In fact, he's here now; he's been on leave, but he goes back tomorrow.' Mrs Muirhead's smile had faded. 'He's taking me out to dinner tonight and I've just been buying some new evening gloves – mine were in such a state, pre-war, you know.' She laughed tremulously. 'Must look my best, for his last night.'

'Will you ... will you give him our best wishes, then? Say, from Mrs MacLean and Miss Rae? Tell him we wish him well?'

'Of course, my dear – how kind.'

'And maybe our congratulations, too?'

'Congratulations?'

'On his engagement.'

A change came over Mrs Muirhead's face, as

330

though a cloud had covered the sun.

'Did you not see the announcement?' she asked stiffly. 'The marriage between my son and Miss Glenner will not now take place.'

Elinor felt as though everything was moving round. The glove counter, Mrs Muirhead, women shoppers turning over merchandise ... Elinor felt she must be moving, too. Such news, such news – she couldn't believe it! Please God, may his mother not see how much it meant to her. Without good reason, maybe, but suddenly everything was different, for before there had been no hope and now...

She stood straight, steadying her thoughts.

She must face it; nothing might have changed at all.

'I'm very sorry,' she heard herself saying politely, telling lies, crossing fingers, but Mrs Muirhead was pursing her lips.

'No need to be. Miss Glenner is a charming girl, but she had some foolish idea of ... Well, I won't go into details, maybe just say that what happened was all for the best. Stephen has other things to think about, anyway. He's a captain, you know; he has his responsibilities.'

'I'm sure,' Elinor murmured. 'Well, I'd better be going, but it was nice to meet you, Mrs Muirhead. Do hope...' Her voice began to trail away. 'All goes well for Captain Muirhead.'

'You can speak to him if you like,' his mother said kindly. 'I have to go home now, but he's in the Gentleman's Outfitting Department, choosing some civilian shirts.' She laughed indulgently. 'Says he might need them soon. The war is

331

going to end this year, he's sure of it.'

'Gentlemen's Outfitting,' Elinor repeated dazedly. 'Well, it would be nice to wish him luck.'

'Yes, my dear, I'm sure he'd appreciate it, he loves meeting his students. It's just on the next floor, you know, you can take the lift.'

She saw him before he saw her, her eyes drawn immediately to his tall, spare, uniformed figure bending over a pile of folded shirts, his hat under his arm, his face so gaunt, so worn, her heart sank in dismay. Then rose. For he was there. She had found him. No matter if he didn't care to see her, she had seen him, and would have this image of him to remember when she was alone again.

She was about to speak his name when suddenly he looked up and saw her, and their eyes locked.

'Elinor?'

He took a step towards her.

'Hello, Stephen.'

'Well, this is a surprise!'

He came closer, put out his hand, which she briefly shook, remembering its firmness, and still they kept their eyes on each other, hers large with wonder, his hard to read. But warmer, she thought, than the last time they'd met. More as they'd been in the old days, if she could believe it.

Be careful, she told herself, don't expect anything. Don't see something that isn't there. He might appear more friendly, yet at the same time mean nothing. In any case, his manner seemed to her to be uncertain. As though he couldn't decide how he should be.

'How did you know I was here?' he asked.

'I was shopping when I met your mother. She told me you were here.'

'My mother?' He was mystified. 'But you don't know her.'

'I heard her name, I spoke to her, told her I'd been in your evening class, and she said if I wanted to speak to you, you'd be here.'

'And so I am, surrounded by shirts.' He smiled and shook his head, as an assistant approached. 'Think I'll have to leave them for today. I don't need them yet, after all.'

'I don't want to interrupt your shopping.'

'No, no, it's all right. Would you like a cup of tea, perhaps? Or to walk?'

'Walk?'

'In Princes Street Gardens?'

Princes Street Gardens ... Where they'd once walked, long ago. Long ago, before the war.

'I'd like to walk,' she told him, adjusting her hat, to give herself something to do, to calm her nerves.

Together they left the shop, making their way, as they had so often done before, to the gardens across the road. Wintry-looking today, of course, but still filled with light, and almost empty. Just as they had always wanted them to be.

Sixty-Four

'Plenty of seats to choose from,' Stephen remarked. 'Though might be too cold to sit for
long. Shall we keep walking?'

'Maybe we should.'

Amazed to hear herself still sounding reasonable when she felt so light-headed, Elinor kept
looking at Stephen to make sure he was really
walking at her side. After all these months of not
knowing, she could scarcely believe that for the
time being at least, he was safe. Safe and with
her. Walking as in the old days. But be careful,
she told herself again. These are not the old days.
This is now – and things have changed.

'Does it bring back memories?' he asked, turning to look at her. 'Walking here?'

'Oh, yes.' She wondered – did it mean anything, the question? Was it significant? Was she
clutching at straws?

'And for you?'

'Of course.'

He said no more. Looked away. Kept walking.
Rather slowly, as she was beginning to notice,
but didn't like to comment.

'What's been happening to you?' she asked
carefully.

'This and that.' His tone was light. 'Enduring

battles. Cambrai, and such. Managing to stay lucky.'

'It must have been terrible.'

'Had its compensations.'

'Heavens – what?'

'Well, I suppose I've learned a lot.'

They halted for a moment, standing together to look up at the castle on its vantage point of rock above the gardens, above the city.

'Not about warfare – God, no.' He shrugged at the idea. 'We just do what we can there. No, I mean, other people – my chaps, for instance – the Tommies. Elinor, I'd no idea what life's like for some. I thought I had, working at the WEA and all that, but in fact I knew damn all.'

'What did you find out?' she asked a little wryly.

'To begin with, half of my men are under-weight – malnourished, I suppose – and have known so little comfort, I swear they don't even mind the trenches. I'm not talking about all soldiers, of course, but those from some of the tenements – they've never had a chance, Elinor. Never had a chance at all, for a decent life.'

'Stephen,' she said gently, 'I live in Friar's Wynd. I know what some tenements are like.'

'Sorry, of course you do. But the thing is, this eye-opener's given me an idea of what I might do when the war's over. Because I feel sure it's going to end this year. Germany's getting tired. We're all getting tired. And when it's all over, what I'd like to do is work for people who need help. Set up some sort of centre where they can come for advice on jobs, welfare, all that sort of thing, and maybe combine it with a hostel.'

They had turned to pace on, down the still-frosty paths, Stephen glancing often at Elinor, she trying to stem a feeling of rising excitement she couldn't be sure she should have.

'Won't all this cost a lot?' she asked shakily.

'Yes, but I think I can manage. My uncle left me a bit and you remember I was going to buy a place of my own one day? This centre could be it.' Suddenly, he grasped her hand, then let it go. 'Don't you agree? Don't you think it could be a success?'

'There'd be a lot to think about.'

'I'll have the time. Haven't exactly finished fighting yet.'

At his words, carelessly said, a great cloud of darkness seemed to descend over her, as it sank into her mind afresh that his fighting wasn't over, that he must return to the front.

'Oh, don't!' she cried. 'Don't talk about it. You have to go back tomorrow!'

There was a silence between them, broken by sobs she couldn't hold back, and Stephen, pulling off his glove, gently dried her eyes with his handkerchief.

'You still care, then?' he asked softly. 'About me?'

'You know I do.'

'Look at my handkerchief.'

'Handkerchief?' She turned it in her fingers, saw the initials she'd embroidered, raised her tearful eyes. 'Oh, Stephen, you've still got them? My hankies?'

'I've still got them. Put them aside once. Took

336

'em out again.'

'And I've still got my scarf. Always will have.'

Gently, he drew her into his arms, holding her close, pushing back her hat so that he could brush her brow with his lips.

'Elinor,' he whispered, 'we've both been pretty foolish, haven't we?'

'I was foolish, Stephen. I was the one who made the mistake. Threw away something precious.'

'I know how it was. You were dazzled, that's all. It happens.'

'Dazzled? Yes, maybe. It's no excuse.'

'I made mistakes, too,' he said after a pause. 'I knew you and Barry had parted. I knew – I could sense it – that you wanted to come back to me, but I was too proud. I wouldn't forgive you.'

'I don't blame you. I'd let you down; I would have felt the same.'

He gave a long, troubled sigh. 'I thought I could be happy with Frances, but she was wiser than me. You know she broke our engagement?'

'Your mother told me. She seemed upset.'

'No, she just didn't understand. Frances was right to do what she did. Told me she knew there was someone else, even if I didn't know it myself any more. I realized what she said was true.'

He put his hands on her shoulders, made her look at him, for she had been lowering her eyes.

'I realized I'd never stopped loving you, Elinor, and that was the way it was going to be for me, come what may.'

'Stephen, I didn't know. How could I? When I saw your engagement in the paper, I thought

337

there was no hope. No hope at all. So when Barry asked me to marry him, I said I would.'

There, she had said it. What she knew she must. As her great anxious eyes searched his face, Stephen was silent.

'It was to look after him, Stephen, that was all. He'd lost his leg, he was in a very bad state – they were even thinking he might ... try to take his own life.' Elinor's voice trembled. 'He'd been a footballer, you know.'

'Poor devil.' Stephen shook his head. 'I see how it was, then. But you're not ... you're not ... going to marry him now?'

'No, no. It's all over. When he got his artificial leg at Queen Mary's, it was wonderful, really, he seemed to take on a new lease of life. Didn't need me any more.'

'And you didn't mind?'

'Stephen, I was never so relieved.'

'You truly don't love him?'

'I'm here with you,' she said quietly. 'Where I want to be.'

That was when their mouths met and, after so long apart, they tasted passion again, both as though on wings in the darkening gardens, oblivious to a man walking past them with his dog, oblivious to the castle, the lights ahead of Princes Street, to everything except that they had come full circle, back to their love.

'You have to go,' Elinor said at last, pulling herself away. 'You're taking your mother out tonight, remember.'

'I want to take her out, but I wish I could have been with you.'

They began to walk slowly back, her arm in his, their eyes constantly meeting.

'You liked her, didn't you, when you met her at Maule's?' Stephen asked. 'My mother? I know she'll like you.'

To talk to, maybe, but as to more than that, Elinor wasn't sure.

'Don't say anything about me tonight, Stephen. Let her have you to herself, eh?'

'And what about your mother? I want to meet her, you know, and your brother, as soon as I come back.'

If you come back, she thought, and sensed again that great cloud of fear waiting to consume her as soon as Stephen had gone.

'Corrie's been discharged,' she said bravely. 'His right arm's pretty well useless now – he's had to take a salesman's job at a tailor's.'

'Oh, no, Elinor – oh, God, I'm so sorry. He wanted to be a draughtsman, didn't he? That's just one more life ruined by this war.'

'At least he's safe.'

'At what cost? Oh, what's the point of protesting? No one listens, no one counts the waste. But it will have to end soon, Elinor, it will have to!'

Even though they were in sight of the shops and the pavements crammed with people, Stephen flung his arms round Elinor and held her so hard she could scarcely breathe.

'It'll end this year, Elinor, I promise you. This year, some time, I'll come back to you.'

But she couldn't believe him, and saying goodbye to him when they had just found each other again was like feeling her heart wrenched from her body. He had said she couldn't see him off; he was leaving very early in the morning with a number of people from the regiment. Could they bear it, anyway?

'No,' said Elinor. 'Oh, no.'

'But I'll write,' he told her, on the steps of the Primrose. 'I'll write whenever I can, and you must write to me, and send me knitted mittens and tins of chocolate and anything else you fancy – promise?'

'I promise,' she cried, tears gathering again, and because it was dark and because they couldn't help it, they clasped each other close again and kissed and kissed for the last time. Then Stephen drew slowly away and turned, waved, and left her. And Elinor, as stiffly as a jointed doll, walked up the steps and in at the door.

Just as long as no one sees me, she thought, I'll be all right.

As though no one would see her! Of course they would see her; wasn't she here to work?

'Why, Elinor,' said Brenda, finding her. 'Aren't you going home? I thought you weren't on duty tonight?'

'Oh, Brenda,' cried Elinor, and resting her head on Brenda's shoulder, let the tears flow.

Sixty-Five

'This year, sometime, I'll come back to you,' Stephen had promised.

But both he and Elinor had known it wasn't in his power to make such a promise. He couldn't know how the war would go. He couldn't know if he would come back at all. What his words meant was that he wanted to come back to her, and though that was what mattered, though that meant everything, she had to face it every day – all she really had was hope.

'Ah, lassie,' her mother said, seeing Elinor poring over the casualty lists in the paper, reading up about the latest battles, 'now you see what love can bring. Heartache, eh?'

'It's better than having no love at all.'

'Why'd you never tell me about your Stephen before, though? Why'd you keep everything secret?'

'It was because of Dad. I thought he'd never approve and might – you know – get into a state.'

'Aye, he might've done. Or he might've been pleased. You never could tell with your dad. Anyway, when do Corrie and me get to see this laddie of yours?'

'As soon as he comes back.'

Their eyes met, and the words hung in the air. 'If he comes back...'

341

It was a great help to Elinor that Brenda now knew about her relationship with Stephen, for it meant she had someone at the Primrose who shared the anxiety she was otherwise keeping to herself. Of course, Brenda told her, she'd always known there was something between her and Stephen – hadn't she once said so? And now that they were together again, in spirit, anyway, she couldn't be happier for them.

'Oh, it's such a shame, though, just when you should be so radiantly happy, you've had to be parted, eh? Life's so cruel.'

'I do feel sort of radiant inside, though I know I don't look it,' Elinor murmured ruefully. 'No, don't say I do, I'm sure I look as though I've been ill.'

Only one person, in fact, had asked her if she was well, and it was Major Henderson. Stopping her in the hall one morning, he gave her a long, sympathetic look, and said he hoped she wasn't overdoing things, she was so pale. Perhaps she was anaemic? He could arrange to give her a test.

'No, no, I'm fine, sir, thanks all the same. Just – a bit anxious.'

'It's not Barry worrying you again, is it?'

She smiled and shook her head. 'I haven't seen Barry for weeks. No, it's ... well, there's someone in the army I care for ... he's at the front.'

'Someone you care for?' His expression had subtly changed, from one of kindliness to one of surprise. 'Forgive me – I had the impression there was no one.'

'I knew him before. We had ... drifted apart.'

342

'And now he's in France? I'm sorry – no wonder you're anxious. Let's hope there's good news soon.'

'You think there might be?'

'Everyone believes the Germans are tiring. So are we, of course, but we have the Americans now.' The major shrugged and smiled. 'Can but hope, Elinor.'

'I live on it,' she told him, and they went their separate ways.

There were in fact some good things to take pleasure in, mainly Stephen's letters which were as comforting as Elinor had expected. Well written, never downhearted, often amusing, with little drawings and stories of trench life, and always gratitude for her own letters to him. She worried at first that she wasn't as good at writing as he was, but as time went by, found she was improving and came quite to enjoy putting her thoughts on paper to him. As well as sending him his knitted mittens, of course, and small parcels of chocolate and biscuits, if she could find them.

'It really helps, sending things,' Brenda remarked one day in March. 'And Tam loves goodies. Will be getting something else soon, though.'

Something about her expression made Elinor's interest rise, and at her look, Brenda couldn't contain herself any longer.

'I mean news, Elinor. News that he's going to be a father. It was that Christmas leave that did it – I'm going to have a baby in September.'

Oh, that really was good news! Wonderful news! Elinor hugged Brenda over and over again, and almost shed a tear or two, she was so happy

343

for her.

'But you'll be leaving, eh? And I'll miss you so much. Don't leave too soon, will you? Keep well and keep going as long as possible.'

'Hey, I'll be wanting to put my feet up!' Brenda laughed. 'But I'll stay as long as I don't look like a house-end.'

'You'll be one of those neat ones, I'm telling you. Oh, but this is such lovely news.'

There was more good news a week or two later, even if not quite as personally interesting, except to Miss Ainslie, who brought it.

'Elinor, Elinor!' she cried, when Elinor was fetched to meet her in the hall. 'Splendid news, my dear! Did you hear? Have you read about it in the papers?'

At Elinor's blank face, she drew her to one side.

'We've got the vote, Elinor! We've won the day! Women over thirty are to be given the vote – it's been approved by parliament. Oh, I'm so happy, I can't believe it!'

'That's wonderful, Miss Ainslie. I think I did read about it now you mention it. But it's no' for everyone, is it? I mean, don't you have to own property, too? That rules out a lot of women.'

'Well, it's true, there are those qualifications, but it's a start, isn't it?' Miss Ainslie's eyes were shining. 'After all the work women have been doing in the war, it's no more than common justice that we should be given the vote, and I'm sure it will come to everyone eventually.'

'You're right, it's a start, and I'm very happy for all the people who've worked for it,' Elinor

344

said truthfully. 'But are you on leave just now, Miss Ainslie?'

'Yes, but I'm not idle.' She laughed. 'The war news is good – we may see an end to hostilities this year. Which means, my dear, that this place will be coming back to us.'

'Back to the club?' Elinor asked, astonished.

'Well, it has to come back and I'm making plans already. I don't think I've a hope of getting the old staff together again – they're all doing something else – but I am hoping you will consider an offer I'm going to make?'

'An offer?'

'You remember Miss Denny, my assistant manageress? Well, she's now married to someone in the Guards and won't be returning. Her job will be vacant and I want you to take it.'

'Me? Assistant manageress?' Elinor was stunned, her eyes on Miss Ainslie's face enormous. 'But I couldn't do that!'

'Of course you could! Didn't you do that office management course? That will be very valuable for the sort of work you'd be doing, and I know you'd do it well. Now you just think about it and we'll discuss it later. There's no hurry; we're not quite ready to be moving back yet!'

Leaving a bewildered Elinor staring after her, Miss Ainslie flew away, seeming so keen and energetic, it was clear her years of war work had changed her not at all.

Assistant manageress, though? At one time, Elinor knew she would have been over the moon that she could ever be considered for such a post. Now, though, the only words that were really registering with her as she turned away, were those Miss Ainslie had mentioned quite casually: 'The war news is good – we may see an end to hostilities this year.'

Words that were an echo of others that scarcely left her mind. 'It'll end this year, Elinor, I promise you. This year, sometime, I'll come back to you...'

This year? It seemed too much to believe that Stephen might be proved right, that this year, the war could be over. Better not think too much about it. Better just keep on. Wait and see. Have patience. Hope.

Yes, and better get back to Private Norris. She'd been halfway through cutting his hair for him when she'd been called down. Not that he'd be wanting her to hurry back, had probably been smoking ever since she left.

Slowly, she began to climb the stairs.

Sixty-Six

On November 11th, 1918, a beautiful word entered everyone's heads, and it was 'Armistice'.

Though its meaning was truce, a truce could be temporary, and to the damaged people of Europe, the real meaning of the Armistice was peace. Permanent peace. The time when the two sides realized they'd had enough. When the Kaiser had abdicated, the guns were silent. And when the soldiers would come home.

Not at first, of course. There would be formalities. Demobilization couldn't take place overnight. But, sooner or later, the men would be back, the main thing to remember being that they were now safe.

'Thank God,' said Brenda, bringing her baby daughter, Tamsin, round to the Primrose just before Christmas. There were hugs and kisses and exchanging of little presents, before fond farewells and promises to keep in touch the minute anything was heard from the loved ones, who would be coming home as soon as possible.

'Can't believe that this place will soon be returning to a ladies' club again,' Brenda remarked as she left, with Tamsin in her pram. 'And then the hospital will be as though it had never been.'

'Don't know about soon,' said Elinor. 'These things take time. Now I'd better change and dash – it's my afternoon off and I've to do more shopping.'

But on the steps of the Primrose, she looked across to the gardens, still handsome in the severity of winter, still with enough light for a quick walk round to clear her head before she faced the shops. And, of course, she still had her key. Wouldn't have that for much longer.

She walked quickly across to the gate and let herself in, succumbing at once to the peace of the haven she so much enjoyed. How tranquil she could always feel in this green space – at least, when she knew that Stephen would be coming home, and was safe. No more battles. No more

347

reading of casualty lists, heart in mouth, trembling fingers turning the page...

Armistice, she murmured. Oh, thank God, it's come!

Brushing a bench with her gloves, she decided to sit for a while and sank into a reverie that brought Stephen to her now. Not officially demobbed, but simply spirited into her arms, a figure from a dream – her dream.

Was she dreaming, then, when she thought she heard his voice?

'Elinor, let me in! Elinor, open the gate! Elinor!'

She sprang to her feet, instantly terrified that something had happened to him, that it was not he calling but his spirit, for she'd heard of things like that, everyone had stories, in wartime—

'Elinor!' she heard his voice again, so strongly, she knew it was no spirit's, and ran, stumbling, to open the gate.

'Stephen, Stephen!' she was crying, and he was there, painfully thin in his uniform, leaning on a stick she hadn't seen before, but smiling at her as only a real-live man could smile.

'Elinor!'

He let go of his stick, gazing at her, as she gazed back at him, each dwelling on the other's face as though they could never see enough, never be sure it was actually there.

'I thought you were a ghost,' she whispered. 'I thought I'd called you up and you were a spirit. I thought you might be dead.'

'Dead? A ghost?' He laughed and put his arms around her. 'Do I look like a ghost?'

Clinging together, they kissed, strongly and passionately, with no thought of strangeness, as though the intervening years of disillusion followed by the nightmare of war had never happened. So secure were they in their rediscovered love, when they finally drew apart, Elinor was smiling in contentment and Stephen was laughing again.

'Do I kiss like a ghost?' he asked. 'Thank God, no. You don't need to tell me. No ghost could feel as I do, being back with you. I've dreamed of it for so long, you know. So long, because we lost so much time.'

'I know. My fault.'

'Don't let's go into it. All over now.'

'Yes, all over. I'm so glad, Stephen. So glad.'

Her smile, however, as she looked down at his stick and handed it to him, had vanished.

'Why?' she asked quietly. 'Why the stick?'

'It's just my knee playing up after an old injury, that's all. Sometimes I need the stick, sometimes I don't. Look, shall we sit down for a moment? Let me look at you, believe you're really here.'

They moved to a bench and sat close, as close as they could, their eyes still fixed on each other, still seeking reassurance that their closeness was no dream, was real, as real as all they'd been through that now was over.

'Are you still in the army?' Elinor asked, running her fingers down his gaunt cheek, thinking he was as handsome as ever, but different. Of course he was different. What he had endured, what he had seen, would have left its mark, just as their experiences had left scars on the patients

349

she tended in the Primrose.

'You're in uniform – are you just back because of your knee?'

'I'm still in the army. Won't be demobbed for a few weeks; I'm just on leave at present.'

'You'll no' be going back?' she cried in alarm.

'No, no. I haven't had any leave at all for months, except for a weekend in France, and the powers that be decided to let me go. Seeing as I might have to have a small op on this knee we've been talking about.'

At the look on her face, he shook her arm gently. 'Only so that I can do without the stick. Don't worry.'

'As though I could ever stop worrying.'

'Yet you look so beautiful. Just the same as you always did.'

Again, they kissed for a long moment, until Stephen pulled a little away and asked in a whisper, 'When can we be married? As soon as possible?'

'Oh, yes, yes!'

'Would you mind a civil wedding? Mind giving up the trimmings? If you want them, I don't mind, I'll stand the wait somehow...'

'I don't care about the trimmings. I just want to be with you.'

'And then what? Will you come and work with me in my hostel when I get it? Use all those lovely business skills I taught you?'

'Someone else wanted those,' she said lightly.

'Someone else?' His brow darkened. 'Who?'

'Miss Ainslie. Offered me the post of assistant manageress at the club when it re-opens.'

350

'And you'll take it?'

He was so instantly afraid, she immediately covered his face with kisses.

'Of course I won't! I want to be like you, doing what I can to help people like me. I mean, people who haven't been as lucky as me.'

'It might be a drop in the ocean, what we achieve,' he said seriously, 'but I take the view that oceans need drops, anyway. Are you really sure you want to work with me, then?'

'Really sure.'

He took her hands and kissed them.

'You know what – it's freezing here, and getting dark. Why are we always meeting in the dark?'

'What dark?' she cried. 'The gardens are full of light.'

They strolled slowly back to the gate, Stephen saying soon they must meet their two mothers, make everyone happy, and they would be, he knew, but for now, why not make for Maule's and have a Scottish afternoon tea? Another thing he'd been dreaming about all his long years away. It was terrible, he had to admit, the amount of time he and everyone at war spent thinking about food.

'Better warn you, we're a bit the same,' said Elinor cheerfully. 'We've had rationing since February.'

'Oh, no, don't tell me! Surely, Maule's will still have butter for their scones?'

'I'm sure they will. This is our lucky day, isn't it?'

'Our lucky day ... The first of many, Elinor?'

'Of a lifetime,' she said seriously.

But as they let themselves out and she relocked the gate, she gave a little sigh.

'The only thing I'll miss is the square, you know. The gardens mean a lot to me.'

'Why, you could be a member of the ladies' club!' Stephen told her, waving his stick at the house across the road. 'And have your own key to the gardens. What could be better?'

'Stephen, you're no' serious?'

'Never more so. I'll pay your sub for a wedding present. What do you say?'

Smiling, she shook her head, still in disbelief that she should ever turn into a club member, and put her arms around him, just as Major Henderson, having shown out a patient, looked down from his window and saw them. By the light of the street lamp, he could even see their faces, and at their radiance, gave a quiet little sigh.

'Come in, Corporal Armstrong,' he called over his shoulder, as a tap sounded on his door. 'Be with you in a minute.'

'Right you are, sir. Mind if I smoke? Only joking.'

Over at Maule's tea room, Stephen and Elinor, facing each other across their lucky two-shilling tea for two, were so overcome with feeling, it was some time before they ate anything at all.